COMPANY OF THE PARANORMAL

COMPANY OF THE PARANORMAL

THE LORDS OF THE FUTURE

MARCOS MENEZES

authorHOUSE®

AuthorHouse™
1663 Liberty Drive
Bloomington, IN 47403
www.authorhouse.com
Phone: 1-800-839-8640

First published by AuthorHouse   12/7/2009

ISBN: 978-1-4490-5952-1 (sc)
ISBN: 978-1-4490-6274-3 (e-book)

Library of Congress Control Number: 2009913228

Printed in the United States of America
Bloomington, Indiana

This book is printed on acid-free paper.

PROLOGUE

Who would be crazy enough to hike through these landscapes?

Probably someone who should have super humans skills or was trying to commit suicide in a great style, because he or she would be facing one of the worst places in the world. An ice desert would the most appropriated definition to this land, where no animal could be seen, as if all of them had preferred to starve instead challenge the bad weather, since it was the most hard living region of that poor small country, that once had the oil as its only source of richness. But since the alternative fuels were largely being used in the whole planet, the black gold lost its value. As it practically had no other significant exportable product, the people lost their way of life and began to live by agriculture, hunt and ecological tourism. They depended of international help to continue existing as a nation. The border countries were equally in the same misery, and with no other choice, they used to exchange manufactured goods, handcrafts and farm animals. This winter hadn't been too hard and the spring was at the moment the coolest of the past years, but even though, the temperature often decreased to an unbelievable freezing weather, and the great number of mountains didn't make easy the life of those who were looking for adventure in these lands.

In that freezing and monotonous scenery, the white of the snow vaguely detached the asphalt of that old road that apparently came from nowhere and was going to anywhere. No animal could be seen, as if all of them had preferred to starve instead challenge the bad weather. The most amazing thing was that some bad luck man decided or was compelled to fight against this outstanding nature power. His name is Peter Moll, and he walked with the stumble step typical of the people that are out of their mind. He seemed to do not know what he was doing or where he was going to. Sometimes he turned backwards as if someone was whispering his name: Peter! Peter! Unfortunately he was completely alone and the voice of the harsh wind was the only sound, and with an dread noise insisted in showing that it was the owner of that lonely place.

Peter kept walking, with thousand thoughts burning his confused mind:

_ Where am I? What hell am I doing this shit? I know that my name is Peter, at least is this name that I hear within my head. But I have no clue why I am following this way. Who is calling me? Why I didn't get sick after eating some rocks and roots? And why I was compelled to eat that? It looks like that the devil had no imagination when he created this snow hell. Or he was very naughty and wanted to torture his enemies, sending them here.

But he had more urgent concerns to solve, such as the unbearable pain that was increasing every minute, indicating that the cold was breaking the resistance of those lousy clothes that he was wearing. They were totally non-appropriated to this climate. He knew that if he didn't find shelter, even with all sort of strange things that were happening to him, he wouldn't be lucky enough to survive another night.

Tired and feeling his legs weaker and weaker, Peter sat on a stone along the road, wondering how the strength of his body was leaking quickly. Peter! Peter!. Again this damned voice calling, tormenting him. But he was too weak to waste his energy trying to locate an imaginary person, and he just ignored it. He had figured out that it was his imagination. Looking at the horizon he thought:
_ This is a female voice. I know that it is only in my brain, but I can't help thinking that I know this woman. Who is she? Some how, when I hear this calling a strange vibration runs my body, fulfilling me with hope and trust. As if someone was helping me in this situation.

Suddenly, the growing noise of a vehicle waked him up from this numb. Looking towards it he was able to distinguish the shape of a small truck coming his way. He sat in his knees in the middle of the road, begging for the help of this unknown fellow, praying that the driver wasn't distracted at the moment that he was passing near him. Slowly it began to stop, and the passenger door was opened, showing the face of an old woman, however beautiful and weird at the same time. He could see that she was tall, and had strong and thick hands, indicating that she had spent her life working in the field. Her long red hair, huge lips and bright blue eyes betrayed her age showing that she still had a great passion for like. Even in his confused mind he could note that she wasn't exactly a woman, but a very special kind of human being, that he couldn't realize which one. Instantly he felt safe and secure, as if her kindness could be sensed by distance. She told something, but he didn't understand her language, so she made some gestures, and he got in.
_ That is heavy! What a chance of that happen? One in a million, probably! Can you see that? I am very luck! A hitchhike just when I needed the most! I just understood that her name is Gilda, or something like that! What a damn. I thought that I knew how to talk, but I must be a complete idiot, because I can't communicate! But I can't complain! I am alive! – he thought with some sarcasm!

The truck began to move. Inside it wasn't very comfortable but was warm enough, and the sympathetic lady offered some food and hot beverage, that he ate very fast. For some time they tried to articulate a strange conversation:
_ Oh, I know! You're trying to enhance the qualities of this din can! My grand dad had one in better conditions when he was young. But who am I to make fun of this old toy that is taking me out? I must tell her that I am not a criminal! I may not know who I am, but definitely I am not a criminal!
_ Speak slow, young boy! I can't follow you! Do you know that you resemble to "Brad Davis" in the "Midnight express"? I don't understand a word you're saying, but I can tell that you are not a criminal or a simple hobo, poor guy. I don't know why, but I want to take care of you. And I promise that I will! I like you! You remind me my dear son, Sazzor. If he hadn't died, he'd probably be in your age. You could be friends! Don't worry, I'll take care of you, whatever you have done to be in this situation! And my husband Glen will help me.

After an exhausting time, they notice that the conversation was going nowhere and they gave up, remaining in respectful silence. Peter enjoyed the silent, and rested his head in the seat, looking through the window glass. He tried to rest, but couldn't sleep. He was looking for some comprehension in the solitude. Peter! Peter! Once again, the voice annoying his thoughts. This time, without major concerns, he decided to let himself go through this calling, and slowly he closed his eyes, going deeper and deeper in this kind of trance. Flashes of memories started to sparkle in his mind, flowing as water running between cracks of a dried soil.

He was recovering his memoirs!

CHAPTER 01

===

20 YEARS BEFORE

_ Peter! Peter! C'mon lazy boy! You have to put your clothes on! The doctor is about to arrive! Don't you know that is not polite to let a gentleman like him waiting to long for a naught lad as you? Don't make me lose my temper! You know that I am not that healthy!

_ Mom, please, I don't wanna go! Don't make me go! I wanna stay with you. Who is gonna take care of you, mom? Don't let them take me, please?

_ My heart is bleeding, my dear Peter, but there is no other way. I wish I had. It is the best for your future, and I can handle myself. You're just making things more difficult. Besides, in that school you'll have things that neither me or you dad, when he was alive, ever could give you. Someday you thank for everything that I am doing now. Trust me once more, my love!

_ But mom, I just want to stay with you! I don't want fancy things, and I never will. I promise that I will be a nice boy from now on. I'll even take bath regularly, and will eat all that horrible vegetables that you put in my plate. I won't complain anymore, of nothing! But, please, let me stay, mom! I love you! Please, send them away! Tell them that you made a mistake or that I am not your son, that you are my maid, and that my parents are traveling!

_ What a imagination, my son! Unfortunately it won't work! C'mon, don't make me lose my temper! It is our last day together for a long time. Let's enjoy it.

She turned around to do not see him cry and to do not let him see her tears. She left the poor bedroom with a huge weight in her chest, squeezing her heart, talking to herself:

_ My dear precious, I'm sorry for everything, for making you suffer like that. I just hope that one day you will forgive me. Someday you will know that you're the light of my life, and I want you to shine like the sun! And I am sure that you will!

For some minutes she lie her back down on the wall, whining her bad luck since the death of her husband. She had worked too hard to support the house, but it wasn't enough, and things went worse when the physician said that she had a terrible disease in her heart. It was getting bigger and weaker every year, and the pension was barely providing some of the several remedies that she had to swallow every day. Peter was her only child and her greatest concern. Who would take care of him after she had gone? Nor her or her husband had near relatives who would apply to this task.

That's why, when the secretary of mister Jardell Vasconcellus, came to talk to her, two months ago, telling that test had been realized in the kindergarten where Peter studied, and that he was chosen to receive a scholarship in one of the most important schools to gifted children in the Europe, she felt a great relief. After all he would be headed to the future that she had always dreamed to him, and he wouldn't need to witnesses her debilitation, and her certain death. Immediately a gathering was scheduled, and professionals came to her residence for signatures and explain the procedures. Few days later, mister Vasconcellus, himself, came to meet to little phenomenon of only five years old, who had strongly impressed his technicians.

_ Doctor Vasconcellus, I want to be sure that all of this is free of charge. You know, I am a poor widow, and I couldn't afford this. We have nothing left to be snatched.

_ You have nothing to worry about, ma'm! From now on all the expenses of yours will be our concern. Better saying, a concern of my foundation. We will provide everything that he may need until he is graduated in the university and able to live on his own.

She send a gratitude look to everyone in the small living room. Her son's teacher, the principal and the counselor of the kindergarten, the lawyer and the crew of the foundation. All they seemed honest people, and she felt that she could rely her son's life to them. They were also happy with the agreements, and she finally assured with them.

_ That was the best decision, Ma'm – said the lawyer, and everybody nodded – we have the best school in the whole world to children with the talent that your son had shown. We have international reputation, and we won manifolds awards. We have all the qualities required. Even studying abroad, your son will be authorized to visit you in his vacations. We provide the tickets. We have students from all over the world. If you wish, we can provide transportation wherever you want to visit him and check our venues. This way, you will help him to settle down easier.

He wanted her to be sure that the foundation had all the facilities to make his like and her life better:

_ I don't know if you are aware that from this day forth you are included in our health insurance. All your treatment is covered, and so your medicines. You will have nothing to worry about. She agreed with a sad smile.

He was ready to go. The car was waiting outside, but her legs trembled and she couldn't move, and the driver came in to pick him up. She even had strength to see his departure through the window, while the impatient man closed the car's door, and left skidding the tires.

Peter was an extremely obedient boy, and he had stopped crying when his mother ordered to. That was his main characteristic. He always obeyed. His greatest diversion consisted on creating his own toys, with rags and rests of other toys, because he knew that his mother couldn't afford new ones. Even when his father was alive he didn't received many presents. He was able to spent hours playing alone, with his rag armies. He used to play in his room, in the living room's corner, behind the building, or every place where he wouldn't be bothered by other people. In these moments someone could say that he was completely happy. He wasn't envious of the gifts that his mates used to receive on Christmas, anniversaries and children's day, such as bikes; videogames; mini robots, computers and all sort of toys used to make the children eyes glow. He was a very disciplined boy, a good observer and incredibly smart. At the age of five he already knew how to write and to read

Into two languages, but wasn't that good at math, despite his logical thinking well developed. In classroom he used to behave, because he wasn't very popular with the mates. He was excellent at sports and normally won all the competitions and was a good player of chess. He was even better than the teachers, and nobody got surprised, when some foreign researchers came into the school proposing to apply tests on the students in order to offer scholarships, and he was the only one that passed in all the exercises proposed. The technicians were very impressed by the fact that he had scored all the results while he guessed hidden figures of several ways. They decide to apply more difficult tests, and he passed again. No one in the foundation could believe on what was happening. Only another boy, so far, had achieved such performance, some years ago.

The president of the foundation was told what had happened, and admired with the fact, had decided to go himself to talk with the boy's parents, what was very unusual, because he was a very busy man and did not have time or patience to deal with his students. He could count with experts to that. But he didn't want to risk losing this little prodigy to another school, or that for religious motifs his parents could impose some barriers, what was very common in those current days.

Mister Jardell wasconcellus was, in a certain way, used to the poverty of the third world, after all, some part of his pupils came from countries from South America and Central Africa. Even though, he couldn't help felling a little distress with all that misery, and the excuse to his conscience, for being very rich, was that from his revolutionary work the level of life of the population would increase considerably. In certain way, he was a bit more distressed than the costume when he arrived in that city, probably because he considered that it wasn't proper to a child so talented as Peter. As if such event only could occur in a certain society and a certain class of people. After all his efforts to became a better man, he still conserved some rests of bias. The ugly place, mainly the big condo, with 30 buildings of six floors, each one in a different color, surrounded by muck and in ruins, with no conservation, shocked his style sense. To make it worse, there were bunch of filthy children, with sick look, with their bellies inched by worms, running and playing throughout the streets full of garbage and stinky water, and looking amazed to the fancy car. They had never seen one like that. He was disgusted and talk to the driver:

_ It is not an excuse to poor people behave like pigs. Dignity and neatness cost absolutely nothing.

The people on the sidewalks peered with such curiosity a tall blond elegant man, dressed in a well cut dark green suit gets out of the vehicle. They felt such satisfaction when he stepped in a stink mud, remains from the last flood. He cackled with then, thinking that it was a punishment for his prejudice. There were so many people in front of the building, that was evident that was no secret that the son the "trash barons", as Peter's parents were dubbed by the neighbors, was to receive the visit of some foreign authority. In their poor imagination, they believed that the Moll family would gain some heritage from a distant rich relative, because their extravagant behavior only could indicate that they once were millionaires and lost all their fortune. In their envious soul, they desired that something bad occurred, because they didn't want to see the little Peter awarded with a chance that their own kids probably would never have in their miserable lives.

The women and the men were whispering that the trash baroness's bastard; they used to refer to them in such scorn and mockery; didn't allowed his little prince to play with the their children, and because of that, some bad luck would haunt his destiny. The fact that Peter was coy, polite, kind, very gorgeous, was always clean and well dressed, and preferred to play alone didn't make him a popular kid among his little neighbors.

His teacher, who had gone with the procession, went up ahead to indicate the path, and while they were going up the stairs, Mister Vasconcellus felt the sadness return to his chest. The walls with the plaster falling apart, the steps almost without tiles, and the bad smell of the piles of rubbish on the corridors represented all the complaisance, marasmus and lack of initiative that he longed for eradicate. When young and idealistic, he thought when had his family fortune was in his hands, he could diminish the poverty of a considerable party of the world by creating non governmental organizations that would act in manifold fronts to combat misery. Long time after that, he was obliged to admit all his money wasn't enough to scratch the surface of the social problems and that they were much more complexes than he could suppose. Besides it, would have to step up groups of people who raised great amount of currency by exploring the suffering of others. Sadly, he concluded the best way to face that would be creating a manner to set free people from the yoke of those baneful interests. He just didn't know how to achieve it. Yet.

Peter's mother opened the door. By on looking at her someone could realize her profound state of debility and penury. Her face, formerly could have been cute, now was marked by deep wrinkles and speckles around the eyes. The disease had taken away the blush from her face and the glitter from her hair, leaving the yellow tone in the skin as to assure that everybody could recognize how terrible her problem was. But that woman smiled in a humble way to the group, and despite her fragile appearance, they noticed how strong she could become to support all the probations life had imposed with such dignity and tranquility.

_ The gentlemen and the ladies would give the honor to accept a cup of coffee? Don't you worry, it is not the bad one that I am used to. It is one from the package of food that your foundation sent last week. I was just waiting for you to make a fresh one – she showed so much satisfaction in that gesture that noone could refuse.

_ We will be grateful for that, ma'm. thank you very much – replied Morgana, mister Vasconcellus's secretary.

Mister Vasconcellus was peering everything, curiously repairing that despite all the mockness outside, inside it was impeccably clean and neat, and the kid, anyway resembled the bad impression that he had with the local children.

_ It looks like to me that you, madam, appreciated all the supplies that we had prepared. Is that all that you needed? We can provide some more, if you wish!

_ Oh no, sir. I mean, yes sir. I appreciated every single good you've sent. And I have more than I need. I pray every night for you because of that.

The president of the foundation was touched by the statement, yet his face just demonstrated a pleased smile. His assistant, Morgana, with the authority in which she was invested, knowing that her boss wasn't efficient with words, completed:

_ We are very satisfied with that – she said with a friendly smile – If you need anything else, we will be glad in providing. Just keep in contact with our local employer, Mister Aaron Mendell, who is present here today – a gray hair man nodded his head – now that we have chat a little we are able to discuss the subjects that brought us here. As you know, the president of our great foundation, Mister jardell Vasconcellus, came to explain to you what is the school in which you son will study from now on. I believe that I have removed all your doubts in our previous conversations. But if you've any further questions, you can talk directly with him.

_ Yes, lady Morgana. I am very aware about your institution and about doctor Vasconcellus. It is a pleasure to meet you, sir. And now that I could look into his eyes, all my doubts have vanished. I 'm quite sure that my beloved son will have a great future with you.

_ It is a pleasure to meet such respectable lady – greeted the president – I must confess that your kiddo impressed me a lot. He possesses extraordinary skills that the majority of the world population can barely conceive. Rare times I have seen so outstanding results on the tests that we have being applying for the past three decades. And I have reasons to believe that without an appropriated education and specify training program those innate skills will soon disappear, changing him into a frustrated adult without a reasonable place in the society.

_ You must know, as any other mother, I worship my boy, and I would do absolutely everything in my grasp to give him a chance to achieve his dreams in this life. Only another mom could comprehend how painful is to me to be apart of my dear Peter. However, I am sure that there is no other way, and I submit myself to the fate's will – she said mourning – I am aware that in this city, in this country, he will become like those rejected hobos that live among us in this hole. Me and my husband never thought that we would raise our son in so precarious conditions. we worked too hard to offer him a good education, but like had other plans and the death took away the life of Peter's father in a bus accident. And after my illness, all my dreams faded away. Did you know how good electronic technician my husband was? He was a hell of a professional with a good job and his own repair shop. He worked all the time, often working till late at night. And now, with this precarious pension I can't support even the minimum necessary to your subsistence. I am not naïve, I know that I won't live much longer, and I can only praise you came into our way – she dried her tears with the tip of her clad.

_ I understand your reasons, ma'm. I know what you've been through and I am by your side. You can have peace in your heart, because your son will be cherished by me and all my crew. And when he leaves our school, he will be graduated and well prepared to be the man you've expected to, and will occupy the place that he deserves. And I am sure that you will see all that happen, because our physicians will take care of you, with the ultimate treatment – declared Mister Vasconcellus.

_ This foundations is very famous and reliable. Their reputation is recognized everywhere. - Said the kindergarten principal – I looked for information about it and received excellent references. You may completely trust on their good intentions. I hope you, mister Vasconcellus, understand my concerns, that's why I needed to certify all your data. Peter is our best student, and everyone in the school cares about him. Nowadays, you know, there are many crazy people around the world, doing all sort of nasty things, we can't be sure!

Mister jardell Vasconcellus used to talk in a very confident manner, with low voice and always looking his speakers in the eye.

_ I understand and admire your precautions, it is more than natural that you check on our credentials. There's no need to be embarrassed.

Peter's mom argued again:

_ I believe strongly on you! Since you arrived I felt like angels had fallen from heaven to give the good news, and I was taken by such joy that I can barely hold my tears. I am sure you came to help my kiddo to fulfill his destiny.

Mister Vasconcellus had a deep relief's breath. Everything has gone as planned and he didn't have to waste his precious time by convincing superstitious people about his ideals, as he had sometimes, and after some more talking about the details over the scholarship, he added:

_ All the required documentation to the boy's travel must last some weeks, and I believe he will read to go right after that. My secretary, Morgana, will be in charge of his reception at the airport. And as my lawyer said, this was the best decision you have ever taken about Peter's future. Be sure that we will never let him down. You have my word on that. Thank you very much.

_ I am the one who have to thanks. God bless you, mister! God bless you all, people!

_ God bless us all repeated Morgana.

CHAPTER 02

PETER MOLL

Peter had never traveled by plane. Otherwise, he had never traveled by any kind of transportation. But he wasn't afraid. He was proud for have being nominated as a courageous boy by his parents, and had a certain love for novelties. Two years before, when he was at the age of three, and his parents took him to the zoo, by the first time. When they admiring the elephants, one of them came closer and with its trunk took out the doll from the armies of a little girl. While everybody around was mocking about the weird episode, Peter passed among the rails and ran towards the elephant to try to rescue the toy. His father and mother were in panic, the other kids began to scream. To his luck, one of the tamers were nearby and got into the enclosure to save the boy who was pushing the doll from the trunk. His mother was so traumatized that she decided to never come back to that place, although the little Peter always asked his father to take him back to the zoo.

The eight hours flight ran without any problem. The flight attendants all the moment came to bring food or play with the cute polite little boy, who impressed them considerably with his unprotected care needed manners. At any time he acted as it is usually expected from children in closed ambient. At their arrival, as mister Vasconcellus had promised, Morgana Helen Tantty, director assistant, was waiting for him. Despite she wasn't any model of beauty, she used to captivate people with her dainty sympathy. She had been working at the foundation for many years, and one of her duties consisted on receiving and locate the students who didn't have the support of their parents. But she didn't treated Peter like a simple student. Since the very first moment of contact there was a huge empathy between them, when Morgana, with a warmth smile, kissed him on the forehead, and he greeted her in a funny way, bending on his knees and kissing her hand. After that, feeling well sheltered, the coy Peter trusted her the most perfect laugh, the one was reserved only to his mother. Her resemblance to his mom and her eyes full of tenderness touched him. He remembered the cherish he didn't have since he left his country, and all the new things happening and all the rush, for some hours he completely forgot his progenitor, and when her image came to his mind, he began to weep, a low cry, almost unperceptive, of a reserved person who is abashed to drop tears in front of people he barely knew. Touched, Morgana hugged and embraced him, and proposed to have a hot chocolate.

_ Very well, little Petey. I am not used to children, specially the crying ones. So let's make a deal, you have the right to ask anything you want if you stop crying for a little bit, at least.

_ Everything I want to? I already stopped. You see? No more tears in my eyes! – he never had in his life the opportunity to eat whatever he wanted. He always had to eat what the parents could afford or what there was in the fridge. And the food was never tasteful, and the most of the time it had the taste of shoe sole. But peter had to be grateful because at least he had what to eat, while many of his neighbors had nothing. – Now I want milk and coffee and that flan over there. I always wanted to prove a flan. What flavor is it?

_ I believe it is cocoa and cranberry.

_ Cranberry? What is it?

_ It is a sort of fruit.

_ Okay! After that I'll have that hot chocolate and maybe a hamburger. I tried it once and it was delicious.

_ Everything you say, master. – Said Morgana, laughing at his sudden change of mood. – The chocolate in here is simply wonderful.

_ Aunt, why do you talk in a funny way?

_ Because you're not used to our accent yet. Despite you speak our language beautifully, you do not have conversation experience. Now eat your pastry.

_ When can I see my mommy?

_ First of all, is not polite to talk while you're chewing. And it is too early to thing about it. You just arrived, and there is a lot of things for you to know, but I am sure that in your first vacations you'll be allowed to visit her.

_ I understand. Other question. Aunt, is my mother going to die?

_ Of course not, Pete! Who gave you this idea? Your mother is a little sick, but I am sure the doctors will cure her, and everything will be fine again.

_ Hey, aunt! I must be a child but it doesn't mean I am stupid. You don't need to talk to me like a moron. I have a good understanding of how things work, and I know my sent me away because she didn't want me to presence her agony. She never thought about herself, nor for a minute. Her priority was always my future.

_ Alright, Peter. Let's talk right, you deserve this. I didn't think you are a moron. I just don't think is fare to a child like you to behold this sad reality. Excuse me, please. I knew you were a very gifted boy, but I couldn't imagine you were so mature.

_ I had to do so, to help my mother when daddy died.

_ I know. What is happening is that your mother is really very sick. Her heart is dying and the doctors want to replace it for an artificial one. You know, a bionic heart.

_ I read something about it in the internet.

_ So, She didn't have the resources to afford this surgery, but the foundation health insurance will cover everything. And we have very good healing psychics, who will make everything they can to help her recovering. But you're right, she never thought about it, and I believe she didn't even know she would have these rights if you were our student. All she wanted was to assure your future, because she loves you so much. I am sure you two will be very happy together. Trust me.

_ Thanks, aunt!

_ You're welcome, dear.

She had brought a new coat to him, because she knew in his country he was used to another kind of weather, and his mother didn't have money to buy a new trousseau. In this moment she decide to give him a present and when could be possible she would take him to buy new clothes. He would be crazy about it. During all the way to the campus they were talking happily, and she even taught some famous lullabies, and when they got there, Peter felt in his chest as if he was already related to that protective woman, as if he new her a long time ago, and they shared the same spiritual family. The car stopped in front of the big gates. They were really huge metal structure, stuck to walls equally very high, that didn't allow a glance to what was happening inside, this way, giving total possibility to the workers and students to exercise freely all the rigorous training they should be submitted. The central computer authorized their entrance after identify the license of the vehicle, and slowly the heavy gates moved up, permitting to the passers by to satisfy their curiosity peering for some moments the exuberant fame of the inside of the campus of the foundation. While the car was rolling in the great property, the little Peter was being amazed by the profusion of trees, grass and gardens very well taken care that surround a total of nine buildings. They stopped in front of the third one.

_ You see, Peter? This is where you're gonna live from now on. You can play and amuse yourself in all this space, and there is much more behind that hill. I am sure you re'gonna be very happy here with us, and make great friends. If you are a good boy, you'll receive lots of presents, toys you can never imagined. Wait and see.

But the boy wasn't paying heed to her words, because he was so excited with all around him, specially the yellow brick three floors building, very different from those he was used to. Richly decorated, well conserved and illuminated, the construction had a pleasant aspect, cozy and infantile, as if it had been taken out from a fairy tale's book. He didn't believe when she said he would dwell in it and invited him to get in. inside it kept all the enchantment of the outside. The same impression caused in him the bedrooms, that were shared by four kids. The boys occupied this and the next building and the girls the two ones beside. There was a bathroom for each two bedrooms, and the students until the age of nine lived on the first floor; those until the age of fourteen were on the second and those from fifteen till eighteen dwelled on the third. The older apprentices lived in a annex, outside the campus.

On the front of it, there was a reasonable size hall with three coaches and two armchairs, for those kids who wanted to gather is small reading groups. On the corresponding spaces of the second and third floors there was a great study room with four six places tables provided with core screens, which allowed them to connect to internet, to promote holographic conferences and to watch movies or shows.

_ This is here, Peter. The room number seven will be your new den. Be my guest and open the door, gentleman. Said Morgana, while she leant forward.

Curious and euphoric, he immediately obeyed the order, and when he entered, his eyes sparkled of such joy and incredulous satisfaction. He had never got into such fancy ambient. Two big beds were on the right side and two on the left, and all of them were very different of his ancient sleeping sofa, high; large; beautiful with thick and comfortable mattresses, idleness soft pillows and colored blankets portrait the bed of every child's dream. Just like those from the television advertisements he used watch, so cozy they made him asleep. Under the window, on the center of the room, a big desk with a computer and eight drawers, on the door's wall there was a closet with four places, and to the left the access to the bathroom, which had a special brown ceramic floor. The directory assistant passed to show and to explain to Peter all the rules of the dormitories.

_ As you can have noticed, you'll divide the room with three other boys. They study here since last year. At the moment they're on vacations, visiting their families. Therefore, for the moment you'll be here alone, but you must respect their space as if they were here. You are a single son and are not used to share things with other people, however you must learn quickly to avoid any problems with your mates. I believe you'll fit easily. Look, here is your part of the wardrobe, it is big enough to keep your stuff. There on the desk, the two drawers down on the left are yours to put your school material and anything else you want, the computer is for all you, and you must decide how to use it. Do you know how to use one? No? Don't worry, I'll teach you. At night, if you want to use it, you must certify that your mates agree with it, and use the flashlight glasses to not bother them.

_ Flashlight glasses?

_ It is a special glasses made to be used in the dark.

_ cool!

_ Going on, the beds have drawers to accommodate all your toys, blankets and sheets. Any doubt, handsome boy? No? so must take a long bath, because you must be very tired, put on the new pajamas I bought and try to sleep a little. Don't forget to close the door, that gives access to the other bedroom, when you use the bathroom. I'll go to my home to do some things and at afternoon we'll go out to buy some clothes and other stuff you may need.

At noon she woke him up, chose a nice trousers and shirt, dressed him up and they were walking forth to the second building, where the refectory was. It was a huge salon with dozens of long tables, with long benches attached on them. On the enclosure some students and some employees who didn't travel had lunch. They peered the new one and smiled, nodding their heads as if they gave welcome to him. The most of the workers and apprentice would only begin to return on the next week. On the following days, Peter knew the rest of the foundation campus, and the deans of his school believed he was getting adapted easier and faster than the expected, in great part due to be a child very clever and extremely observer. He perceived the great unique opportunity he was been given and understood he should to do his maximum to do not bother noone, avoiding this way to be send back. His incredible capacity of memorization facilitated the knowing of the property, and The most Morgana showed to him the most he wanted to see more. This way, the days flown by and he almost didn't have time to get depressed when he reminded and missed his home and his mother, and even his boring neighbors, who tormented and despised him, but in certain manner were part of his short life.

On the first building was located the administration and a auditorium to 900 people and on the other floors functioned the school. On the 7th and 8th were the research laboratories, development and training of all the students and volunteers. With seven floors each, these were the highest constructions of the complex. Woods and small artificial ponds completed the celestial ambient of the place. People could sit on the manifold orthopedic plastic benches; which fitted to the bodies, spread around the area. Behind some hundred meters from the 8th building, was located the sportive center, formed by a complex of two warmed Olympic pools; one of them covered, some fields to soccer; football; baseball; lacrosse, and some courts to basketball, volleyball, badmington and tennis. On the 9th building were three salons to dance, workout and do gymnastic, a 4th salon was dedicated to yoga and martial arts, and a multi sportive gymnasium adverted that the physical exercises should not be interrupted because of the weather conditions. The good fitness and good health were extremely important to the goals. A large running track surrounded all the sportive complex, symbolizing the Greek ideal of a sane mind, sane body should be a rule among the students. On the truth, the firsts years of the development of the special capacities, the physical conditioning was preponderant factor to the full success of the realizations that would come after.

The little Peter wasn't worried to understand the purposes of all those installations, his main purpose was to run free among them and the immense green spaces and to squander on the toys of the infant park. Due to be the only child at that moment in the campus, he received all the attention from the part of all the adults, which let even more satisfied. The girls and workers took him everywhere, always disputing his presence, enchanted with the fact that he looked like a pet, that didn't bother, and the boys usually were very patient to answer his questions. The climate was peaceful and serenity, and everyone enjoyed the maximum the last period of rest, once the rhythm of the academic year was intense and exhaustive.

The boys and girls began to return to the accommodations with the proximity of the initiation of the classes. Peter was very animated with the idea to finally meet his roommies and make friends of his age, once wasn't the same thing to play with older fellows. He even made new puppets with the rest of the material Morgana gave him, and learnt to use the computer, and he used to play with Sven, the janitor. He was becoming proficient on the language. At last his roommates arrived. Victor Nerd, the director of relationship of the entity, a person very friendly and cordial; who was always trying to find out the needs of the intern students, was in charge to make the presentations between the fresh ones and the junior ones, who would share the accommodations and to look after their adaptation. With 62 years old, the funny and witty former circus clown, was the right person to the job, because he knew how to relax an ambient as anybody else. That's why he did this function for 20 years.

Peter was laid down in his bed, reading a digital comic book, when he got into, followed by three other curious kids.

_ My friend Peter, your days as the lord of this room are over. Now you'll have to share your reign with these other princes. Now I introduce you the cousins Mick and Tommy Hagar. They're from Australia. And Argos Numi Buzollor, from Somalia, Africa. Boys this meet Peter Moll, from America. I'll let you alone give you the opportunity to know each other better. I have other noble kids to settle down. Arrevoir!

Argos was six years old, the same age of the other two, but was far taller than they. He was always attracting attention for being robust and for being always showing his big bright teeth in a constant sympathetic smile. That's why he was dubbed "Joker", in a reference to the laugher Batman's foe. He was the first one to "break the ice".

_ Do you have any choco, pal? I have double ball gums if you wanna trade.
Peter didn't understand his accent, but tried to guess what he asked.
_ I am not chuck. I am not even buck.
_ Bulky? Not if you put just one in your mouth.
_ My month is march, and yours?
_ No, here we don't need to march! We are not militaries.
_ Would you two please shut up? - Replied an angry Tommy - I am getting sick with horrible communication.
_ Syrup? What is he saying for God sake?
_ Don't worry, Peter. He is Australian. Even I don't understand his accent sometimes.

The red hair from outbanks cousins were confused with problems with the language pronunciation, but they decide to get into the conversation too, and give their hints.
_ Where do you come from, Peter? Is it too cold in there? How is your family? Can you introduce me to your pretty sisters if you have? I have three, and they are the most beautiful girls in town. I am always gaining candles from the boys who want to date them. But Tommy's sisters are not cute.
_ How dare you? Vic and Layla are prettier than your grim siblings. Even I am more handsome than you, Shrek!
_ Keep dreaming, folk.
_ Stop it boys! I am tired of this dispute. What Peter is gonna think about us? Would you like to play outside, pal?
_ What?
_ Are you deaf, fresh boy? I asked if you wanna play outside?
_ "It's late". Let's go to play. By the way, I am not daft.

Quickly the boys became inseparable friends and wandered by the dependences of the foundation. But the joy last few days. The classes began and a total frenzy took over the campus. Hundreds of intern and extern students circulated everywhere, as in any other school, looking for information about schedules and classroom numbers, meeting old friends, talking, laughing loudly, fleeing from former flirts and searching new woos. Almost nothing was different from another teaching establishments, with teachers and assistants in a lazy rhythm that barely could remember the names of their former pupils who were more interested in knowing when would be the next holiday, and complained about how fast the vacations used to pass. The main difference was here, people were psychics, and could do amazing things. It was common to see someone flying over the buildings, students vanishing or appearing instantly, objects levitating, lights flashing, and all sort of manifestations that is expected to be produced by paranormal people. The population was already used to these happenings, but to witness them in a place full of such capacities still remained something amazing.

As used to happen every year, after the last class of the first day, all the students, workers and the teachers were reunited in the auditorium to listen a speech that would mark the official begin of the school year. Peter was a little dislocated in this hall full of people. He had never been in a such place and laughed a lot when someone offered him a pair of headphones so the foreign people could understand easier the lecture.

_ Thank you, but I am not deaf.

_ It is not this sort of phones, boy! These are to the simultaneous translation, made by a robot. Do you think you understand very well our language? Try to follow the speech without these things. Don't make me waste my time, kid. Take it here, now! Don't play games with me!

He needed only a few minutes to perceive that he couldn't comprehend the most of the words said and have to use the device. When the huge salon became quieter he felt intriguing the fact that a large number of young boys and girls do not make any kind of disorder, and even his three fellows, who were usually hyperactive, were strangely calm. Even between the senior students, who knew practically everything that would be said, the climate was of total respect, tranquility and mainly silence. The simple presence of Mister jardell Vasconcellus on the stage, who worshiped the discipline above everything, probably was enough to intimidate the most rebel of the students. Despite the fact that the president of the foundation have never needed to use his authority to restrain someone or impose his will, or even to punish somebody, he was respected by the admiration everybody felt about him, an outstanding man who dedicated his life and fortune to a dare and challenging project which everyone believed to be integrant part of it. Even the youngest felt the intuition of the importance of what is "on the table there" and didn't want to do anything that could exclude them somehow of this historical process.

CHAPTER 03

THE FOUNDATION

The first to talk was Mister Reubens Éolo, principal of the school and a psychologist with a successful career over than 30 years. He was responsible for the adaptation of the school subject grades into of the demands of the rigid training program developed by the scientists of the foundation. He was very sever, but fare enough to keep the friendship of the major of the students, always participating of games and events proposed by them, and respecting their opinions and complains. He knew how to make himself obeyed by the fresh kids. As he had always done, he began by exposing in a clear and compact way to the new ones, all the behavior conduct rules that ran the life in the installations of the school and the whole campus.

_ Very well, ladies and gentlemen, I hope to have been clear like crystal about the rights and duties in our establishment, and if some of you have yet any doubts over the subjects treated here, please wait until tomorrow, because will be released a folder with a small manual about these matters and many others. I'll ask you to have it always in hand when you wish to make any complain. Proceeding, the student quality that we appreciate the most in our school is the discipline, and I warn the fresh ones from now on we won't tolerate any disobey to our determinations. This institution is not public and do not work with any government help, so we cant afford to deal with rebels and pranksters. The course is too much long to be wasted with someone that should not belong here. You were decorated with the prize to study in here and you must do right to our trust. We do not want, and I repeat, we do not want and we will not waste our precious time, money and knowledge with those who do not with to give their best to accomplish our goals. Who do not want to make many sacrifices the best is to give up as soon as possible. All and any breach will be noted and on the fifth in the current year, the student will be invited to leave our school. You will responsible for the conservation of all the materials and equipments given to you, we will not have expenses with hoboes, and who damage anything will pay for it. Anyhow, I hope you enjoy everything and all the opportunities that are here given to you. Study, have fun spend you energies on things according to your ages. But keep always in mind that you have to think and act in a rational healthy and instructive way. Respect your community, school, your and your schoolmates and you will always be successful and happy.

If you are sufficient persistent and patients, the foundation will offer you in the end of your efforts, a wide world of wonderful choices. You are in the verge to experience things that never happened in all the history. What you've learned until now is nothing in comparison to what is ahead of you. You're being prepared to take the reins of the world in your hands, and you'll be able to fix what have been done in a wrong way to our most precious good, the earth. You are fare and honest, nothing will stand in your way to build a better place to live. When you're grown up, the civilization will be totally different of this rotten husk our society is soaked in, and people will look at you with pride in their eyes, because of your extraordinary actions and will feel in their hearts a little bit of envy for did not have had the chances you've been offered now.

At this point of his speech, his secretary approached and whispered in his ear:

_ Mr. Principal, did you forget the most of the students in here today is in the age of five years old? Neither of them is understand what you're talking about. Hold your enthusiasm in.

_ Of course, Mrs. Levinsk. Thank you. – Turning to the audience – It looks like I am a little stimulated and I forgot we have too many children presents today. Of course they can't understand yet what I'm trying to pass, and I'd like to ask the help of the parents to talk to them, when the opportunity comes, about those important issues. My apologies, I talk too much. Let's just follow the guidelines. This year we'll have something new, besides our well known discipline keepers, we'll have the reinforcement of surveillance robots, who will take care of the dependences of the campus 24/7. With this support we expect to avoid the breaks in of hooligans, that happen occasionally. Also, any emergency can be reported directly to these machines, which are equipped with the ultimate generation devices, and be solved faster. Their intranet system can access the foundation employers at any time.

At this moment, six three feet tall machines got into the stage walking like any human being. They were white and black and had four arms and four fingers in each one. Their head was round and could move in any direction, and had three camcorders that worked as three eyes. They nodded to the audience and stood still behind the principal, who made a signal to one of them, that stepped forward and talked to the people, in a metallic funny voice.

_ What's up, Bros? All green? Groovie! – Nobody understood a thing it said. – our main concern is to make your life as comfortable as possible. We are here to help and serve.

_ I present you mister roboto, the ultimate technology in support. Excuse its vocabulary! The technician who programmed it wasn't updated to the latest slang. Of course adjustments will be required, but I believe we were successful in our intention to portrait what is it about to come, weren't we?

Proceeding to the activities, was the time of Mister Vasconcellus to talk. It was the first time peter saw him since he had been in his mother's residence. On the photonic microphone he made his firsts considerations and let Peter very embarrassed when Mister Vasconcellus made him some questions.

_ I can see the little Peter Moll over there. Hello Peter, how are you? Are you having a good time in our institution?

The kid shyly nodded.

_ Very good, my lad! In here you're going to see, learn and do amazing things. Soon I'll visit you, to have a nice conversation. Be well.

Driving his attention to the audience.

_ People, I'd like to introduce you the young promise Peter Corona Moll. Keep this name in your memories. He is going to do great things!

This special deference awaked the general curiosity and a whisper took the ambient, while everybody writhed to try to see the new one who deserved such consideration. Something Jardell had never done before. Two twin brothers, who were some lines behind , Tharus and iullus Vendra, looked at him so hard that little peter felt the heat of their eyes in his nape, and automatically turned on their direction. For some instants they deeply peered each other, as if they were doing some kind of recognition, but them Tharus made a grimace and showed his tongue. The three boys began to laugh and returned to pay heed on the lecture.

The president continued with his imposing voice.

_ My dear kids, the main finality of our institution is to forge good citizens who can contribute to the evolution of our civilization and the planet as an all. We want to educate consciences that will harmonically interact with the nature, creating an ambient of peace; equilibrium and respect to all the creatures that share this world with us. The society requires good professionals, such as good doctors; engineers; politicians; farmers; artists and believe me; even lawyers. In sum, requires workers in all areas of human interests, but it requires mostly men and women who can use their citizenship with solidarity, integrity and dedication. These are the pillars of our foundation, SID, solidarity, integrity and dedication. You're going to see it everywhere. Our goal is, no matter the profession you choose, you will have dignity to conduct it as good citizens. That's why we are so exacting in relation to your duties, in this time when people are only worried exclusively with their rights, once we are aware there's no right without a respective duty. The life in our planet depends on unique conditions, and any alteration in the equilibrium of the forces that maintain us can signify our destruction. However, remember this: all our success depends on one thing, the equilibrium. All the process you will be tested can only be reached by the use of it. And when you achieve all your potentials, with equilibrium you will be able to do amazing things. This premise I learnt long time ago, with much effort and suffering, some good apprentices died on the process, but finally I understood, and I am passing it to my students since then.

He kept talking after a short break.

_ Thirty five years have passed by since I graduated in psychology and had no idea of what to do with my life. I know that for the most of you, to keep listening to this mambo jambo every single year is very boring, but I consider my own experience may be of great value to the fresh students. So, let's go on. A only son of a very rich couple, I had no vocation to be in charge of the family business and had all the perks money could buy. And this pretty life last until the day after a horrible discussion with my mother, who had all the reasons to charge me a more serious attitude with my life and future, I decided to travel without communicate them and pass the new year's eve in Aspen. I not even wished happy new year to them, who only thought on my well being. For several times I dialed the holographic phone that everything was a non-sense, that they were right and that eventually I would be adapted to the grown people life style. However, the pride and the slot made me hung up all the times. Something told me I should not care about it, that when I was back we had enough time to settle things, and other bullshits that keep us apart from those we love. So I went to the ball escorted by a beautiful actress and some friends, and I had a great time the whole night by any possible means, even some considered illegal, and I do not remember when I went to sleep. The sure thing was that I had a very vivid dream on which I was at home when my parents arrived. At first moment I felt embarrassed because of the discussion we had before, and instinctively I leant my head. Then they came closer, hugged me, kissed me on the cheek, and my mother just said: "my beloved son, I want you to know that there's no chagrins between us. The fights we had were part of a health relationship. Be in peace, because we know your good heart and good will, and we are aware about your love for us. We are sure we will be proud of you and so will the whole society. Have judgment, and remember how much we love you". After those words they turned around and left. At afternoon, I was having breakfast with my friends when I remembered this dream, and I was just talking it to them when the vice-president of our companies called me to give the tragic news. My father and my mother had passed away in a car accident the night before, while they were driving to the community center where every year was shared a supper with the indigent people. Since I was a kid they used to spend the new year's eve in that place. They weren't satisfied on just give financial support to the organization, they wanted to participate, because they believed that the most precious gift we could share with somebody was our time. In their beliefs, time wasn't money. Time is much more valuable. Money you can always regain, but the time spent can never come back. This tragedy let me devastated for a long period, but little by little, that dream was giving me strength to enjoy life again. In the deep of my heart I knew it wasn't creation of my mind. The encounter was real. I had seen my parents right after they died. It was clear to me, and I had to do something about it. First my duties increased a lot because of their death. I had so many things to take care, and my priorities changed without I had noticed them. The will to continue their beautiful work took over the void in my heart, and the desire to discover how was possible that supernatural encounter put me on the right direction. I should dedicate my efforts on studying the phenomenon that gave me the chance to meet them by the last time, and the official science didn't have means to explain. I had to search, dominate and reproduce the cerebral capacities that produce so many mysterious and inexplicable facts. But the most important reason was this phenomenon helped me to support the loss of the people that I love the most in this world and to overcome the remorse for did not have said good-bye to them tenderly, in the way we were used to. This dream avoided my life had become bitter and distressed, and I wanted to teach and develop these gifts on general people, so they could remake their lives after great losses.

He made a pause to certify the effect his speech was causing on the audience and them continued.

_ So I elaborated the project that ended on the creation of the foundation to the study and development of the paranormal(FSDP), with the main goal to develop the greatest number possible of young people in their sensitive abilities, creating this way, a fellowship of psychics who would embrace the mission of helping the mankind to step another degree in the ladder of the evolution of the species. Exactly thirty years ago, we set our first laboratory, and after three exhaustive years of many and many researches and experimentations, we formed our first classroom of paranormals. After ten years of efforts, uncountable sacrifices and studies, me; my team; the students; and the large number of collaborators, were able to prove scientifically the function of the extra sensorial perception as any regular activity of our brain. Finally, the mind super capacities were no longer considered as superstition, coincidence or illusion created by professionals. Today we can see good psychic schools practically in all the countries of the globe, and the techniques developed by our crew are used in large scale. Can you believe that I almost won a Nobel prize because of it? Recently, the UN suggested to their members to adopt procedures to approve laws that would regulate the control over the use of this new work power. Today we have former students working on the most distinct areas with their capacities, such as doctors; astronauts; firefighters; consultants; security officers; politicians; mine managers. And I say that only to quote a small example of the positive impact we are causing in the social behavior. Some countries are already implementing some conduct norms to the paranormals, to avoid future problems.

He noticed the audience began to show signs of tiredness, and before they get bored, he decided to end his lecture.

_ Very well, my dear ones, thanks for your attention and excuse me if I prolonged too much speech. I am very excited with this theme and I don't know when to stop. Now I will give the word to Hermes Vasconcellus, my son, who is in charge of the infantile research center. Good evening!

During some minutes, the audience cheered stood the touching relate of the man who faced many troubles and bias so they could be there in that moment and place. Asking hush to them, alleging the end of the lecture was close, the young Vasconcellus began his speech.

_ Don't you worry, people. I won't be long. I'll just talk for some three hours and nothing more.

_ What? – Someone shouted.

_ I'm just kidding! I want to finish it quickly because I am starving. – He said that laughing, what was unusual to his behavior, and who had met him knew he was more serious than his father. – The extra sensorial perception is inherent to the living beings, dogs; cats; turtles; spiders; mosquitoes; bees; elephants; and humans, inclusive. Only the manifestation degree varies from specie to specie, and from person to person.   With time and dedication all of us can achieve the maximum of our potential, and those who have strength enough can even trespass a little their biological limits. And is justly during the childhood that we find the best conditions to begin the process of training. So, as an athlete trains since early age to overcome his physical boundaries, our brain can, in this same form, achieve the objective of developing itself sensitively. The years of precise measures, made by our technicians permitted us to create with total certainty, an scale to detect the degree of the mental powers. This table goes from 01 to 10 points, and each point is divided into five sub-divisions. One hundred per cent of the people of this planet and the others we are conquering can develop their capacities until the first stage. Of this total, about 50 percent can achieve the second stage. 20 percent can reach the third level. 08 percent of the world population can reach the fourth level. 03 percent will be able to complete the fifth stage, and 01 percent can finish the sixth. From this forth we can only suppose. It is incognito, for till the present day, none of our students or from other schools have reached the levels from 07 to 10. it means that we have excellent challenges to the future, don't we? Well, till now, we could prove the existence of 97 different types of paranormal phenomenon, and each psychic manifest a quantity of these capacities equivalent to the double of his degree. What means to say that an sensitive level three possess six abilities and one level five has 10 different types of paranormal phenomenon. And the mental powers of someone can be alike of those of other people or completely distinct, once the babies already are born with their gifts pressed in their brains by their DNA, and everything we can do is provide the tools to them achieve their goals.

He interrupted for a while to drink a glass of water.

_ To give you an example, I will quote the case of the young Joseph Prometeu Souz, of 14 years old, who have been studying with us for nine years, and till now have reached the level 6.4. Much probably for have been gone so far with so little age, the most of those who achieved this degree did it close to the age of 20, he still will surprise us by boldly going where no man has gone before. Since his beginning we were very hopeful, because he was the only one to score all the tests he was submitted, and the curious thing is that so far, only two little kids got closer to his points. The third one is the fresh kid my father referred to. We will keep an eye on his development. And the second one is an older boy, a little rebel, who do not treat seriously his gifts and his potential. Would be sad if this slovenly behavior muddle his growing. I do not want to name the person, because I know he understood the message, isn't "little Bat"?

Cackles echoed through the big hall, but the little Peter didn't understand the gag.

_ Let's continue. Prometeu holds between his already known 12 abilities the technique of telepathy, telechinisys, bylocation, phyrogenis, transmutation, retrocognition, hidrogeny and vital suspend. We have to emphasize that unfortunately, the most of the capacities are not useful, and they serve only to show how astonishing our brains are. But some few are very helpful to our lives. These powers of the young Joseph are really amazing, and it is our responsibility to take care of this special boy. He is the only one in the world to possess these capacities and all the other schools and governments greed him. To those who do not know him, we will provide a little demonstration. Can you come here, my friend?

In this moment, a boy who was sat in the back of the room stood up. It was a lean black hair boy. Extremely shy, he didn't felt good under the peering of so many people. but he knew what he was capable of, and that feeling gave him courage enough to face this challenge, and with a satisfaction smile he began to levitate almost to the roof. At this point, he also began to glow, into different colors. Everybody looked at him amazed. Nobody could fly that high. Enjoying the moment, he idling slid forward, heading to the stage, while that, his hands illuminated some viewers as if they were flashlights, and slowly approximated his feet of the floor, to then, back to behave as a simple mortal again. The fresh students, that somehow waited for something like that, made a great alacrity. The older ones, that in a certain way were already used to these kind of spectacles, reacted as if it was the most common thing in the world. After some minutes of tumult the silent took over the place again, and Hermes used it to end the meeting.

_ These demonstrations were only to depict to you what is awaiting for those who accomplish our goals. There's still a lot to be done and discovered and all of us are extremely important to the success of the piece-pork. The potential of the human brain is something formidable. This energy generator plant has revealed itself more potent than any nuclear reactor, and I believe we are just in the beginning. Thank you very much and good bye.

On the next day the classes indeed started. The new students got used to the routine in a few days, which began with the breakfast at 06:30am, and it was followed by regular classes, from 7:15 until noon. At 01:30pm, right after the lunch, more classes till 03:30, and from 04:00 to 06:00pm the students dedicated their efforts to the training and development of their mental skill at the research centers. At night, they had free time to spend as they wished, to play; to watch television; to use the internet; to stroll through the woods; or any other activity they wanted, however, at 10 o'clock pm, they should be in the bed, preferentially after take a bath.

The introspective Joseph P. Souz was the sensation of the school. His shy behavior, clumsy and his lean figure worth the dub of Ziggy, and the fact he did not captivated the sympathy or the affection of the girls with his lack of beauty, made him use his talents to call attention. The adolescence that for itself is a very strange time, of difficult adaptation to the new body posture and behaviors dictated by growing hormones, when the sine of a simple spot have the potential to become a Mexican drama to them, and the fast growing of legs and arms made them look like puppets manipulated by a drunk puppeteer, became much more complicated with the manifestation of their powers. And what should be a motif of proud, many times took the shape of a great embarrassing, for, before they could learn how to control their abilities, they passed through bizarre situations. It was common their capacities manifested spontaneously, making them pass through ridiculous situations in public. A simple sneeze could unchain unpredictable reactions of their sub conscience, and the power released could rip their clothes, for instance, or break something around them, or even create small fires, or move objects, promoting light accidents. The appearance of lights or smells was the simplest events. A sudden gesture or the nervousness in front of the opposite gender could also create situations of great troubles, like the melting of some materials; spoons let askew; electronic devices working randomly or ghosts poltergeists, who used the forces of the rash young students. And what should be faced with good humor, many times made some of them abandon the project. At this time was vital the support of the psychologists of the foundation who would show that it was only a transitory period, and soon they would let behind the awkward ducks they thought to be, and would see they are truly beautiful swans, capable of miracles that would amaze the whole world.

Contradicting the determinations of his instructors, Ziggy practically only commuted through levitation. Each day he was becoming more and more prankster, just to impress his fellows. Certain time he tore the clad of a beautiful teacher, after a bet with a mate, only to show the tattoos in her butt. A supervisor saw everything and understood he was the responsible. It cost Ziggy three days of probation. In exchange of a kiss of a girl or some money of a classmate, he demonstrated his abilities any time and anywhere, like a young Uri Geller, by changing the shape of tiny bangles or lifting thing with his mind, making them fly some dozens of meters over the campus. At the age of fifteen he was changing into a phenomenon who attracted the interests of the media, scientific community and the governs, requiring by the foundation a huge effort to keep him relatively safe of the proposals of these entities, granting a minimum of privacy so he could go on with his development.

Other two students who were attracting too much attention were the brothers Tharus and Iullus Vendra. For being very handsome identical twins, and for being always together, they were celebrities also because they were awaking their abilities very early, by the age of ten. Very blond with blue eyes, very vanities and sociable, and with few desire by the academic studies, the two were only interested on the trainings, because they wished to be the best of all. They loved to participate of games and plays with Ziggy because they were amazed by the powers, sooner or later, they would possess. Tharus was always the leader, and undoubtedly he was developing his skills faster than his brother, but this wasn't motif of dispute between them, for they loved each other, and the success of one meant the success of the other. Unfortunately it didn't happen with their mates, mainly the fresh ones, and they were into a incited competition. Everyone was a rival to them, and Iullus was always checking the new abilities of the other students. This way, it was very natural their approximation to Peter Moll, due the treatment reserved to the little boy by the directory and to their feeling that he would also develop quickly, and so become friends of the five years old boy.

The life of the students was quiet and happy. All the teachers, technicians and scientists of the foundation were also paranormals by at least the level 01, graduated in the foundation or some other famous school, and it was very difficult to the apprentices to break their rules without being caught. As they couldn't evade their surveillance, the students had to enjoy what was offered to them. To avoid that any frustration took hold of the student spirits who could not go home on the weekends, the direction of the school concerned about keeping them always occupied and satisfied, to that, they were always programming jaunts and interesting group strolls. Night thematic parties were realized always by the "SAC" (students academic center), games and championships always were happening, and the best players and those with the best behavior were awarded monthly with tickets to the best games, shows and events. The direction even tolerated the existence of a secret society formed by the students, dubbed "the young paranormals". This group was created when the second the number of the students in the foundation raised the number of 50 children, and their powers began to be manifested. Their main goal was to provide things to the members of the group, by using their abilities, that wasn't allowed by the foundation, and mister Vasconcellus pretended it didn't exist, just while the "young paranormals" didn't do anything to harm someone or put the members in danger.

With the same rigor they charged the duties of the apprentices, the directors used to compensate them. This politic worked perfectly well by instigating and stimulating the young ones to dedicate hardly to what was proposed. And all seemed to live in an ambient of perfect integration, without the promiscuous sparks of the common boarding schools. Drugs, alcoholic beverages and cigarettes were never source of temptation to the major of the students, who seemed to be, at least in these points, members of any religious group, due to their "square" and "straight" behavior in relation to these topics. All this alleged moral attitude had an explanation. On the very beginning of the works of the psychic development, the apprentices should maintain their physical organism the cleanest possible, under the risk of compromising the results. Later, after have achieved the absolute control of the bodies and faculties, they can decide what to put inside of them, without someone to point the finger or judge the way they live their private lives. But while in the school, they should cooperate with all the norms to do not damage their development.

Since early age, the children had to learn to live under the philosophical basis created by mister Vasconcellus, once there were people from every country and religion, and they should live harmonically. The president of the foundation believed that someone could only covet to rest when the duties and works were integrally fulfilled, and to try to escape out this compromises, to enjoy pleasures weren't deserved, would only postpone the execution of these works, that would inevitably return raised by sad consequences, accumulated by the fact the ideal time to realize the duties was lost and the time wasted. Only when the person had honored the duties, he or she could have the usufruct of peaceful vacations, that only the honest workers can deserve. During this time the person would become lord of his or her destiny, deciding the best way to enjoy the occasion.

Mister Jardell Vasconcellus liked to exemplify to the students, when he had the opportunity to talk to small groups, by quoting the history of a middle class retailer man, who after become widow decided to get married again. During certain period everything "ran at one thousand wonders" between his three children and his new consort, until the moment to her first child was born. The kids of the first marriage became a hindrance in their own house, and things went worse when she got pregnant again. All the attention, cherish, dedication and money were reserved to the young girls, and the older three, relegated to the second plan, slowly lost everything, the private school; the free courses; toys and space in the house. Even their alimentation was damaged, once the little girls always wanted all the pastry to themselves. The father didn't have time to perceive or interfere on the impertinences of his young beautiful wife, even if he could, he wouldn't, because he was afraid of losing her, and little by little he detached from his older kids and became more connected to the selfish and spoiled little ones. Revolted with the situation alongside the years, the three boys began a dangerous relationship with the drugs. To do not compromise the relative peace in her house, the shrew made the husband to send them away from home. Each one followed a different path, which unfortunately and tragically headed on the same direction, the marginal life. Decades passed by and the rebel adults returned to their father's house searching support, once debilitated by drugs and discriminated because their time in jail, they no longer could provide by their own. Before this tragic situation, of the constant scandals, threatens and discussions, the father realize he has to take care of them to the rest of his or their lives. It changed his marital life into a hell, once nor his wife or his daughters accepted the fact, and because the remorse for seeing his boys in that terrible state. In his heart he knew if he had done the right thing, took care of them properly, giving love and education, today they would have success in life, and he would be free to enjoy his retirement as he wanted, without further headaches. And the wife, he was so afraid to lose, finally went away.

Chapter 04

Back to the present I

During eight hours, the truck had only stopped twice, to a prompt relief of the bladder. For all this path nothing beyond the road and the iced hills had been seen. Peter already knew how to speak some words of that spooky language of Gilda's people and he was feeling almost like home, and he thought he was a luck bastard to find someone carrying so much good food, once he didn't eat human food for several days, and didn't have a decent meal in his stomach for long months. Little by little he felt his strengthen being invigorated physical and mentally followed by a remarkable recovering of his memoirs, and all the happenings began to make sense now. He needed to reunite his group as fast as possible, even though he yet didn't know exactly why, however, he had to let it down for the moment, because his strengths required some more period of time to get completely recovered and he was able to make things by his own. For some time he would still need the aids of that lovable "lady". Whenever he looked at her, he remembered a phrase of a very old movie: "There's no woman like Gilda".

The intuition rang his "mental alarm", it was a strong sensation he used to feeling his chest indicating something was wrong, although it wasn't developed enough to permit him to prevent or even understand what it was exactly or where the hazard was coming from. He just knew he was in great danger. Looking forward on the road, he could notice the motif of his concern, a great barrier with many soldiers strongly armed blocked the path. He understood that he was being looked for, and sufficed a glance among them to Gilda guess he had to hide. She indicated the floor, under the seat. While this she would put her make up to entertain the soldiers. The truck got closer the barrier and slowed down the speed until stop completely. Immediately several threaten face men, from the new government but still using the old uniforms because there wasn't enough time to concoct new vestments, surround the vehicle, pointing their thick caliber guns. A lieutenant cam by the driver's side and ordered her to present all the required documents. With tranquility she gave him what he asked and yet offered them delicious biscuits, what was quickly accepted by the agog men, who didn't even express a signal of gratitude.

_ Your papers say you came from far way! Meanwhile have you seen anything unusual on the road? No man wandering alone? Inquired the coarse man, with a coarse face of someone who neglected to shave for several days because of the lack of inspection from his superiors, who were very occupied with the installation of the new regime in the frightened period the country was passing through.

_ No sir! Unfortunately I can't help you. You know, I can see fresh meat miles away. – Se replied gently. And certainly if I had seen it would be a ghost or a walking dead body, because everybody knows no one by foot can survive in a such frozen place. And if weren't my "ABBA'" holographic DVDs I would have nothing to distract me in this boring trip. You know a woman has needs! Usually my nephew comes with me in these kinds of transportations, we are an artisan family, but he got hurt and here am alone. Me, myself and my cookies! There is a long time I do not cross country like this, and my hands are killing me. Look at those hardened fingers!

_ Shut up, woman! I am sick of your blabbering! You that if you help an enemy of the state you can be charged of betray, don't you? - Shouted the suspicious man. – C'mon, get off this vehicle! we don't have all day! If it is okay your travel can proceed without further troubles. C'mon we'll make a detailed inspection!

Scared to death and paled like a character from the Japanese movie "the ring", Gilda thought she would lose everything she joined in a entire life of sacrifice, and for nothing, because the mysterious guy would be caught anyway, and probably killed or worse. What could she do? Probably nothing, but nobody would drop her out from her high heels easily. She'd show them her big stature wasn't only to garnish. Sometimes she could scare people too, and she'd prefer to die struggling those toy soldiers instead to beg for mercy. The fibers her guts were made could be pink, but indeed they were very hard to rip. Stunned, she tried to look into Peter's eyes to show him she'd be there for everything, but she didn't see him and got yet more confused, what hell would he be? He couldn't have left the truck, because it was surrounded by militaries, but she hadn't time to thing about it, once a strong soldier came along, opened the door and pulled her out. After the detailed search, which she remained praying the whole time, they didn't find out anything suspicious and decided to release her. Her determination and loftness made them show some respect when her wheels began to roll. After a few minutes she was still intrigued with what had happened to her hitch hiker when suddenly she saw Peter in the side of the road, making hand signals asking for a ride again.

Despite he couldn't make himself understood by words, some gestures were enough to explain his eerie disappearance.

_ So he is one of this freaky paranormals. – She thought. – Yes, mister. I am pretty aware of this kind of people. This country is too far from everything, but the information comes here. I have seen something on the internet television.

She knew about some of the spectacle feats of these men and women, she even knew that in many countries they were already part of the ordinary life. However she had never seen one of them in action. She had heard some rumors about paranormals helping the new government, but till the present moment she wasn't aware of their existence. What if he was one of them? She couldn't know, but she was so proud for helping him, that she didn't care. This feeling was alike the one people feel about artists and celebrities, a mix of admiration; curiosity and, in this case, a felicity because she was chosen to help such a man. Her country was very poor and technological late to invest in this kind of project. Mainly because the former Dictator was only concerned about finding new ways to steal people's money. As she and her friends lived in a community too far from the urban centers, where the action took place, they didn't give much attention to the happening. After all, they didn't care about who is in the command, because if they didn't work hard to earn their lives, no govern or politician would put food on their tables. She kept wondering if Peter was part of the guerrilla, but it couldn't be, because the revolution happened one year ago, and if he was there all this time, he could have already learnt how to speak their language.

The rumors should be true, because the circumstances that evolved the fall of the dictatorship were really very weird, by the fact there had been a few number of combats to a govern that invested hard in the army. Also the vanishing of the presidential aircraft , a real flying fortress, generated many speculations on television because of the alleged death of the president, many of the ministers and their families. Gilda was already with a terrible headache of thinking too much in politics. She had lost the habit a long time ago, once the regime forbade any kind of political manifestations, and the new govern hadn't shown yet they would follow a different guideline. That's why she didn't care about who was in charge and which side Peter was in, if the right or the wrong side, if there was a difference between them in all that mess. What counted was she felt sympathy for him, and he looked at her with more tender in his eyes than her own nephews, who only came after her when they wanted to borrow money or anything else.

While the tall lady was immerse in her thoughts, Peter also was consuming his mind in uncertainties. The desolation of that white landscape created a felling of loneliness, bringing up emotions that seemed under control, but at this very moment took a proportion that suffocated his throat. All this time he thought the Vendra brothers were completely wrong, but he was beginning to question his points of view. Didn't they have the right to use their powers to correct the injustices that otherwise wouldn't be changed? Were they really trying to mitigate the suffering of this poor people? And he reminded his own country, what had he done about it? Nothing. Can the governors have the right to take decisions that affect drastically the life and destiny of the citizens to their heart content and remain unpunished just because they have the power? Can a few men deliberate the fate of the nations according their own sleazy interests and don't suffer the consequences of their mistakes? Peter wasn't naïve and knew that behind of the humanitarian ideals there were strong corporative interests that defined the luck of the sub-developed countries, and, therefore, wouldn't be licit people like him or Tharus could take attitudes to defend the oppressed people, and also change the destiny of the unfavorable classes? With all the certain the temptation was huge to a person with the faculty to become judge and executor of those people who believe themselves above the law. But , unfortunately, one of the reasons to the long process of development of the paranormal people was the intense study of the moral and ethic, not those conduct norms dictated by hypocrite bias, but those that had been proved to be universals, so they could have a better discernment about the planet and to know that any action, right or wrong, generates an unpredictable reaction on the contrary way, that can change completely all the result expected. All decision taken must be carefully analyzed, because the best of the intentions do not achieve the right goal by a dubious attitude. For the most "square" it could seems, Peter was a politically correct pacifist, who believed that only the straight observation of the universal laws could define signifying world changes. Even that it take long time, the life conditions would only have a considerable increasing by the responsible behavior of the citizens. The planet was crossing a period of great social instability, and he believed the problems would go even worse, but it didn't give the right to people to act like they wanted, without thinking a lot about the consequences.

However, even invested by the conviction to fight every psychic who used the powers against the law, in the deep of his heart he couldn't help to admire the Tharus Vendra and his group, "the blue jackets". Besides, all this quarrel had a personal side. During many years, he and Tharus put on the brake a veiled dispute to find out who would be the most powerful, and the fact that the blond man was apparently winning made Peter effort harder and harder in his intention to become the best. The friendship that linked them didn't allow this row to turn them into enemies, but the freedom of action Tharus permitted to himself, bothered a lot the self controlled Moll, who knew his disciplined character would never set him free to enjoy this kind of behavior so out of proportion. For all this, his intuition showed the rolling of the things would lead them to a definite struggle, and probably very violent, and would be necessary the help of the teams of both sides, and this let him very upset.

When they arrived to the little hamlet there was a certain movement of troops. Peter had remembered a lot of things, and even felt a sort of vanity because of the huge effort to capture him. However, the great number of curious people on the streets and the lack of training of the soldiers, worked on his favor, allowing him to pass unnoticed. After parking, while she was taking out the merchandises, Gilda made him understand he should stay with her for a little longer, what let him very pleased, once he knew the dangers she would be in. and certain he would need a den until he was strong enough to organize an escape plan. Some days later, farmers who were passing by and some neighbors, distrusted that young man could be the one the soldiers were looking for, but they believed on the old lady's judgment, and tried to help her by finding clothes, that would fit better in that rough winter, to him. On the next weeks, the serviceable lad, who desired to help on what he could on retribution to what they were giving to him, conquered the sympathy of all the villagers, and so, everyone wanted to help in his plan.

Gilda felt tranquility for knowing her protégée was relatively safe. Despite they have met for so little time she cherished him as a member of her family. The decreasing on the difficult of communication helped this mutual feeling. At this time he was already aware that in his invested on the fight against the out-law of that country, the single fact that nor he nor the militaries of his task force had worried about the habits of the people they wanted to set free, was crucial to their defeat. Therefore, he decided to know everything he could about the locals to correct this flaw. Due to his facility with languages, he quickly learnt the vocabulary, and this way, comprehend better the lack of satisfaction of that poor people. Glenn Ariel Fuond, Gilda's husband became his tourist guide, escorting him everywhere, mainly in the local pub, where they used to spend hours talking to who had time to.

_ I'd like to say that Gilda is the one of the most spectacular human beings I have ever met. Her dignity is outstanding, and if it wasn't her help I don't know what had happened to me. – Said the grateful boy.

_ I agree with you, Peter. There has never been a woman like Gilda!

_ Everyone in this hamlet is aware of that, Glenn. That's why we wanted to help this boy since the beginning. – Said one of the locals.

_ How a so tall woman can be such funny and charming? The children love her. Is a pity what happened to our foster son.

_ What?

_ Don't you know? I had imagined she wouldn't say anything about it to you. Is very painful to her to remember this. A long time ago, right after we get married, we decided to adopt a child, and when a former girlfriend of mine died, we had the opportunity by taking care of her little son, but a few years ago he decided to join the rebels and was killed in a firing with the troops of the govern. We couldn't even bury his body. A very sad episode, he was a very good boy. – His eyes became red, and tears wet his face.

_ Stop talking about this, poor man. It won't bring your son back. Let's talk about more mild things. And so, mister Moll, people say you are capable to defeat this new regime, can you?

_ No, not at all! A task of this magnitude requires the concourse of hundreds of paranormals. If they could support the task!

_ What a pity! But you will at least try, won't you? Because they seem to be worse than the old govern. You know, this new politicians look like crazy people.

_ Well, there is a resolution of the United Nations in this sense, but I doubt they will send armies to this task.

_ I knew it! Since I had heard about the existence of this paranormal folks, long time ago, I realized the world would become a better place to live in.

_ We are not gods! We can only to help people to live better.

But you have the power to set things in their right place by sending behind bars all those who want to explore citizens good will, haven't you?

_ Absolutely not! That is not our main intention. Besides we are not in the necessary number to this overwhelming work. There are too many felonies being committed, and we can only take care of those done by psychics. The rest is concern of the regular police. Sometimes we can even help them, but it is not common.

_ Anyhow, the simple presence of you in this world indicates that we are living wonderful times.

_ I think so! Our primordial function is to stimulate each individual to try to perfect more and more, by recognizing a world of opportunities can be opened to those who desire to overcome stingy interests.

_ I see. These two recent great conquers of mankind, the mind powers and the colonization of Mars, prove that we are in the right path to solve the mysteries of the universe.

_ Exactly! We can't say yet about colonization because we are still in the first stage of the fertilizing of the soil and purification of the atmosphere, but the conquers are really amazing and open a world of possibilities. And when people finally understand that and stop fighting for small things, like money; sex and properties, then we will have advanced a great step.

_ I understand what you mean. I see on the television all the time, this escalation on violence in the whole world and it makes me wonder where we are going to!

_ Probably you have been feeling this situation here in your own country. The politic and religious intolerance is leading to attitudes each time more radical by people who can not or do not want to see the greatness the men can achieve, or they simply do not want to let us get there. And this is quite hazardous to the dainty equilibrium of life in our globe. Powerful and extremist organizations are putting in danger all the advances we reach in the last few decades.

_ I believe that if you freak paranormals can not hold this giant wave of destruction, the only possible solution will be sending to the red planet who want to live in peace and all those criminals killing each other in here.

_ Freak paranormals? Do you think we are a bizarre type of people?

_ No, not really! It is just a way of talking in here. Don't take me wrong, please. I apologize if I hurt your feelings.

_ Don't worry, I have heard worse. But anyway, I believe that 98% of the world population is compost of worker and honest people, who just eager to live and take care of their families in peace. So, we couldn't relocate almost eight billions of people to other planets, even if the long process of revitalization was near to the end. It will be impossible even in a hundred of years. I understand that would be much more simpler to unite efforts from everybody who want to the sake of the world by eradicating evil and preparing a bright future to the new generations.

With this kind of conversation, Peter could feel the way of thinking of the locals about the new govern and the foreign people who were helping them and to practice his points of view. In his heart he felt he hadn't talked to people this way for a long period. He was sympathetic with their delusion with promises of democratic elections and politics who after they reach the power, begin to create projects to remain there for a long time, even using the military force if needed. But he started to feel like a prisoner in that hamlet, once he couldn't move freely by the streets because he was from a different ethnic, and would be easily identified by the spies of the police, and he didn't want to use his ability to appear and disappear wherever he desired, without attracting too much attention, despite this was his favorite ability, because he knew how dangerous could be to his brain the regular use of it. He remembered making use of it when he was in the college and was late to some class or simply lazy of walking or catching a bus under a pouring rain. Whenever the occasion appeared he exercised this gift, until the day he became sick, and the doctors detected it was caused by an overload of his energies. Fortunately, right after that he bought his first beloved car, and it became his main commute transport, an sportive model with all the optional items offered in the market. He exhaled a deep breath when his automobile came in his mind. How he wanted to have the chance to drive it again, through the large streets and avenues of his city, of excellent asphalt. Principally during the winter, when he stopped in the traffic lights, sat on the leather seat, and kept staring at the windshield and silent moves of the cleaner, while feeling comfortably protected from the cold wind inside of his car.

That hamlet was a portrait of the whole country, the life conditions were very precarious, and the citizens had to work hard to have the minimum necessary of heating, to face the extremely freezing winter. Most of the time they had to live feeling the cold aching their bones, and Peter wasn't used to it, and he felt nuisance all the time, missing constantly his cozy newly acquired apartment; his king size bed; his holographic DVDs and books. He would give everything to have his ointments; shampoos; perfumes and fashion expensive comfortable clothes. But, the most unbearable pain was in his heart. He missed so much his girlfriend, since he remembered her. His pretty and sweet Denise Tanner. More than the love of his life, she was his great companion, always dedicated and solicitous, who had joined the company of paranormals only to have the opportunity to work with him and spend more time by his side, participating in his adventures. The sensation he experienced when she was with him, was she would follow him in the most dangerous situations, if he asked. Besides, she was always a delight to the eyes, because she was almost as trend as him.

Despite everything that happened to him, Peter was happy. He reminded how many dangers she was exposed to, and even so she tried to save him. If wasn't for her, he couldn't have gathered enough strength to escape from that filthy prison. He knew she hadn't gone away, and probably would be waiting him anywhere nearby the border. And he thought.

_ If she hadn't come to me I would be dead by now, because even don't recognizing her face, due to my mental confusion, it was crucial to see her for some moments. It made my mind fight against the effects of those poisoning remedies.

Peter didn't have the gift of talking from mind to mind, the telepathy, and required the help of ordinary devices of communication. Internet was still forbidden in that country, and long distance cell phones or radios were constantly spied by the secret service. This way, he didn't have the meanings to contact his agents to warn he was alive and kicking, and to know where they were planning to rescue him. Only his intuition could guide his steps,. However, as the police siege was each day more strong, he was sure some "blue jackets" were among the soldiers to track his energy, and use his powers next to one of them would be very dangerous. Indeed he would have to risk, sooner or later, because the flee was more than necessary, once he didn't want to expose those helpful farm people to more hazard, and because he knew if he didn't give notices on the next few days, more drastic attitudes would be taken by the United Nations.

The locals perceived his preoccupations and concluded he had to go. So, they got an authorization to travel to a city next to the frontier, by the allegation to take some craft works to be sold here, to their community old bus. It would be a good disguise to Peter's intentions. Many of them volunteered to give more credibility to the task. They were so anxious to participate of this adventure, because they wanted to be as famous as Peter, when he finally defeated the govern, and because they wouldn't be in danger with someone so powerful by their side. Everything was prepared to the combined day. With tears in his eyes, Peter thanked for all the help and cares he received from that humble and helpful poor people, that gave him so many demonstrations of charity; friendship and sense of duty. He swore to come back to set them free, and help them to conquer the right to become a more fare nation, with equal treatments and opportunities to everybody. Gilda felt like she was losing a son.

_ You don't have to worry about us, my son. We did what we did because we wanted to help you, without any further interest. You have to do what you have to do, and we will be here praying for you. We know how dangerous will be for you if you decide to return, and we will understand if you decide not to. I will be more relieved knowing you're safer at home.

_ Thank you very much, Gilda. What you did for me I won't be able to repair even in a hundred years, but I'll try. And I'll be back.

_ Go in peace, my lad. And when the UN decides it is time to act, we will prepared to help you. It is time for us to do something. We can't let other people fight our wars. We finally understood we'll have to shed our blood for the sake of our beloved nation.

_ I'd like to believe you're wrong Glenn. These things could be solved easily, and the suffering avoided. But I can't. I do not see any other solution but the war. I just hope to have the condition to make the Unite Nations take the less terrible decision. I'll have to figure out the best plan.

_ That's right. – Said one of the villagers, an elder man. – We are old but we will prove our guts, and we will honor the blood in our veins. When the time comes, I'll show I can be as smart as master "Yoda".

_ Master who?

_ Yoda. Don't you see the old cult movies, Peter? Like "star wars"?

_ That movie is from the time of my grandmother, but I think I have ever watched it.

_ So you'll be our Jedi knight.

_ May the force be with you, Peter.

_ May the force be with all of you, my dear companions.

Using this time, more proper clothes to walk on the snow, and a backpack full of supplies, and prepared to get into action, he embarked in that thing that could resemble to a transport vehicle, with good will. Peter had left behind his Yuppie style, and had another conception of life. Since the death of his mother he hadn't contact with a community as miserable as that, and it touched him. The years in Europe had erased of his memory the how much life could be hard to those who haven't cable television, shopping malls; household robots or microwave processors.

CHAPTER 05

THE RETURN

The bus left full of people and farm animals. The group had the perspective to participate of a risk and exciting mission. They were all poor little farmers who had never, in their quiet and servile life, thought some day such a thing could happen to them. Forty minutes after the departure they were stopped by the soldiers in the first barrier, and as had been previously combined, Peter dematerialized himself and was waiting few miles ahead. The same thing happened in other two road inspections, once none of the passengers saw the presence of the psychic cooperators of the police officers, who could sense energies emanated from other psychics; all of them dressed in dark blue raincoats, and so, the young paranormal could use his powers freely. The travelers talked happily while exchanging snacks without further concerns because they believed the mere presence of the most powerful man in the world, in their humble opinion, would be enough to prevent any trouble. Several times the young Moll tried to explain to them that unfortunately there was another one more powerful than himself, who in the truth of the facts deserved this title was the one they were in the verge of combat against, and that's why they should take care, because there was a clear and present danger, and indeed, some of the followers of this potent man were very capable in the sensitive arts.

Feeling very comfortable in the presence of such singular people, Peter contradicted his introspective nature and told them some stories lived by him and his companions. Narrated the time when Tharus and Iullus took him, and other boys, to a brothel. He was in that time in the age of 14 and the twin brother were the only boys over 18 years old in the group, and at the door of the establishment, everyone tried to look like older, while holding the chill in the belly and the anxiety of being just to get out of the roll of the virgin lads and get into the category of experienced men, but the eager boys suffered a total deception. The doorman didn't allowed their entrance, because he didn't believe in their pretended age. Amused by the general frustration, Tharus decided , after bother each one of the poor guys, to transport all of them to inside of the brothel, using to that his outstanding capacity. Once there, the boys quickly forgot the incident and treated to relax the ambient by making fun of their lack of ability with the working girls. The clumsy and coy Peter got into a room with a beautiful mature escort girl, who helped him to strip down his clothes and laid him down on the bed, trying to hush him. As much he tried to look like an experienced boy as much she noticed he had no idea of what he had to do. At the end, cherish, she hold his horses and gently showed the way not to paradise, but a better place. The boys, who now believed they were complete men, left the establishment in a euphory state and a bit drunk, fact that attracted the attention of the body guard, who didn't understand how they were going out if he didn't allowed them to get in, and decided to ask for explanation. However, before he could say anything, Tharus suspended him to the roof, while the guys made a big racket, now raising the attention of police officers, who were patrolling the area. Irritated by the lack of respect of the boys, who cackled at each question, the police men decided to take them to the police station and there punish their disrespect.

_ You, funny boys, will learn a important lesson today. And I assure you will keep it in your memories for the rest of your miserable lives, you little nasty punks.

_ Wait a minute, dirty Harry. We have the right to a last wish, don't we? – Gibed Iullus.

_ I didn't know that was against the law to be happy. – Replied Tharus.

_ We may cry, may not we? – Gibed another boy.

_ Keep on laughing, bunch of pranksters! Down there, in the station, there is a jailer who loves pretense comedian "daddy's boys". You're gonna love his gags so much you're gonna leave there traumatized. – Answered one of the police officers in a threaten voice.

_ Wait a minute, "dynamic double", I can see you're very stressed. Who knows a stroll on the beach could do you well? – asked Tharus with a dangerous glow in the eyes.

_ Are you crazy, punk?

Without giving them time to think, Tharus held their arms and disappeared with them. Within a second they reappeared on a seaside nearby town. While the dazzle police men recovered from the fright, and understand what was happening, the Vendra wished good luck and returned to his friends. Because of this nocturnal folly, Tharus was three days in bed in fever, exhausted of his energies.

The tranquility gave space to anxiety when the driver slowed down drastically the speed. Ahead, rocks of considerable size impeded the passage. Suddenly a band of rag hoboes, hidden into the snow, leapt over the bus, with guns in their hands. Simple bandits, the type of those who infect the roads where the authority is weak and subsistence becomes more difficult. When more and more people lose hope of better days, it is inevitable the rising of violence and riots, where common people decide to fight with nails and teeth, leaving behind social, moral and religious values. Peter looked at them with pity in his eyes. He didn't want to harm them. They kicked the side of the vehicle, trying to indicate they were in charge, and the door should be opened. Probably they didn't want to waste their bullets, but even so, that old rusty weapons scared the passengers. But, after they noticed Peter was quiet and calm, they became more confident.

The paranormal was already concentrating on the 17 smugglers, who were referred by him as "the incredible army of Brancaleone", an old Italian movie he saw when child. He noticed the group was agitated and could put in danger the life of his adventure mates, so Peter decided to act. The rag hoboes didn't understood what was happening when their guns; axels; knifes and hammers began to crack. A few seconds later all these things broke into pieces. When they perceived themselves destitute of their weapons in a strange happening, they became confuse, and did know what to do. They wanted to run away, because in their simple minds, without instruction, they could believe it was work of some kind of demon, but, due to the starvation, they were compelled to stay. After the celebration of the victory, the occupants of the bus felt pity. The thieves inspired more compassion than anger, and the villagers decided to divide the food with them. Peter and other two people put the supplies over a rock on the side of the road. The hoboes didn't fell safe to get closer until the bus has gone. The Moll went to the front of the vehicle, and simply looking at the big stones that impeded the passage made then lift above the soil, and removed then aside. After that, he and his friends continued the trip.

The episode let the passengers very excited, and for over than one hour there was no other subject between them, when Peter intuited there was a police siege some kilometers ahead. The difference is this time he sensed the presence of some "blue jackets" using their abilities in that place. Immediately he asked the driver to stop, and explained if he continued with them he would be detected, and their cooperation would be exposed, what would bring serious consequences to the community he learnt to value. Even if he just used his skills to transport himself forward the siege, they could track his energy. He didn't know if they had paranormals powerful enough to this task, and he didn't want to risk his friends. So he decided the best thing would be to allow them to go on with the travel as combined to do not raise suspects over them, and continue his journey alone, by foot. They understood the situation and regret their adventure ended there, but they had already enough material to relate to their neighbors, and they agreed. For some minutes Peter thanked one by one of his friends, for the inestimable help.

_ My dear friends, I can't express how proud of you I am. You have systematically risked your safety since I got into you lives, and I thing I'll never have the means to pay this debt. May you have my eternal gratitude, and know that you will be always on my mind. God bless you all.

_ So we are even, my friend. – Said the driver. – Because you gave us back the hope of a better future, and the motivation to fight for our beliefs and values. God bless you too.

_ You bet it, Peter. – Replied one of the villagers. – This is the general thought. In these weeks of familiarity we were able to perceive you're an outstanding guy, not only because of your powers, but mainly because of the person you are, and the generous heart you have. We are also proud of you.

_ May our souls remain linked. A link that is not made of interests, doubts or fear, but made of a deep friendship and fraternal love. Be aware that sooner than you thing our fates will cross again. Our adventures are not over. See you, folks.

Peter wanted to give them a last show, and left the place levitating thirty meters over the soil. But right after he was out of sight, he landed, because the cold weather was terrible, and he needed to exercise his muscles to become warmer. As his power of instant transportation was limited, he could only disappear and appear 14 miles ahead, and besides, he couldn't make frequent use of this ability under the risk of drawing off all his vital energy, what would put his physical and mental integrity into serious danger, in case his forces weren't recovered in capable time.

Again he found himself , walking lonely throughout open ranges covered by snow, as a sort of "dejavu". The main difference was this time he was well prepared to the long journey, protected from the cold wind by a thick jacket; enough food, and most important of all, lord of his mind, by knowing who he was, where to go and what to do. Now he could appreciate the solitude and beauty of that place, that resembled the surface of a hostile planet. Whenever he was ahead of a difficult trespassing place, due to different obstacles, like avalanches, rolling stones, huge rock walls, thin iced lakes or steep mountains, he made a break to drink or eat something, sat on the ground, and right after he inhaled a deep breath and before exhale he was already 14 miles forward. . by the end of the day he had traveled 75 miles, and thought it was time to stop to have dinner and sleep. The villagers didn't have instant tents; which had only to be put on the ground and pressed a button; and in 30 seconds it set itself, instead they gave him an old fashioned one, and he had some troubles to set it. After solve this problem he lit a fire and prepare some food. Peter always enjoyed radical sports and constantly did tracks, hiking, rafting, snowboarding, sailing and others, but nothing had prepared him to face such a horrible weather like that. Besides, he hated extreme temperature. As the excess of heat as the lower chill always bothered when he was in a mission.

Twisted in an old blanked, made by hand by the artisans of the hamlet, he tried to warm his bones beside the fire, while remembering some funny jokes he used to play with friends. They used to declare themselves jealous of some of his abilities, like levitation; instant transport; the balls of energy; telechinesis; transmutation and bylocation, and he understood why, because these abilities were considered active powers, while the most of the paranormals had passive powers or subjective ones. At that very moment he would like to exchange some capacities with them.

_ With Argos, for example, I willingly exchanged my levitation by his gift to increase the temperature of the body. I remember that day when we put him into a bathtub full of ice bars. In some minutes all of them were melted and after a while the water was boiling. Or even Pablo, who was always interested in my power to blow things with my energy balls, I'd take his ability to decrease the corporal temperature. Once he almost froze an entire room. He would feel like home in this hell made of snow.

He knew it all was just a delusion to distract his attention for some moments, until get to sleep. The real fact was if he couldn't cross the border, getting to the village he believed existed there, until the dusk of the next day, probably he wouldn't see the daylight again. He would die due to the cold conditions or the wear away of his capacities. He calculated that if began to walk very early and without stop, using his transportation ability twice, and had any further trouble to complicate his path, he would accomplish his goal. At dawn he woke up, after a freezing night, where he barely slept, ate something and prepared to start walking again. At this moment he fulfilled his lungs and shouted. Trying to astonish his ghosts:

_ For those who think I am defeated, know that the dices are still spinning!

After this relief he began the march. The ground was worse than he had supposed and Peter couldn't hike in the necessary velocity, and he saw himself forced to use the instant transportation ability more times than the planned, to get to the border on time. On the other side he found out the climate does not respect diplomacy and territorial limits traced by men, and he kept been terribly chastised by thermal sensations that only Eskimos can stand. Always guided by his intuition or his "spider sense", as he used to play with his preferred comic book character, "spider man". Unfortunately this ability indicated he miscalculated the distance to the village, and he had to overcome his strengths to continue walking in that nightmare place. Luckily, in the end of his resistance Peter he saw at distance some dots that indicated there would be the place he was looking for. He didn't believed when he saw some kind of goats and shepherd. He praised God for being there, and for some moments he distrusted what his eyes were seeing due the fever was burning his body. He wouldn't dare to use his gift once again, the consequences could devastate his mind. He almost crawled to the entrance of that tiny village, when the shepherd boys saw him and ran to help.

_ What am I doing? Why did I risk my life coming to this place? If I am wrong and nobody is here to rescue me I'll be into serious problems. I don't know if these people have the ways or intention to heal me. I even don't know if they are hostile.

The boys came closer and almost carried him on their arms. Fortunately their dialect was very similar to Gilda's, and he was able to talk to them. Peter didn't believed when they informed about a group of western people that was hosted in the small hotel. He let them conduct him, because his legs were aching so badly and the rest of his muscles weren't better, as if he had fought the all the champions of the "ultimate fight wrestling", at once. Sore and drained, he saw the entrance of a very old two floors building, with a rusty plate indicating it was a hostel. Completely exhausted, he tumbled down on the porch steps. Immediately the front door opened. Denise Tanner had sensed his energies, and ran to the entrance to verify if her intuition was correct. She cried when saw him, and held him in her arms, kissing his face, intense and franticly.

_ Thank god, my dear, you came to me. I missed you so much!

He gathered his forces to talk, before the imminent faint took hold of his conscience, and he babbled.

_ Did you believe I would leave a such pretty woman like you alone for a long time? I know how many "Alfies" would like to replace me. I have to take care of my estate.

_ Why did you take so long, Peter? Do you know how much money we are spending in here? – Joked Hermes Vasconcellus.

_ I had to plan a dramatic entrance, my friend!

Those were his last words, before lose conscience. They took him to inside, where was considerably warm. Denise began the firsts medical and psychic aids, avoiding his condition became worse. On the next day, a rescue plane came to pick them up. Two days later he woke up, and before opening his eyes thanked God for keeping his mental health. For some time he thought he would have the same fate of Ziggy. The pleasant sensation of being in a cozy warm room, laid down in a comfortably soft bed and pillows dido, covered by smooth sheets, gave him the certainty of being back to the country he made his home.

_ It is very good to be home. To be protected, well treated by nurses and physicians. God I am lucky. How I missed these simple things!

Soon later, a sympathetic doctor came by, and verified he was in very good conditions.

_ Now I'll ask the nurse to bring your lunch, and after it you'll be permitted to receive some visits. You must be some kind of celebrity, mustn't you? There are many people in the lobby, trying to see you.

_ and my girlfriend Denise?

_ She didn't leave your side since you got here. She went to the canteen to talk to some mates and must be coming back.

As the doctor said, in a few minutes Denise was back, and she was very happy when saw him awaken.

_ Hello pretty girl!

_ Hello, handsome guy! You can't imagine the bliss I am in. but I never gave up hope.

_ Neither do I!

_ Later you'll tell me everything about your adventure. Now there are some friends who want to see you.

Peter couldn't hold the tears when he saw the people he loved the most in this world, Morgana; Argos; Jardell and Hermes; Tommy and Mick; Suzanne Binoche.

_ What frighten you gave us, pal. – Said Argos.

_ Did you bring anything to me? – Asked Suzanne. – Forget all the excuses, you had plenty of time to provide it.

_ If you wanted vacations, you could have asked. I wouldn't have denied it. – Replied Mister Jardell Vasconcellus.

_ Did you rest a lot? – Asked Mick.

_ And the girls, are they pretty in there? – Tommy wanted to know.

_ Now you can pay me that loan, can't you? Hermes joked.

_ Shut up you people! Let him breath. It is very good to have you back my dear son. – Completed Morgana.

_ Let then talk, aunt Morgana. Their jokes are music to my ears.

_ You wouldn't say that if you knew how many debriefs you'll have to do.

_ Did you know our team won the championship?

_ I moved to you office, Peter. We didn't know when you would come back.

For some minutes everyone tried to update him, mainly with bad news. Just to annoy him.

_ I think I want come back to that stinky prison. – He replied, joking.

_ Don you worry, my love! These people are jealous because you have a girlfriend like me. – And she whispered in his ear. – When everybody has gone we will celebrate properly your return.

_ The doctor said you may go home tomorrow.

_ My home! I had forgotten about my apartment. How is it?

_ Is everything okay there. You maid-robot took care of it. I verified the maintenance. Don't you worry!

_ It's alright. After months sleeping in a stinky filthy cell, sharing the horrible food with rats and cockroaches, I believe I won't be as neurotic by cleaning as before. I'll never make that poor robot take out the dust three times…

_ After all maybe this experience may have produced something good.

Later Peter received the visit of other friends and mates, as Pablo; Dan Lee; Diana and Kim, who brought flowers; candies and cards of who couldn't be there, and the day elapsed as normal as it could be, with them chatting about what had happened on the world during his absence. In the beginning of the night, mister Jack Similos, secretary of justice, Peter's immediate boss, came to show his esteem to someone he had delegated so many responsibilities. Despite his early age, Peter conquered his respect and friendship with his determination and dedication.

_ You scared us all, boy. It's good to see you in good shape. I wanted you to know that I never lost the faith to find you alive. The rescue team will be awarded. We can never leave a companion behind.

_ Thank you sir. – Interrupted Denise. – In the name of all the volunteers I'd like to express our gratitude on your cooperation.

_ I just did what any of you would have done for me. And so, Peter, how was it?

_ Well sir, it could have been better if I was in Disneyland.

_ You're right. – He laughed. – Unfortunately I can't stay any longer, I have a reception at the embassy of Micronesia, and as I see you're in good condition, I'll be straight.

Denise became apprehensive. She knew the boss wasn't known for being diplomatic, and she guessed the issue was very important, and as he was very despotic, she didn't asked him to leave the conversation to the next day.

_ The militaries are preparing a contention plan to eradicate the threaten this organization, "the blue jackets" has become. I am deeply worried about what they intend to do. They don't share too much information with us, and all we can do is fill in the blanks. I believe they are considering the use of a terrible alternative, and are just waiting your report to set the details. I hope you have suitable information that can avoid the taken of command by these militaries, because if they do, I do not know they will be reasonable. The day after tomorrow there will be an appointment of the task force, inclusive the Vasconcellus senior and junior are aware, and they are as worried as me. Therefore, rest a lot because from now on "the grill will heat up".

On the next day Peter went home. His first thought when he was outside the hospital, was how wonderful was to live in a rich big city, with a pleasant weather. He stopped on the sidewalk, just to admire the continuous flux of elegant cars and pedestrians on the large and well paved avenue. As usual, it was raining and weak chill increased the sensation of cold, but he didn't care, and was even feeling a little hot after bearing the lowest temperatures for so long. During the way he was analyzing the peaceful expressions on the fancy and beautiful people's face. It was certain they had their own dramas, in more or less intensity, but nothing as the tension printed on the physiognomy of a people that suffered situations of extreme privations and violations, as civil war and starvation. And the bright of the eyes was different. Citizens who have faith in the future have a different glow. He decided to help that poor population to have hopes alike those outside his Denise's car. At his building, he tasted each instant since the front lobby, where he was cheered by the doorman and the receptionist, and in the elevator and in front of the door of his wide loft, where some neighbors awaited. Denise had prepared a romantic lunch, with his favorite food, once they would finally have a private moment after months. He saluted each corner of his home, and didn't pay heed to the greetings decoration. After the meal they went to the living room, which had a glass wall in front of a balcony, and remained some hours talking and dating. It was a great relief to liberate sexual energy held after a long period of abstinence. A collateral effect, much appreciated by the paranormals and their partners was that the years of physical and mental conditioning, where the apprentices acquire total control over each muscle of their perfect bodies, sex reaches a performing level never imagined by people who depends on their hormones.

At night, after the visit of some friends who didn't go to the hospital, he could surrender to the pleasure of sleeping on the arms of his beloved woman. Before close his eyes, Peter peered lovely that beautiful and perfumed body, that smoothly laid down besides him, with an angelical expression in her perfect face. By the morning he retook his hygiene and dressing habits with immense satisfaction, prepared the breakfast, woke up his girlfriend, ate looking at her. He couldn't wait to go to the garage. He wanted to greet his steel friend, "James". James was the name given to his dark green car, which was a mixture of James Bond and Mad Max cars. His first automobile, acquired after a long save. Since he was a child this was the great hobby he would like to have if he had money to buy the toys. When he began to study at the foundation he started the collection, and his friends used to help him, by presenting with some miniatures, mainly Morgana. Probably he inherit this passion from his father, for since the early age used to listen his progenitor talking enthusiastically about everything that possessed wheels, and his great frustration was never have had condition to buy one, even an old one. When Peter closed the deal, and left the agency driving his machine, he felt on his side the proud presence of his old man, who probably came to check his son's acquisition, and share with him the pleasure of the first travel. They rode for hours, talking about personal issues, and as it could not be different, about the newest vehicles, and peter explained to this being of another dimension all about the new car technologies. And when they finished, both left with the sensation they had lived by the first time a real experience between father and adult son. It repeated for other times, indicating the bonds that unite the hearts trespass the barrel of death.

Peter was a person who enjoyed the routine. To commute to work by the same way, to lunch in the same restaurant and eat the same food, with the same mates, to train at the foundation three times per week after work and come back home to listen his CDs; Dvds and books beside Denise, were habits that didn't caused tedium, on the contrary. But it didn't mean he didn't like to vary, and enjoy unusual programs or new adventures. He used to frequent raves that lasted three days, travel to unknown jungles or volunteer to rescue teams when some natural disaster occurred. However, above all, he enjoyed punctuality. To respect the schedule was almost an obsession to him, and he preferred the bureaucracy of his office instead field word, which he applied only when it was extremely necessary. He liked to command his agents without leaving his wide and fancy workroom. Maybe the painful adventure of the last months didn't lose ardor of his routine impetus, and most probable it became stronger, making him desire to strengthen even more the links with his beliefs about the world.

Despite to work to the secretary of justice, in a special agency, the company of the paranormals, since his graduation in psychology two years earlier, would be the first time he would have a reunion on the building of the minister of defense, once the militaries had their own psychic agency. As they didn't have majored paranormals over the sixth level, they were forced to accept the help of more experienced civilians. People like Jardell and Hermes Vasconcellus, Peter Moll and mister Anthony Arrays, the UN justice specialist. As always, Peter was the first to arrive, and decided to wait the others outside the building, because he wasn't tired of appreciating his familiar landscape. He only got in after the arrival of the last one on the forth floor, at the gathering room, where the general Nilt Deslock was initiating the deliberations.

_ Ladies and Gentlemen, this case of the rebel paranormals has reached such level of seriousness that it became a world security matter. As you well know, on a first moment we tried to solve it using only our own resources. The only outsider was Peter Moll, who acted as a consultant. We failed magnificently, and lost the lives of several of our best men in this campaign. However, we believe now it is time to use conventional weapons, and use the maximum power where diplomacy haven't brought results. we can't run the risk of being on mercy of an army that become stronger each day, which will put in danger the established world order sooner than we thought. As some of the present people today can not be understanding about the clear and present danger represented by an uncontrolled paranormal, I'd like to ask mister Vasconcellus to give us a brief relate about the situation.

_ Very well, my friends. I'll began by depicting promptly the fundaments of paranormal activity. I won't make you sleep. About 50 years ago, I created a foundation to develop researches about the phenomenon known as extra sensorial perception or ESP. I hired and trained excellent professional to develop devices to measure and amplify the capacities of the volunteers in this jog work. I sent teams of researches wherever there was a place with fame of being a mental energies catalyst center, such as India; Tibet; China; Bermuda triangle and Amazon rain forest. Inside the brain there is a gland called pineal and we discovered that inside it existed what we called neural battery or NB, which works as a receptor, processor, amplifier and emitter of a back ground energy present in the whole universe, better known by the religions as UCF or universal cosmic fluid; God's breath; primordial force; ectoplasm; philosophic stone; residual energy and other weird names. Well, the battery captures this UCF and configures it into different shapes to different finalities. This capacity of the brains of any animal specie, mainly the human, had already been indirectly perceived by the quantum physics, when during experiments with sub atomic particles the observer interferes on the results, proving the mind can interact with the physical, even in a infamous part in the beginning. My gadgets demonstrated that after a determined size this neural battery begins to influence not exclusively the micro cosmos but also the macro cosmos. We detected as well a relation among the size of the NB and the capacity of interaction with the ambient, and as the biceps can be worked and exercised to it's maximum, this gland also can be, and it could be raised to ten times it's initial size. Each mass gain was measured and classified into a level table that vary from 01 to 10, and each increase of the level, the NB becomes five times more potent. Fir instance, let's take one of the identified paranormal capacity, the telechinises, that is the ability to move objects just using mental commands, one of the phenomenon that enthralls the most of the people's imagination, despite it's less utility in a world dominated by remote control. The psychic of level 01 can move an object weighting 50 grams that is in his or her interaction field, which is the reach of the eyes. In this case, a distance of 10 centimeters to all sides. To you understand better see this projection n the holographic screen:

Level	Weight	Distance
01	50g	10cm
02	250g	50cm
03	1,25k	2,5 m
04	6,25kg	12,5m
05	31,25kg	62,5m
06	156,25kg	312,5m
07	781,25kg	1.562,5m
08	3.906,25kg	7.812,5m
09	19.531,25kg	39.062,5m
10	97.656,25kg	195.312,5m

_ Tharus Vendra, the leader of the group we are fighting against, is a paranormal level 08, and now you can have a better picture of the problem we are in. he can elevate three cars and their occupants 90 feet above the ground, and if he wants, let them fall, and what is more serious, he possess other 15 abilities, such as the capacity to appear and disappear whenever he desires carrying with him a burden weighting 2000 kilos until the distance of 150 miles, the capacity to create an energetic barrel around him so strong that it block the passage of bullets, explosions and even liquids and gases, the frighten ability to create balls of force that keep condensing until they blow up, destroying everything around them. The control of his organism makes him immune to the action of any poison, including cigarettes and whiskey, that why he appreciates a Cuban cigar. This way, dear friends, it is totally understandable the apprehension of the militaries of governs of practically every country in the world. The potential of destruction of this young man is overwhelming and unpredictable, even more with the help of this group with paranormals of great powers. However, just eliminate him is a task, as has been revealed, highly complex and extremely risk, by the simple fact he could kill anyone who was hundred miles away, for the most protected this person was. But I ask you to pay attention on this. Tharus Vendra isn't a simple criminal that threats the society, and he doesn't have the ambition to dominate the world or anything alike. His mind is more complex than that. I have accompanied him for almost 16 years, and can assure you he is not a bad nature person, on the other hand, he could be the perfect husband to ours daughter. If he wanted, he could have became a billionaire, after all, there's no one that can measure forces with him in the whole world. His greatest mistake was to get indignant with the lack of justice and impunity that have been the ordinary pattern in our civilization, and become a sort of punisher, as if he could exorcise all our ghosts, and let himself be seduced by the extraordinary power he possess. I want to emphasize only the company of paranormals agency is capable to neutralize him without shed too much blood of innocent people, and that's why we should be in charge of this mission.

_ Naturally your concerns are fare. – Agreed general Deslock. – But you have to understand that this man can't keep going on unpunished, harming people according to his desire. Imagine if he understands some of the leaders of the world are criminals and decides to act, what could happen? While he remains released nobody will be safe. He can get in and get out of any country without being detected or controlled. Obviously we, the militaries, are against an over reaction, and want that all the possible measures are examined. That's why we'd like to hear from Peter Moll, the only person who faced this group "the blue jackets" and escaped alive.

_ I do not know if my information will be useful, once you are already aware of almost everything about this organization. But I will narrate everything I find relevant. This group "the blue jackets", created by the brothers Vendra counts with the participation of 80 paranormals very well trained, varying from the level 02 to 06. Tharus took hold of an old military installation and transformed it in his headquarter, and a big mansion on the suburbs of the capital became the blue jacket's seat. It is worth to enhance the warlike power of the mountebank army is almost zero, and the govern just keep the control thanks to the works of the sensitive ones, who divided into 20 cell of four agents move constantly throughout the country, inspecting and coordinating the effective actions. Practically all the information I raised were gathered before being arrested, because after our anti terror group was eliminated I was without conditions to verify, and is almost certain the established order must have changed from that moment on. When I was hidden in the hamlet, waiting for the right moment to escape, the farmers could perceive a kind of tension being formed between the new regime and the "jackets", who began to abuse of their prerogatives. In each group there is at least one telepath, to make the communication easier. Because he is not one of them, Iago, the third in command, keeps always on his side someone who is, to be in charge of things. Tharus does the same, and only occasionally he leaves the bunker, and when he does, uses one of his manifolds motorcycles, despite the climate. I don't know if this is useful.

_ Of course it is. Any information about his chores is relevant. – Completed the general deslock.

_ he lives isolated with his girlfriend, Kiria, and surrounded security guards, provided by the local police, and as I suppose, the ministers and politicians are very afraid of his mood, and follow his will as if it was a tacit order. Despite do not get drunk, each time he drinks more and more, what indicate he is passing through moments of mental unbalance, caused maybe by the excessive use of his powers. I would say this is his weak point, which we should skilful use to defeat him. In my opinion the best way to deal with the present situation is pushing Tharus so hard he will be forced to use all his sources of energy, taking him to exhaustion. While that we should attack from another side, his brother Iullus is always moving, trying to follow the come and go of the cells or serving as bridge between the cupola of the "jackets" and the govern. He is the most reasonable of the entire group, and I think is really interested on the end of the conflicts. He is very worried about the hostilities and would like to find a peaceful negotiated form to return the authority to the people and to fix things with the UN. He was tempted by our offers to reduce the accusations against him, his girlfriend and the special treatment to his brother if he cooperates. This way, I thing to the moment the best option is to follow this path, and keep insisting in a less violent solution, general.

_ We entirely agree with you, Peter. – Replied mister Vasconcellus. – I had thought about something alike. This path is very dangerous, and will cost some lives, but is the less bloody, and it is worth to try. Don't you agree, general Deslock?

_ I think I am forced to agree. I have some rendering nulls, but I agree. Don't you think that my military mind compels me to opt always by the way of weapons. I always try to use only the required force to solve the problem, and I don't see anything wrong when we use the cooperation of civilians like you, now and then. – His eyes peered at Jardell. – From now on, in the name of the ministry of defense, I transfer the command of this operation to the agency company of the paranormals, and I deeply hope the men of doctor Jardell may elaborate a detailed strategy that makes this plan fails proof, because if you do not succeed, I am afraid we will not have the luxury of a third try, and we will be forced to the maximum power to destroy these Vendra boys. You know what I mean, don't you?

_ I am afraid so, general – Said Joanna Angels, the second secretary of the UN. – You mean to use atomic devices.

_ Exactly. And I do not need to tell it will cost the lives of hundreds of thousands of poor people. May God be with you.

_ We have two options, to win or to win! – Completed Peter, trying to make the ambient a little less heavy.

The real possibility of using of nuclear bombs was too shocking to those people, and none of them would like to get into the history by that way. Besides, the fact that measures so extremes could be used against such a small group of paranormals would cause a huge panic in the world's population due to the possibility of others sensitive ones could be as dangerous, disseminating a crisis of paranoid, and a the hostility against this minor would be inevitable, what would lead to another world persecution. The reunion went on for some hours, with the participants deliberating about the details of the operation. At afternoon, Peter and Hermes gathered on the building of the COP(company of the paranormals) , a regular construction of nine buildings, where they disposed of the necessary infrastructure to the coordination of all the agents involved in the task. On the round table, beside the directors of the company, were present the secretary Joanna and her assistants, and the general Deslock.

_ I'd like to emphasize how dangerous the present situation is. – Said the general. – We must use tough measures. However, I want to let clear as crystal the UN sobriety can't be tainted. The high command is particularly concerned about three main factors that can bring horrible consequences. The first is possible illegal attitudes we can take mustn't get to the public opinion, the second if it gets; probably it will generate an international crisis, and third, we must avoid the world can be shaken in its social structures by the ideals of the movement of these Vendra brothers. It is imperative we contain the growth of the members of this group. At any cost! I do not want to be informed by the details of this mission. I just want to know about the results. I just recommend that it be clean and precise as a surgery. Now excuse me because I have other thinks to do.

After a short relate, Peter put all his subordinates side by side about the facts, and exposed his strategy.

_ Since I left the hospital I have put my crumbs to work.

_ I do not recommend you to do it, if you're not used to.

_ Very funny you, Argos! I think I found the solution. To this case we will need the cooperation of thousands of paranormals volunteers, and the direct participation of at least 160 agents, the most capable and experienced ones, who will be divided into 10 groups. We will get into the country from different points and will act in quick incursions to immobilize and capture all the members of the "blue jackets", trying at all cost a direct confront with Tharus. We will try to attract the help of his brother, Iullus, and only then we will attack with full power The "Bat", forcing him to spend all his energetic resources until exhaust him completely. This will be the most complicated part of the plan, once none of us is able to stop the strike of this man. I believe it will be indispensable the precious aid of Joseph Souz.

_ What? – Complained Dan Lee. – Are you asking us to trust our lives on that crazy whack man?

_ Technically yes! I am afraid we won't have other alternative,

_ Now I have seen it all! – Argued Suzanne.

_ Calm down, you people. – Asked Denise. – I have been treating Ziggy for a long time, and I assure you he is reliable, despite his condition.

_ The thing is not as you are thinking. I am sure Denise will be able to prepare him to help us when the time comes and we need his intervention.

_ Pretty sure I can do this. – She looked at Peter with a proud look for his confidence. He is getting better each day, and I think this kind of work can be very helpful to him.

_ You know this is not a therapy, Denise. Completed Diana.

_ I am afraid it can not be so good to us. – Said Pablo.

_ Relax pals! – Said Kim. – I think I am understanding what the boss is trying to do. Each one of us would be leader of a group, correct Peter?

_ Exactly! Can't you see the whole picture? That's why I love this girl.

_ Thanks, boss! Anticipating your request, I raised the files of each one of the "blue jackets" psychics, by using the latest reports. With this we will elaborate an energetic profiles that will permit us to catch them more easily.

_ Very well, my dear friend. – Peter said that with such smile in his face, that it let the others more calm.

_ C'mon people. – Completed Suzanne. – After all we will twist some necks and punch some faces of this lunatics jackets.

_ This is a good point! I can't wait to kick some asses!

_ She is so excited because she wants to see her great love, Tharus.

_ Shut your big mouth, Argos! – Suzanne said angrily. – You don't know what you're saying.

_ Let's show these people we are the best. – Shout Dan.

_ Slow down, people. I am sure every one of us wants a revenge from what they did to Peter, and other personal motives, but we must keep in mind lots of innocent lives will be wasted in this process. And many of our enemies were our schoolmates. – Argued Hermes.

_ You're right, Hermes. We can't forget it is just another mission, just a little more dangerous. I believe the total obedience to the guidelines will bring us victory. I am touched you are worried about me, but I do not want to see any of you committing a crime to repair what they did to me. See the case of this new sect, "the owners of tomorrow", everything tells me soon they will bring us as problems as the "blue jackets".

_ Who are these people? Asked Denise.

_ We know about this group a few months ago, while Peter was captive. And when he came back, he brought us some more information, provided by Tharus Vendra. For the moment, this "owners of tomorrow" is just another religious group. They believe when the world is ruled by their leader, a new age of prosperity will begin. And to achieve this goal any mean can be used. From spontaneous conversion until terrorism.

_ Tharus confide me this group belongs to a secret society, who wants to create another kind of human beings, the "Andronoids", by using the synthetic biology. I don't have further information, because the Bat told me it would be too dangerous to me.

_ This sect was created in the beginning of the 19th century by a French- Portuguese archeologist professor named Joaquim M. D. Duran – Continued Hermes. – He developed a theory, based on the studies of ancient civilizations, God and the devil do not exist the way we conceive them. he had a predecessor, an old prophet from the 15th or 16th century, named Milo Rambaldi, who predicted a new race of men would raise. Duran believed the spiritual world do not have only one great leader, but an uncountable number of them, who are responsible by our evolution, and in determined times legions of spirits unite to impose a conduct line to other groups. Right and wrong do not exist as we understand them. What prevails is the point of view of the strongest and most intelligent, therefore any method is valid to achieve the purposes. Duran said he was connected to a powerful "egregora", which is the energy condensed by an association of similar consciences, a very powerful one that possess enough knowledge to make the mankind to dominate the whole solar system and even the galaxy, and each person who helped in the process would have his own planet to rule. About three months ago we were called to investigate an eerie murderer of 4 busyness men and we found out they were killed by a paranormal level 03, because they were involved with this sect but refused to give more money. Millions of dollars! Unfortunately, before we could raise more information this psychic committed suicide, closing the case, at least for now.

_ This is frightening.

_ Yes it is, Kim. But let's come back to what interests to the moment.

_ That's right, Diana. Lee and I will be in charge of the division of the teams. In each group there must be agents with specific abilities to the work to be done. Hermes, you and your father will be in charge of recruiting other schools and paranormals agencies to ask their cooperation. In a determined day, indicated by us, they must organize their students to provide mental emissions headed to that country. The main finality is to block the power of the Vendras and their associated.

_ Yes, captain, my captain. If everything runs properly these jackets won't be able to do much, and when they comprehend what is going on it will be too late. To this task will be necessary the help of thousands of psychics. It was never done before, but I think it can work. Said. Hermes.

_ Yes sir! To prevent leaks is essential they receive only the necessary information to their participation. You, Hermes, and Argos will be responsible to set a base where we will neutralize the prisoners.

_ I believe the best place to set this is in the desert of the neighbor country.

_ Excellent idea, Argos. This way we will have relative freedom and tranquility to act. – Completed Peter. – Once they are dominated they must be drugged to remain inactive, and nobody better than my sweet Denise to take care of it.

_ No problem!

_ When the teams are mounted, it will begin a training to a perfect development of our activities. I want everybody dancing in the same groove. I believe we will have 20 days to be prepared, so let's work!

On the next day they initiated the preparations. Every morning, they participated on physical and strategy trains, and in the afternoon they participated on lectures about relevant matters, and to learn the local idiom. The rest of the functions of the company of the paranormals were under the direction of those ones who were not directly involved in the case. The proximity of a combat of such magnitude generated much excitement even when the agents were on their spare time, and they used to gather together to discuss about the smallest details about the mission. Peter was by far the most anxious, because he would fight against his former idol and friend. In a certain way, he was puffed up by the fact his strategy could defeat the most powerful alive paranormal, and their 20 years personal dispute would end with his victory. The fact of a disciplined psychic level 07 be capable to face a level 08 one make the fight a little sweeter.

Chapter 06

How to raise a paranormal

The first school years ran without any further facts worthy of mention. Peter watched the classes regularly by the morning, including the study of three other idioms. By the end of the high school, he would be able to speak at least other three languages. After the lunch time there was a one hour gap, for a little nap, where the students had to rest to be prepared to the difficulties of the second round. At 01:30pm the second journey began with two classes, one theory and other practice, of several technician coursers, such as electronic; web design; nursery; agriculture techniques, music; cuisine; accountant; computer animation; chemistry and some others. These courses, besides spread the knowledge of them, had the finality to help on the development of the brain connections. At 04:00pm, after a brief snack, had begin the training of the extra sensorial perceptions, when 200 different types of exercises were systematically practiced alongside the years.

The firsts exercises had for finality to raise the maximum the perceptions of the five senses. To enhance the peripheral vision were made use of games where the participants had to practice activities, like soccer and football or baseball, without the use of the frontal vision, obstructed by a small device. The senses of touch; taste; smell and audition were improved by plays executed with this four perceptions blocked. The young children just loved this stage, when they could freely enjoy the playful side of the paranormal development, with activities like identify objects, food and animals using only one of the senses. At the end they learned not only to not be so dependant of the eyes, but the conscious use of the nose; skin; ear and tongue, all together, and this way try a different manner to relate with the world.

After this stage, which lasted about three years, began the training to control the physic organism, on which they learnt yoga; kung fu; judo; tae kwon do; breathing techniques; "chacras" rotation; bio energetic; do in; chiatsu; chromo therapy and reflexology. This phase was split into two, with each lasting two years; and the second part of it was studied together and practiced with the third phase. At the end, the apprentices should be able to recognize and control all their physiology, and could even be able to remain still for hours; decrease or increase the flux of oxygen on the blood; increase or decrease the heart beats; the intern temperature; the sweat; suspend for undetermined time the need to pee or lee, without damage to the organs; to prolong the need for food or water;

strengthen the defense systems of the body, in order to be free of cold and flu; decrease the painful sensations; increase the pleasure perceptions; elevate or low down the blood irrigation in certain organs; increase the strength and resistance of the muscles, bones and hair for a certain period of time; expand the capacity of memorize and learn; accelerate the cicatrisation of wounds; accelerate or low down the metabolism, increasing or decreasing the calories burn and to prolong the resistance to the cold and heat.

On the third stage, the apprentice learnt techniques of concentration; meditation; emotional and mental control and hypnosis, along a period of four years, executing exercises that in the begin lasted about thirty seconds and, while as were having success, the time was being extended until reach some hours, on the final phase. Was begun by tests where the student passed pre-determined periods with the mind empty of thoughts. First, the clock 's fingers should be watched and in another, a white wall. Won these obstacles, the next step would be to be free of ideas with the eyes shut in an ambient with much clarity, and after that in one without light. The brain was scanned throughout the executions of the exercises to have pinpointed all the moment of naps and frenzies, and when had completed the required time controlling the flux of spontaneous thoughts the student was allowed to continue the studies.

After that it was time to execute the tests where the apprentice should have the goal to remain hours only observing a given object until get to reproduce it mentally with shut eyes without losing the focus for any moment. First was given things of simple memorization like needles; plates, spoons and forks or pendants. Later with objects much richer in details like paintings; landscapes; homes and big gadgets. The tests began in sound and light controlled ambient, and next to the end of the phase, in ambient with much noise and other factors to make more difficult the concentration.

By the end, the student would have total control of the windings of the his mind and would be able to interrupt for a long period of time the whirlwind of thoughts that afloat of the unconscious, and even, direct his attention only to specified points and realize what was necessary without the mental tire interfere in his discipline. This way, the apprentice became the master of his thoughts, and not the contrary. So, his imagination got the necessary strength and freedom required to a paranormal.

On the fourth stage had finally begun the training on techniques of development of the extra sensorial perceptions. The initial exercises were common to all the students, starting with the use of flashcards, the apprentice should be able to recognize them before the selection, and later, to anticipate the instructor on what should be worked. They were trained to move with only the power of the mind a needle in a pan full of water; or move small polystyrene balls; or use the brain like a remote control, turning on and turning off, electronic devices, switching the dial; volume; color or intensity of TV sets, radios, DVDs or holographic systems. They trained with pendulums the exact location of hidden objects, and to score the answers of prepared to this finality questionnaires. The crystal should spin to the right when the answer was correct, and to the left when it was wrong. Games especially created to stimulate the intuition were developed by the department and largely used, like one where the students should cross a dark 3D maze in a short time, and in another, should detour the character out of traps and random attacks. By the way, the most of the exercises where executed in a virtual reality ambient, which was largely used by the psychic schools. Great part of the initial program of paranormal development required the participation of at least two students. They had to help each other strengthen. In one of these, they sat in front each other and extend the palm of the hand in the mate's direction and irradiate enough energy to create a shining ball of manifold colors, which should be detected by the other students and later described to the instructors.

They learnt relaxation techniques, trying to achieve the astral projection, also know as astral trip, bylocation, spiritual unfolding. It is simply the capacity of the spirit to leave the body by free will, for a certain period of time, and realize the works the person programmed to, and the conscience is direct as well to other landscapes and even other dimensions. This part of the learning was extremely important, for the apprentice verified by self experience the existence of live outside the material world, that death wasn't the end of the human essence, that there was intelligent life in other planets and even in ours, the evolution continues in other levels of existence and some of these levels are identical to the physical world; with cities; woods; oceans and people searching the happiness or preparing to return in another flesh body. The biggest obstacle to this technique was in few seconds of unfolding, the spirit began to lose conscience and slowly began to sleep. However, after some years of dedication, the most of the practicing got to remain outside the body the sufficient time to quick meetings with dear relatives, who were already dead or not, and they lost the fear of the inevitable transition. Some of them achieved a stage where they could spend hours absent of their flesh organism and realize great feats, such to know the whole planet; inside and outside; to study directly the energy that compose the orb, and to help the livings and the dead people. this studying had no connection with any religious cause, it was pure philosophy, as a order created by a Frenchman in the 19th century, named Allan Kardec, the spiritsm. This technique developed the specific capacity of projection as any other as levitation or telepathy.

On the second stage of the fourth phase, the training became individual and directed to each one of the extra sensorial perceptions of each apprentice. The degree of difficult increased as the obstacles were being left behind, demanding more and more dedication, discipline and patience from the students. However, not everything was that boring, after all, this was the part where the powers began to manifest more physically. The apprentices were so excited they didn't care about the sacrifices they were doing. There was also a special care about the alimentation, so they could have all the chances to achieve the maximum of their potentialities. The food served on the campus didn't have any portion of meat; chemical conservation or industrial fertilizer, to let the organism of the students always light and not intoxicated, to support the weight of the whole process of development. To compensate, they had always on their disposition, an incredible range of fruits and vegetables at any time of the day or the night. Special juices, shakes, food supplements, vitamins, teas and mineral pills completed their diet. Nobody complained about this forced feeding reeducation because twice a week they were allowed to have a special dessert, plenty of pastries; ice creams and all kinds of chocolates, and always they were outside the institution, there were no control about what they ate, just recommendations they usually followed. Even their relatives used to adhere to this diet.

Several scientific studies attested the efficacy of this alimentation method on the psychic development of the students, and the earliest they began, the best the results would be. Free of food based on animal protein, except eggs and mil, the body spent less energy on the digestion, and using the exceeding one in other organs and functions, specially in the brain, where the pineal gland was privileged, which reacted better on the influence of more subtle fluids, gaining more agility. The brain was less overloaded by the digestive tube protection against the poisoning effect of the rotten meat. And last but not least, the student didn't receive the negative emission of suffering, which impregnated the animal tissues on the time of a violent death. The skin remained more beautiful and luxuriant, the hair won an extra glow, the nails and teeth were yet stronger and organism defenses recovered more easily from wounds and illnesses, the power of concentration raised considerably, and the studies weren't interrupted by megrims and stomach problems. While this, the fruits, vitamins, vegetables; mainly the soy; which was the principal aliment, increased the immunity and strengthen the muscles and bones. Teas, roots, seaweeds and herbs opened the perceptions of the students, letting them more easily adaptable to the new mental posture. However, once completed the development process, the graduated paranormals had free will to chose meals from that day forth, without considerable damage to their abilities, once they were on control of all physiologic activities. A considerable parcel of them, well adapted on this reeducation, kept the most of the nutritional values learnt in the school.

When entered the forth stage, Peter already counted thirteen years old. Time ran by normally, almost without great tribulations worthy to be noticed, he made new friends; studied; played a lot, practiced sports; joined the young paranormals club, dedicating his energy on activities which would be unthinkable case he had remained with his mother. She had always been the involuntary motif of the few sad moments he had alongside those years, and it was the reason of the sadness in his eyes. Every school vacations he was sent back home for some weeks, nevertheless, each year he was becoming stranger in his own homeland, due to the fact he was getting well adapted to his new life and social condition, and for that felt very uncomfortable regarding to the lack of structure of his ugly city, neighborhood, dwelling conjoined and his mother's home. The garbage on the bored streets, the excessive heat, bad dressed non-educated people, the fattening food, the mosquitos, the lack of hygiene awaken on him an ambiguous felling of repulse and cherish. For it, always when he arrived at the airport with the heart beating fast, missing his mom, while he was on the traffic, grew in his chest an indignation with that filthy place and every moment all he could think was: " What a horrible city". To that contributed the fact that throughout the years, the tiny friendship between him and the neighbor boys raised into a hostile indifference, and the kids used to call him "nut professor", and on each travel the ambient was heavier. The excellent education created on him habits then unknown by his ex mates, and his genuine will to talk about subjects that weren't comprehensive to them and the undeniable fact peter was growing each time cuter, smarter, cult, skilful on sports, elegant, self confident and charming only increased the distance among them, and consequently a rejection feeling and despise from both parts that many times ended on fights.

As he always had done, on the same day he finished one more school year he embarked home. This time he didn't care about the unpleasant look of the nasty hometown. His only interest relied on his sick mom. He was a gallant teenager, who attracted the greed peers of almost every girl and envy of the guys. The degree where his abilities were generated a great proud on his mother, who was always asking him to demonstrate it to the neighbors. The fact of a poor boy reaching a so elevated position, made the suffering woman forgets her hard life and thanks God such gifts. Against all odds her boy would win in life. If weren't his demonstrations about martial arts on the square, and the rumors about his abilities, the jealous guys would have curried him all the time. One day the contained anger exploded when he was going to the bakery, few days before his return. A group of boys decided the fact the most beautiful girl in the region was seen kissing him the night before. They wanted to tear his nice clothes, which contrasted with their rags. On a first moment peter was terrified with the possibility of being beaten by so many boys and to be humiliated on daylight. Trying to avoid the conflict, he remembered them his kung fu skills, and even showed some amazing movements. It made the impressionable adolescents hesitate a bit, but it was enough to open space so Peter could run. When he was almost being reached by his stalkers, his feet unfastened the ground and he began to levitate by the first time. This gift had already been manifested once, but only the sufficient to be detected by the instruments of psychic activities measure, and the technicians believed it would be necessary some others years of training so he could fly as Peter Pan. The young Moll graciously floated on 30 feet high, while group of brats just observed. If desired, he could use one or another resource to dismiss the small crowd formed below, but he didn't want to hurt anybody, and besides, he was to euphoric with that conquer to be shy, and simply ignored those people. he began to slid amidst the houses and buildings enthralled by the new angle he could admire the landscape. Because it was dusk, he didn't attracted much attention, and went shopping and came back home this way, getting in by the window, to amaze and joy of his mother.

When returned to the school, he joined the select club of the students who could transit around the campus gliding above the constructions. He became more popular, because besides him, only Ziggy and Tharus had begun to levitate in an early age. The "top gun", as the flying paranormals dubbed themselves, used to form teams to play in several air games on Tuesdays and Thursdays, after class, what always attracted the cheers of great part of the students and employers. The instructors didn't see those activities with tender eyes, once they considered it a dangerous and unnecessary waste of energy, which could bring serious consequences if some of them trespassed the critical point, overloading the brain. As any regular teenagers, they didn't consider the advices. The participants enjoyed to play "burnt ball", where one of the players tried to hit, by throwing a ball, each of the players of the adversary team, and return it to his companions who were behind the enemy lines. It was a great crossfire. Some telechinetic students, who didn't have the ability to fly, were responsible to do not let the ball touch the ground. These disputes usually happened about 45 feet above the soccer field, a little bellow of the limit reached by the most of the psychic kids. The power to domain the gravity law, as any other, wasn't the same to all the students, somebody from the level 02 could raise less than 02 feet from the ground, another from the level 04 easily levitated 36 feet high, and one level 06 reached the maximum of 208 feet of height.

The "guns" usually played cop-thief, chasing each other through all the air space of the foundation, sometimes even crossing the limits of their neighborhood, and sometimes caused small accidents, which only increased the emotion of the radical sport. Another modality also much appreciated by the them was "steal the flag", where a team had to rob all the pennants from the adversary spread over the roof of the buildings of the campus, while protected their own streamers. The internals reunited to cheers and watch the spectacle larks, and unbelievable scenes of young people flying around trees; spinning on incredible jugs and funny stumbles. Now and then some television networks appeared to try to capture images to their evening news, but the principal never permitted the exhibition, pledging they should preserve the privacy of the under age minors. Only distant pictures where allowed, because the foundation directors understood this kind of documentaries could be a great form to introduce the sensitive practices on routine of the common people.

Some day, after an air rugby game, where Peter was chosen as the best player, despite being too much deranged on the air, and constantly twined himself on the branches of a tree. He was saved by the beautiful Suzanne Binoche, a charming happy talkative and sexy adolescent, two years older, who had the typical confidence of the girls who know very well the strong impression they caused on men. He was gathering his belongs and boasting to the mates when saw her passing by and arranged courage to go there and thanks to the girls who saved him too much in that evening from a great embarrassing. He got together to the so popular chick, and nothing came to his mind, he only could stutter.

_ Tha..than..thanks.

_ That's all you have to tell me, young fellow? I risked my pretty skin to save your ass, and can only think about a poor thanks? No baby, you must come up something better.

_ What! – Said the petrified boy.

_ Take it easy, handsome boy. I'm just kidding.

_ Wow, thanks. I almost had a heart attack.

_ Don't say that, boy. Are you always so serious? Look at here girls. – she called the attention of a group of friends nearby. – this boy is not only very cute but is also much more interesting than the wind head guys we have in here.

_ Thanks for it.

_ Stop saying thanks. By the way, my name is Suzanne, but call me Sue. And you are Peter.

_ How do you know?

_ It is my duty to know about interesting things in here.

_ Now that we are officially friends may I kiss your cheek?

_ Only my cheek? What a poor thought! Yes, you may.

And gently she offered her right face to the boy, but the moment his lips were getting closer, she turned her head, grabbed his neck and smacked his mouth, introducing slowly her tongue. After that she blinked and wishing him a good night, turned around and went away with her mates, leaving the incredulous boy frozen. Life was pretty to the young Moll. He was not only famous for being an outstanding sensitive, but also for being one of the luckiest boys who had the opportunity to prove from the most coveted thick lips in the whole school.

Peter and his young mates lived his life far from the problems that concerned the rest of the world, when in a certain pleasantly cool afternoon while studied biology under a tree, another girl as pretty as Sue came closer visibly worried.

_ Is everything alright, Peter?

_ Yes, it is. I know you. You are Gisele Demeter, Sue's friend, aren't you? – He didn't understand why she looked for him. – Had I done anything wrong? – Her expression wasn't good, he thought. – Can I help you?

_ No. Not really. Actually, I came here to help you. Unfortunately what I have to say will not please you.

_ You're making me nervous. Spit it out!

_ You have to go immediately to see your mother. – She finally said after hesitate a little.

_ My mother? I don't understand. What is wrong about her? We spoke by the video phone last Sunday.

_ I do not know exactly, so I prefer not to speculate. What I can assure you is when I saw you from over there I saw her image besides you, and my intuition tells me she is in great danger and needs you.

_ But she lives too far, in other continent. I won't have permission to go. – He replied with his hands shaking.

_ Yes they will permit. Morgana will have everything prepared when she hear it from me. She believes in my gift. I had never committed a mistake to the present. I am very responsible regarding this.

In a few minutes they both were sat in Morgana's office. The assistant heard the whole relate, and at the same moment she picked up the phone and set everything in motion to this travel. On the first flight of the next day Peter departed home, escorted by his dearest friend and almost an aunt, Morgana Helen Tantti. Peter did not possessed the ability of premonition, however his intuition was strong, and for some days he had felt a distress in his chest, and couldn't identify the reason of such apprehension, and because of this tried to do not pay much heed to that, until the moment Gisele told him about her visions. Even without meet her or know about her skills Peter had conviction she was telling the truth. It was the worst travel he had ever done. The time didn't passed and the plane didn't seemed to fly over the speed of sound, and nothing that Morgana or the flight attendants tried to remove him from this state of anxiety and prostration seemed to work. Everything was annoying him, and he didn't held the sad tears that wet his child's face.

During all the way to the residence he remained in silence, chewing his tragic expectations, and after another traffic jam, the young Moll in an access of impatience that wasn't from his character, turned his head to Tantti.

_ I'll wait you at home. – And by the first time he made use of his capacity to transport instantly, and before she answers he disappeared from her sight.

When she finally arrived at the condo the front door was open. Inside a desolated boy, sat on a rag armchair, waited for her.

_ What happened, where is your mother?

_I don't know. There's no sign of her. There's muck everywhere, that's not my mother. She is poor but likes everything neat.

_ Don't worry. We're gonna find out what happened and find your mom. – Morgana hugged him. – Have faith. Now tell me about this your new ability. I didn't know you already could use it that way.

_ Neither do I. I had an idea, let's ask the old lady on the 13th floor. She was the only person my mother had some level of friendship. Probably she knows something.

_ You first!

They went up and knock on the door several times. After some minutes an old woman, dressing humble clothes, but well chosen, what revealed a person who wanted to have the style and the life of a higher social class.

_ Hello, Peter! You came earlier this year, didn't you? Or am I getting dazed and confused? I think that the excess of hemp damaged my brain!

_ NO, you're far from confusion. I came here to ask if you know something about my mother. We went there and she wasn't, and it seems she left a long time ago.

_ Your mother? Oh yes. Your mother! I truly don't know where she is. I don't news from her over than two weeks. The last time I saw her she was going to the doctor because of a bad flu. I thought she had traveled to see you. Maybe she is in the hospital. I just made a coffee, come in and have some with me.

_ NO, thanks. We have to locate this kid's mother.

_ Ok. Let me know about my dear friend.

Back to the apartment Peter thought about trying his intuition. He got some objects from her room, those she was very attached, and laid down on her bed, closing the eyes and entering in profound concentration. Little by little some shuffled images came to his mind, but after thirty minutes, subtly, behind his eyelids, as a movie projection, clear portraits of a hospital were formed, and he could see his mother in the nursery, sleeping deeply. The impression was too vividly he was able to read the name of the institution in the sheets. Leaping from the mattress, he grabbed the phone catalog to look for the address, and they two headed there right after. In the big and precarious healthy treatment building, they had much difficult to receive suitable information. There were too much patients and too few attendants. Peter stopped a nurse who seemed sympathetic, because Morgana Helen was very confused in that lousy place.

_ Excuse me, lady. Can you help me?

_ No I can't, but I may! Speak up quickly! I have too much to do!

_ Wait a minute, ma'm. This poor boy just need some information.

_ What is this "aunt Sam" saying? Get out, boy. I am not the super nanny.

_ Morgana, I am in the verge to break everything up in here!

_ Why don't you hypnotize her? Just keep low profile.

_ Good idea!

Peter got closer to the healthy professional, who was distracted by some paper work. For some minutes he stared at her forehead. After that he just said.

_ You're gonna help me find my mother. Now!

_ I am going to help you find your mother. – She replied.

For some time she tried to locate the lady, without success, but another nurse remembered about a woman who was found fainted on the streets, a couple of weeks earlier. She didn't carried documents or they were stolen, and she got into as an indigent, that's why she didn't receive much attention, despite her clinical situation was very serious. She was bitten by a new specie of mosquito. The whole country was passing through a bad epidemic crisis. There weren't care to everybody. Peter went into the worst nursery of the hospital. from the door he could see his mother's face. People were amounted there only to wait for the death. The windows didn't even have glasses, and the floor was wet and dirty. He found a small bench, and pulled it to the side of her bed. She was in coma. He held her hand tenderly and began to pray. Meanwhile, Morgana went out to provide the necessary documentation to remove her to a proper institution, once the foundation healthy agreement offered her the best doctors and clinics. Tantti was disgusted by the way poor people were treated in that hospital. During hours peter was beside his mom, talking to her as if she could hear. All the time he kissed on her cheek while cherished her hand, crying in silence, trying to avoid her to notice his sadness. Looking to that suffering woman, very fragile, laid down in that uncomfortable bed, regarded as a street dog, he regretted for his good life. He wished he could have spent more time with her, and couldn't help thinking if he was there, taking care of her, as a son should do, it hasn't happened. He felt guilty for living in a cozy place, surrounded by rich people in a rich country, while she wasted her youth struggling against the adversities. What the advantage of being so powerful and famous between his friends if he couldn't heal her, he thought. At this moment she opened her eyes, and looked at him.

_ My pretty boy. How I missed you. It is very good to wake up and see your face.

_ Mom. Thanks God! Please forgive me for everything. I wish I could be a better son. I promise from now on it will be different. You'll have all things you deserve. I am so sorry I don't have the gift to heal you.

_ Please, my baby, what are you saying? Stop it. You are the best of the sons. Don't blame yourself what happens to me. Each one of us has a proper destiny. I want you to know how proud you let me. This foundation rescued me, because I was feeling terrible for not offer the best education and opportunities when they chose you. They relief my heart, and I know your father's too. I know he felt happy in heaven when you went with these nice people. to know my dear Petey is going to accomplish everything in life I always dreamed about made my life have a purpose, and that I did it right. May God take care of you from now on. I want you to be very happy. My heart is light because I could see you before I pass away and give you a last kiss. Don't feel sorrow for me, because I am going to be with your daddy. He is here to pick me up! I can see him clearly. So I can only be heading to heaven, and there aren't unhappy people there. Always have in mind how much we love you. Now is time to die.

Right after say that she had a last breath and the brave woman died without further sufferings. A smile depictured how peaceful she was. For a long moment Peter remained still beside the inert body of the woman who gave him life, lost in thoughts, trying to understand the meaning of that painful loss. To mourn wouldn't be enough express the void in his soul. He wanted to cry it out loud to the whole city hears his grief and his anger.

_ How could they to scorn just because she was poor? – He asked to himself.

It wouldn't help. Nothing could bring her back, time won't retreat so he could recover the years he was absent, and permit him to all this time on her side. And then, he simply laid down on her bed and embraced her chest, like he used to do when a child, imagining he wouldn't have opportunity to know her better, what she enjoyed, her dreams and desires, what was going on her heart, her opinions and wisdom. He supposed to have an entire life comprehend her soul and learn more about that woman he admired the most. A woman who was always quiet and talked low, who almost never smiled or laughed, who was always feeble by a illness since he was a toddler as if her weakness was part of her personality. On the next day she was buried. Few people were preset to see her for the last time. During the wake Peter practically didn't talk to anybody, and never left her side, nor to eat or go to the restroom. Were his last moments with the woman who gave birth to him and Peter wanted to stay together while he could. Peter requested to Morgana to provide the simplest burial and coffin, likewise had been her short life. The fact he believed in life after death was a great comfort and relief to his heart, when, a few days later, he had to deal with the sale of the few values she possessed. A falling into pieces small apartment, some old furniture, some bangles almost worthless were all the hoarded up money of an entire honest existence. The raised currency would be sent later to Peter's savings by the lawyer in charge of the inventory. This way he could return with Tantti to the country and city he would call, from that day on, home. On his way back to the airport he looked melancholically at the buildings and the people around him, as if he was saying goodbye, as if he hadn't any other reason to come back there.

Now and then his life was regaining the natural path. The vigor of youth and new challenges were beating the sadness and prostration. In a few months, Peter was already playing, joking, laughing and making plans as before. Morgana was practically his foster mother, and took him to her house every weekends and holidays. They made company to each other, reading books, watching television; while eating chocolate cookies under the blankets, on the cold and rainy days, visiting her relatives or simply strolling throughout the parks and museums of the city. Mister Vasconcellus was also very attached to the obedient boy, who never asked or complained about nothing. And always when the occasion permitted the president of the foundation took Peter in his researches and entertainment travels, trying to mold his character, by passing wisdom and life lessons. Even his son, Hermes, despite the great difference of age, treated the young Moll as a younger sibling, and constantly took him on his diversions with friends. This way, surrounded by cherish and attention, the adolescent was understanding his mother was sure when she affirmed he belonged to that place and to that people, and despite the initial suffering, his life would fit in the right way. The boy was So Grate to Gisele, who made possible his last goodbye to his mother, all the time Peter saw her wanted to express his gratitude, with gifts; words or just a tender smile. From her part, she was so touched by his misery, she asked a friend, who as a strong medium, to look for notices about the poor woman, and all the time Peter had good news from her, that she was in peace and happy, reassured the best to do was to return to his beloved chores. His powers were becoming stronger on each day, and he, more wise and mature. Now Peter was as popular in the school as Tharus, the bat, or Joseph Souz, the Ziggy. His discipline forged in iron and the dedication to the mental exercises compensated the fact he wasn't in the same level of the other two. Always obedient, calm and studious, never exceeded the established limits by his supervisors, and all the teachers loved him. He passed hours connected to machines that scanned, stimulated and thickened his sensitive capacities with the submission of a budhist monk, and long physical exams and boring tests did not bothered him. Peter did not even thought the monotonous and slow routine of enhance of the ESP were tiresome.

Great part of the students did not stand the long way to walk and the rigorous growing system and gave up of their purposes, and were satisfied by the results already accomplished, and abandoned the foundation. It occurred mainly on the time they reached the adolescence and the hormones were blowing up in their veins, pushing them into infatuated adventures, absolutely incompatible with the Spartan abnegation that was required from the apprentices. The Vendra brothers succumbed to the mundane temptations and quit the institution, and after the mysterious sickness of Ziggy, the young Moll, at the age of 14, became the main paranormal of the school.

CHAPTER 07

THARUS VENDRA

When the family Vendra found out that they would be parents of twins they got into a completely state of euphory. To raise a large family had always been their main goal, and had passed a long time since the birth of their first daughter and son. They were in the age of 14 and 09 respectively, and the couple didn't they could be able to realize another dream. Besides, it would be a perfect crowning of a happy marriage and a emotional and financially stable life family. With the two kids well raised and almost independent the arrival of the stork in a double dose would give a new meaning to the spouses, and with the experience accumulated they would do better to the twins than they did to Idice and Iones.

The boys were born strong, handsome and very healthy, surrounded of all the comfort and dedication possible. Since the early age the identical twins were used to be the core of all the family attention, and were growing shrewd and despotic, but also caresses and charismatic. By the age of two they already knew how to read and write easily, and were soon enrolled in a kindergarten specialized on over intelligent kids. But as time passed by it became clear that the hyperactive boys possessed a different kind of brightness, and they generated so many troubles and confusions to the mates and teachers their parents were nicely invited to look for another school. The same thing occurred in other infantile centers along the years. The psychologists said they were precocious rebels and didn't fit in the rigid teaching methodologies, based on ancient formulas that did not take in count the individuality and the needs of each child. All the time the twins were questioning the pedagogues, always trying to test the limit of patience and knowledge of them, and even the schoolmates didn't understand the strange behavior of the little ones, who thinking it was only to catch attention, end up by discriminating the Vendra boys. This way, Tharus and Iullus lived in strives with the other kids, including and mainly the older ones, who they considered envy and not as smart as themselves.

Tharus was always the leader, and loved to shine more than Iullus, who preferred to follow the steps of his three minutes younger brother, who was always the mentor of the pranks and all sort of jokes that drove their parents crazy. Inseparable companions, they never fought each other, preferring to share equally all the toys and candies or simply giving up on the other's favor. Outside the scholar domain they were always surrounded by lots of friends. All the girls were in love with their blond hair, blue eyes and angelically devilish symmetric face. Among their street little mates there wasn't competition, rivalry or someone trying to show up to the teachers, and the only tension was in the healthy dispute on the games. The small devil kids won the sympathy even of the neighbors who suffered the most with their tricks, and always they looked their parents to complain about them, end up by praising more than reprehending.

They didn't have much in common with their older siblings because of the difference of age. However, the lack of affinity was compensated by the cherish between them. Idice and Iones constantly protected the youngest from the rage of those who were bothered by them, and loved to take Tharus and Iullus to the cinema, parties and theaters. All the family, including, uncles, aunts, cousins and grandparents lived in harmonic sociability and in all the contacts they were always fondling the little ones. This way, they were growing with strong family values, what defined their character. In a certain manner almost all their future problems were caused by their defense of the family principles they considered the most important and true.

On the party of their fifth birthday, a guest noticing the preoccupation on their mother's face, asked nicely:

_ Is there something annoying you, darling friend? Have you discovered a mistress of your husband?

_ Of course not! My marriage is wonderful! Why, do you something?

_ No! I was just kidding, darling. Your husband is faithful, what I can't say about mine. But then, what is it about?

_ I am a bit worried about the future of my two kids. No good school will accept them, and I do not want they go to a regular one.

_ If you accept an advice, I believe I can help you.

_ Please. I really could use some help.

_ Why don't you ask the visit of the researchers of the foundation to the development of the extra sensorial perception? They will apply some tests and if the kids pass in, Tharus and Iullus will study in an excellent institution.

_ But how would they pass on these tests? Do you think they possess any special ability?

_ This I do not know exactly. Along these years I have seen them making some strange things. I believe their behavior is not caused by hyperactivity, they do not show all the classic symptoms. There is something else that needs to be worked. I have a niece and she was the same as them, and now she is studying in the foundation school. She is another girl, so nice and centered. Now imagine, if they become paranormals how it would improve their resumes? I mean, they will have a very high status. Anyhow, some people say that when a innate paranormal is not educated properly, he becomes a problem to the society, like an alcoholic for example, darling.

_ That is true! Do you have the email of this foundation? On Monday, first thing in the morning, I'll call them! I won't even tell to my husband. It will be a surprise if they pass in these exams.

During a whole week the two kids were submitted to several tests, and despite they did not have taken it seriously, and did not have made much effort on scoring the most possible, the technician were amazed by the results. After the family approval, they would begin their studies within a month, and as they lived in a small town only 15 miles away from the institution, there was no need for them to become internals. Since the first class day the twins felt very comfortable with the campus, once they never had studied in a such big and luxury place, full of many distractions to be explored, once they were too young to understand the real purposes of the foundation, which for them functioned as any other school, only in a better installation. Other twin siblings studied there, and this way they wouldn't be always attracting too much attention, what was fundamental to their socialization, and soon they made lots of friends. They enjoyed so much their new school they decided to take it easy with the pranks, to do not be expelled.

The firsts years ran without big stumbles, with the boys playing and studying just like any other kid in their age. The only difference was they had a intelligence over the average of the children and required a different curriculum. So they were set in older students classrooms, and many times they used to make more pertinent comments than the rest of the group. When their perceptions began to give the firsts signals, Tharus and Iullus were so glad, as if now they comprehended how important it would be to their lives, they decided from that day on to dedicate the maximum on the exercises, a thing they hadn't done till then, and they wouldn't say anymore the training was so boring they rather die. To be hours sat still in a uncomfortable chair full of wires suddenly became a pleasant way to overcome their mates, and they stopped escaping from it. They finally understood the huge spread field of opportunities was open ahead, and this way, renounced freely to their good life to accomplish the object of their ambitions.

The demonstrations of the capacities of the most potent students, mainly Ziggy, frightening powerful, made the blue eyes of Tharus glow of such admiration, because they were example of his own future capacities. Day by day the brothers were getting to participate on the games and diversions that were accessible only to the more advanced students. The power of their ESP was incredibly high to the age they were in, as for example the telechynisis, which allowed making their heavy backpacks float behind while they walked through the campus. But what attracted the attention of the instructors the most was the fact, despite they were identical twin brothers, their abilities weren't all the same and weren't in the same intensity. To amaze the supervisors, who couldn't explain the fact, on each three months became a little more developed, sensitively, than Iullus, who, at least in thesis, should not have any discrepancy from his brother. The arrival of Peter Moll, who rumors had was the mister Vasconcellus"s new protégée, let the brothers yet more competitors, and this jealousness let them curious and approximate to him. They liked the little boy, and Iullus decided to keep him close, so they could see if the gossips had any basis. The Vendra were very amazed by the fact a little child could already be talking their language as a local. The empathy was immediate.

_ Come here, kid! Do you want some candy bar?

_ Why are you giving me this? Are you a kind of perverted?

_ Shut up and take it quick. Are you out of your sick mind, crazy boy?

_ I am just kidding. You know, aunt Morgana told me to do not accept candies from strange people.

_ But we are not strange, crazy boy. I am Tharus and he is Iullus.

_ The Vendra boys? I heard about you. In this case I'll take some candies.

_ Come with us, we'll introduce you to some friends. You'll be our mascot.

_ Where are we going?

_ We are going to play soccer.

_ Cool! Can I call some friends? Argos, Mike and Tommy? They are very good players.

_ Ok, but go fast.

After that day, the twins began to take Peter everywhere after school, and he was always escorted by Argos, Tommy and Mike, and alongside the years, the four roommies became really the mascots of the Vendras and their friends.

_ Today we're going to the shopping mall. – Said Iullus one day to Peter. – Unfortunately the principal only allowed us to take you and your mates if we take together Morgana " the bag without handle" and other two monitors.

_ Why did you call her bag without handle?

_ Because she is boring. Do you know how boring is to carry a bag that had the handles ripped off?

_ No!

_ Forget about it! We'll catch you all at 04:00pm. Don't be late.

_ Very cool, Iullus! Your parents should let you stay here in the weekends more often.

Iullus noticed the angry face of his friend, Diana.

_ what is wrong, Di?

_ Nothing! I just wanna stay here. I prefer to play soccer instead hang out with these kids.

_ If it was up to you, you could do what you please. - Replied Tharus. - But I am in charge here, and I decide who do what. Ok? You are going with us, lady. Besides, Ziggy is going out with us. Do you know how difficult was to convince him? It will be bizarre!

All the group was so excited by the perspective of great diversion, and at the combined time they embarked in the foundation's bus, escorted by expert "hack messy" trio. Once inside the immense shopping center, the first providence of the teenagers was to prepare a trap to their supervisors, and Tharus stopped the elevator while the three ones were in there alone. At least for some hours, until Morgana and the other two woman were rescued by the mechanics, the boys and girls would have enough time to do whatever they wanted, free of any kind of control. Peter was the only one who clearly demonstrated his disagreement to what they did to Mrs. Tantti.

_ Don't you forget, Ziggy, that we have to inspect the girls on the beauty pageant. – Said Tharus. – I think they are trying clad, and it is an excellent time for us to transport to inside the backstage.

_ "For yesterday" my friend!

_ While these two horny go to satisfy their passions, I want to see who can manipulate the vending machines. – Replied one of the girls.

_ Let's go. – Said Argos.

After they were stuffed of chocolates and other pastries, the group decided to do other things.

_ Let's do other things, people. Those two are taking to long. It's time to play.

_ Somebody missed us. – Asked Joseph Prometeus, when he sudden appeared in front of the guys and girls. His fade denounced he had done something really bad.

_ Thanks Gosh, Ziggy!

_ You have no idea how wonderful those chicks are. We were hidden in the roof and saw everything and something else.

_ Stop blabbing. We have something to do. – Complained other girl.

Every place they were things were moved away. The prank season was opened. Chairs were pushed in the right moment somebody was sitting, clients had to run after their purchases, plastic mannequins were flying over the salespeople's head, fire extinguishers were sprayed; leaving everything around covered by white dust, merchandises crossed the galleries, security guards ran from one side to the other trying to figure out what was happening. The chaos took care of the mall, but nothing could openly demonstrate the action of the paranormals. Joseph, the Ziggy, and the others prepared all the tricks without leave evidences to accuse them. the evening was so bizarre, the direction of the mall decided to close doors and call the police. Meanwhile, the firefighters got to open the elevator and set free Morgana and the monitors, who did not suspected the pranks their pupils were doing. The trio looked for the kids and found them rolling on the floor, cackling and joking. They didn't understand what could be so funny. Once again, the little Peter did not involved in such tricks, because, despite the fact he was only 06 years old, he didn't like to make other people look like silly, and did not want to harm anyone. After be noticed of what had happened in the mall, about the odd thinks that scared so many people, Morgana suspected it was work of her protégées, and decided to end the stroll. However, for some weeks, the occurred fact in the mall, was the main subject in the foundation, as for the students; who were not tired of talking the exaggerated situations, as for the directors; who shared the suspicious of Morgana Helen and were afraid the Hero glow of Tharus and ziggy influenced the behavior of the rest of the school. And they decided to increase the polite, justice and honest lessons, and gave the episode closed.

Time flew by and the twin brothers were already 14 years old. They kept behaving as 10 years old child, because they wanted do stretch out their childhood the maximum they could. Their main concern was still jokes and games, instead woos and sex. Frequently they changed programs with girls and raves by games with their mates. They didn't have patience to stay with the same girl more than two weeks. Their fan club was enormous, and they were vowed the most handsome guys in the school. They didn't conceive a long relationship, once they had an entire life to enjoy. They knew their infantile days were counting down. Their way, whatever they chose, would be replete of beautiful and interesting women, but soon the tricks and plays would lose glow, and so, to enjoy this period was priority to them, and they did not pay much heed to flertings as their friends less favored by Apollus, the god of beauty. In the other hand, chicks used to be upset by the excessive self confidence of Tharus, what was in the verge of arrogance, and his careless attitudes let them very annoyed, and then, they pended more to Iullus side, stimulating a certain competition among the twins. It made then slowly search more and more adventures in the fascinating adolescent world.

During many years, Ivana Minerva had a crush on Iullus, but the poor girl began to lose patience and considered finding a real boyfriend, once he did any move and she was too shy to take the initiative. Their mutual friends tried to push one into the other's arms, because they would form a very beautiful couple. Unfortunately Iullus had no idea the friendship of the green eyes blond was something else. His friend Hitchie had to alert him.

_ And Ivana, what do you thing about her, Iullus?

_ Ivana, the "big ant"? I do not know, dude. She is skating very well and has some very crazy capacities.

_ No, you potato head, I am talking about her as a woman.

_ I don't know, man. She is only 14. She still has to eat too much porridge to become a woman.

_ That is what you see, you moron. There are a lot of guys trying to catch her. She is already a woman, and one of the best, if you know what I mean.

_ Is that true, man? I don't see it.

_ That's because you're a retard. She is in love with you since we were kids, but you're delivering the gold to the bandits. Besides, big ant was a dub from her childhood. Nobody but you calls her like that. Keep your eyes wide open, pal!

_ Now you mentioned it, I am beginning to see it. She is really very beautiful, a real "Gisele Bundchen".

_ And so, man. Make a move.

_ Later I'll invite her to go out.

_ But do it as a man, pal, not as a boy. She thinks you're too silly to your age.

_ What are you talking about? – Asked Tharus, entering in the conversation. Who thinks my brother is too silly?

_ Do you know the big ant?

_ Stop calling her this way, Iullus.

_ What is about her?

_ She has a crush on me.

_ What? I don't doubt it, after all you look like me. The only difference is I am cuter.

_ Keep dreaming, dude! Chicks say the opposite.

_ Shut up, kid! Just because you lost your virginity before me it doesn't mean you're more experienced than me.

_ Stop saying shit and give your opinion, brother.

_ Ivana is a nice girl, and I think it is time for you to stop calling her big ant. Dig deep, brother.

_ That'S what I intend to do, brother.

Iullus had never thought about dating Ivana, but from that day on he obviously began to consider the hypothesis, due her extreme beauty and nice way. He reminded the form he used to talk and treat him. And soon he felt for Minerva an infatuation, and decided to take a decision when they hung out the next day.

_ Hello, Ivana, what's up? Can I talk to you?

_ You already are.

_ You got me. Now let's talk serious.

_ Can you?

_ Yes I can, and you?

_ Spit it out, boy.

_ Well, what do you really think about me?

_ Really? You're a cool guy, but kind boring. And such a child. A big toddler. You do not want to take responsibility, is super convinced, your left eye is a little askew and your feet are weird. I've been told you're not a good kisser. What else? Let me think for some seconds and I tell you more.

_ I didn't know you hated me. Wait a minute, I'll look for a tree to hang myself up and I'll be right back.

_ What a pity! C'mon, boy. Say what you want. I have more important things to do.

_ Alright, I'll be straight. Do you want to date me, despite all my qualities you spoke about?

_ Yes, I do. I must be a sort of masochist.

_ Now I can kiss your mouth.

In that moment their friends were passing by and applause the scene. Despite being embarrassed, Ivana was too happy, and did not care about the jokes people played around them. the relation floated on the surface, because Iullus did not want to go deeper, but it was a relationship anyhow, what was a progress to the Vendra boys, despite Iullus only dated when they were hanging out with the rest of the group, what began to bother Ivana. As time passed by she got used to the superficiality of the relation, and as she believed she wasn't yet prepared to have a sexual life, took advantage of the slow motion of the situation.

On the contrary of his brother and other friends, Tharus was more reserved concerning to the girls. He did not have a romantic soul, and preferred to approximate them when there was possibility of easy sex or when he missed to kiss a beautiful chick. Most of the time he was satisfied by the greedy eyes they stared at him. The simple fact of knowing that great part of them desired him was enough to let Tharus proud, and he needn't to waste time with the futilities proper from people who are in love. Being more ambitious and pragmatic than the others, his priority was the development of his ESPs and the pleasure the use of then gave him. While Iullus strolled with his girlfriend, Tharus made a huge tattoo in his back, a colored bat. It was so perfect it seemed real. And when he showed his trend mark to the friends they dubbed him Tharus, the bat, and he enjoyed the new nickname. At the age of 15, Tharus achieved the level 06. Only Joseph Prometeus Souz had reached such level in a such early age. However, Iullus was still level 04, what was a impressive fact, but that was dazzled by his brother feat. But it didn't bothered Iullus. His main concern was his two minutes older brother was lonely, because he didn't have company to the kind of diversion he intended, because the most of the students didn't achieve his level. Tharus enjoyed to transport himself to several places of the city, in unexpected moments, such as when he asked the teachers to go to the restroom and disappeared, going to some snack bar; pet cemetery; medieval museum; craftwork fairs or old bookstores, taking care to do not appear in crowded places to not attract attention, and after some minutes of solitude, came back to the classroom. At night, after everybody is in bed, he used to go out to fly over the city. And as usually was cold, principally at certain height, most of the time he wore thick black pants; soldier boots; black jumper; scarf; dark blue raincoat; gloves and black hood. Dark blue was his favorite color. He materialized outside the building took a deep breath, appreciating the night freedom, began to walk, and slowly was going up, until reach the maximum height he could. Then he remained some minutes still, just observing the admirable landscape. Always in erectus position or sat in a yoga style, he started to move forward, without much speed, to do not increase the air friction. In this night flights he liked to escort the flux of cars and the passers –bys right bellow, and sometimes he got so close to the people he could listen their conversations, without letting them notice his presence. And although this was not a violent city, many times he saved some girls and old people, avoiding crimes, like rapes or assaults, by sticking the criminal, twisting them with iron bars, removed from grids and calling the police. These hero acts were made by distance, just using his mind powers, and the most of the rescued ones did not notice his participation. Duty accomplished he returned to his lonely stroll, heading to some sky – scratch and stayed there for some hours, thinking in his life. Sometimes somebody approached the window when he passed by, and was big scare, when lights were lit, shouting. Many times he was identified as the "mothman", a supernatural bird, half man, half moth. In these occasions he just disappeared to do not have to give any explanations. The wide sensation of liberty he experienced in these hours no other sport could provide. The loose in the air was higher than any other called radical activity. Tharus wasn't a lonely wolf. On the contrary, he was a group member, and appreciated to be surrounded of friends and fans, but he valued highly the moments he could be alone.

At the age of 16 Tharus had already reached the 7th level. With the thicken of his abilities he was able to include the brother into his favorite pastimes. This way, the gearing between them, which already was strong, became yet deeper, and the young Iullus had such admiration on tharus, he would be capable to follow the Bat wherever he'd go, in any kind of job work, for the most insane it could be. They woke up late every day, had breakfast with their parents and siblings, and in an instant the Bat and Iullus, who did not possess this ability, appeared in the school. Many times, before it, Tharus used to let his family in their jobs and colleges. At this time he was more sociable, and to amaze his friends, he even dated for some times the gorgeous Gisele Demeter, and they were always together, acting as any conventional couple; also doing what only enchanted paranormals could do, as moon night strolls, but 600 feet above the ground; private visits to museums and art exhibitions, when the access to the visitors was over, and trips to the most dangerous and inaccessible spots on earth, by using the mental instant transportation; which didn't required visas or any other type of bureaucracy. Even the Bat was guessing very spooky this, till then, "non manifested romantic spirit" and became surprise after spend hours materializing small gifts to his beloved, as jewels; little crystal sculptures, which so perfects seemed true fairies and goblins; sugar inscriptions carved in metal and wood boards. During some time they believed being completely in love, predestinated to each other, but once again the Tharus frivolous and inconsequent spirit gave its grace again. Sick of the constant presence of his no more so beloved Gisele, who was already making venturous plans to the future, he began to flirt with another girl, who also had an infatuation on him, Suzanne Binoche. The two chicks used to be very good friends. None of the two lovers tried to hide the romance, and when the official one, Gisele, found out what was going on, feathers flew everywhere, as Ivana, one of the two witnesses, said later to the others. They fought with teeth, nails and mind powers, with chairs, vases and many other objects flying around, while the discord motif watched it all impassible.

_ Bat, won't you do anything to end this? – Ivana shouted. – They are fighting for you, and sooner or later one of them will be hurt. Probably Gisele, because Sue is very strong. Do something, man!

_ Hush, woman. Too much hush in this hour. Nobody is in danger in here, and no one will be hurt seriously. So let them express their feelings. I have decided, the winner will have me as her award.

Ivana called telepathically some friends to help, and after some effort, by using their capacities, they got to separate the wildgirls. When the animosity settle down, seemed a tornado had swept the venue, such was the mess of broken objects and torn clothes. Practically naked, the competitor ladies still peered each other with threatened eyes, cursing mutually, with accusations of fakeness, lack of friendship and excess of libidos. After a while they both noticed the ridiculous of the situation and the tranquility in which the "motif" watched it all, and they laughed for being such sillies, by passing through a great shame for someone who was amazed by the rolling drama, and finally they comprehended the true guilty of everything was Tharus. So they gave him a "banana gesture" and hugged each other, and went away. For some time Gisele and Sue stopped talking with him, but after he insists for so long, they capitulated and forgave him, but never more the friendship was the same between they three.

The Ziggy's sickness, Tharus became the most powerful sensitive in the world, and according to the researchers, the only one in condition to compete with the Peter Moll, the little promise, who at this time was 12 years old. Aware of it, the Bat approximated yet more of the pre adolescent, trying to show to peter they were members of an exclusive club, as if he was Öbi Wan Kenobi, and Peter his padawan. In the deep of his heart he felt threaten by Moll's discipline and dedications and was afraid to be left behind. The right thing is a courteous rivalry began among them, and all the moment they were testing each other, to measure who was winning to the moment. Many times Tharus used to forget to age difference, such was his will to be the number one. Obviously, when there was a tough dispute, the Bat usually was the winner. But he was always recognizing the merit of his opponent, and showed him to be the second was a honor, and Peter was cheered by the other students by the simple fact to be the only one with real chances to beat Tharus. However, this rivalry was only on the paranormal field, for Peter admired Vendra as an older brother, and respected him for it, and not because he was so powerful. When they were not competing, Tharus used to treat him almost as a younger brother, and loved him as a good friend. But most of the time they were provoking each other.

_ I don't want to make you jealous, Bat, but today, during the class, I dematerialized a book and materialized it in the other room. Teacher Carmen, do you know her? The judicious one?. She made me a lot of eulogizes.

_ Don't you tire me, boy. I agree, what you did isn't a feat worth of anyone. For that I praise you! But in your age I used to do the same with a bicycle.

_ You don't need to tell me that with a such superiority.

_ I am just giving you a purpose!

Peter was the only person, besides Iullus, Tharus enjoyed to share his ideas with. The Bat's thoughts sounded very odds to the ears of his companions, and they were always arguing against him. That's why Tharus used to talk with Moll, despite he didn't have enough comprehension to understand his concepts and points of view, but was a very good listener.

_ What's up, Tharus? Are you annoyed by something?

_ I really don't know, Peter. I guess I am bored of all this shit! Any day I'll blow it all up.

_ But you already do it.

_ Pay heed, boy. I am not talking like that. I am talking about quit the foundation and be gone. I don't want to go to college anyway. I want to travel and meet different people, spree life, dude. In a few months I'll be 18, and what interesting things have I done? And the people in here are so gauged!

_ But what do you really want. Here in the city is full of different people, and besides, life is great in here. You should have seen the poverty in my country. In there, people have to work hard to get the minimum, and most of time they don't even have that!

_ That's another thing that bothers me a lot. Why some people get things so easily, and the most of the population have to struggle to try to get a little bit? In the most of their efforts they just eat shit.

_ I believe each person has a fate, and has in life what was previously planned. You know, the past lives can explain why we are suffering in the present days. To ransom old debts, I don't know exactly. I understand you do not believe in it all, and I respect it.

_ I do not. Those little children that live in these poor countries, like yours, and die of starvation and sicknesses, those old people forgotten in the dark corners of our streets, would all that be just a matter of other lives ransoms? If that's right, there wouldn't be injustices, Peter, and I know they happen all the time around there. Don't you tell me it is just a matter of fulfill the destiny. And why us, who were born with these fantastic gifts, can't do more to repair this process of injustice? Can you tell me why not? After all, these powers must have been given to us for a reason, and I have to use them to other purposes but flirt the girls. There must be a major sense!

_ I think so. But we don't know exactly how things work, and if we don't study hard and act with caution, we'll never make the right thing.

_ I agree with you, and I also think we can use our gifts to fix things we know are wrong. There are lots of people practicing evil and hurting innocent people, and who tries to face them dies. If we can stop these people we should do it. This is not our right is our obligation.

_ I don't know what to say, I still have a lot to learn. I think it is too dangerous, and you're not superman, you know.

_ Superman is a jerk. I always preferred Doctor Destiny. He is much more interesting.

_ So here is a free lesson, my friend: the evolution is up to us, is on our cargo. Only ours. Do you think God is worried about what we do? I don't think so! He created this world and all the chances to develop life, gave the directions to the monkeys evolution till us, and let the rest on our hands. Since then we have done nothing but crap. The crusades, the witch hunt, lots of wars, the continue destruction of the nature, the ozone layer we vanished it. You must have studied about the world wars I; II and III, the middle east war, that began with the terrorist attack on the twin towers. My father lost an aunt on that atrocity. No my friend, I believe God no longer control the Earth, and let the work on our responsibility. That's why everything is falling apart. Nor even those light spirits, you believe totally, want to know about us. we are our own guardian angels, judges and blackguards. And what is the purpose of all this? Can you tell me? The people who can answer this question have already abandoned this shithole. What is the advantage in the evolution in this dimension, so materially poor and stifling?

_ I have no idea. I think this conversation is to hard to a silly boy like me. You should talk to mister Vasconcellus, he is very bright and wise.

_ Let it be, dude. I am just giving vent to my thoughts. That's why I like talking to you, you don't try to prove I am wrong. I think I smoked too much weed.

_ What?

_ What about a delicious chocolate ice cream, with caramel and marshmallow covering?

_ Now you're talking my language.

At the age of 18 Tharus reached the 8th level. At this point, the guy was passing through a conscience crisis. The excess of theory in his studies, measuring, exposition, puberty concerns and psychological counseling he was submitted to, by the fact he was entering into a phase exceptionally challenging, and principally, the pressure by the fact the only human being had reached such level was handicapped by an eerie illness, which revealed the fragility of the human brain forced by such energetic efforts, let him extremely stressed with the special attention he was receiving. He was also too frightened by the Joseph Souz drama, imagining it could happen to him at any time, and he decided to enjoy life while he could. He wanted bliss every moment. The most the researchers and supervisors tried to hinder the use of his powers, the most he rebelled against their determinations, thinking everything was under control. However, certain afternoon, after take the friends to a quick visit for several countries, the medical director, after being notified by this dangerous extravagance, determined he would be suspended for two weeks from the activities in the foundation. Contradicted, he decided to talk to Hermes Vasconcellus.

_ What is it all about, Hermes? Do you think you're dealing with a child?

_ Unfortunately we found out we are!

_ I am old enough to know what I can or can not do. Nor my parents control me that way.

_ Maybe it is because your father and your mother don't have absolute knowledge you are exposed to, when you act like a child. If you want to be treated as an adult you have to act like one.

_ Take it easy, Hermes. You already had my age, and I know you used to lark to.

_ I don't deny it. I am very proud of my juvenile pranks, that are not so distant in time. Even now I sometimes make some tricks. Thanks god! But I never exposed myself as you are doing, and I always accepted my punishments. You can do what you want, and it is recommendable you do it, but everything has a limit, and you constantly trespass it. You don't have criterion. Please, help me help you.

_ I do have criterions, I just do not accept impositions and stupid rules. Did you hear it well? I do not accept them. it is my life and I decide how to live it.

_ Life would such wonderful if everyone could do only what they pleased. But unfortunately there are rules to followed, because that is the way life is, and I am not talking about mankind social rules, I am worried about the nature rules, the universal rules that fries who contradict them. We may even not to agree with some of them, but we have to live according to them, otherwise we must suffer the terrible consequences, without cry or pity. The laws of the universe hardly give us a second chance. You belong to a cast and must know it well and give the example to the population. See the case of our poor Joseph Souz, we don't know what he did, but he will suffer the consequences of his extravagances for the rest of his life.

_ I am aware of it. I am honest, I am not violent and I do not use much drugs. Therefore, what I do with my privacy is my own concern.

_ I am afraid it is not like that, my lad. To be honest and peaceful is an obligation of every citizen, you're not doing anything else that you were supposed to do. To stand out you must show other qualities that are not required from everybody. And to finish this quarrel, I want to say you've a talent maybe nobody else in the world has and probably nobody will, not even Peter Moll, but even though we will not keep our eyes wide shut to your odd behavior and abuses. While you're in the foundation you'll have to follow our determinations. We are in this business long time before you were born, and we know what is best to you to the rest of our students. That's why we are the first and most important institution in the world. Did I make myself clear?

_ Crystal. You're the boss!

In that afternoon, Tharus invited Peter to walk a little. They transported themselves to the top of a very high building, and talked a lot, while they ate chocolate.

_ Peter, I know how smart you are, and that you will become a powerful paranormal, just like me.

_ You think so? Cool. I'd love to get where you are now.

_ And even more, who knows?

_ I keep staring at the incredible things you can do and I wonder how many good things I could do to the entire world if I was in your shoes.

_ That's exactly what I think. You just have to pay attention to the people who are trying to manipulate you, as a puppet. I am so cutting the strings.

_ Would that be true, or they are just trying to give us guidance?

_ Guidance my ass! These people are not worried with me or you or anybody else. They are just interested in our powers. Ziggy was fucked before they could map all his abilities, and now they want to do it with me. I am not a rat lab.

_ I think mister Vasconcellus just want us to be wise.

_ The priests and nuns must be wise, not me! I am free to do what I want. They should have more confidence on the education they gave me. I am prepared to life. Besides, how can they teach us how to act if nobody never had what we have? I am level 08 and only somebody who know how is to be a level 08 should tell me what to do, don't you agree?

_ I don't know. You are level 08 because they made you get there. They constructed the basis and the tools to make possible our development. And I think he trusts us, otherwise there were lots of students complaining about him. He must have motives to have a close control over you. I think there must be a lot of unscrupulous people trying to use you. Do you have more chocolate?

_ Take it. In one thing you're right. There are some people trying to hire me. They offered a huge amount of money. But I didn't decided yet. I am not an asshole. Nobody uses me. Be sure of that.

_ What kind of people?

_ You don't wanna know. There's this man, mister Ivan, he is one of the richest men in the world, and since I was a kid, when I participated in a lecture of one of his companies he is harassing me. He offered to pay my studies if I trained in his school. From time to time he sends me a message, offering a job, and lots of stuffs. I never accepted because I think he is evil. There's something about him I don't like. But he is very sympathetic. I used to talk to him on internet, and his ideas are very similar to mine. Last year, during a dinner, he confided me he was member of a secret society. Something very dark.

_ What kind of society is it?

_ I don't know. He said they rule the world, I don't know what it means, but it is scary. I must warn you, this is for your ears only. Not even Iullus knows about it. Ivan told me if somebody else knew it, would be my death penalty. He believes they represent the strongest force in the universe.

_ Don't worry. My lips are sealed. And I believe love is the strongest force in the universe.

_ Don/t make me laugh, boy. Stop chanting what they put in your mind, as a tamed parrot. Doubt of everything you were taught. Use your reason. For instance, if love is the strongest force as you say, show me where is it in the nature. Can you do it?

_ Everywhere, I don't know. What is your point?

_ Visualize a deer having a cub! Imagine the moment of the birth. It is cute, isn't it? Imagine that little cub discovering life, springing around his mom. In a few minutes it is already learning how to run, with other nestlings. It looks like a scene from "Bambi", doesn't it? And then, from nowhere raises a big lion and kills the nestling while the others flee, breaking the idyllic picture. Moments later the mom is already trying to get pregnant again, and the other cubs playing as if nothing important had happened. Where is the love? And this is not an isolated case in the nature, it happens all the time. It is evolution. What pulls the evolution laws is not love, is the force of the strongest. What keeps the universe together is not the love, but the force of the strongest. It is worth for me, for you, for the simplest animals, as for the planets; stars and galaxies.

_ I believe you're right in the surface. I don't possess elements to reply your ideas, and if we didn't have an immortal spirit I would agree with you. For me, the love is in the fact this little animal spirit survived to the horrible death of his body, and in a next encarnation he will be back with the experience and strength to survive to another lions attack, and will grow up and reproduces and has his owns nestlings. I still see love in the work of the invisible beings who take care of this cub, so he has as many opportunities as required to win his obstacles in life and step another degree in evolution. I don't know much, I have to study a lot yet.

_ You're bright and funny, dude. I like to talk to you, and I will miss it. I am practically out of school.

_ What are you saying?

_ I don't know. I already graduated in high school, and I am thinking about traveling a while around the world. It is just an idea. Just me and Iullus. You are aware in the last few months we are working as models, and we are receiving many invitations from abroad. I don't know, maybe we'll dive in this world, there is a lot of money if this meadow. I don't know yet, Iullus keep saying it is up to me, and all I can say is I already raised my limit in here, and I want to step out. All this is suffocating me, and I want to breath new airs. I know you understand me.

_ I think so. I'll miss you guys. You know, I never had siblings, and you and Iullus are what I have the closest of it.

_ Don't you worry, boy. Even if I quit the foundation I won't abandon you. I promise I'll come back to visit you often. And as you also have the instant transportation, will be able to visit us whenever you want.

_ it won't be the same thing, but everything will fit.

Some days later, the Vendra brothers officially communicated the foundation directors they were leaving. This notice was already expected, but anyway it caused uneasiness between the researchers and instructors, who wanted to scan the twins for some years yet. But not even mister Vasconcellus, who was very worried about their future, was able to remove their decision, by the argument it was still to soon to interrupt their work, once probably they could raise higher levels. But it was in vain. In the next day they did not return. Tharus kept his word and from time to time he appeared to visit his ex mates, inviting them to long strolls, where he spent hours telling the news about their new challenges on the catwalk or taking shoots to publicity campaigns or recording television advertisements, and about the eccentricities of the top model girls they had met. In one of these meetings, the twins celebrated the 14th birthday of Peter Moll, by taking him to a thai massage house. It seemed they were the older brothers and wanted to provide everything his father should have, but didn't have time to do. During the next months, the Vendra boys didn't do anything but have fun. As the works as models were sporadic they usually spent the spare time sleeping late, riding their huge motorcycles around the countryside, or transporting the friends to secret, dangerous or inaccessible places. Tharus enjoyed to proportionate to his friends who weren't paranormals the experience of a night flying over the buildings, and was very amused by the scared expression on the faces of the boys and girls, when they were free of the gravity slashes about 400 feet height.

At this time Iullus had already broken up with Ivana Minerva. However they were still very close friends and frequently had long excursions throughout the fields. She remained his safe port. They appreciated doing picnics on the heights.

_ What a view, huh? It is really a privilege to enjoy the phenomenal landscape. The river down there, the top of the trees, the mountains far away. All acquires a new perspective from this angle.

_ That's true, Iullus. But it is also an inconvenient this cold wind spreading our food.

_ Stop complaining! Today the weather is helping.

_ Sure, my dear. Do you remember that day when a condor crashed on the fruits basket? What would have happened if was one of us?

_ I don't know. That day was sinister. If we kept the concentration and the focus, probably we had avoided the fall.

_ From now on we'd better keep an eye on the big birds or planes.

_ You're absolutely right.

_ Do you want some more flan?

_ Not now! I'd rather do a better thing. If we made love up in here, with all the stuff to keep under control such as the towel; food and beverage; the sound machine, would we be able to maintain the focus and avoid the fall?

_ Interesting this question. I do not have the answer, but as we both have the levitation capacity, we probably will keep everything under control. But there's only one way to be sure.

In a short time the international career of the Vendra brothers took off. There were so many millionaire invitations they concluded the best to do would be to move to New York. Their older siblings took care of the business administration and they could enjoy the new beginning phase, taking advantage of the pleasures that a glamour life could provide, with much lark; money and wonderful women. Was really a time of great discoveries to the teenagers who were just free from family control. They met too much interesting people and also to much crazy ones; businessmen; artists and politicians. They met the fancy side of the wealthy; with lots of fans trying to please their tiniest desires, but also the despicable side, which is always around who is getting well, like greedy; betrayal; envy and slander. Thanks to the classical beauty of the twins and their natural talent to entertain people, in a little more than a year they gathered some millions of dollars. However, the monetary matter was their last concern, what they wanted the most was to party. Tharus and Iullus never liked car, they said it hindered freedom, but they loved motorcycles since they were kids. The first things they bought with their first money were two old fashionable two wheels vehicles. This was a real passion shared by them, and it was in the verge of the obsession, and after a year they had a fancy collection with dozens of motorbikes, to let envious any motorcycle professional racer, and wherever they traveled, They used to take at least two ones with them. if wasn't the good management of their older brother and sister, they would have spent every dime they earned in a brief time. To the paranormal brothers, to invest in real estate, stocks and savings was a great rubbish, once they couldn't, as any adolescent, imagine themselves old and retired. They believed their good life would last forever and ever. This way they traveled always by first class, and lodged in the most luxury hotels and usually paid the sprees of their friends, girlfriends and friends of friends in the trendy nightclubs. The group that used to escort them everywhere was practically the same from their childhood times, once they didn't like to relate with new mates, principally the ones they met in the fashion world, who were a little afraid of their gifts, and couldn't act naturally near Tharus and Iullus, so the brothers avoided intimacy with these people. even the toadyism and exploration were barely made, because these kind of people who are in everywhere usually were intimidated by their penetrating eyes, as if the Vendras could see the licentiousness they tried to hide from the world, and frequently these parasites fled from the twins company. In the deep of their souls, the brothers hated the bough they were working in, they considered it just as a temporary step to their main goal, to raise money to accomplish their dreams. They didn't have patience with people they didn't comprehend the behavior and considered too much namby-pamby, futile, greedy and priggish. And it was becoming very common they quit works in the middle, annoyed by the swoon of some super model; shooter or sponsor, and little by little they began to lose the joy that made them so famous and granted high contracts. They knew, some other day, they would quit definitely this life style, and would miss it. Even with all the rebel behavior and lack of professionalism, they were still the super paranormals Vendra boys, and remained the sweet hearts of the most trend marks in the fashion world, that kept shut eyes to their rudeness, and made every effort to please them, and keep them on the catwalk. Also, many fashion divas, former girlfriends or simply friends, fought with the producers to have the brothers on their jobs, and with a lot of stumbles, they continued working as models for some more years. But Tharus was always worried about what they would do after that.

_ Tharus, do you know that sometimes I miss the foundation? I miss the quietness of there and the healthy ambient of the school, without the snakes we have to deal in here daily. There we used to have more reliable friends.

_ That's exactly how I feel, brother. There's only three years that we work with fashion and it seems an eternity to me. I really don't know how long else I am gonna stand.

_ Dido! I think our days in here are in countdown, because if we don't quit they will fire us. the incident of last week was the last drop.

_ That was a joke! I only dematerialized the clad of the top models.

_ But it was in the middle of the catwalk, and the chicks were totally naked in front of the cameras. Some of them want our heads in a silver plate, because they had swore they would never pose without clothes. It was wild.

_ I don't think they are that mad. I know they want other part of our bodies. Anyhow they deserved it! I think I had never worked with such nasty, pretentious and boring women at the same time. But nobody knows that it was my guilty.

_ Of they know, brother. Firstly, we were the only paranormals in that parade, and secondly if it was the first time such thing happened, they could think it was sabotage. Some enemy, maybe. However I have lost the count of times you did these things.

_ I didn't know you were a saint. Probably you forgot that many of these pranks were your work.

_ But my tricks are not as messy as yours!

_ That's right, you won. You're an "hollow angel". The car that was dismantled with the sponsor inside it. Just because he hit his girlfriend who was having an affair with you, it can't be faced as an innocent trick, can it?

_ But it was hilarious to see that Porsche falling apart while the poor bastard was driving, wasn't it? And besides, that daft man deserved it. He thinks just because has a bunch of money can punch a defenseless girl? If he believed himself as a powerful man, I proved I am more.

_ I am not censoring you. If I was in your shoes had done worse.

_ But already have.

_ Yes, but that was different. The problem is the people are afraid of us, and the ambient is becoming unbearable.

_ I don't care about these insect people. "phunk them all"!

_ Yes. If someone bothers my patience in the wrong time will regret a lot.

_ I could leave the jerk without a single hair in the body.

_ That would be very funny. But don't you think it's time to break away? Before something bad happen?

_ I couldn't agree more!

_ So this will be our last campaign. After that will be long vacations. Deal?

_ Deal

As they had planned, after that work they traveled on vacations, without care about their further compromises, and didn't attend the pledges of their siblings. For three years the did nothing but rest on paradise islands all over the world; practice aquatic sports; ride around on their potent motorcycles; drink a lot and love the women. In this matter, The Bat was much more eclectic than Iullus, and appreciated all kind of chicks, of different nationalities; ages; religions and sizes, and sometimes several at the same time. He didn't want to be attached to no one, but his brother couldn't' do the same, though he tried to. Sensible an romantic Iullus couldn't be as scenic as Tharus in his affairs. He wished to fall in love with a good girl and settle down for a long period. Always in the end of a relation he was very sad and dull, as if he would never have another infatuation. During one of these love hangovers, while the Bat sparked all the time, the young Iullus retreated in profound melancholy, and spent his days on lonely walks on the sands or reading around the hotel swimming pool. In one of these afternoon readings, he observed a paranormal man exhibiting his abilities to a group of girls. He found it intriguing, for they almost never saw other psychic using their abilities for fun at daylight. To break the monotony he decided to get close to the man that apparently was about 30 years old.

CHAPTER 08

THE SHOP

_ What's up, man? Is everything ok? I couldn't help to listen you conversation with the girls, and I am a little curious.

_ No problem, Pal! Feel free to ask anything you want to. My name is Jean Luc Termis Shatner. I am Canadian, and as you can notice, I am as paranormal as you!

_ You must be very good to notice it!

_ I can nor take the credit. Your energies can be sensed far away. You are neglected. Maybe it is related to your blue face, probably somebody just broke your heart. Am I right or am I right?

_ Wow, you are really good! Nice to meet you, my name is Iullus Vendra.

_ I don't believe it! So you are Iullus Vendra, twin brother of the great Tharus Vendra?

_ Alive and kicking! - He answered without much conviction, once he wasn't animated with his brother's fame.

_ Boy, I heard a lot about you two! Girls, Girls! Come here, you won't believe who I am talking to. You are face to face with the brother of the man who is simply the most powerful man alive in the world! – Noticing his fail, Jean Luc tried to fix it.

_ But he is also very powerful, ladies!

_ What interesting! I love might men! What sad face is that, cowboy? C'mon, have a party with us and forget all your problems. I bet you have big qualities!

_ Today I am your slave, princess. – Iullus replied.

In the subsequent days, Iullus and Jean became great friends and spree mates. The Canadian knew exactly how to please people, and was always preparing a surprise to entertain the Vendra guy, principally in the female query. The gallant Termis seemed to be related to all beautiful women in the Caribbean islands, and money apparently wasn't a problem either, who was spending with more eager every day, renting expensive yachts and promoting 48 hours raves, and drinking only the world most famous trends of champagne, whiskey and cognac.

Curious with sudden change of behavior of his always introspective twin brother, Tharus decided to approach of Iullus newest friend, who seemed to be anxious to meet him, and there was no better place to do it than participating of one of their fancy parties.

_ My friend, Iullus, this time you surprised me! I was beginning to lose my hopes of meeting your brother! He is more inaccessible than the president of the United States!

_ He is a little paranoid with his privacy, but finally he accepted to honor us with his presence. Jean Luc this is Tharus!

_ I don't believe that I am in front of the phenomenon! Dude, you are my idol!

_ Nice to meet you too, Jean!

_ Dude, I am wordless! There are many years I follow your development. Today is a very special day for me! All expenses on me! Let's party! Your brother told me you have good taste and know how to appreciate the female company, isn't it? Let me be your host. You'll see the most amazing group of chicks ever.

_ Haven't I told you, Tharus? This guy rules!

_ I can notice that! But we came here to drink or to chat? Let's get it started!

_ The party is about to begin!

All Tharus preoccupations vanished in proportion they were hanging out together, surrendering themselves to the craziest diversions, and talking about their ideals. For several weeks they even lost the notion of time. It was a party followed by another, in a moisture of faces, bodies, alcohol and other complements to improve the disposition to fun. In one of the several gaps between a night riot and another, while healing a huge hangover with a round of strong beverages, to reboot, lazily laid down on the seashore, with the crystalline emerald green water to portrait the hot dusk, the twin brother had a serious conversation with the Canadian. At the time they didn't perceived that, but this dialogue would change forever the fate of the Vendra brothers.

_ My dear friend, Jean Luc, I am a little intrigued, and I'd like you to clear it to me.

_ Spit it out, dude! I am here to serve you!

_ until the present moment we do not have any idea of what exactly you do for living. Iullus believes that you are some sort of a multi millionaire playboy heir. But, despite I do not possess the gift of prediction, telepathy or the vision of the past, I can notice that aren't rich by birth, because you have all the grimaces of somebody who became a wealthy person from overnight. I have a theory you set a huge defalcation in a multi national company and now just want to enjoy all the pleasures of the life. C'mon, boy. You can trust us. We won't turn you in to the authorities.

_ You have a great imagination, dude! I wish I had done such a thing. Unfortunately I have to "work as a donkey" to pay my life style, and since I am a bachelor without children to support, I am doing well. Now we are close friends I can rely on you my secrets. I have a very well paid job, but it is also very stressful and whenever I can, I take some weeks of vacations and enjoy it the maximum possible, I need to be numb from time to time because I have to deal with some stuffs really hard. It's blessing when you don't need to think about anything else but where you're gonna drink tonight. Thanks god I earn a lot, because I hate poverty and economic class.

_ Who doesn't enjoy perks? I wonder if someone really would prefer Mcdonald's instead a French restaurant.

_ That is my philosophy, dude! And how about you two? Do you want to remain in this place forever? I heard you are not modeling any more.

_ I don't about Tharus, but I have no rush to get out of here.

_ I am touched, but you didn't say what exactly is your job, Jean!

_ Well, you know, I was trained in a navy psychic school, and after my graduation, at the age of 18, joined the mariners seal troops, where I remained for eight years. After my military service I was invited to integrate the team of an agency of professional paranormal investigators, and I am in this bough for seven years. It is an interesting and gratifying job, if you know what I mean. I do not intend to change it! I am pretty satisfied.

_ That is interesting! I never heard about such companies. What exactly do you do? Tharus and me are very interested on it.

_ First of all, you never heard about us, because that is our prerogative. Secrecy is required on our work, and, of course, we don't need to do advertisings of our service. – Jean Luc took care to do not be heard by anybody else. – but basically we act on defense of those who require our services and are being threaten by more powerful people, the type of person who believes is over the law. You could say that we are a kind of group that act like a sort of Robin Hood or Zorro. We protect the weak and the oppressed citizens. We solve kidnappings, industrial spying, fraud, great thefts and murderers. We also locate criminals, recover missing people and protect those who believe their lives are in danger. In short, we regard the interest of those who can afford, and we are consultant on many areas. We have very, very rich clients in all the continents.

_ But you work under the law, don't you?

_ Let's say that our function begins where ends the law. That stay clear we are not a bunch of gangsters with mug shots. But our cases usually are those the common police is not able to solve.

_ Yeah, we enjoyed this job of yours. It must be challenging!

_ I knew you would! This company is your face. You haven't seen anything yet. I work traveling surrounded by strong emotions, and what is the best, I earn a lot! To you comprehend better, know that I was in this island by duty, and when I had it concluded, took some weeks off. I really work, I do my schedule, I am independent and owner of my nose, did you copy?

_ Sure! This is fantastic! And what kind of things did you do here?

_ That dudes, is confidential, classified, secret. This is the most important attribute of our sort of operation. When some other task shows up, the "shop" calls me. Till there is only fun!

_ The "shop"? what is that?

_ That is how we denominate our company.

_ That is beautiful, pal! You punish the jerks and still raise money with that. – Replied Iullus in a state of joy, as if he had finally found a purpose in his life.

_ My dear friend, Jean. I think you are two steps from paradise. – Tharus wasn't less interested than his brother.

_ Now you're getting the hole picture! Would be possible for you to consider the idea of accepting an invitation to know better our company, and see it from the inside? At least you would meet very interesting people there. We have incredible analysts who could give you another perspective over the world.

_ That's an interesting possibility! Maybe we can find some spare time in our overbooked agenda.

_ Yeas, Jean Luc. Tharus and I would very much like to know better this "shop".

_ Sure thing! We have been looking for a purpose for our abilities, because what for having these power and do not have a real opportunity to use them in something useful? There are so many daft people around the world, thinking they are God, that is already time to show them just one is right, me!

_ I couldn't agree more with you, dude! I knew that we weren't equals only for the taste of a good lark. We also share the same ideals!

_ My friend, if your ideal is to get the world rid of so many parasite no scruple human bugs, then we are really alike.

_ So, Tharus, be aware that is exactly this what I do for living. And I am only a paranormal level 05, and the most capable agents in our "shop" reach the maximum the sixth. I can't even conceive what you two could do for the world peace.

_ I'd like to know if your superiors would share the same enthusiasm of you.

_ Are you kidding, Tharus? There's no one in that company that wouldn't do anything to have the opportunity to meet you. You are our hero. I am sure of that, and if you want to, I can schedule an appointment, as fast as I can, with the president of the "shop". And besides, almost all of our agents are civilians.

_ What do you think, Iullus?

_ I'm in!

_ So, it is show time, Jean Luc!

Two days later, one of the executive jets of the company came to pick them up. A whole scheme was orchestrated to give the Vendra brothers a special and warmth reception, with limos, cicerones, receptionists and red carpet at the entrance of the building, after all, the acquisition of the most important paranormal in the world and his brother certainly would raise the value of the enterprise on extraordinary levels. The headquarter of the company was in Vancouver, Canada, and the twins had spent so many time in hot spots, when they arrived they suffered a little with the extremely cold weather, and were annoyed by the snow that didn't stop falling, but they were so excited with the new perspectives after sometime they forgot completely about the climate. As the president of the company hadn't been warned on time, he couldn't participate on the reunion, because he was in Australia, and Tharus and Iullus were then introduced to the three vice-presidents, and they barely could hide the satisfaction on hiring the brothers. The executives nor even were concerned about making purposes or ask about their background. On the first moment they let very clear what the Vendras wanted they would have. And that's all. Ended the paper work, the brothers were sent to the most luxury hotel in town, only for a short time, once the would in brief install them into wide and fancy lofts. Tharus found on his bed a wood box with finest cigars in the world, and in the freezer, his favorites beverages and on the coffee table specialized magazines about motorcycles. Some days passed by, with the twins riding around the best places to party in the city, escorted by jean Luc, and then, Tharus and Iullus were summoned to began their new functions. They started by studying in a boring investigation techniques course, shooting practice and data analyze. They were also submitted on sensitive measuring, so their missions were planned according to their abilities. The directors, managers, supervisors and general workers couldn't believe in the extension of the powers of Tharus Vendra, who overcame all the expectations. They were amazed by the results of tests where he was sat down on a little bench, drinking hot chocolate calmly and reading a book, while a rain of bullets of thick caliber flew around his body. Nor even an explosion of some grenades could shake his confidence or his mental shield, that was keeping protected from the weapons. They were as well perplex by the test where he simply looked to blocks of concrete, and they immediately Imploded, as if they were full of TNT. Or the time he increased the temperature of objects, including metals, so high, they began to burn and then melt down. Iullus powers were much weaker than his brother and didn't raised enthusiasm on the bosses, once they had many others psychic level 06 as him. But due to Tharus they showed certain satisfaction with the reach of his abilities, as for example, his capacity to alter the vibration of the atoms of his body and could pass through and be passed through solid objects. The only problem was he had to do it naked, once he couldn't do the same for his clothes. This way, he could penetrate almost everywhere.

After an endless training, the Vendra brothers were ready to their first mission. The plans would be reviewed directly by the president of the "shop", who was anxious to meet them. Escorted by Jean Luc, they headed to the luxury yacht of the enterprise, anchored in the Iceland sea. In the small ship worth 7o million dollars there were facilities to make envious kings; sheiks and the young billionaires from internet, and was far more fancy than the most expensive hotels in the world. With six Jacuzzi suits, eight bedrooms, meeting room, gymnastic room, games salon, two lounges, party lobby, two kitchens and chopper point, the mega yacht "Namor" was the ultimate in sailing technology.

Permanently rounding the globe, it became the main housing, between his five official dwelling located in three continents, of mister Willian Hades Price, creator and CEO of the paranormal investigation agency, also known as the shop. When they boarded, the three incredulous men soon conceived a great reception was prepared to them, however, as the ambient on board was constantly partying, with lots of very important guests as well as unknown beautiful people, plenty of excellent food and exotic beverages and much diversion, they comprehended it was the regular situation on it. Mister Price, 56 year old, who with the looks of a 36 year old healthy man, was waiting for them on the deck, and personally wanted to show the installations to the brothers and introduce them to the other guests. Despite he was treating everyone with extreme sympathy and politeness, was apparent his enthusiasm upon the presence of the imposing Tharus Vendra, who Mister Price didn't know how to please more. On the next day, after lunch, the secretary came to warn mister William H. Price was waiting for the three in the meeting room.

_ Did you pay attention this mister Price likes you, Tharus?

_ He is a real gentleman. What this filthy mind is insinuating, Iullus?

_ Take it easy, brother! I have no point. I just think it's weird the way he treats you. Just that.

_ You're jealous! Confirm it, you're jealous.

_ Shut up!

_ I can assure you, guys, this man is a real "stallion", if you know what I mean. – Said Jean Luc. – Did you see the great number of beautiful chicks in here? The man knows how to enjoy life. Rumors has it he is father of more than 40 sons and daughters around the world. I don't envy his expenses. The thing is he is obsessed by the paranormal phenomenon, and as our friend, Bat, is the greatest star of it, is more than natural mister Hades treats him as an idol.

_ You have a point!

_ Yeah. Believe me the man is a "sword".

They arrive at the door, and Jean Luc knocks gently. The secretary came in and allowed them to get into the wide ambient, decorated with the finest furniture and equipment to provide all the necessary to the realization of any kind of business deal. Mister William H. Price was sat in a huge armchair, in front of a great glass window, through what could be seen the imposing glacial sea, wearing a scarlet robe and red slippers. The president smiled at their entrance.

_ C'mon, my lads, don't be shy. Act as if this was your boat. I hope you have appreciated our humble sea transport.

_ I had never seen anything like that before. – Jean Luc had never been invited to that place before, and he was there just because of the Vendras acquisition.

_ Me neither! And you Tharus, what did you think?

_ Yes, sir, I must agree with my friend and my brother, you have such bathtub. The only flaw is that it doesn't fly.

_ You are hilarious, my boy. Anyway thanks for you comments. Now, to fly I prefer other kind of transportation.

_ What I appreciated the most were the planes landed besides my bedroom. Those are a real piece of art.

_ And they can take off and land on the vertical, and are quite silent. Feel free to use them, my friend. They are here to amuse you.

_ Just him? I'll begin to be jealous of my brother.

_ Of course not, Iullus. These aircrafts are here to those who knows how enjoy them. you want so, you can also use them.

_ You bet I know how to enjoy these machines.

_ Now I am afraid we must discuss some boring issues. I believe you're well aware about the details of our shop, aren't you?

_ I think so, sir.

_ Don't call me sir, because sir is in Washington. I'd rather to called just Bill. It is very important you know all the meanders of our organization, so you may have a real dimension of your duties and privileges, and this way you'll be able to work hard and have full dedication. Our good partners are very well awarded in here. Fidelity is crucial. I may say we form a loyal and united family that walks in the same path, stalking the same goals, and for that reaches uncountable richness. You may not believe it, but I came from a very humble family, with few chances to raise socially, when I was selected to study in the foundation of mister Jardell Vasconcellus.

_ I don't believe it have you studied in our school?

_ Yes I have. Why do you find it strange? I trained with the bests. In that time, Mister Vasconcellus was also a teacher, and he was one of my instructors. I graduated in his first classroom, as a psychic level 03. it was a great time to the paranormals who knew how to take their chances. The world was taken by a great commotion because of the impact of the discovers and applications of the ESPs. Within a few years I became a prosper man, who was always attentive to the opportunities presented. So I became an associated of two other men, former mates in school, and we created the "shop" as I prefer to denominate it. In the beginning we were only three private investigators, hence, soon our fame grew up, and we were required often, and were forced to spread constantly our board of employers and branch of activities. Today we count about 230 workers and 110 paranormal agents, as you. We generate an annual income about two billion dollars, which come mainly from governs of several countries, who pay us stratospheric sums to be freed from some kid of problems, such as corruption; betrayal; conspiracies; espionage. Our main fountain of rent is the search and arrest of justice outlaws, and the due restitutions to the public safes of the usurped quantities. In second place comes the industrial counter spy. You have no idea what some companies are capable to protect their secrets, and what others want to risk to steal inventions of somebody else. It is a "fight of bid dogs". That's why all our cooperators receive beyond a fat paycheck, an individual participation on each mission. This way, the success of an investigator becomes the success of us all. Work team, eyes wide open and mouth wide shut, is our motto.

_ Does the shop accepts any kind of client?

_ Of course not! We have principles. We are not a mercenary army. We do not accept any kind of client and we do not accept any kind of work. Before take a case, the possible costumers pass through a rigorous preliminary investigation, and a contract is not signed before the guarantee of an ethic commission. Any how, we aren't involved into shady negotiates. We know that in our segment nobody is completely saint, and there isn't a defined line between good and evil, right and wrong, noble or knavish intentions. Is very frequent we have to break some local rules or even international ones to reach untouchable criminals that, most of the time, were responsible for the creation of such rules. The world is gray, nor black nor white, but gray. There are powerful people that modify the constitution of a country just to accommodate their sordid interests. Always keep in mind one thing, gentlemen, our world is perfect, but we aren't, the otherwise, every instant somebody that controls the power manipulates the rules of the game, according to theirs desire, and the reason is only on the strongest side. However I hope you maintain your mind and perspectives open, don't be tuff judges, because if you do, I'll think you are morons or naives. And so, my future agents, that I, invested as the more experienced and wise than you, will always know what is the best way to conduct our business. I am an old fox. I am the head and you are the arms and legs that will execute the work, and all of us will gain a lot with this agreement, principally the planet, which little by little will become a better place to live in. but the most important is to do all we have do to without let vestiges to do not raise suspects. We don't know where lie our enemies, and we must take care. Any doubts?

_ Not to the moment, Bill.

_ That's better. Let's move on. Your first mission won't be easy. Have you ever killed someone?

_ Are you kidding? Of course not. Why? Have you?

_ When was necessary. And probably you'll have to, sooner or later. Is that a problem to you?

_ Not for me. I am not an assassin, but to save someone's life, I don't care. Depends on the context.

_ Tharus pretends to be tuffer than he actually is. I wouldn't like to murder anybody.

_ Don't worry, Bill, Iullus will do what is necessary to do. I know him better than he thinks. He pretends to be smoother than he actually is.

_ Well, you'll have to deal with it later. Your conscience won't hurt when somebody aims your head with a laser gun. This mission will be risk, sure thing, but nothing such radical boys as you won't overcome. I calculate in 100% our chances of victory. Here, in these briefcases you find out more suitable information about the man you have to capture. This case will definitely depicture our *modus operandi.* This monster is a former dictator, who after a bloody civil war was deposed, fled, and now has to answer for his hideous crimes and return some hundreds of millions of dollars to the poor govern. For years he has been living in the exile, surrounded by everything money can permit, protected by a friend governor and equally corrupt, plotting a return to the power. Until some days ago nobody was capable to track him down, once he is always moving, and as in that country everybody fears the regime and he is always protected by a huge security system, is very difficult to the UN put the hands on him. If we do nothing, he will began a new war to install a new dictatorship. The weapons industry helps to protect this genocide.

_ I have seen this gangster on television once. Will be a great pleasure to catch this assassin. That's what I always wanted to do.

_ Very well, Tharus. I couldn't hope less. I like this juvenile enthusiasm. The day before yesterday our rangers located him in a farm, 300 miles away from the capital. The service is quite simple, you get in; grab him and get out. A helicopter will let you on the border, about 600 miles from the target. We can't risk our intentions. From there Tharus will be in charge of the transport, and once in the farm, Jean Luc will pinpoint where he is, and Iullus take care about the security guards. Tharus will freeze him and bring him to us, and everybody will be happy and lots of greens in our pockets. When we deliver the merchandize 45 million dollars will be deposit in one of our accounts. Each of you will receive the praxis commission. Tomorrow morning you must be ready to leave. That's all! Let's enjoy the rest of our day!

They followed the schedule, and in the middle of the afternoon they were let in the border by the supersonic helicopter. They some minutes ahead of the stipulated time, and Jean Luc, the responsible for the mission, wanted to follow all the procedures.

_ I think we'd better stay here. The security has a routine and we must not permit the minimum mistake. The devil lives in the details.

_ That's up to you, Jean. I am ready to get into action.

_ Me too, Tharus.

_ Did any of you bring a repellent? I hate bugs. I hate bushes and I hate nature. I am not a tick to enjoy staying in a stink swamp like this.

_ Take it easy, Jean. We are almost leaving.

_ Do you know where to take us, Tharus?

_ Yes, I've been given the coordinates, and I memorized the map.

_ I'm just checking!

_ Don't you worry, Luc, I know what to do.

On the right time Tharus put his left hand on Jean's shoulders and the right one on Iullus's, and in less than a second they were 300 miles ahead. He took a deeper breath and instantly they ran the rest of the course, and only one mile away the farm's big house. Jean Luc then began his mental sweeping, which his was specialist, and within few minutes he knew the exact location of everyone in the house, including their target, and he draw a plan of the residence and right position of the victims, and gave it to Tharus. Suddenly, coming from nowhere, three men strongly armed showed up, following two enormous silent dogs. Speaking a strange language they gesticulated to indicate the intruders should lie down on the ground, while one of them tried to contact the security chief. Before he could do it, Tharus dematerialized all the gears and weapons of the guards. He and Iullus wanted to practice their kung fu abilities and decided to fight them with their bare hands, and quickly the Vendra brothers put them to sleep, while Jean Luc looked for another guards.

_ Wouldn't have been easier if you two had just immobilized them with your minds?

_ Yes, it would. But wouldn't have been as funny!

After certificate everything was back to normal, the three agents disappeared and appeared in a dark and empty living room. On the back, an old shaggy man, sat on a couch, wearing pajamas peered sadly outside through a cleft in the window., while swallowed a milk glass. That wasn't exactly the image they expected to see of a man who had spread terror for a long time in his homeland. A bit disappointed, they hesitated for a while, as if they doubted the identity of this "king Lear", and this time was enough to the old man get up, with an amazing agility and shoot at them with a revolver that was in his pocket gesticulating the security. The agents didn't expected such reaction and almost were hit, once Tharus or Iullus didn't have to raise their mental shields.

_ What a hell was it? This decrepit man almost shot my head!

_ Who walks around the house with a gun in the pocket?

_ Expect the unexpected!

_ Keep blabbing, master Iullus!

Jean Luc tried to grab him but it was too late, five men holding gun machines entered shooting, covering the dictator's retreat, but now the agents were prepared, and Tharus neutralized the bullets with his shield. When they stopped shooting, he just looked to their weapons and they began to melt, while Iullus with a peer threw against the wall the five body-guards. It wasn't enough to immobilize them, and the Bat had to threw them again with more power, and the wall almost broke. Meanwhile, Iullus ran after the target, who was locked in a safe room. The Vendra undressed his clothes and Passed through the thick structure as if it was made of smoke, the young paranormal easily tied up the incredulous fugitive, opened the door and took him to his companions, and they gave for finished the mission. In this moment another 10 security guards entered the room, pointing their guns, but it was too late. The four men just vanished without leave any vestige of who they were or where they were going. Iullus still had time to, sarcastically, make continence to them. After two instant transportation, Tharus headed them to extraction spot. The first mission of the Vendra boys was accomplished successfully. Tharus and Jean Luc were very excited during the return, while Iullus seemed sad and thoughtful.

_ I didn't know it could be so wild! Man, I liked that. The adrenaline discharge is outstanding! This mission started me up!

_ I know what you're feeling, Tharus. It happened to me in my first work. Take care or you'll get addict into it.

_ I want more! It is not the kill, is the thrill of the chase!

_ Yeah, but it seems your brother didn't digest it well. I am worried about him.

_ Let my brother alone! He is fine.

In a few days they were back to Vancouver, where they would pass to dwell in. the keys of their apartments were waiting for them. Tharus would live on the 10th floor and Iullus on the 12th. the luxury 600 square feet estates had all the facilities to make easier the life of bachelors, and had been decorated according to the profile of each one, provided by the human resources department. Tharus residence, for instance, was all painted in dark blue, and the few furniture had dark colors. Iullus's had a standard decoration. For some time, Iullus wasn't fine, he was shaken by the violence used in the mission. Constantly he kept thinking what had happened to the former dictator and his family, how they were dealing with the situation, and if he was being judged, and how serious had been the wounds of the security guards, and even if they had rights to do such operations. The great amount of money he had received, was another source of regret. He felt as if he was prostituting his gifts, profaning sacred abilities, so hard developed throughout his best years. However, the linger attitude of his brother and the lack of guilty in his face, who interpreted all that happened as duty of his work and his duty as a citizen worried about the impunity around the world, and the unconditional support of his parents and siblings, who came to live in the same city to better manage the business and the estate; and who believed they were in a fair crusade, made his dubious feelings were slowly vanishing. The passing by of the years and the missions made his concerns about the possible damage to innocent people and moral consequences to be substituted by a void of emotions and regrets.

Time kept passing by, and after each solved case, the twins surrendered into a period of celebrations and rest that could vary from weeks to months, depending on the money involved and gravity of the situation. During this phase of tentative to forget and self forgiven they all tools on their disposition, and let their bodies numb by enjoying many types of pleasure, throughout entire countries searching opportunities of diversion, as in the United States, the richest nation in the world, which provided all kind of perversion they were looking for, while riding their potent motorcycles. Sometimes they joined giant sea cruiser ships or sailed alone with some female companies. They also related very well along with their "shop" mates, and used to promote huge raves that lasted days. Always when they came back from a mission, the prestige of Tharus with the directors increased, because of his incredible feats, and the larks he sponsored turned him into a living legend among the investigations companies throughout the globe, and a real fan club was created to celebrate his accomplishes. However, the young Bat was still the same introspective and lonely boy from the times of the school, and with part of his profits he bought a small ranch in a very difficult access venue in the Patagonia, Chile, and from time to time he appreciated to isolate himself there for some days. Wild places with inhospitable nature always attracted his dark side, and in his ranch he enjoyed to jog in the woods and cold deserts and to observe and approximate to the animals, principally the most dangerous and aggressive, as the puma, once they mean no hazard to his physical integrity. In this private world, a totally rustic venue, without all the facilities of the modern life, where the intense chill was stood with firewood cut in the bushes, and the less dangerous way to bring supplies was by air, Iullus was the only person with full access permitted by him, by the simple fact they almost never were apart. Tharus never considered the suggestions of his superiors to work alone in some investigations, and never agreed to let his brother works in another team. Tharus knew Iullus was weaker and always wanted to protect him. The mere hypothesis his brother could be seriously wounded or even killed, usually left him completely overthrown. Now Iullus made question to escort Tharus constantly for fear his temper leaded him to commit excess, and wanted to be next to him to avoid Tharus did something he would regret forever. In the moment the Bat felt more confident into the shop, more owner of the situation, he began to invite his old school mates to join the company. Soon almost all of them were working on his side. One of the few ones to refuse the invitation was Peter Moll, justly who he wanted the most to work with. For several times he personally tried to persuade the young Moll, but his efforts were in vain. Peter seemed unshakeable in his decision. In his last tentative, the

Bat intimated him to spend in Vancouver his 21ˢᵗ anniversary, thinking about to impress him with his fancy life style provided by the Shop.

During one week Tharus strolled throughout the city with his former protégée, showing to him all the tourist spots as well as his influence and ascension over the local inhabitants. One day before Peter's departure, an urgent phone call took Tharus of serious. The brother of his actual girlfriend, Bruce, had lost a huge sum of money in a poker table, to a revengeful local drug dealer. As the young gambler had no condition to pay his debt, he was threw away from the window of the fifth floor of his apartment. For a miracle he survived, but had dozen of bones broken. He ran to the hospital and took Peter with him. There, his girlfriend related him all her brother's misfortune, letting the powerful paranormal furious with the lack of consideration for the human life showed by the bandits, and angry with the boldness of them on harm someone who was always a relate, and who Tharus had great esteem. Completely out of his mind and claiming revenge, he didn't worried about the negative image he was passing to his former foundation company, and even without notice his presence, he lit a cigar and thought out loud, trying to calm down a little.

_ How these venomous insects dare to do such atrocity to a harmless friend of mine? This boy is always helping me. He's gonna need months to recover from all the successions, while these hoboes are walking freely, abusing of their impunity and their friendship with part of the local police. I think it is time for me to do some cleaning.

Peter decided to follow him, once Iullus wasn't in town and he was worried about what the Bat could do. They went to several spots until they finally locate the group of whackers. They were drinking and sniffing, in the ranch of their leader, when the two paranormals materialized into the meeting room. For some time tharus listened their conversation, where they were bragging about what they did with Bruce, and complaining, as he didn't die, he still would have to pay them, or they would complete the service. Invested in his cold calculated and distant behavior, typical of a shop agent, Tharus went to the kitchen, put some vodka in a crystal glass and walked around the house, trying to attract the attention of the gangsters, who didn't guessed the trap and came after him to the pool, while Peter remained hidden. When everybody was reunited, with their guns in hand, aiming in a threaten way at the Bat, the mighty paranormal level 08 with a tiresome look threw them all into the swimming pond, and with another look he broke almost every bone in their bodies. Listening their pain howl and the background music, he turned his back and stepped out slowly, trying to avoid the indignity and bewilderment in Peter's eyes, who had never witnessed such a violent situation in his whole life. Tharus knew what he was doing was very wrong, but no way he would accept any kind of reprimand. This demonstration of total emotional fail to observe due proportion reinforced Peter's resolution to refuse the tempting offer. He didn't understood what could have happened to his former idol, and he didn't want to fall in the same hole. A little before embark home, Moll went to him to explain his reasons.

_ Tharus, I'd like truly you understand and did not get angry with me, but unfortunately I have to say that I deeply disagree of you acting manner, and I can not take you generous offer

_ You disappointed me, Petey. All those years have had patience with you, but I have to confess that you are still a mystery to me. Did I hurt your feelings and sensibility the other day? I'm sorry but I don't give a damn! The world is not the amusement park you live in the foundation. Things are happening outside your glass-shade, very nasty things, and sooner or later you'll have t deal with them. There are people so bad, they are capable to hideous behavior you would never believe, and I have to do with them all the time. I am sorry if the fact I am trying to kick them out of this planet offend your beliefs, but someone has to do it so you can continue to live in your colored fantasy island. I thought you would comprehend my motives, once we used to talk a lot. I always thought you were ambitious, you wanted to raise in life by using you capacities, and at the same time do something useful and relevant to the mankind. Just like me.

_ But I do. And I thought my pretensions were just like yours. I just think you misjudged me. Before everything I want to respect the law, not you aren't, only our vision about it is different. I know that I won't fix the world. The task is too complex. I just want to do my part. Besides, I am committed to an old project of mister Vasconcellus.

_ C'mon! I don't believe you bought that crazy idea of that "Don Quixote". It won't work. It is too idealistic. In my time he tried to convince me, but I will never be a government's dog.

_ Me neither. In a general way my job will be much alike yours. The main difference is I'll act into the law, strictly, and my targets will be exclusively the paranormals outlaws.

_ I hope you never come after me.

_ It won't be necessary. You never cross the thin red line.

_ But you'll have to face the truth. You never have the required freedom of action to impose the proper justice, working to an organization controlled by politicians. You have no idea how good is to punish those who believe themselves above the law, protected by their expensive lawyers, who are responsible for the creation of the rules. Sometime ago we took the leaders of a traffic organization in the south of Asia. We took every single one. They are now in jail, without the need of trials and corrupt judges and police officers. Besides, we still destroyed all their weapon supplies, and found out their banking counts and passwords and sent all their money to the families of their victims.

_ I imagine how good can it be, Bat. That's exactly why I am so afraid to do as you do. And I am so afraid of what it can do to you. All the people has this dream, to put order in the world in a fast and efficient way, but unfortunately it is not possible. Civilization is too damn complicated, full of people with different behavior, needs and desires. For more tempting it may be, we can't act like criminals to punish criminals. This is called vengeance. Democracy requires respect for the rules, and nor even the justice can run from it. All the structure of the society is based on that. That's what I think.

_ This speech is very beautiful. I would like to live in this world you imagine that you're living in. look around you, boy, people are tired and sick to see every single night the news on the television about impunity to another big bandit. Only chicken thief goes to jail. Economic power rules the world, and only radical measures can broke this cycle.

_ And the consequences of these measures? Because sooner or later others will get up to use this measures, and in the end we will have returned to the law of an eye for an eye. The best way to guarantee the success of any measure is by submit it under the approval of the population, after it be evaluated by specialists. The effect can be slower but more effective. What we have to do is to mobilize the public opinion.

_ It is pity you have such square mind with so narrow perspectives. You have always been like that. I just didn't see or I thought that I could make you want to change. I just hope our differences never put us on opposite sides someday.

_ Don't say such a thing. That will never happen. We both have a very solid ethic basis, despite it all. We can walk through different paths, but we're in the same direction.

_ So be it, my friend. I hope you have found you way and be happy in it. I'd like to apologize for what I made you experience. I hope we keep in contact.

_ So do I, brother. I wish for you the same things. Give my regards to Iullus. I'll call you on your birthday. See you!

Their friendship ended that day. They didn't kept contact. Only Iullus kept talking to Peter from time to time, but seldom. Tharus didn't like the refuse of someone he considered could be his best follower, and never forgave him for that. On his turn, Peter's heart was broken, he left Canada sure the man he saw there wasn't anymore the guy he learnt to respect and to love as a brother. Tharus was a great deception. In his intuition Peter knew that he would end for assume more extreme attitudes, and feared it would be inevitable life put them against each other. For some days, Tharus' mood showed he was shaken for what he considered a huge ingratitude from someone he considered as a younger brother. However, his day by day chores made him forget the episode, and concentrated only in his present and future realizations. His past and everything it represented should be left behind. The foundation became to him only just the beginning of his journey. His glorious time began when he joined the "shop", this truly his most important school.

Throughout the years, the Vendra brothers assumed not only the most dangerous and profit missions, but also the most polemic ones. With the routine of the cases, they, and mostly Tharus, were losing the scrupulous on solving craggy situations or that involved extreme violent measures. He didn't hesitate when he was given the incumbency to erase a band of bloody criminals. As this group worth more dead than alive, once would be very difficult to keep them in jail, the client wanted the case was solved outside the courthouse, and the Vendra boys felt on remorse on the intentional killing, their first time. Once on their den, Iullus caught their attention, trying to keep them occupied while Tharus concentrated on their necks, precisely on their jugular vein, slowly obstructing it, until they fainted, without blood in their brains. Few minutes later, they were all dead. Besides the huge reward, something else let the twins very satisfied. They believed they were doing a public utility service, as if they were terminating rats and cockroaches. They also live hallucinated, but some differences of behavior were being enhanced alongside the years. Even physically they weren't so identical anymore, what was giving a lead of their rising lack of sintony. Since children they expressed their desire to be alike by keeping the same hair cut, always long, until the shoulders, and even their closest relatives usually confound them. however, in one of their last job as models, the client demanded at least one of them had the hair cut, and Iullus accepted the tip, once he knew his brother was too proud and would never accept it. He enjoyed his new look and decided to retire his old visual new hippie. Another important factor on the definition of their appearance was the fact since they quit the foundation, Tharus stopped the weight lifting, preferring to dedicate only to the aerobics and full of adrenaline sports. Also his preference for alcoholic beverages and tobacco, and his taste for fast food, let him always under the ideal weight, while Iullus kept the sculpted body of someone addicted to the work out, and was fanatic for vitamins supplies. Many people who knew them recently doubted they were identical twins. They were always averse to free publicity, but opposite Iullus, who never made any effort to avoid the press harassment, the Bat developed an efficient way to face the surround of the *paparazzi,* that were always behind them since their puberty. He just posed to the cameras, or gently let them interviewed him, and when the professionals were back to their offices, believing they possessed exclusive material to edit, they discovered all their equipment was damaged and all the photos or recordings lost, without any suitable explanation. This way, loss after loss, the journalists learnt to avoid issues about the Vendra family. the lack of physical and mental synchrony wasn't causing problems to them yet. Professionally they were becoming more and more important into their organizations each year. Until the point the unique person above them was mister William H. Price, what bothered many older companions who believed they didn't have enough experience or dedication to such responsibility. Even the CEO of the shop was worried about their fast ascension, despite the exorbitant profits proportioned by them, and feared to lose his empire to them. all his attempts separate the Vendra brothers, so he could have more control over them, were in vain. Their link was very strong and they seemed two ticks stuck. He believed Iullus wasn't so important to his schemes, and that he had a dangerous influence over his brother, with his constant conscience crisis, and decided the only way to have complete ascendancy over Tharus would be erasing his weaker twin.

Determined to take his dangerous plan to the end, once he knew Tharus wouldn't agree easily with that, mister price accepted a case he usually discard, because the profit would be tiny. The risk involved to his agents would be very big, and with a proper help his torment would have the final he desired. His client would do anything that would be necessary to do not allow Iullus came back from that mission. After that he seduced, with a huge reward, many of his best employees, who Tharus trusted totally, included Jean Luc Termis Shatner.

_ I convoked this secret reunion, here in my house in Swiss, because what we have to deal is extremely dangerous and confidential, and very important to the future of our company. For some time I have been keeping informal and private contact with each one of you. And I couldn't help noticing your displeasure with the status of these Vendra brothers inside our organization. Many of you had the right pretension to occupy their position, once you are not satisfied with Iullus acquittal. I understood you showed yourselves very receptive to my ideas, and so I felt comfortable to invite you here. My situation in my beloved shop is unbearable, and so is yours. All that due to the unmeasured ambition of Iullus Vendra, who not satisfied to reach a high position in our organizations, wants to keep control over all the structures. I m sick of his intromissions in the model I shaped with my sweat, blood and tears.

_ We comprehend you completely, sir. – Said Jean Luc.

_ Iullus hasn't the guts to deal with the cases we deal. Sooner or later he will fall apart, and take the shop with him. We must prevent this to happen. – Argued Peyton Sloane, another agent.

_ Exactly my dear. Many of you have been working with me for over 10 years, and know how loyal and grateful I am with who help me in my purposes. I treated this boy as a son, and he reciprocates this way, trying to steal my company. If there is something I do not tolerate is ingratitude. And I tolerate less yet who puts in jeopardy the works of a whole life dedicated to change this world into a place better to live in. this company is bigger than me or any of you in here, because it serves to a greater cause, it means life or death to hundreds of thousands of people who claims for justice in the whole world. And such task can not simply be threaten as the shop is.

_ Of course not, boss. – Replied other agent.

_ You're a hundred percent right. We have to do what we have to do to avoid this to happen. – Completed another.

_ Now that we are in the same position, you're allowed to call me Bill.

_ You have our unconditional support, Bill. – Completed Peyton.

_ I couldn't expect another reaction from you. Now I'd like to know what exactly the shop means to you.

_ Well, I am sure I talk for all my companions here. – Said Jean Luc. – The shop for us is more than a source of payment. It is our reason to live, the family we don't have and the tool to accomplish our goals. For it we could do everything.

_ Are you sure you could do anything for the shop? Even betrayal?

_ To protect our organization is not betrayal.

_ That's what I wanted to hear. I am very satisfied with you, my friends.

_ We are here to serve, Bill.

_ You know how much I am attached to the Vendra boys, don't you?

_ Of course, Bill. What other explanation to their quick ascension on the company? We believe they are not worth of the opportunities you gave them, at least one of them, we know who. – Argued Solomon, the oldest agent.

_ Very well. As must be of the knowledge of all the presents, Iullus plots against me, and I have it documented in several reports.

_ One of these reports is mine, Bill. – Completed Jean Luc. – He doesn't approve the way you have been commanding the company.

_ I am aware of that, jean. I appreciate it. Iullus Doesn't like my methods, or doesn't have stomach to deal with what we deal. I can't allow this kind of mutiny. I won't allow it.

_ I understand what you mean, Bill. You're right. – Said Solomon. – Iullus is the mentor of this plot. I believe Tharus would never betrayal us, and when we get rid of the source of our problems, he will keep with us, and even become a better agent.

_ My concern is about here and now. Hence, the next mission must be decisive. I have all arranged, I just need your cooperation. There is a very poor small country that is crossing a bloody civil war. The president is my personal friend, a very sensate gentle man, who asked for our help. He doesn't want to see the suffering of his citizens, and agreed to help us whatever we need. You Jean, will be in charge of the team that will eliminate the focus of the guerrilla, and in the other hand, the president will help us to erase once and for all our problem. While Tharus is occupied with the rebels, all of you will in charge to kill Iullus Vendra. The guilt must fall back over the rebellion. I am so sorry for this sacrifice, but there's no other way. With this behavior he let me no choice, and I must do it the fastest I can.

_ We will follow your orders, Bill. All the presents in here have a great affection for Iullus, but the shop comes first. – Completed Jean Luc.

_ I thank each of you from the bottom of my heart. I want you to know, as soon as the routine has returned to the due place, you will be promoted. I want loyal people as you in my directory. Of course there will be also a great reward in the end.

_ We are not doing this for the money or the promotion, Bill. We are doing this for our beliefs. However, no one will refuse your generous offer. – Completed Solomon.

_ I am aware of it. I just want to show all my gratitude for your risk for my company. From now on we must keep our lips sealed about it. We need a password. I think it can be operation Trojan. Nobody outside this group should know about our agreements. Never. Thank you very much!

Tharus had developed such taste for the power, after the first year in the shop, he decided to have his own organization, some day. The excess of mister Price just precipitated his decision, which he never tried to hide, although many of his mates had credited it on Iullus account. He began to disagree on the criteria on the chose of the clients, and the exorbitant prices charged on each mission. Only the very, very rich had access to their justice. Alongside the years he perceived his boss was more interested on set an influence net around the world, by pleasing politicians; union leaders; businessmen, than help the whole society. Through these people he could exercise his domain over the fate of hundreds of million citizens. Tharus became as well to create his own net of connections throughout the years, by conceding favors to important people on several sectors of the society, in some countries he considered essential to his goals. He wanted to set a web of influence and favors to whom he could charge later. The main difference between his and mister Price plans was he believed his purposes were nobler. He dreamed about to establish a new world order, based on the glorification of the honest work and on the incessant combat against all kind of corruption and abuse of the economic power. He wanted to see implanted in the whole world a politic of zero tolerance to all kind of crimes of those who believe they are above the law, untouchable, and this would stimulate other felonies to avoid this life. Tharus considered himself the right to punish those who weren't punished. The money saved from the crime would be enough to increment social programs and help to eradicate misery all over the globe. To achieve his goals, where many good intentioned men had failed, the participation of a great number of paranormals would be decisive. They would guarantee the correct fulfill of all the required determinations to moralize the relations among the citizens, by controlling with iron hand the sectors of society necessary to such operation, using their specific powers to do not give chance to the enemies. He wanted to see created the EWO, ethic world organization that would work as an arm of the UN, invested with the powers of police and public justice in each country. It's workers should have the power to map, investigate, control and punish all the suspects of breaking the law. With full access to the privacy of the population, none detail would pass unnoticed, nor even in their minds, because specialized psychics would scan the brain of each one, bringing to the surface the most hidden secrets. All the citizens should pass through a brain mapping every year, on which all their bad tendencies would be cataloged, and this way crime could be prevented.

The population certainly would lose a considerable parcel of privacy, mainly the most sacred of all, of thoughts, but he believed soon they would perceive they would gain much more, and freely would give up their rights to reach a fairer honest prosper world, without almost none violence. The control used by the sensitive ones achieved a level that would never be reached by the use of simple technologies devices, once after each scientific advance, rise as well the means to swindle them. Certainly it could be also done with the mental abilities, but it would be much more difficult. A system maintained with the best trained psychics would be hard to be manipulated, once should be developed a new technology to reach the intangibility of the energies emitted by the human mind. Tharus openly called his friends to join his projects. He set an office in New York, managed by his sister, to keep in contact with sensitive people from all over the world, and also created a site in the internet to gather more participants in all layers of the society. his ideas were being diffused from mouth to mouth, and every day grew up the number of sympathizers of his movement. The most of them were teenagers, who used to discuss Tharus proposal in large groups.

Iullus shared the ideals of his brother. However he was very skeptical about the implantation of such measures. He new a great part of the population would be happy to adder to this new order, but another great part would fight it furiously, and would name Tharus as the new age big brother. He was the great follower of his brother ideas, but his loyalty wasn't unconditional, and he had serious restrictions about the use of the violence in large scale, to obligate the world to fit in the axle. In the beginning he believe his twin was joking, and when he saw Tharus was being very serious, he believed his brother was getting crazy, and just after that he began to see some coherence in all his beliefs. They used to spend entire nights discussing the details of this new world order, and how to proceed in relation to the "shop". The Vendra brothers were convict Bill wasn't seeing with good eyes the recruitment of many of his agents, despite he had never touched in this issue with them. they knew sooner or later there would be a frontal shock. They just couldn't conceive the proportion of it. They wanted to deal with mister Hades and get to a good term, before something bad could happen. For the most experienced they were, the brother were naïve enough to believe the president of the shop would never plot against them. for several times, Iullus with the guarantee of his brother, who didn't have patience for negotiations, looked for mister Price to talk about their plans. He believed if he took the initiative in the conversations it could make the boss understand, without shadow of doubt, he had no reason to fear their inevitable removal. That they would never damage the organization or would try to compete with him, even though he knew after the new order was implemented there wouldn't be places for such companies as the shop, but it would take many years yet. He conceived probably mister William Hades would be thinking they would raise a company in the shape of the shop, and that a good quarrel would put an end in the things that weren't properly understood.

However, mister Hades avoided on the maximum any kind of negotiation with Iullus. He fled from situations that would put them face to face. He didn't want to point out the problems, once he wanted to solve them on his way. For him this was the perfect moment to separate the twins. He never sympathized with the other, and considered him too weak to work in his company. He believed without him, Tharus would be able of greater feats under his control. In his opinion Iullus was so mediocre and would never be in the same level of his brother, who he worshiped as a Greek god in flesh and blood, and believed he would take Tharus to the top where he belonged. William imagined while he would be linked to the incompetent brother wouldn't shine in the due intensity. For a long time he supported his brother presence for having no other alternative, but now it fell into his lap and he wouldn't lose it.

All the details apparently set to the fatal mission, the Vendra brothers embarked escorted by a larger group than the usual, for what they believe was an ordinary case. The intriguing points, besides the number of integrants, were the fact Jean Luc was leading a huge group in this mission by the first time since the twins became the second in the shop's hierarchy, and the fact they couldn't include any agent of their confidence. Jean argued he wanted to create his own work group and wanted to test some people. These aspects weren't sufficient to them distrust a conspiracy was being played in their backs. With the spirits unarmed for suspects they arrived in the capital, where they were expected by the republic presidential secretary, Kiria Eolo. An exuberant 24 years old woman that emanated charm with her cult and sober style. Immediately Jean Luc and Tharus shivered in their basis enthralled by the girl's beauty, and they soon started the flirting, trying to impress her with what they supposed were their main qualities, the jokes, and during the whole way to the hotel they were in a veiled dispute to decide who would have the pleasure to share her bed. However, since the beginning, the beautiful girl tried to let no doubt of whom she was impressed by.

At night, a secret reunion on the suburbs of the cold and semi destructed city, with the defense minister and his main assistants, put Jean Luc Shatner and Tharus aware of the real state of the situation. During several hours they heard a detailed relate about the rebel activities and their main leaders, about their warlike power and their intentions, always under the govern optics. They were instructed also about the interests of the new administration and what should be priority to the shop agents. For last, they were informed about the life conditions of the inhabitants, with a real class about the work of the president, and the conquered social advances, and how the prolonged civil war was jeopardizing all that, pushing the population to a colossal abysm, where the most wouldn't get out alive. The leader of the team was very sympathetic with the cause and touched by the poverty state of the sick women, children and old people, who were being caused by a bloody rebels, who were trying by any cost to destroy a legitimate govern, that was only working for the citizens.

Tharus Vendra didn't buy that version of the facts. However he was being paid for them, and should give them some credit. A little bit intrigued by the excess of eulogizes to the president and his feats, he guessed it was a great excuse to arrange a private meeting with the beautiful secretary, and early in the next morning he asked her to show him the city. During many days, the poverty of the locals in contrast with the members of the party and government cleared his mind, and the Bat understood he was dealing with a band of savers of the worst specie. The kind of people he despised the most, what caused a profound irritation with the way things were functioning in the shop, and he felt loathing for being defending the wrong side. The sympathy and the generosity of the citizens created on him the will to do what was the best to the people. and pretending he was trying to figure out real condition of the guerrilla, he deferred for some weeks the begin of the tasks. While in this time Iullus, who shared the indignation of his brother, seized to learn the local idiom so they could obtain more precise information.

Annoyed by the lack of action, and without distrust Tharus attitude, who was believed to be only thinking about his relationship with the beautiful secretary, and without conditions to rival with him, Jean Luc decided to use the extra time to perfect the Iullus elimination plan. He made contact with troops , searching ideal venues to ambushes, and enjoyed to good life proportioned to those who were working to the powerful people. With a great consume of alcoholic beverage, he and his subordinates used to break the monotony of the wait escorted by very sociable women, who didn't hesitated on satisfying their darkest desires.

Noticing the Vendra boys will to seriously know the two sides of the situation, Kiria felt a great relief for knowing the man she was deeply in love with wasn't a mere mercenary. Decided to test him, she began to invite him and his brother to watch meetings of the guerrilla sympathizers.

_ I didn't understand the most of what they were talking about, but I enjoyed your invitation, Kiria. They are not the children killers they were depicted to us.

_ I am glad to hear that, Tharus.

_ I comprehended a little of what was told inside. I am beginning to realize if in this story there are good guys, they are the rebels.

_ I agree with you, brother. This is serving to clear my last doubts about Bills behavior. He is trespassing all the frontiers for associate with kind of people. it is clear all he is interested about is money. And you, lady, you're surprising me every day. I could never conceive a perfect "Sabrina" as you could maintain narrow connections with the guerrilla.

_ I guess I must tell you my secret. You two have been so reliable I can trust you. I fell safe to tell you I am part of the revolutionary movement. That's it!

_ What? I don't believe it! Your father had been minister of this govern. At least that's what I've been told.

_ That's true. I ever sympathized with the movement, but I couldn't do anything to do not compromise my dad, a nice and honest man, who was really trying to do the best to the people. But since he died of virus infection three years ago, I felt free to defend my beliefs. However, the command decided I'd be a better help if I remained undercover, infiltrated in the heart of the enemy. I've been working for this administration for five years.

_ Creep! Aren't you afraid of been discovered? Probably they would torture and execute you. I can't even imagine what they could do to such gorgeous revolutionary girl.

_ I am not afraid, exactly. but what other options do I have? I can't just lay down and close my eyes while friends of mine are being brutally slaughtered, without any fair defense or judgment.

_ Since the first moment I saw you I realized I was in front of a great woman. And every great man needs a great woman besides him.

_ And behind her his wife.

_ Shut up Iullus. The conversation here doesn't winds.

_ And that great man would be available for a dinner tonight?

_ Of course I am, pretty lady!

Since the first moment she saw Jean Luc, Kiria felt a natural profound antipathy, which kept growing while he continued wooing her, even knowing she was dating Tharus, in a rude and filthy way, which served to demonstrate his treacherous nature. And distrusted of the several secret meetings between him and the high cupola, which she noticed weren't related to the twins, Kiria began to spy these reunions, by using the freedom her job proportioned in the corridors of the power. Certain night, the president of the republic, with the vision her short skirt revealed of her amazing legs, covered by silk socks, which enhanced her perfect curves, broke the protocol and kept her inside the lounge while received Shatner in the next door. He was so horny, the only think in his mind was to get rid quickly of this foreign man, who dared to look for him personally, to come back and try to satisfy the desires his pretty assistant awaken on him. The old dictator was relapse with the security and didn't close the door, allowing her to listen the whole conversation. The paranormal didn't notice her presence and went straight to the point.

_ Sir, I decided to come here personally to inform you within two days we will begin the attacks against the rebel forces.

_ At last! I started to wonder what were you doing here. But why didn't you give that information to one of my assessors?

_ No way, sir! The situation is too dainty.

_ And this paranormal of yours? What is his name, Iullus? Have you arranged everything for his elimination? My troops are on your disposition.

_ Thank you, sir! Everything is already set. Tomorrow morning he will participate of a meeting and the ambush is meticulously prepared. Twenty agents on my order and an elite troop, disguised in rebels, will be waiting for him. There's no chance of escaping.

_ Very good! I am glad to hear it all will be over soon. Now, if that's all I have much work to do. Good luck.

When the lascivious president sought Kiria in his cabinet she had already left for a lateral door. Cursing against the Canadian agent, who he blamed for do not get to satisfy the tension among his legs, the man who named himself as sir doctor great general president of the republic; that had never been military; but titled himself like that for being fan of an old fashion Japanese cartoon, where there was a character with this title,; and without think that she could have heard his conversation, went to the bathroom to remedy the situation with a naked women magazine, before go home and to a wife who didn't awakened him anymore. The young lady Eolo searched the Vendra brothers the entire night in vain. She didn't have the number of their cell phones, and even if she had she couldn't communicate with them, because the agent Peyton used her skills to interfere in the devices receptions. While they strolled around the inner cities, talking to the locals and experiencing the cuisine, trying to figure out a manner to help to put an end in the combat that brought nothing but suffering to that poor people, and trying to understand if the rebel movement would be a good alternative to the actual regime. After receive his orders through a last holograph email transmission, before his phone stopped working; late at night; when Tharus was already sleeping in his room, Iullus took a shower, changed clothes and went out to meet the convoy that would transport him to the venue that should be inspected. Believing he was just rolling a little more the shop operations, he spent sleeping the next three hours of the long way to the ambush place.

When he felt the vehicle had stopped for a long time, he woke up, less than a second before a strange noise that preceded an explosion of a laser bazooka that reach full the cabin. All the other occupants died instantly, while Iullus, after heard the noise, changed his atomic structure, and was trespassed by the splinters, without any harm. Leaving the vehicle, the paranormal stood still when he saw members of his team wearing military uniform side by side with his aggressors. Before he was able to do or say anything, a violent weapons and energy attack let him paralyzed, trying to protect himself. He could clearly feel the attack of his companions, who were trying to make return to his normal state, so he could be hit by the artillery. The Vendra had perfect notion he could not hold for a long time the violent stroke of people who should protect him. He kneed in the ground covered by a sliver layer of ice, and putting the head among his legs and the hands in the nape, he tried to chill out to spare energy, by concentrating in the maximum on his defenses. Before to shut his mind in his mental block, he could distinguish the physiognomy of people he trusted, people who had participated in so many successful missions in the past years, and now betrayed him in a so vile way. Iullus had no illusion he could escape from that strong siege, and if he didn't receive help from outside, what would be much improbable, he could just postpone his death for a little longer. And he doesn't want to die. At least not there, and not that way, but each minute passed by was like an eternity, and his chances were being dragging as his force in his hopeless tentative to do not surrender to the fatality. He still had a card in his sleeve, Tharus.

Meanwhile, the Bat was taking his breakfast normally, despite it was almost lunchtime. Few minutes earlier he talked to Jean Luc, to know where his brother had gone, and this one informed Iullus had left to a routine inspection, and he should not be worried, once he was strongly escorted.

So he relaxed and began to read his electronic magazine, when a shaggy and visibly tired Kiria entered the salon.

_ Why didn't you answer your mobile phone?

_ I don't know, it had a problem and it is not working. Calm down, little girl. Why are you so despaired?

_ Because at this moment your brother might be killed! There's a plot against him. You have no time!

_ What are you talking about, woman? My brother? How come? Speak up, please!

_ Yesterday I heard a confidential conversation between the president and Jean Luc. They had planned to kill your brother this morning in ambush. And the revolution should be pointed as the guilty. It doesn't matter now, we have to save him immediately.

_ Thank you, darling. The son of a bitch just left, but I know where Peyton is. She is responsible for the transportations, and surely knows where Iullus is. That filthy snake! I never trusted in her. She'll have much to talk to me, or I'll take her skin out. You did what you could, now is my turn. Go to rest for a while. Now is show time, and I guarantee many people will regret have been born!

_ Good luck, my love!

Right after she have said that Tharus appeared in Peyton's bedroom, where she was talking to someone on the phone.

_ Don't you knock anymore? I am in a private conversation with my husband! Excuse me!

Without giving her a chance to do or say anything, the Bat grabbed her by the neck and raised her, beating her back violently against the wall.

_ You daughter of a bitch, what did you do to my brother? Where is he?

_ I don't know what you're talking about! He is on a routine mission.

_ You're gonna tell me right now, or this will be your last breath!

_ I don't know where it is.

He just peered at her and her left eye dried as an old orange. She cried out loud.

_ I gave you a chance!

_ I don't know what is going on. My eye! What did you do?

_ you still have the other. Chose carefully your words!

_ Wait a minute. I can take a look, where he is.

He put her on the ground. He knew she knew she could do anything. He transported her some places, until she finally showed in a map where Iullus was.

Some more minutes and Iullus would have capitulated. He was already in the edge of his strength, and some of the bullets were already entering in his shield. Tharus looked up from distance and breathed relief. There was a fog caused by the smoke of the funs, but he could distinguish his twin. At least he was still alive. On the next second he was beside his brother, creating another mental shield to protect them both. Then he pushed Peyton out of the protected area. She was instantly whitened by the explosions. For some time the paranormal agents didn't notice his presence, because they couldn't hold the fire, risking the mission. But they had to do after a while, to check it out. When they perceived Tharus was there too, they got into panic. The commandant, noticing the consternation of the shop agents, tried to argue with the Vendras, but it was already too late.

The Bat put his hand in his brother's hair, and gently asked if he was okay. With the confirmation he turned his attention to the troops, where some people began to flee.

_ You can run but you can't hide!

He told his brother to remain where he was, and calmly began to walk towards his opponents, concentrating in his hands, where balls of energy started to grow. While the balls grew up, the soldiers and the shop agents became to panic and began to cry, begging for mercy. Tharus sipped their distress with such pleasure, with a smile in the corner of his mouth. The opponents finally understood he would not forgive them and tried to run in many directions, but in this moment the rounding spheres where were big enough and he sent them against the fugitives. Magnificent explosions liberated the fury and rancor kept in Tharus heart, destroying everything and everybody that were in their reach. When the cloud of smoke vanished, he could see the size of the devastation, wrecks of vehicles and trees and bodies indicated the only survivors there were the twins. In triumph he returned to his brother, and tenderly embraced him.

_ Man what thrill! That was awesome!

_ You took too long, brother! I always trusted you'd come to rescue me!

_ I almost had a heart attack.

_ That's fine, but is everything okay now, so quit the tears.

_ Thanks for resisting for so long, brother. I don't know how would be my life without you.

_ That's fine, Bat. I have to thank you too. Man what damage! I didn't realize you could do such magnitude action.

_ neither did I.

_ Now can you explain me what a hell happened in here? Why our people were working with the rebels?

_ There's only one explanation. The shop betrayed us. and those weren't the rebels, were soldiers disguised.

_ What?

_ Let's walk for a while, and I tell how Kiria saved your skin.

_ This interests me.

They walked for some time in the road covered by snow while talked, and Tharus explained to his twin all the details, and they conjectured about sordidness that leaded the president of the shop to warp a loom against them. they were still very tense, mainly Tharus, who by the first time felt he could effectively lose his twin, despite they had already experienced dangerous situations before, but none like that. He never worried much about it because he was always by his side, but he never conceived a betrayal of his own kind, and if wasn't for Kiria he could have done nothing. His chest was full of hate and chagrin. By the first time in his life his heart and mind were dominated by destructive feelings. Killing for him wasn't anymore an immoral act, but was the very first time he felt pleasure on it. Certainly to eliminate everyone involved in this plot wouldn't be any hindrance to his peace of conscience, on the otherwise. In his actual state of spirit, he was absolutely convict would be essential the total extinction of his newest foes, including the members of this government who collaborated in this episode.

By nightfall, already recovered and rested, after being hosted by a friend of the young Eolo, the twins more lucid, sat down to talk about the details of the new task.

_ Don't you think you should see someone?

_ What?

_ I don't know, a shrink for example. You may be traumatized.

_ I am a grown man, brother! I can handle myself. I've been shot before.

_ But not by friends!

_ I am fine, don't you worry. Why? Do you need some treatment?

_ Me? Kiria's arms provide me all the therapy I need. You should use some.

_ What, Kiria's arms?

_ Shut up, you idiot. I mean you should use a girl's lap to lie your head on.

_ Oh! That I can use. I'll arrange someone to hugs me.

_ I hope so, Iullus.

_ Have they already known about what happened?

_ Sure thing, Iullus. Even Jean "the scrap" Luc must be aware we know everything.

_ What we're gonna do from now on?

_ I still don't know yet. This betrayal precipitated everything. "By the walk of the carriage" I'd say our plans will have to be modified.

_ I agree.

_ I think we should act in phases. What is closer we realize first, and so on. According to this point of view, what we should do first is to vanquish this horrible government. Later we will destroy the shop, and then set our things in motion.

_ I see you're in touch with your inner anger. But I can't disagree. I even thought about it and I got to the conclusion, even allying to the rebel movement we will need more support.

_ So it is time to convoke our people. I am sure they will answer quickly.

_ Exactly! Let it roll!

_ It is time to fight!

_ Hold your horses, brother. I know we were set up, but we have to chill down to think straight, because what we suffered doesn't give us the excuse to act with refinements of cruelty.

_ I know, brother. I'll take it easy. But one thing I can assure to you, those people who participated in this filthy plot will suffer the consequences of their acts, bit for bit! I won't give up this!

Within a few hours, Kiria Eolo provided safe mobile phones so they could initiate contacts with their helpers, and in the next ten days, 80 paranormal people got into the country clandestinely, disposed to become revolutionary. They arrived from several parts of the planet. Were former shop agents, former schoolmates, friends from other psychic schools, or just sympathizers they had met by mail. All of them were installed in a difficult access camp in the eternal snow woods. The recruits brought as well all sort of supplies, tents, medicine, clothes and coats enough to keep on a long invested. Parallel to all these movement, the Vendra boys initiated negotiations with the rebel leaders, so the brigade formed by them took active part in the process of destitution of the actual regime of government. Tharus had programmed demonstrations of the capacities of his allies to the guerrilla so they could acknowledge of the amazing offensive capacity of his paranormals, and this way be more respected by them. the chiefs of the tattered militias, who had been fighting for decades without any success against ragamuffin troops, exulted with the join of people as capable and powerful. Now they had full conviction they could beat Idi Koppel Cerbero, the facinorous dictator, and celebrated the alliance with the Vendra brothers as if they were celebrating the final victory. Tharus and Iullus also celebrated with great joy the alliance, because this pact would represent the beginning of a new journey. A journey headed to the destiny they had traced for themselves when decided to create this new order. And they believe that there was nothing better to begin a new path than mash their foes. The pay back time was coming.

CHAPTER 09

BACK TO THE PRESENT II

Every dusk, Peter and Denise met to see the sunset, talk and have a snack. More often than they would desire, they were obliged to use their powers to deal with the worse side of the human beings, and those jaunts to the dark side of the society imbued the energy of the aura field of the paranormals that did not attune those very low vibrations. And to them there was no better way to deal with all this and yet clean their mental emissions than a daily thanksgiving to the gifts the nature had given to them.

They usually met to have a snack in one of the manifolds cafeterias next to the work, and have a pleasant conversation about their hopes to the future of the planet, and how they could help to make these dreams come true, but only in a positive perspective, because Peter knew that Denise had a inclination to depression, this way, they talked about poetry, literature, music, philosophy, politics. He avoided subjects that could have related to violence, once the world was passing trough a frighten era, without perspective to come out this rage that took over the most of the nations in a relative short time. It seemed the human being had never been so rough and disregarded with the others. Juvenile gangs were causing riots everywhere and the criminals had never been so aggressive. However, when there was enough spare time and the weather was nice, Peter transported Denise to the suburbs and they had a picnic some meters above the treetops that surrounded a beautiful lake. Despite Denise do not posses the tele-transportation gift or levitation, Peter's energy was enough to sustain them both for a long period. To dupe the gravity, he created a ectoplasmic energy field which should keep all the objects up as if a invisible table was supporting them. Certain time, during an experiment, Peter created a so strong field around himself that he was able to remain above the soil for over than 72 hours. He didn't stop the procedure nor even to go to the bathroom or to be fed, and even while he was sleeping, he remained floating. Another time, he kept in indefinitely suspension and spinning, 6 feet above the ground, a 30 pounds stone. Four months later, the stone was still twirling without any addition of energy, until after some more time it began to stop and lowed down slowly, proving that once generated, the ectoplasmic field, the psychic can simply eliminate it or let it vanish by itself, by exhausting completely the force used in the process. After everything that had happened to him, Peter enjoyed to remember when he first met Denise, as if it helped him to recover his strengths.

Despite being admitted in the foundation only two years after Peter, they practically barely noticed each other for many years. She had heard about his feats, and by distance, knew his fame, and him, for several times paid heed to her beauty of that young red hair girl, but never had the opportunity to get closer to her. They just began to have some contact when she started her studies in the same university as him. One day, in a casual meeting, he recognized her and came along to talk to her.

_ Excuse me, lady. Is everything alright? You are student in the foundation, aren't you?

_ Just like you, Peter!

_ That's nice! And you even know my name!

_ That's obvious, after all, aren't you the most famous student in that school?

Nice to meet you, my name is Denise Tanner.

_ The pleasure is all mine, Denise. I didn't remember your name, but I'm sure I had seen you many times, but unfortunately nobody had introduced us before, and I didn't want to keep waiting somebody do it.

_ It was really a pity nobody had introduced us before, because I always heard good things about you.

_ Don't trust in everything you're told. But I am afraid I can't say the same thing about you!

_ How's that? What were you told about me?!?

_ That you were a gorgeous smart responsible good daughter, and that you were also a funny good friend reliable charming comprehensive girl. Only nasty things!

_ I didn't know you were a comedian.

_ And you don't know many other things too! But I think you will someday. Say, what are you studying in here?

_ I am in the medicine school.

_ Congratulations. To me, medicine is a profession to priests. I respect very much those people who relief the suffering of the others.

_ Thanks! That was always my dream, and as my main gift is the healing, there was no other way.

_ What is your level?

_ I am a paranormal level 06.

_ wow! a physician with that capacity is remarkable! It is a sensational mix. I believe that healing is the most noble of the gifts. You really must be a very special girl, and I'd like very much to become your friend!

_ I couldn't agree more!

_ So, friends?

_ Friends. What are you studying?

_ Psychology.

_ Yes, you look like a shrimp.

_ I don't know if I take it as an eulogize or an offense, but thanks anyway.

_ It was a praise, believe me.

_ But I do not have intention to have a clinic.

_ why not?

_ I have other plans. I'll use my abilities in other direction.

_ May I know how?

_ On the due time, yes. For the moment it is just an idea. I am not superstitious, but I prefer to wait. Changing subject, what are going to do tonight?

_ Whatever you're going to do.

_ Cool. Some friends and me are going to a rock concert.

_ That's fine to me.

For the next two years they remained just as good friends, sharing confidences and dividing good and bad moments. However, slowly, a new feeling was sneaking in their hearts, until the moment wasn't anymore possible to witness each other romantic affairs. Their mutual friends, without patience with their delay on recognize the obvious, set an operation to make them see they were undoubtedly in love, by arranging a blind date, where they didn't know it was with each other, at the same time they tried to enhance their jealous. The tentative was an success, when Peter arrived at the restaurant and the girl who was waiting for him was Denise. Dido to her. The relief they felt indicated a latent infatuation. And they decided to do not ignore it anymore. And from that moment on they surrendered from body and soul to this strong safe and mature union, fulfilled with much love.

From that day on, the life of these two became much more colored by a healthy cooperation relationship and mutual respect, covered by a huge physical attraction, once they were both very attractive. They didn't lived a ravisher passion; of those kind where there are tiring highs and lows; full of ecstasy and suffering; as the tales of the love stories, but a constant and pure love, based on a steady emotional ground, which proportioned a feeling of protection and safety, which satisfied completely the eager of them both. They knew very well their own limitations, as well as the other, and accepted them without hard feelings the differences, what resulted in a familiarity with few quarrels and charges. The adult and frank dialogue was the essence of the love-making, and there wasn't forbidden issue or dainty matters that could not be raised and openly discussed. And to complete the equilibrated affection, for they were naturally sensible; cherish and thoughtful, qualities the long training enhanced the maximum, their sexual life was a full and gratefully float of desires and satisfactions.

Peter lived alone, and so Denise used to spend much time with him, because she still lived with her parents, who did not interfered in her decision of spending some nights per week in his apartment. Extremely romantic, the young Moll liked to present his beloved all the time, and not only in special events. As he wasn't a millionaire, his graces were almost always of low cost, but highly conceived, as vintage poetry books; old porcelain dolls; love cards; fancy bangles; pictures and a some garnishes and other presents made by him with his mind skills or his artistic ones. One day, intrigued by his weird behavior, when he asked her to do not get into a room in his loft, she was reluctant on accept his request, but agreed, believing he was preparing a nice surprise. Some weeks later, he showed up on her house, bringing a present package.

_ Hi my love! What pleasant surprise. I like it!

_ If I could I'd do it more often. But what brings me here is a very special mission, to bring this gift to my Martian princess.

_ To me? But it is not my birthday, nor any other special day!

_ by my side all days are special.

_ I hope so!

_ C'mon, girl! Try to guess it!

_ This is the motif you kept me out of your office?

_ Precisely.

_ So I have no clue. Then give that soon. I am too curious to keep playing games.

_ Here you are. Open it

_ What noise is that? Oh! It's a pussycat

_ Yes it is. I found this cub almost dead another day, and I found out this snoopy is your face. So I took it home, treated it, and then I began an energetic work on it, so it could grow up strong healthy and smart. His name is Puywacket.

_ Puywacket? I like it. It is an original name.

_ Actually it is from a movie.

_ It doesn't matter. You see? He already likes me.

_ he has a good taste.

_ Now I have two cats in my life. It is too much luck.

_ I hope he can be a good companion to you, after all we won't be able to have kids for the next years at least.

_ I am sure we will be good friends.

_ I am *nip* too. Why do you think I gave him to you? Every witch needs to have her own magic cat.

Denise revealed herself as a great animal caretaker, demonstrating she would be also a great mother someday. She raised Puywacket so well that within few months he was already twice bigger than any other of his specie. The feline only needed to speak to be more intelligent. He used to follow her everywhere, and many times was caught hidden in the back seat of the car when she was traveling with peter. She used to talk to him as if she was talking to another human being, and he seemed to understand and answer. The friends used to joke, saying the pussycat used her on her spells, and he was also becoming a paranormal, the first psychic, a mix of Felix, the cat with the cat in the boots. If he doesn't like someone, this person couldn't be next to Denise or Peter for more than a few seconds, but if he sympathized, then the person could even cherish his fur. Differently of other felines, who have aversion for affect demonstrations, Puywacket constantly looked for his owners, when one of them seemed tired or sad, by making company, twisting in their lap tenderly. Some times it looked like he was trying to give some advice to them, about how to proceed in some subjects, by walking around them, or simply dropping things, trying to catch their attention. Peter's energy had an amazing effect over the cat, who really stood as an witch auxiliary, of those kid that seemed sent by the beyond, to help her in her sortileges. Denise loved to stroll with her pussycat, which seemed a tamed small jaguar, due to his extreme facility to learn new tricks. Who witnessed these presentations wouldn't believe he was just a cat. He didn't enjoy to chase rats or fishes, nor to spend the most part of the day sleeping. What he really loved to do was to help Denise on her tasks, bringing to her pens, pencils and other objects or reminding her of her compromises, or taking care of her security.

_ Puy, where is my note block?

_ Do you really think, he understands everything you say?

_ Yes, mother. So what is that on his mouth?

_ Your note block? I don't believe it?

_ Why not, mom? He is *nip*.

_ What?

_ Forget about it! It is just a poor slang!

Even in the hard and stressful preparation to the mission, the couple didn't let aside their routine. At dusk they were in their "tea time", while had a snack lazily sat over a great towel few inches above the surface of a calm lake, and threw rest of food to the fishes, and watched the Pyuywacket pranks on a tree.

_ This life is so good!

_ Petey, do you know what day is tomorrow?

_ Yes, Thursday.

_ That is not what I mean, silly boy.

_ Do you think I could forget a so important date?

_ I hope not. After all, is not every day a couple celebrates two years of love-making.

_ That's what I meant.

_ As time flies by when we are happy, isn't it? It is scary.

_ This is relative. Who believes in God and makes what is in his possess, doesn't need to be afraid of the future.

_ I know, but I am always a little bit afraid when we are in the verge to deal with forces more powerful than our recovering capacity.

_ Danger is always around us. Even when we are sleeping in our own beds! There will be always somebody stronger than us. The secret lies in the discipline. When we are strongly determined we are unbeatable. Now if you are referring to the Brothers Vendra, I want you to know I am certain of our victory. Remember I survived the first clash. I passed through a very bad time, but I survived.

_ I hope you're right. I think the problem is in me. I believe I wasn't born to deal with such violence as I have witnessed in the company. I hope things could be solved differently.

_ I wished it too, my darling. Unfortunately there are people who only understand the language of power. They react against any tentative to solve things through diplomacy. Tharus is one of those people. He showed us how terrible his powers can be. The power can corrupt who is falls in its illusion, and the absolute power can corrupt absolutely, and the Bat is very close to reach such level of force. There are many people who fear such might in the hands of a emotionally instable man, who is highly anarchist. They believe he can represent a serious danger to the world peace. In some level I agree with these people. I know tempting all these capacities can be. To try to modify the order of things is so easily, but we can't let it control us. We can't act as if we were in the god's business. The limit of the acceptable is so easy to be crossed by, and Tharus had already left this limit behind, and nothing indicates he will turn back.

_ It may be, but I continue disagreeing with the use of such violence. I believe I do not have the guts to be a police officer. I am seriously thinking about quitting the company after this case. My will is to save lives in a hospital and to teach in the foundation, far from these events.

_ Are you considering mister Vasconcellus invitation. What *dabrat*! I am glad for you. To teach is so you! It won't interfere in your work in the hospital. Who knows someday I'll be a teacher as well.

Despite being so young, Peter had accumulated many responsibilities when assumed the charge of the company of the paranormals. He was too methodic, and even enjoyed all the compromises that came with the job, as press conferences; reunions with politicians and authorities, to take care and coordinate the work of each single agent, and even to coordinate personally the conduction of some missions. He had self-conscience of the importance of his function to the direction of the paranormal phenomenon in the world context. He knew the way the psychics would be accepted by society would depend on the way he would play his roll, mostly.

A very common feeling to almost all paranormals, mainly those over the level 04, was the pride they had of their abilities, and Peter was no exception. To be the leader of an organization so powerful and influent worked as a huge vibrator in his ego. His success was mixed with the company and vice-versa, as much credibility his agency raised the most would be his own ones. And he pawned all his forces to everything works perfectly as an atomic watch. Every morning he ran the building rooms, talking to as much workers he could, about the tasks and difficulties of the day, offering help. In his comfortable office, he used to sat in his favorite chair to dispatch, looking from time to time at the portraits of his mother, Denise and Morgana, which where on his left briefcase. After that he called his helpers who weren't around to know about results and to give guidelines, and when there was a spare time in his schedule, he enjoyed to remember his goals while tasted a hot coffee, as the years flew by calmly, without further trouble after the quit of the Vendra boys, when he passed to dedicate even more tenacity to his trains., the growing number of friends who made his life become more agitated, and the friendship of mister Vasconcellus and his son, Hermes, who were actually his family, proportioning a normal affective development.

When Peter achieved the 7th level his ego went to the stratosphere. As Tharus had left the foundation a long time ago, and wasn't any more measured, and had never enjoyed to be in the core of the attention of scientists and researches, the Moll passed to the condition of psychic world biggest star, becoming some sort of celebrity in the academic centers, celebrated by his kindness and willing to cooperate with the advance of the knowledge. He always traveled with mister Vasconcellus, as Ziggy had done before, in his lectures and conferences all over the world, and was treated as a reality show star, and despite his serious and analytic nature, in these occasions he used to let himself go with the fun, and amused the audience with comic tricks, as when he was stalked by a group of *paparazzi* and excusing he had to go to the restroom, he just disappeared and went to a snack bar have some ice cream, while the photographers were stood still at the door of the restroom. However, his greatest challenge began when after 13 years of studies in the foundation he joined the university, to course psychology. During all those years he hadn't prolonged living with people who weren't also paranormals, and in the beginning was kind of difficult to interact with an ambient where the regular students had to do their chores by only using their hands and feet. He wasn't even used to negative answers to the manifestations of his abilities, and found strange when his ordinary mates and teachers had bias and fears regarding to his paranormal condition. However, with the pass by of time, he were more adapted, and avoided to use his gifts in public, and was seeing by the other students as a common one. He took a sort of double life, were by morning; from Mondays to Fridays; he used to behave as any other college student, and in the afternoons and nights; and in the weekends, he was compromised with the psychic trains. He seemed to enjoy this life style.

Few people around him had exact comprehension about the extension of his mental resources. Some had just a vague idea, and the major had no clue about what he was able to do. And in the semi anonymity, he had the freedom to enjoy the kind of life proper to young boys. The wage he earned from the foundation to participate on its compromises, despite it wasn't much, allowed him to be integrated on the passage rituals of the university world. However, he wasn't pleased by the light superintendence of the teachers and the dean's office, over the sensitive students, by the allegation they had to be under surveillance to do not try to use their capacities to obtain improper advantages. He felt as a suspect who had to prove his innocence all the time. But he knew he could do nothing about it, and his discipline made him conform and to submit himself to some embarrassing situations, once the legislation had created some norms on this regards, in practically every social activity, despite the protest of entities linked to the defense of the human rights. Some times this vigilance was funny to the sensitive people, due to the precarious resources on the police disposal on the wrong side to avoid crime, they offered chances to the psychic ones to dupe the law. Peter never tried to acquire advantage by using his abilities in a illegal way, once he was extremely ethic, but many of his friends and colleagues used these stratagems to revenge their humiliations. Many times he felt his mates reading the minds of the teachers searching answers to the tests; one or another more powerful, who had the ability to detour the light and this way become almost invisible, trying to copy results or those who could change the chemical composition of the pen's ink to alter notes and observations. By the simple fact his capacities were stronger than anyone else, he could capture the mental emanation in the exact time people were making use of their abilities, and how they were doing it. However, he avoided to point out his colleagues, and they knew he was this kind of person. He tried to see these felonies as small pranks, that didn't do no harm. But when he noticed someone was trying to get advantages under somebody else's belongs, he usually interfered. One day, he witnessed a student confounding the fotonic circuits of a vending machine robot, to steal some goods, and instantly grabbed the prankster and threatened to deliver him to the authorities if it was repeated again. The poor guy didn't want to pay to see, and apparently renounced to the criminal life. When Peter initiated his relationship with Denise, he became more active in the campus, once his beloved was member of the student directory, and was always involved with the police of increasing the study conditions, specially from the psychic students, many times by the use of her mental abilities, and her incentives finally convinced him to do the same, and he enjoyed to give his powers a more social connotation. To help more damage to students who paid no attention and were involved in stupid accidents, who had tried the suicide or were under aggression or threaten, enhancing his superman side, making grow in heart the possibility to consider the solidarity a way of life. He spent hours with her in the emergency room, and often arrived in the accident local before the fire fighters, and normally avoided a bigger tragedy.

With great joy mister Vasconcellus perceived the his pupil was becoming a mature man, and even before his graduation invited him to be a trainee for some months in a special unit of the justice department, which had been created one year ago, and was under the supervision of the president of the foundation. Immediately Peter was identified with the project and its purposes, and didn't even think for a second to accept the invitation and become one of the most enthusiastic cooperators of the agency. He dived by head, and wore the company's shirt, and in a brief time he was as experienced as mister Vasconcellus about the meanders of the division. From trainee he was promoted to effective agent with praises.

His first concrete case was the investigation of the eerie death of three people. they were been found at home, in advanced stage of decomposing, and the autopsy revealed the two men and the woman had sudden death due to a compression of the respiratory system. However, their clinic file didn't show any physical problem that could result in such tragedy. And their general health was perfectly. That's why the police suspected of a psychic crime and asked for the help of the company of the paranormals. Peter began to assist the diligences of the investigators, without catch any energetic chink of the action of some mental criminal. For several days he had no progress, and the detectives began to doubt of his professionalism. He asked for patience to his partners, alleging if some paranormal had something with those deaths he would find him, without any possibility of mistake. Insisting they should trust in his judgment, he asked for a new crime scene investigation in the houses of the victims. A bit annoyed, the detective agreed, once they had no other clue to stalk, and when they arrived in the first residence, while Peter was in the kitchen, trying to feel the room, he had his intuition headed to the trashcan.

_ What are looking for there, boy? We had already seen the garbage. There's nothing relevant in there. It should already have been thrown away. You'll have to update your supernatural powers, David Blair. – Said James Stark, an old policeman, and a little moody.

_ Everything is possible, sir. For example, what is this can of milk doing here?

_ Try a hint, Sherlock Holmes! – Completed Steve Genaro, the other detective.

_ I'll get it. I think I've done for here.

_ And now you want to search the garbage of the other houses, don't you?

_ Of course, My friend Austin Powers!

_ I deserve. Probably I threw a stone on the cross! You're beginning to piss me off, Brat boy. – Mumbled Genaro.

In the other two residences, the same milk mark was found.

_ Do you know what that mean?

_ This is the most sold milk mark? I think I'll complain with your bosses. You're kind of nut. – Muttered Stark.

_ Before we have a quarrel, I'd like to go to the milk factory. Are you going with me?

_m What for? Do you want to arrest the owner for selling too much?

_ This is the last time we follow you crazy instinct. After that we'll let you in the mental hospital. Threatened Stark.

_ You have a deal.

In the factory, peter informed about his intentions to the manager, and he authorized a complete search. The workers didn't understand much when they saw a young man dressed like Fox Mulder, with a penetrating look and an arrogant and cadenced step, silently inspecting each pasteurization stage to the packing, examining deeply the behavior of each employee, while his partners had a snack offered by the manager. Looking for clues he couldn't even know how to say, Peter was only sure that if there was something there he would notice. After some hours, without no success, he reluctantly decided to apologize to the president of the factory, who had been so nice with his boring investigation. And when he was walking in front of the office of the financial manager, felt a disturbing in the "force", as he enjoyed defining the capacity of sense energetic unbalance. Calling for the detectives, the owner and other witnesses, he entered the office and began a search in it, under the protests of the financial manager, who was a paranormal level 01. When he found a hidden safe, he wanted it opened, but the man argued he had forgotten the key at home, and offered to go there to take it. Without answer, Peter just peered at the steel box, and the door began to stew and to creak, until it fell down with a great roaring. Inside were found bottles of unknown substances, which the later exams proved was a potent poison, used in black magic rituals. Immediately he understood it was being used to sabotage. The poor man understood he was hopeless. He had seen what Peter could do and imagined he would reveal his darkest secret, and became desperate, and took a gun he had hidden in his desk. He seemed out of his mind, and threatened to kill everyone in his way.

_ Frederic, it is your fault! You've stolen me all these years! This factory was supposed to be mine. It was my idea! You pushed me into this! If this company can't be mine it wouldn't of anybody else. I prefer to it goes to bankrupt rather than see it make you richer! I wanted to be the best psychic ever, but That nasty school didn't made me nor even reach the second level! My very special dreams never were realized! There's always somebody trying to sabotage me!

_ Fargo, you're my brother in law! You've been working with me since the beginning. I recognize it was your idea, but you didn't have the money to invest in it, so I had to make my moves.

_ Shut up you idiot! You've been pretended to be my friend but you're nobody's friend. You've cheating my sister. You're having an affair with that nasty sales woman. I know it. I have been watching you, stalking you How could you do it to us? I hate you. I won't kill you because it would be so easy, but I'll turn your life into hell.

_ Shut up, you queer! You're nothing but an incompetent! You're a heavy burden to your family and to me! I hope you rot in jail!

Fargo looked at Peter. He knew the paranormal wouldn't let him shot his brother in law, so he decided to try to escape, quickly with a gun in his hand. Screaming he was being stolen by Frederic. He had to make his brother in law to lose everything he owned. Before he could flee or hurt somebody, Moll stared at him, and he was pushed into a yogurt drum, flying over the heads of the workers. Peter wanted to give a private show to them, who cheered the young hero. The detectives had to agree they were deceived by Peter's natural instinct to solve felonies.

_ You're good, boy. I want you to accept my apologies. – Eulogized Genaro.

_ You can be my partner any time you want, brat boy. I hope you excuse us. We are so naughty and old fashioned. Completed Stark.

_ Don't you worry, there's no hard feelings between us. I kindda like to work with you, guys. You're tough, some sort of Dirty Harry. Keep on like that!

The mayor himself came to thanks him for solving a crime that could have had catastrophic consequences, if the assassin had remained in his intention to contaminate other packages. Peter enjoyed so much of this experience he decided to do a post graduation on police criminal scientific investigation methods. All this theory knowledge, summed to a vast field training, made of him a specialist on solving the most complicated and hideous cases, committed by psychic criminals or highly dangerous bandits. Even the most incredulous police officers respected his opinions. When he majored as special agent, he was assigned to be the assistant of mister Dennis Hoover, area supervisor, a former cop and paranormal level 04, who at the age of 49 was the most experienced investigator of the company of the paranormals. During one year they worked side by side, sharing the same room and solving several small cases. His tremendous dedication and pawn on solving crimes without any importance showed to his superiors, beyond his mental power, he possessed the required qualities to the highest job in the organization, and after some other months he finally was raised to the cargo of general director, under unanimous approval. On the prestige the job conferred summed an excellent salary, and he could finally realize some of his consuming dreams. Very touched, he gathered to his economies the money saved by the sell of his mother's apartment, and bought his first loft. Few months later he felt completely happy when bought his first automobile, feeling like a real man. Fulfilled of these professional and personal satisfaction feelings, he began to defend with more dedication and vigor, the moral values that made possible his social ascension. Naturally he understood many things were very wrong, and would be necessary radical changes to eradicate unfair and cruel precepts. However, he believed these changes, for the most legitimate they were, would have to respect the rules of democracy. He was completely against any tentative to use the force to do what only could be done by people's agreement and sustained by the current laws. Convict he defended the most sacred human rights, as if he was participating of some divine project, he usually didn't feel no remorse by putting in jail people who passed through the same training as him. Nor even face moral dilemma when the target of his investigation was someone he had known in his school time. Peter didn't feel any satisfaction on somebody's punishment, he just believed to be doing what was correct, and guarding the rights of the honest and worker paranormals of being integrated without further problems to the ordinary life.

Hence, wasn't with such tough purposes he faced the one who had been his school idol, and who he considered as an old brother, and his group, which counted with many of his former mates of the foundation, many of them worthy of his admiration. Even with all the pain he had passed through on the long months of confront, his convictions hadn't been cracked, and now he was completely prepared to the fight which was being put in front of him. His only scruple was to hurt innocent people, was afraid this weak side could be used by his opponents, otherwise him, who wanted to preserve the life of everyone under his command, the "blue jackets didn't care about dying or killing to defend their objectives. Every day he reviewed exhaustively the action plans, trying to find out hidden flaws. On meetings with his assistants he always enhanced the need to analyze calmly all data and how they should cooperate with each other, giving suggestions to minimize the possibility of obits. By the fact of the huge number of paranormals involved in the operation, and despite of it, he tried to keep the focus of the members, and tried to avoid the "already won" spirit, for didn't matter the size of the force they had gathered, the clear and present danger wouldn't decrease.

_ Peter, with all due respect, man, I think you're over reacting a little bit. After all, Tharus isn't any "captain Marvel".

_ A lot of people who thought like you must be very sorrow now, in the cemetery. You must keep in mind this can be, maybe, the worst mission you have ever faced in your lives. If it depended on me I would have never involved you into this, but unfortunately, if the mission was in the hands of the military the consequences would be even worse. Lots of people who have nothing to deal with this story would suffer.

_ This is no good. Why this should be happening right now I am in the verge to get married?

_ Don't be so "Eminen", Argos. Think positively. Now you have a good excuse to flee from the church. Said Diana.

_ I'd prefer to fight a real war, if you want to know, Argos.

_ Take it easy, Sue! The man has a point. Now let's get back to the issue. In a few minutes I have a play in the school of my little daughter.

_ Don't you worry, Dan. We'll finish on time.

_ Thanks, Peter. So let's continue. Within four days, the first group will be embarking, and the countdown will begin, to the end of the operation. Diana, as the team leader, could you give us a report about the on goings?

_ A hundred and fifty percent! You know me, and know that I do not enjoy unpredictable situations. Each member of my squad is ready to play. Our basis will be set on the top of one of the highest and more difficult access mountain, where already there is a hut, which will give us conditions to remain there for a long period. On the same day we'll initiate the mental emissions to total or partially block the psychic activities of the blue jackets, mainly their premonitions. The password will be "Brokeback mountain".

_ Very good, lady! And you Debbie, is your group already prepared?

_ "Zero bullet". Three days after Di, we will head on. To do not attract attention we will be in the other side of the country, as planned. Our shelter is already done.

_ You have to keep in mind how important your task is. Everything has to work as an ocean's 11" job.

_ Chill out, Petey. We are aware of that!

_ Under the command of you two there will be four subgroups, with eight components in each one, and I do not anyone calling in the middle of the operation to call for more toilet paper.

_ Everything is in motion, dear boss. – Completed Kim. – Anyhow we know how to improvise. What do we have two hands for?

_ Cute! If you want to use your hands to clean shit is your problem. I just won't take any food from you, anymore! What I want to emphasize is nothing can interrupt the movement of the mission, once it has started. The Vendra brothers just need of some minutes of negligence to take over the situation.

_ Everything was exhaustively trained. The kids are alright!

_ No, the kids aren't alright, Sue! Bad things will happen, and we can only expect them to happen. Remember the devil lives in the details. The unexpected things and the reaction of each agent may compromise the whole operation. I have already passed through this, and I know how difficult is to confront people who had lived with us for a long time. The temptation to bring them to our side is too much. I committed this mistake and paid for it. I do not want you to do the same.

_ That what Peter said is too serious, people! we are going to fight against a group that is willing to do anything. Thanks God they didn't kill Peter in their first invest. However they must be aware now it was a huge error, and be sure they will not commit it with none of us. Any indecision will be punished with the death. – Argued Denise.

_ Kim and Pablo, you're the next. Is it "Pin"?

_ Yes it is, Dan! Our groups will be responsible to locate and map the habits of each blue jacket.

_ All the training is complete. It's time to play. The agents have learnt the local idiom and the habits, beyond all the geography of the country. I think our disguises will be perfect, and none will notice we are foreign people. Only the agents that have resemblance to the population will be allowed to mingle with them. We'll pass unnoticed.

_ That's good Kim. That's exactly what I wanted to hear. All the information must come quickly to my group. We will collect the data installed in an old basis in the suburbs of the capital. From there we will coordinate the actions of Suzanne and Anne Moss. Besides, we will responsible by the support to the other groups, sending supplies and providing transportation to the wounded ones. The venue couldn't be better, an empty and abandoned beverage factory. There are several warehouses to stock our equipment and for being a place frequented by criminals, even the hoboes avoid going there. Nobody will suspect of our actions. And you Sue and Anne, are you ready?

_ We can't wait for the rock and roll, Pete. Our team is formed by the most aggressive dudes we could gather. When you pass the coordinates to us we'll fall over these jackets. They won't even have time to understand what hit them, if a double deck bus or a pack of wolves.

_ That's it, Anne. While we didn't enter in action, we'll keep rounding and rounding the country, to keep up our agility of attack. When we put them down, they will be let to the cherishes of our friend Argos, who will be responsible to keep them immobilized.

_ You spoke a little, but you spoke everything, Suzanne. Just let the package with me and I'll dispatch them faster than the UPS.

_ Avoid being so confident, Argos. Your part maybe will be the most difficult. You'll have to cross that frozen desert from hell carrying many powerful and dangerous paranormals, and let them under the cares of Hermes, on the other side of the frontier. Have no doubt if they have an opportunity, they will do anything to get free or warn their companions.

_ I know that, Dan. Take it easy. The hot grill is always in my hands. I am used to that. But as I am the best in here, you can lay down your heads in your pillows and sleep without worries. If it's with me Then it's with god!

_ Everyone in here no it so, dude. But remember, you'll be only safe when they're with Hermes. He is preparing all the infrastructure to receive our guests. They will neutralized and finally out of action.

_ That's it, Pablo. About me, my unique concern will be the capture of Tharus Vendra and other two jackets, the most dangerous. I'll be in constant moving throughout the groups, to check them out and to give a better assistance. Completed this first phase, we will reunite and go on together to conclude the task, to capture the Bat. In this stage we will count with the decisive help, however a little volatile, of Joseph Prometeus Souz, the Ziggy. Denise how is he?

_ We are doing all we can to have him prepared, but he is still not responding the stimulus properly. I have faith he will be ready when we need him.

_ We count on it. Without his participation our chances are very reduced. You must put him on his feet.

_ Thanks for the pressure!

_ That's not what I meant, sweetheart. I wanted to say that you're the only one that can make him cooperate with us.

_ With God's little help the victory will be ours!

_ I couldn't say victory, once I believe nobody will get out of this battle with the victory, Sue. The defeat of people we carry in our heart can't be celebrated as an award. We can only wish everything goes right, accordingly to what we have planed, and if more dramatic measures won't be necessary I'll give myself for satisfied.

_ I understand you, Peter. There's someone there I consider as a sister, and I must do everything to bring her unharmed.

_ I know who you are talking about, sue. I am also so afraid for her. I have a debt with her. But as a friend used to say, in the end everything goes right!

_ So be it, Peter!

_ So be it, my friends!

In the deep of his stomach, Peter felt bothered by the fact once again he would leave behind the comfort of his home and his loved routine. He had always been proud of his abilities and the facilities they could proportion to his life, but in this very moment he wished to be just a common person, which only compromise would be to fulfill the work chores, come back home and have dinner with the wife and kids. But he knew that problems and sacrifice weren't prerogatives of paranormal people, and that there was a great part of the population suffering in the hospitals with terrible diseases, facing professional problems and living personal dramas. And soon his ego began to swell, when came to his mind the fact he was considered the most powerful man in the planet, a sort of superman, and it comes with its responsibilities which he couldn't simply flee from. He was proud to be a living laboratory to the science, opening a range of possibilities to the human kind, despite the burden over his shoulders such responsibility brings. Charges and more charges over his behavior, actions and even thoughts, which sometimes he considered exaggerated and inconvenient. For several times he considered the possibility to be as irresponsible as the Vendra boys, and disappear, to change his identity and move to some peaceful isolated village, besides Denise, and live placidly, using his capacities only when was extremely necessary. to raise a dozen of sons and daughters, and have as main goal to create them well. But he had notion this was just a dream, his conscience would never let him take a selfish existence like that, while the world was passing through a horrible transition, in one of it's worst moment, surrounded by violence, misery and corruption. He couldn't disappoint the people who invested in his formation, and his capacities should be used in benefit of those who were suffering. Besides, he couldn't give up all the facilities his life style proportioned in cosmopolitan city. His philosophy consisted in the belief that everything in life has a good side and another bad. The felicity beneath on search the equilibrium between both sides, adjusting to what comes from negative, and that can not be changed and enjoying the positive things that happen. He didn't agree with many aspects of life that revolted his sense of right, those any religion could offer a reliable explanation. Nor even his powers had condition to obtain exact and convinced answers of those people who had already left this world. For the most wise some spirits looked like, neither they could totally elucidate the need of utility of the human sufferings in a universe full of powerful energies, which could easily create an ambient of eternal peace and prosperity. There was always dark spots in the answers he got, what made evident even the most intelligent entities the living men could contact didn't possess all the information about the mysteries of the evolution. This vacuum gave cause to many speculations, and this way, were created lots of approaches on how to conduct the reins of human destiny. According to his concepts, the most interesting was the one that put all the human evolutional process responsibility in the hands of the men and women, incarnated or disincarnated ones, and that the angelical beings; masters of light; divine messengers; spiritual protectors; avatars or any other denomination by which were known the consciences that had achieved the a great level of perfection they had no need to live in the material world anymore; and began to take care of the orb, only granted the means to us, and only used to interfere in our actions when a large number of lives were in danger, such as an overkill or global heating. To Peter, all the mistakes and success should be put in the moral credit of the people who were still stepping in the ladder of evolution, while helped in its continue construction.

Peter became an adept of this philosophical chain, as well as the most of the paranormal people, and lost interest with the interchange with the beyond grave. Neither the spirit of his parents kept his interests on making contact, once he new they had their occupations in their new dwelling dimension, and the simple fact he knew they were happy let him satisfied, and he didn't accept frequently their contact. He preferred to obtain knowledge by the living beings, in his own existence level. He believed there was too much to do and learn in the material universe, and people had so little time to hang on with those ones who were breathing on their side, and if they spend more time with other dimension beings, this time would be even shorter. This practical and straight view of the way of life in the known universe was helping him when he had to take crucial decisions regarding to his profession; to the cases under investigation; and principally to his actual mission. By the intimacy he which he began to have with the social problems of that miserable country, he decided beyond neutralize the fugitives, he would help whatever he could to minimize the sufferings of the population, caused by the actions of the psychic people, and he would fight to obtain help from international entities to sponsor the reconstruction of the infrastructure. Trying to put in motion his will, Peter had frequent meetings with the defense secretary, to convince him to negotiate a help package.

_ Mister Semelo, I am worried about the direction we will give to the police of that poor country. I do not know how to remedy this, and I do not see anyone interested on knowing. External actions had already damaged too much the life of those citizens, once if there wasn't the intromission of the blue jackets, the guerilla would have never taken the control of the government. And for what I have noticed, they aren't prepared to rule. I tried to take the problem to the Un, but so far nothing effectively happened. In two days we will begin an offensive action, and we do not know the proportion it will take and how it will affect that nation. And there's no plan prepared to send any kind of aid to the day after. If it was up to me, after the capture of the criminals, I'd still throw down the actual regime, forcing general elections.

_ Take it easy, young man. Ideas like these put your friend, Tharus, in the present situation. You're not prepared yet to the meanders of the diplomacy. Everything must be exhaustively negotiated. There's no other way. And when things seem stopped, it is when they really walk on.

_ What do you mean by negotiation, exchange of favors?

_ You're a smart boy! Don't get me wrong, but in the political world you must give to receive, and when the result is good to the both parts, then you have an arrangement.

_ But the problem, mister secretary, is the population can't wait. While the powerful ones play their games, innocent people is suffering and dying.

_ You can't make an omelet without breaking some eggs. The help will come, trust me, but to someone put money, and we are talking about a large sum, there must be guarantees. Great companies want their slices. The vultures are flying over, and we must to settle them down first, by throwing some chops.

_ It is too complicated to me. I'll just believe when I see everything written.

_ Don't you worry. This small country never caught attention of the international community, but all this threaten to the world peace is putting them in the spot lights. In the end all this process will be benefic to them. save my words.

_ I sincerely hope you're right, mister secretary. Because, without the effective help of the locals, our chances of victory will decrease a lot. Considerably! There are already many people willing to cooperate with us, and I won't turn my back on them when it is all over.

_ No way we will do such thing, my boy. You work with me for a short period of time, but I think I have been enough to you to understand I am a man of word. I promise you this country will receive all the proper support to restore democracy and maintain a sustainable growth.

_ I trust you, sir. Actually I am relieved for hear all that. I do not know you for a long time, but I could already notice you're a different kind of politician.

_ There are still honest and working politicians. Believe it or not!

_ I do, as I do believe in Santa Klaus.

On the first time Peter had combated the blue jackets he didn't notion of the seriousness of the situation. He thought he was just a mediator, for being a childhood friend of many of them. in his mind were still printed the image of nice joker and funny mates. He had no idea the years of separation had made such change in their personality. He was not prepared to what was about to come. However, he wondered now everything would be different, nothing else could surprise him. He tried to enjoy the maximum his last calm days before the predicted torment. Each night he and Denise went out with friends to have dinner; go to the cinema; theatre and nightclubs. And as the sensitive people were masters in lax techniques, the just required few hours of sleep to remake their strength. Three or four hors were sufficient to let them disposed to face another hard working day.

On the weekends, they went to visit their preferred landscapes and those they always had planned to go, but never had time to. Peter thought, with this behavior he would be prepared to leave this world in case the worst happened. He also intensified his social works. To visit patients who did not have family, donate money to charity, mainly in his birth country, to be a volunteer on asylums and crèches, became an important part of his life.

In the day the first team landed in hostile territory, he abandoned his peaceful routine to become the trained warrior he always wanted to be. He was so concentrated in his tasks, to set the lasts details, until was the time of his own participation. Due to the grandiosity of the operation, never tried before, there were some variables that should be verified constantly, paranormal helpers who needed guidance, confidential information that should be shared and the perfect synchrony, to do not permit an unexpected reaction of the blue jackets. For the very first time, the company used the help of people who do not were part of their boards, and the students and teachers of the 38 psychic schools involved in the task required constant suitable information so they could keep emitting mental signals to favor the mission, by interfering in the quality of the use of the capacities of the paranormal targets, damaging their predictions. And the more precise this information was, with names; photos; descriptions and even personal objects, the better the work would be. Despite the helpers did not know the particularities of the operation, the help of these school would be crucial to everything run as planned, once the group of the Vendra brothers counted with excellent cognitive medians, and if they were not blocked; at least partially; certainly they would discover the offensive, provoking unpredictable unfolding.

Every afternoon, Peter kept contact with the associated institutions, to certify everything was in the right motion, and remind them how important their participation was. He also checked out the send of supplies, mainly medical. He didn't want to lose any agent because of lack of firsts aids. This time there would not be the participation of the militaries, and he wanted to keep them away, and He would be the only responsible if things failed down. He didn't want to have the death of thousands of thousands of people in his conscience. Such pressure let him anxious as he had never been before, and what kept going on was he knew there was no other alternative. He used to have bad dreams in this time, where the fear paralyzed his movements and his reasoning, conducing him to fail, while observed immobilized his agents being slaughtered. If he had option, he'd rather deal with the blue jackets alone. At least this way he would not be risking somebody else's life. But he knew this was not possible and would have to learn how to live with this, with the burden in his conscience. Peter wasn't the kind of man who fled of his obligations, for the most hard and thorn they could be, and had full conviction life continued beyond carnal life, independent of the material world, and even if he lost some parts of his body, his spirit would keep intact. However, he knew still life would end up everything, without a future life, he would act the same way, for he was a fiber man and fought for his ideals. He just didn't want to drag innocent people into his crusades. Once it was almost inevitable, he would have to relax and trust on those who were helping him. And with much apprehension in his belly, Peter embarked back to his worst nightmare.

CHAPTER 10

ORIGINS OF THE FOUNDATION

Mister Jardell Vasconcellus had always been an idealist and visionary man. Since the first moment he notice did not posses commercial sense nor even a slice of interest on becoming the CEO of his family enterprises, he decided to dedicate his energy on another direction, after his parents death, his priority was the search of answers and solutions to the problems that most afflicted the human beings: if really there is life after death; and how it could be, if the reencarnation theory is true, how we could effectively prevent the human sufferings, and the mysteries of the human minds and brains; if indeed the man used only a fraction of his potential and how to develop the innate capacjties. He faced these challenges not as a bothered spoiled rich boy trying to escape the real troubles that afflicted his soul, but as a scientist who believes he is struggling a holy war to head the mankind to the stars, and above.

In this personal crusade he awaked the enmity of several people and institutions. Many of his relatives accused to dilapidate the family estate in a lunatic crazy adventure, inclusive suing him, trying an interdiction on his control over the companies. The quarrel last several years, with his uncles; aunts and cousins manipulating his ideals to prove his madness, using to achieve this goal, the help of many of his foes. Despite these proceedings did not have resulted in full success, they got to hold down his investments for so long while made his life miserable. Tired of that much pressure and willing to do not waste his time anymore with this useless fights, while the real challenge was there waiting for him, he decide to disrupt part of his holding, satisfying the appetite of his serpent relatives and getting rid of them.

The scientific community tended to treat him sometimes with open aggressive critics sometimes with sarcastic commentaries, trying to marginalize his scientific methods procedures, taking any opportunity to tread him to the public opinion. They refused to accept that a large sum of money that should be used on researches to solve real problems of the society was spent with delusional windmills hunt. They refused systematically his participation in many lectures and conferences considered too much serious to open space to a clown scientist. Such rejection made the young Jardell Vasconcellus become totally disbelief to the public opinion, attracting more and more antipathy to his ideas. Many researchers avoided to openly cooperate with his work, afraid to become as ridiculous as him.

Great part of the media used to give to his statements some space only to make joke of them, corrupting his ideas or giving emphasis only the most polemics parts, altering considerably the connotation that he wanted to pass to the audience, this way, his projects sounded even more strange and odds. The most of the newspapers; magazines; blogs and internet news didn't open space to publish the advance of his researches, nor even showed interest in supporting his discoveries, didn't giving him alternative but look for help of the tabloids and sensationalist press, which even reproduced his articles with fidelity, didn't matter much, for they didn't have much credit, and his progress passed by as merely inventions to sell papers. Also, he had to pay for everything with his own money, because no businessman had interest in partnership, and the government didn't give any tax exemption for consider out of purpose his investigations.

Everywhere the paranormal phenomenon was considered old news to the modern science, where manifolds reputation people lost time; money and credibility trying to obtain proves that had never been accomplished. They believed that there were nothing to be discovered about it, and there were no more mysteries about the brain, or they were so inconsistent and frugal that there were no means to measure it with scientific parameters. So many people approached mister Vasconcellus to ironically try to advice to dedicate his efforts to other study lines, less scuffed, such as the flying saucers phenomenon; the conspiracy theory; the seek for the lockness monster; the mysteries of the "Da Vince code", or the existence of the vampires. They argued that would be easier to map the bottom of the sea, or the Mars surface; to locate the lost reign of Atlantis or Noah's arch than crumble the brain to pinpoint the venue where these alleged super powers came from. Despite not been a funny man, Jardell sometimes used to cackle at this mean commentaries, that far from discouraging him, let him more brave on his guts to bring down those bias.

During several years his researches could only count with adult volunteers. The parents didn't seemed to feel safe about the foundation structure or just didn't believe in his goals, and didn't authorized the participation of their children in projects of a man with a reputation of being irresponsible and frivolous and with the looks and the fame of a "nut professor". However, the fearless Jardell didn't gave up, and continued steadily on his purposes, because, more than anyone else, he believed on his works, and his advances made his determination stronger. Patiently was denying, combating and disbelieved all the accusations against him, and letting the time shows to everybody that the words may convince, but the example draws followers, and finally, his good intentions and his qualities of a integer worthy and correct man began to surpass. His explorations took him to the conclusion that only when he could count with the participation of children, mainly toddlers; once the nervous links were not yet totally built and the brain was developing; and when they could train the techniques he was elaborating in the devices that he was creating especially to this purpose, the goals would be fulfilled.

The established religions and some metaphysic secret societies didn't gave him truce, while Jardell was succeeding in his tasks. Unfortunately he began his searches in a time that resembled another one about the witch hunt. The most famous preachers sold the idea that the parapsychology was infected by darkness followers and assured that the real intentions of these evil people were to dominate the minds of the young ones, making them rebelling against their families, the society and God. These attacks seemed ridiculous, but they created many hindrances to the works of the foundation. The calumnies and defamations found echoes on the popular saturation with technical innovations, such as smart clothes, stem cells, photonic gadgets and principally with the household and office robots, that began to replace men in repetitive and tiring activities. To many religious people the science was trying, with success, to take God's place, and they had to stand against it, by alerting the population to avoid the excess of inventions that would apart the men from the divinity, and the ideas defended by parapsychology that the brain possessed hundreds of miraculous capacities, putting the men in the same category of semi-gods, would definitely bury the dependence that linked the mankind to the real God. To defend their positions they used all possible resources to combat what they called the antichrist sinister plan. Everything was permitted on the fight against the extra sensorial perception, that wouldn't be another thing but seduction devices and controlling ways sent by the Satan himself to erase the last resistance of those who stood still and worshiped the divine willing.

Even other adepts of the supernatural and professional of this area were against mister Jardell Vasconcellus researches. They defended so bizarre approaches to the psychic phenomenon, that the intentions of the foundation parapsychologists seemed to them more dangerous that any other life style philosophy. These pretentious masters of the occult did not tolerate the idea their secret knowledge was revealed to the common men in a general way, they preached that for thousand of years only the initiated beings could be taught how to get access and make regular use of these special capacities, and they had to deserve this privilege. The disciple should pass through lots of weird rituals, such as using hallucination drugs, prepare of special offers and physical and spiritual sacrifices to obtain the grace to enter in contact with avatars who would guide their entrance in the multidimensional world, and then, they would be allowed to use these abilities. These masters didn't accept the fact that people could grow their powers by themselves, and they wouldn't need to belong to any religious community. The hypothesis the man could be his own god sounded like a heresy to these mystic thinkers. Many alleged monks and elevated people looked for the foundation offering their services to guide the scientists efforts, but at the same time, making lots of fancy demands, as reasonable payment; acquisition of specific material; and different treatment to the guides. Logically, Jardell was experienced enough to know how to "separate the wheat from the bad seeds", and knew how to find those ones that could effectively have some knowledge to offer. The other he put to run. These rejected deceivers passed to vehemently attack the foundation serious work, raising the list of enemies of their paranormals. One of them was a mysterious man called Ivan Karak, a billionaire who wanted to support mister Vasconcellus researches. He alleged to belong to a secret society entitled the alternative great fraternity, or simply "AGF", but Jardell had already heard about them and knew they weren't reliable, so he refused their cooperation.

During a long time these religious fanatic tramped the development of the researches. They organized public manifestations in front of the laboratories, impeding the passage of the cooperators; convinced or threatened many of the volunteers and put pressure over the authorities to inspect systematically all the procedures and documents of the institution. They feared the new, as they had feared before the automobile, colored television, microwave oven, mobile phone, the transgenic food, the stem cell, the nanorobots and virtual reality. The irrational people always tried to destroy what they didn't know, and they even used attempts against the foundation estate. They couldn't dissuade the tireless Jardell from his path, and in all these occasions, he reacted with patience and tolerance, and when the ambient became more hostile and heavy, he simply moved away. He knew the most of the population was on his side, and would get many benefits from his work. The passage of the years was his best allied, by mining the severe persecution of his adversaries, who were little by little being defeated by his diplomacy and humble manliness, until he could finally work in relative peace at last. With the calm period, the number of volunteers increased gradually, and the best of all, toddlers were allowed to adhere to the program, and this way had begun the paranormal school. Even sponsors started to see great advantages and opportunities on participating the researches, what brought structure to the work, once Jardell was dilapidating his fortune in the foundation, because of the great investments required to the realization of his ideals.

One day, a billionaire of the computer sector, aging just 25 years old, but very famous for his intelligence and competence, booked an appointment, so he could meet personally the president of the foundation he was thinking to invest in. Steve Windows as genial lad, but a while spooky. At the age of 17, after heritage a great fortune, after the suicide of his mother, he created a computing company, which after just two years in the market, released the first personnel computer with artificial intelligence, what elevated the company stocks to the stratosphere, inserting the teenager in the list of the richest men on the planet, with a fortune about 90 billion dollars. Decided to invest in other fields, the intrepid Windows sold 30% of his shares, keeping dozens of billions in the banks while he decided where to enforce. Hypochondriac, he reserved 500 million dollars to spend while he was still healthy to enjoy everything the excess of money could provide. Cinematographic mansions, the most modern yachts, sportive cars and fancy airplanes were his newest toys, while he and some friends larked in travels and parties which could last weeks, riots with the most beautiful women and much alcoholic beverage and other substances. But the sudden death of one o his party mates, victimized by an infection acquired in the savannahs of the Africa, awaken in him an extreme panic to the fragility of the human life against many aggressive situations. Following this paranoid idea, he decided to invest in researches which aimed for achieve the immortality of the physical body or something alike. Obsessed by this purpose, he wanted to put his cards in the foundation. He wouldn't accept to talk to someone who wasn't the great expert in the area, and in the scheduled day he conducted to the CEO's office.

_ It is an honor to have you here, mister Windows.

_ I think I should be honored to meet such scientist. But as I am not given to freshness and neither are you, I'll just say good morning, and that I am sympathetic to your cause. I know what you have passé through. I kind have passed through the same bias, when I created the artificial intelligence. They just can't understand people like us.

_ I'd been noticed about what kind of prejudices you've been target. It is a shame, after all your work is amazing, and is helping a lot our developments. I think you should be awarded with a Nobel prize. But, I believe for the moment, the most proper is good afternoon. Because it's almost 03:00 pm.

_ What? I thought our meeting was at noon. At least was that my secretary told me.

_ Sure it was. But what are only three ours late?

_ Are you kidding me? You're not angry?

_ Not a little. I was working and didn't notice the fact. Besides, your behavior and your deejay style combines with the image I had in mind.

_ Any how, I am so sorry. Truly. I am not used to this time. Yesterday I had a reception in New York, and the night before I was in Melbourne. I am sick of sleeping and taking shower in planes. Now I do not remember exactly if the party was yesterday or two days ago. What day is today?

_ Thursday!

_ Are you sure? Because I could swear we were on Tuesday. What happened to the Wednesday? I've been drinking too much. Serious, I need to stop for a while. I know that I committed a terrible mistake by letting you waiting for so long, but trust me, this hangover is already punishing me a lot.

_ I am so sorry to hear that, my friend. If you want to, I have specialized students on relieving headaches. I can provide you a session. Now don't you worry about the time, sometimes I do the same.

_ Really? Do you like a spree?

_ No. not at all. My days are over. I get late because of the work. That is it.

_ So, let's not waste more time. Do you really believe these paranormal things can improve the life condition in the whole planet, and help to prevent the global heating?

_ Well, mister Windows.....

_ Call me Steve.

_ Well, Steve, I have a dream. And in this dream all the people live in peace and harmony, independently of they are paranormal or not, which level they are in. everybody is equal to the laws of the men, and due to the present situation, I believe to achieve this dream, the help of gifted people will be essential. When a considerable number of men and women is dominating these abilities, there will be no more space to lies, corruption and violence, once the whole population will be aware no crime will be unpunished, and no dark secret will remain hidden. Therefore, answering your question, I do believe these powers will improve the life condition on earth.

_ But can they raise such power? I mean, aren't you over estimating these psychic abilities?

_ Certainly I am not. On the contrary, I think that my expectations are under of what some of them can really achieve. By the files sent to you previously, you can certify, step by step, the on going of my researches, and what I already have scientifically proved.

_ I guess I have seen something like that on my desk in one of my offices. The truth is nothing like that interests me much. What I want to know is if these mental capacities are sufficient to maintain and enlarge youth and beauty, and protect life better than the actual resources of the "nano" medicine.

_ I don't know exactly, to be totally honest. I never thought about it. I believe the esthetic medicine dispose of better equipment and experience. However, I'd say that certainly the occult faculties of our minds can effectively maintain and sustain the general healthy of our body, providing the organism a better equilibrium, and for consequence, to prolong for much more time the good looking. And not only the paranormal people can achieve that, but also the people they want to help.

_ That's what I wanted to hear. I trust in your judgment, but I am a little skeptical. You see, in the beginning of the 20th century, for instance, many researches proclaimed that if we removed our bowels, we could live more than 200 years. Can you believe it? 200 years! Until now I haven't heard of somebody who achieved this age.

_ That's true, I have read something about it. Can you imagine the inutile suffering of these poor people? that's why I am too rigid with my researches. I only affirm what I have already proved many times, under rigorous criteria. I need to be a hundred percent sure to feel safe to announce to the world my conclusions. It's needed to be careful with new ideas, but I can assure you, so far our results show us we're in the right path.

_ I hope so. Your expectations let me eager to know what is about to come. I am no more a child, you know. If you start to think about how many incurable diseases we still fight against, I'd go nuts. And I am not mentioning the hideous accidents that can happen at any time to anyone. Wouldn't be a waste of time if one of the richest men alive died suddenly, without a heir and leaving behind a lot of parties? It racks someone's brain. I just keep wondering about all the mouths that I didn't kiss. As I already spent some hundreds of millions of dollars in the pharmacy industry, I do not see any problem on investing some money in your laboratories. Just to be sure, you know.

_ I understand what you mean, Steve. And I can assure you will never regret this decision. And as you want to become an expert, I'd like to show you some experiences with one amazing capacities, the healing. Once a paranormal has it fully developed, this person will be able of incredible feats, only heard on religious history or fairy tales. The cellular regeneration this ability is capable to promote is something wonderful.

_ Now you caught my attention. I can't wait to see it with my own eyes. I think we should leave the rest of the boring conversation to our advocates. Let's go to the interesting part! I am thinking to invest about a hundred million dollars, what do you say? Is it okay?

_ I think we can handle it!

_ Of course I'd like to give some hints, do you mind?

_ Feel free to speak up.

_ Well, I was expecting something more fancy. I don't know this your lab is kind of shindy. What about we build a super headquarter to the foundation? It could have all the facilities and space to our experiences and trainings. What do you say? We could also enlarge the number of workers and scientists to accelerate the process of discoveries.

_ It is your money, it is up to you.

_ So be it.

The works gained an accelerated path when the headquarter was opened. Specialists from several parts of the globe, and from several thinking chain were hired, offering decisive contribution to the success of the project. With great joy, all the integrants of the equip partied the day when at last would be announced to the world the irrefutable proves of the extra sensorial perceptions. A group of students had been submitted to rigorous lab tests realized by several scientific publishing, which after repeat them over and over again, corroborated all the works of the foundation. With great bustle, the triumphant Jardel convoked all the world media to the best theatre of the city to officially communicate what everybody already knew, that the human brain, specifically the pineal gland, was doted of perceptions that went beyond the five known senses so far. And to demonstrate the veracity of what had been certified by inspectors of many countries, he organized a great show, where some of his best students would provide a more evidences, witnessed by the greatest illusionists and specialists on prestidigitation and optical illusion. Young boys and girls remained flying above the audience, while small objects were dematerialized, lights were seen in the most unlikely places, children passing through solid objects, small colored sparks as fireworks, and many other abilities were demonstrated. All that broadcasted to billions of people in the five continents.

The first impact over the society was overwhelming and ravager. Many of things the fanatic people tried to avoid by violence did happen. No one could speculate how the professional and personnel relations would be from that day on. The ancient religious believes began to be questioned and scurried off on what they had of most sacred, and the contact with the dead started to be more and more common, and the certainty of a life after death very similar to the one on earth shook the moral and spiritual values. Suddenly everyone wanted to study psychology, hoping to develop the mind powers as well, and the name of Jardel Vasconcellus was even quoted to the Nobel Prize. All an industry of entertainment was set overnight with newspapers; books; electronic gadgets; courses; souvenirs; thematic tourism and other opportunism actions to gross with the paranormal fever, which passed to be worshipped by the greatest part of the world population as a panacea that would heal all the diseases, solve all the problems and change the life of the planet. They could just see the material benefits the psychic abilities could provide, and the most of the citizens wasn't prepared to the real change the paranormal phenomenon could provide, the inner transformation, which should come first from the core, to then begin to prevail over the material.

However, the alternations of behavior and thinking was only in the surface, and did not followed the depth of the revelations that should transform the way to face things of practically all the human beings. From all the dark corners, the powerful people, who wanted to preserve their supremacy at any cost began to strike back. Mystical leaders who were against any new approach on the form the universe was understood by their followers, mainly the most true ones, unchained furious attacks of manifolds manners, on the desperate tentative to mine the results of the proves of the sensitive beings. Working in a indescribable gathering of forces, the different religions, who were till then enemies, set a massive campaign of disinformation and denial over the metaphysics aspects about the paranormal phenomenon, once the physical aspects couldn't be renegade. They used the unwonted ignorance of the spirits invoked in the communications with the beyond, who seemed to know less than the living people about the mysteries of the creation of the universe.

After this huge wave of euphory, on the following years, the psychic capacities were losing the fresh air, mainly because the people deposited too much expectations on them, hoping the simple existence of these phenomenon brought structural renewing on the whole society, solving once and for all, the world economic differences. As it was practically impossible to achieve, they began to lose the interest on ESPs, and turning their attention back to the daily issues. The promises in the mental abilities, of increasing of life condition of the human beings, should only promote an emphatic change after decades and decades of hard labor and trainings of a growing number of young boys and girls, linked to an intense use of these capacities to achieve moral and material perfection. However, the fact the great major of the planet population would never possess the required discipline and dedication to the long and rigorous right development, and the urgency to solve the basic needs, made almost impossible to reach these goals, and the life was coming back to the normal flux. The most of the newly graduated sensitive people didn't have slope to the altruistic use of their talents. It was too difficult to avoid a smug proud took over their egos, making them thinking they were above the rest of the mortal people, and possesses of extraordinary abilities didn't give them more responsibility over the weaker. Independently of their level, these sensitive were ordinary people, who had the same character flaws and qualities, eager and fears as the rest of the population. Surely they were improving more, while human beings, than they would if they didn't have passed thorough a wearing out training, which propitiated a better comprehension over their own and the world around them, by learning new universal truths and laws and how these teachings are intrinsically connected to elevated moral values. However, one thing was to know, and another very different was to practice what they knew, and this way, they kept committing the same mistakes. All that taught to Jardell a great lesson, doesn't matter the degree of the technology and the knowledge reached by crafts; sciences; religions and history; the human evolution would still continue to be slow and gradual; and with only too much patience; dedication; control; discipline and love would be possible to help other people to get into higher levels in the cosmic scale.

During the firsts phases of the origins of the foundation, the indefatigable Jardel didn't have awakened other interests but the researches and discoveries about the mysteries of the mind. It was a whole spread field to him, and he was just in the beginning, and he even forgot he should have a private life as well, and the constant attacks and persecutions he was target of, only increased his retraction from the ordinary life, what usually made him spend months without remember he had a home, and he practically lived in his labs, making there his meals and even sleeping in his office. He didn't date anymore, and didn't go to parties, and forgot the way to the cinemas and theatres, and seldom remembered he still had some friends that didn't were his scientists and assistants, and looked for them. However, all this changed when his feats received the due value. It seemed as if an enormous weight had been taken off of his shoulders, made the obsessed working man, who had a behavior of an elder man of 93 years old took out the blindfold and had returned to see life by the eyes of young guy full of life and passion. And he became once again the elegant Nordic green eyes healthy and virile forty years old man, who was undercover by the priorities of a mad scientist. He regained the pleasure of the females company, and felt free as a bird to travel and spend money without further worries on a long vacation, and enjoying, with the satisfaction of who had fulfilled his duties, the good things life could proportionate and he had put aside for so long. Finally he had honored the commitments assumed in front of his parent graves, and they even eulogized him throughout a communication with one of his apprentices; when they could express all their pride and bliss the very important conquers of their prodigy son, to the evolution of the planet. The famous Jardel was one of the greatest beneficiaries of his discoveries, once he used to be the rat lab of his students, and had received for a long time the good application of powerful energies in his organism, what end up resulting in a perfect body, renewed and full of disposition to love, what captivated the attention of several women, until he finally have chosen one to be his journey companion. At the age of 45 he got married with Lara, and completing the infatuated relationship with a handsome son, who they called Hermes.

At the age of 05, the robust Hermes began to study in the foundation's school, and graduated as a sensitive level 02. The odd thing was his four abilities rounded around the same theme, the emission and reception of thoughts. He could capture thoughts of normal and paranormal people who were in his level or bellow him. Sometime he could even sense some of who were one level above. He could send his thoughts to this same group of people, and could even influence the reception of images, sounds, smells and sensations, creating perfect illusions to the receptor, and even alter the mind state of some people, where he many times put them to sleep without their permission or will, creating some surrealist situations.

_ Hello, little Peter. Do you want to have fun?

_ What are you planning, Hermes?

_ What do you thing about putting that doorman in the Morpheus arms?

_ Why, Is there a problem?

_ Turn on, boy. It is just a joke!

_ Oh, I got it!

_ I am just sensing he hasn't been sleeping well lately. So we're just gonna help him.

_ Let's go. Can you read my mind? What am I thinking right now?

_ Let me see. You wanna see the preview of Star Wars IX.

_ Cool! Am I going to have this ability as well?

_ Who knows? But I must warn you this is not always funny as you may think. When you do not have full control of it, you end up listening more than you'd like to hear. Trust me, there are thinks we'd rather not know.

_ And how does it work, you enter in people's mind?

_ no one enters in nobody's head. Only a surgeon can do it. What happens is that our mind is like television network, and when we think about anything we emit a wave what is propagated in all directions, as a radio wave. The more this wave is the far it goes. Then it is just a matter of tuning with the right frequency of this thought and it is done. Each kind of though is in a different channel, we could call it that way. For example, a love thought may be in channel 20 and an angry thought may be in channel minus 10. The elevated or good thoughts are in a positive frequency, and the negative ones are in a negative one. The higher frequencies are for the most altruist feelings, and the lower are for the most hideous human flaws. So we have different channels for hunger; pornography; endearments; jealous; good will and so on. I can not "read" everybody, it is needed determined aspects work together to it.

_ Can you read the mind of those girls over there?

_ That's *glub*! Give me a real challenge.

_ Why it is so easy?

_ Because the most a person is distracted, the easiest it is. It is quite simple. Let's see that short girl. She is worried about the clothes is going to wear tonight in a ball, that cute freckles girl is sad because her boyfriend needs a surgery, and that other one with a big tattoo in her chest is thinking about a loan to buy a new car. She spends the wage the foundation provides her. And the tall one is conceiving if she got pregnant last night.

_ That's bad!

_ Actually it is not. She is doing it on purposes, because she thinks her boyfriend wants to break up, and she loves him and want to do anything to keep him.

_ Awesome, dude. This is really *dabrat!*

_ Come with me. I'll show the practical side of this ability.

The two boys got closer to the group of the young girls.

_ Wait a minute, girls. May I talk to you?

_ Sure you may, Cute boy.

_ I am a paranormal level 02 and I'd like to give you some warnings.

_ We're listening.

_ Ok. Karla, don't you worry about your clad. You'll be gorgeous in the party. Mirna, stop thinking about that your riffraff boyfriend! He doesn't deserve you. Fabritia, here is the address of an institution that provides loans to students, and a course to teach how to administrate your own money better. July, this time you're not gonna be mother, but be cautious, your body is not prepared yet a pregnancy. Something bad can happen. That's all. Excuse my intromission.

_ Hey, aren't you mister Vasconcellus's son? Can you predict the future?

_ Yes to the first question and no to the second. I can sense deep thoughts and analyze and calculate the probabilities of what is about to happen. It is a kind of empathy, you know. It is a little complicated. Premonition is when you see a future event, and I can't see that, I just connect with people's eager and process the possibilities. Kind of. See you.

_ I hope to see you first, boy. Analyze this!

_ Will they hear you?

_ I don't know, Pete. But to increase my chances I also put some ideas in their empty minds. I'd say the probability is about 87%. Now let's go to the movie. My friends must be there already.

The young athletic, who looked like a clone of his father, revealed to be very similar to him in his ideas and projects. Soon he was interested in the institution, what let his progenitor very satisfied. He gave up of a very promising career as soccer player to dedicate to study management, and became assistant of the directory of the first and greatest organization of preparation and formation of paranormal students. Father and son worked syntony of principles, and visionary Hermes was the second major defender of the project of the creation of an federal entity of control and support to the psychics, working hard when it finally was put out of the paper. In this same year he got married to Sara Zukker, his former classmate and also a paranormal level 02. The wedding party was noticed by the media of the whole world.

_ Thanks, dad.

_ I thank you, my lad. After all, your mother and me have too much to celebrate. You took too long to get married. You're just like me. Now remember that I am older, I am more than eight years old, so I can't wait longer to become grandfather.

_ Hold your horses, Gandalf. We are not thinking about that issue yet. You and mom are too hasty.

_ Did your hear that, Sara? Are you going to let him too such cruelty to an old man like me? I just want to see a smile in my grandson's face.

_ Stop with this blackmail! You're young enough to wait for our children. And you'll see their graduation in college.

_ And you, Peter. I could use some help in here!

_ What I think is that Hermes is a lazy man. He took too long to go up to the altar and probably will take the same time to procreate.

_ Thanks, Pal!

_ And you Deni?

_ I think they still have a lot to do before to put a child in this story.

_ I, in the position of future grandmother, support their decision. I have much experience, because I had Hermes right after my wedding, and this "crying baby" complicated our romance.

_ This is my mother.

_ Who would tell the great golden boy would get tight to one only chick for so long?

_ What?

_ Thanks again, Peter!

_ Didn't you know, Sara? Since I was a little brat I see this man parading with an amazing variety of a respectable team of beautiful ladies. When he was a soccer play was a crazy time. The groupies didn't let one minute of peace to him. The poor guy was broken. They were completely drawing his energy. Why do you think he quit? Rumors say he did to study, but I assure you he did it because he was over.

_ You never mentioned this time of your life.

_ That's not exactly like that. This man is lying. I always had too much respect for the girls.

_ Yes, I see.

_ Don't you worry, Sara. I know Hermes for a long time, and I do not remember of too much girlfriends. Peter is just kidding. But who didn't enjoy the adolescence? I dated a lot!

_ Thanks Denise!

_ What? You'll have too much to explain later, Denise.

_ I am just combating fire with fire, my dear. Didn't you try to bother them? Dido did I.

_ Now let's make a toast to the happiness of my son and his beautiful wife. I am not an owl father, but I think Sara made a great choice. You my dear, had an excellent option when you chose this lad, who is an example of man, honest, friend and upright. Few times in my long life I had chance of knowing people like him. I am also sure he did the best choice of his life when he chose you as wife and companion.

_ He is following the steps of his father

_ My dear Jardell, if this is the formation you give to the major of your students, then the world will really become a better place to life, because all the young students I see in here tonight possess the same qualities of our beloved son.

_ I am sure these brilliant minds will spread too much light in this planet!

CHAPTER 11

THE COMPANY OF THE PARANORMALS

After the graduation of the first class of paranormal students, mister Vasconcellus knew that would be necessary a future regulation of the psychics activities, to prevent any negative impact over the structures of the society. He had notion that some part of the psychics would not resist the facilities that their power provide, and the temptation of acting in self benefit despite the rules and the interests of the others would be overwhelming to them. Mister Vasconcellus had full awareness that he was creating a new step in the mankind evolution, and that only those were part of this new condition would be able to stop the criminal ambition of those transgressors ones. These law agents, trained and disciplined, should not only act to punish, but mainly to prevent; educate and intimidate the future mental bandits. To make the sensitive people, less accustomed to honesty, think twice before set themselves in the cunning world.

During several years he prepared studies about this concern and sent them to the federal government of the most important countries, but as always happens, the politicians didn't take his proposals seriously, principally because they didn't believe in the reach of the mind powers, that the paranormals were nothing but a band of magicians, illusionist and pranksters, and yet they were really owners of special abilities, they would merely become future tellers or another circus attraction. Nor even the reputation of some of the most important scientists of the world, who were preoccupied with the rhumbs that the civilization would take after the paranormal events, was capable to remove them from their bias. However, the irrefutable scientific proof of the extra sensorial powers made the governors be taken of overwhelming amazement and dazzle that became almost impossible to convince them some of this medians that were being lifted on the super heroes conditions could represent a serious hazard to the society. They believed that people who endowed with so many outstanding abilities would naturally be illuminated beings which mission would be to serve and protect all the mankind. The euphory lasted some years. Afterwards, the population began to understand that these alleged semi-gods were nothing but ordinary people, just like everyone else, they just were more capable than the rest, and they weren't predestinated to lead the citizens to some sort of holy land, and the better their intentions were, they simply didn't were wiser than the common man, and they shouldn't be simply taken as example of virtue and altruism, for they were subject to commit the same mistakes of those who barely able to use a remote control. And the most important, that they could represent a serious risk to the order of the world.

As always, the humanity was getting used to the paranormal people as they did to anything, and the astonishing of the beginning was decreasing, and the people began to understand that some these psychics were bearer or some dangerous vicious and moral flaws that the major of the ordinary criminals, who didn't deserved special treatment, on the contrary, they should be treat as any other people who commit felonies, with the exception they required specific measures to be arrested and judged. After this moment, the constant warnings of mister Vasconcellus were finally heard. Commissions were created to study the impact of future problems caused by the sensitive people, and due the president of the foundation was the greatest specialist in this issue, he was invited to be the chairman of these commissions. Manifold purposes were sent to the international entities to regulate, prevent and combat the ethic detours of the uses of the ESP. these purposes were transformed into law projects and set to the UN, and little by little they were being debated and vowed. After some time, the need of some kind of control over the sensitive people proved to be urgent. A large number of psychic ones was getting in the work market every year, and a tiny parcel of them, but considerable, was using their abilities to have inappropriate advantages or to commit some crimes. The most common cheats was the capture of others thoughts looking for valuable information, the predictions of the numbers of lotteries, the alteration of games results throughout the telekinesis and industrial espionage. Many psychics used to work as private detectives, and their greatest clients were husband and wives who were suspecting about the reliability of the spouses. These incautious were at the mercy of psychics who scanned their minds and plucked the suitable information without further considerations. A growing number of customers were using regularly these kind of service, and the falling in the hands of criminal savers, who were wining "rivers of money" with their confusion and suffering. The police just paid a closer attention when people began to die, victimized by emotional crimes, and decided to interfere. All a assembly of specific laws was elaborated to avoid the action of psychics with scrupulous. Interests, secrets and estates had to be preserved of these new human abilities, and so as any technological innovation required proper regulation, so does the paranormal phenomenon should be adjusted to the way of life of the society. However, it was almost impossible to normal police officers and district attorneys to take care of people who were beyond their control, it became clear to the government that psychics should investigate psychics, and the creation of an agency to deal with the new legislation about the paranormal phenomenon was imminent, and some time later, when a former student of the foundation was invited to assume the job as secretary of defense. Mister Anton Araujh was adept of the ideas of mister Vasconcellus since he was an apprentice. He acted effectively on the concretization of the projects approved by the UN, and short after his nomination was formally born the Company of the Paranormals.

One by one, the agents were being selected and hired, coming mainly from the boards of federal investigation agencies. A headquarter was specially constructed to the special needs of sensitive investigators, with rooms and offices in shapes and colors to enhance their performance; cabinets of mental recomposing; where they could better regain the energy spent in exhaustive missions; and ultimate technology equipment to facilitate all the process of sift crimes, stalk suspects and maintain surveillance. Investigations methodologies and tactical actions, which were being elaborated for so long, were finally concluded and the works began. The agents should head their investigations according to those assembly of laws, and also help to define new psychic crimes, which weren't covered by justice yet. Proper presidios were being developed to receive these special criminals, avoiding they could escape or to continue committing felonies behind bars. Penitentiary agents, gaolers and all the workers who should maintain contact with these prisoners should be trained psychics, to help to contain the powers of the convicted ones. Mister Vasconcellus and his son were invited to be special technique consultants, with decision power over the rhumbs of the company. Was their duty the approval of each agent, and if they found necessary, could fire or suspend any worker who wasn't keeping an acquitted of responsibility behavior as police officers. The agents weren't allowed to carry and use guns. They should immobilize or defend themselves only by the use of their abilities. They were in charge to analyze any suspect of bad conduct of the paranormal people, and for being associated to the international police, they had disposal of action in practically every country in the planet. The agency was a success since the beginning, and they acquired a lot of credibility and respect from governments and populations alongside the years, due to their impeccable acquittal and good will with the common citizens.

When assumed the command of the company, Peter received a very well administrated enterprise, which was functioning with a very good performing. Even so, he promoted a general restructure, which would allow the company to work in a more rational manner, what would save time and money and even obtain better results. Higher level paranormals were promoted, new guidelines were adopted and the investigations methods were improved and abridged, what allowed the agents to work in several cases at the same time. Since its creation, the company had never lost the life of any agent. The few combats among police officers and bandits had never result in death to any side, and the agents tried to do anything to keep it like that. But it didn't mean they didn't face situations of great hazard, on the otherwise, many times they were in front of very dangerous criminals, who were powerful and well armed and eager to escape by any means, and only the perfect syntony between the equips of psychic agents considerably decreased the occurs of lethal or serious wounds. Each team was integrated by a leader more other 08 agents that would be divided into four pairs when they were in the field. The groups were formed according to the abilities of each component. The leaders were responsible for the distribution of the tasks, to follow each step of the investigation, the safety of each member and to provide information to the immediate director. Thirty teams were distributed in this way, and the quality of each component compensated the low number of agents, once was very difficult to hire new employees when the private work market offered possibility of astronomic earns, and the government couldn't compete with enterprises which offered perks as extra bonus and share options, and no dangerous situation at all. However, the effective number was considered appropriated by the secretary of defense, which preferred to invest in the qualification of the workers. But the great trump of the company was the competency of the directors, who worked with the big star, Peter Moll.

Dan lee, psychic level 06, 38 years old, was the first director assistant. He was graduated at the Mesmer school for sensitive students, the first institution created after the success of the foundation. Chinese, he was the most calm person in the company, and since child had the dream of becoming an agent of the law. As his father, as soon as he completed his psychic studies, at the age of 20, he enrolled at the academy of police, and as a sensitive cop he was responsible for the solution of dozens of cases of drug dealers. His mental powers were always connected to this tenacity and professional perspicacity. All of his brothers and sister were also students at the Mesmer school, and achieved levels ranging from 03 to 05, and as him, they followed the police career. It was very rare to happen of every siblings in a family become paranormals, yet over the level 02, and the Lee family knew how to take advantage of this plenty of psychics. In more than one occasion they gathered forces to solve cases and arrest the most violent members of quadrille of armory dealers. They also counted on each other abilities to protect themselves from possible revenge from the criminals. It became history when they were investigating a death squad gang formed by corrupt cops, who sold protection and confidential information to the worst bandits, what tramped prisons and solution of crimes. Concerned about the participation of some department mates, Dan convoked his siblings to help him in the case, once he couldn't even trust in his superiors, who could be involved with the gang, even some of his best friends.

Dug Lee, one of his brothers, level 05 and specialist on mind monitoring and to obtain felony prove indications, began to stalk the steps and thought of those indicated by Dan, with the proper authorization of the court. Within a few days, he not only had tracked sufficient data, which confirmed Dan's suspects, as also discovered another serious crime. The gang was stealing apprehended drugs and replacing them by chemical products. Dana Lee, level 04, expert on the crafts of psychic defense, and Doc Lee, telepath level 03, were in charge of the protection. Dina Lee and Horatio Lee, the youngest, both level 03, escorted Dan in his diligences, and used their powers to scan each corner of the suspect venues without leave anything unnoticed. In a few days all the legal procedures were ready and all the involved polices, who did not distrust in any moment, began to be arrested. The ambient in the police departments was terrible. Dan and his brothers began to be rejected and discriminated by a great part of their colleagues. Some cop mates, who were not involved with these crimes; but who were loyal to their friends, were revolted with what they considered a huge betrayal with the corporation, and wanted to have them out of the institution, and decided to prepare a vengeance against the family lee. They planned to begin by killing the Horatio, who they considered the weaker of the Lees, and so on, until they could get the most powerful of them. in a first tentative, they had their coffee poisoned in a district where he worked. Two other colleagues of him were killed by the terrible substance. Horatio wasn't seriously harmed because the criminals didn't know his ability of immunization. In the moment he felt something strange slipping through his throat, he entered in profound concentration and isolated the poison until he was helped by the paramedics. Unfortunately he couldn't help his mates. When Dian heard the news, she distrusted it could have been work of some kind of vengeance and immediately called her siblings so they could figure out how to proceed. Without other alternative, the desperate assassins concluded the only solution would be total termination in a single tentative, and tried to elaborate a outstanding plan.

The opportunity appeared when the brothers Lee reunited in an abandoned house, in the suburbs, attracted by the discovering of a drug warehouse, which belonged to the squad they had just arrested. Dan's intuition rang, alerting him about the hazard, when they already inside the place and surrounded by the bandits. He just had time to scream to his siblings to look for protection. The 17 policemen entered shooting their guns machines and laser weapons. In the great confusion installed, were heard explosions and the sound of bullets flying everywhere, but the counter attack of psychic abilities wasn't heard of seen. Dan dematerialized and appeared behind the enemy lines and whacked several of his opponents. Dug set fire on the clothes of others, and Dana, with her capacity of controlling electrical impulses, generated an unbearable pain in the nerves of another group of criminals. Doc finally vanquished the rest of them, by breaking their legs and arms, using his capacity of changing the pressure in specific points of the bodies. In the end of the attempt, five corrupt police officers were dead, and the others seriously wounded. All the Lee siblings were been hit, but without further gravity, and just Dina required special cares. Within few weeks they were already re-established. With the repercussion, Dan Lee was invited to join the task force of the company of the paranormals. As he was disappointed with his department, promptly agreed. His wife Nicca and his three kids; Fhya; Robbie and Shynaya; who were already studying in the Mesmer School, enjoyed his decision. They thought he wouldn't be in danger anymore. Dan wanted to dedicate more time to his family. After some years, all of his siblings followed his steps.

Diana Maris was the second director assistant, and responsible for the accountant of the company. At the age of 35, and graduated in management, she was paranormal level 06, and was in charge to inspect the financial support of the investigations. Spends with hotels, transports, vehicle rentals, insurance, feeding, manifold payments, medical expenses and damage paying passed through her severe sieve. Divorced without kids, she was tender and treated cherish everyone, and loved to use her premonition capacity to advise and help her colleagues on solving their professional and affective problems. Living with a cousin also divorce, Sheyla, and her two kids, Samuel and Sondra, Diana took a peaceful life outside the company. None neighbor could conceive that dainty woman, almost a porcelain doll, who spoke in a soft voice, was responsible for the arrest of a great number of dangerous bandits around the world. With her look of charming gorgeous business woman was easy to her come close, without rise suspects, of criminals who were under investigations, what facilitated the solution of the cases. As Sheyla needed to have two jobs to maintain her high life standard without the cooperation of her former husband; who didn't have any condition to help anyway, Diana participated actively on the growing of the two kids, and usually took them to stroll in the amusement parks, in the club and other places the little ones enjoyed. She also sponsored their education. The children loved the plays She made up with her capacities, what they believed were magical powers, and this way the three ones spent the Saturday afternoons, flying some inches above the living room floor; making the toys to levitate, and pretending they were in a rocket. The two kids loved when she created colored lights around them, and when she materialized tiny clay dolls. Besides, she took care of their alimentation and healthy with the same zeal and attention she used in the company. She wasn't a great fan of woos, and only sporadically accepted males invitations to dinner and dance. Her life summed to the family she adopted as hers.

Normally, she was just scaled to actively participate on a mission when businessmen or people from the high society were involved. Her elegant and fancy aspect didn't suit with cases of different nature. Diana never needed to use her abilities to harm someone, physically, her tasks usually consisted to obtain privileged information and in the logistic support of her team. Each agent of the company should participate once and while on the field work, and combat the paranormal crime. Even those ones that were in charge of the office work had to exercise their abilities. The directory believed it would help them to be prepared to any emergency. Diana Maris was part of this group, and only when was extremely necessary she gave her grace on the battlefield. But when she was fighting, all her fragility disappeared, being replaced by the tenacity and determination of a fearless woman. Since she was a child she had this peculiarity. On extreme situation or under heavy pressure, she became another person, and the shy girl gave place to an aggressive one. It was like that when at the age of 12, in a car travel with her parents, the car violently crashed with another vehicle, which fled without help her family car, which was off road, falling from a cliff and stalling several times. The car was completely destroyed, but at this time the young girl had already some capacities well developed, and she could create a mental shield around her, and she left the accident unharmed, although her parents weren't that luck, and were seriously wounded. Desperate and without get any aid, she had to make a strong effort to pull them out of the wrecks. Her cellular phone was broken, and she had to haul them for about two and a half miles, helped by her yet weak ability of levitation, until she found a police patrol. Even with the aid of her mental skill she had to use all her strength, while she fought against the affliction of seeing her father bleeding to death. Using each fiber in her body she could save the life of her mother, who had multiple broken bones. Diana also had to deal with the scorn of some drivers who passed by them without give any help. Di and her mother took a long time to recover from the traumas and the pain of the loss. With the pass by of the years, the afflicted chores of a productive paranormal adolescent, her life regained the regular path. Her mother got married again, giving her a little brother, Doug. Years later, she was invited by her school friend, Hermes Vasconcellus, to work in the company, becoming one of the firsts hired agents.

Deborah Spitz was a pretty afro-American woman, and at the age of 32 she conserved the perfect body from the time she was a professional dancer in a successful around the world rap group. Despite dance was her great passion, she decided to decrease the tiring work rhythm and make only sporadic presentations, to follow an old dream, to help the world to become a better place to live in. when she was 28, she applied to a job in a governmental agency, which was being created, and thanks to the indication of mister Paracelsus, who was the principal of the psychic school where she studied and closer friend of the secretary of defense, she was immediately accepted. There she found a perfect ambient to develop her humanitarian projects, once all her colleagues shared her ideals. The psychic person who decided to work in the company of the paranormals instead make a fortune in the private initiative, mainly those who were above the 4th level, was before anything an idealistic. It was very common to see psychic people becoming millionaires within few years of labor. And almost all of then had an outstanding life standard, above of the average of other professions in the richest countries. During six years Deborah had a glorious career, traveling through all continents, working in several musical groups. When she was 21 years old quit the crafts college to follow a troupe of performing ballerinas. At this time she had already been graduated in 12 different psychic abilities, some of which she considered completely useless, as the majority of the abilities of the majorities of the paranormal students, as her power to create light rays around her body or her capacity to change the properties of some small portions of liquids, transforming them into something else, as water into wine or ink into wax. Of another ones she appreciated much, as her capacity to decrease her body heat in any closed ambient. This way she was never hot, even when she was on the beach under a caustic sun. She could use the clothes she wanted independent of the season of the year. She enjoyed her ability to sense and analyze smells, better than the most of the animals. She did not need to smell the odors, which sometimes were extremely unpleasant, because she didn't use her not, but her brain to process the information obtained through the scanning of some molecules let on the air. This way she avoided havoc or poisoned food, recognized people who had passed on the same places, and even noticed the odor of some diseases, before they were detected by the exams, and she could tell to the sick people before it was too late. She could also know if her boyfriends had been with other women even if they had already taken a bath. What she considered the funniest was her capacity to see through solid objects, like clothes; walls and vehicles. Her ethic didn't allow her to use this expedient to sneak other people's privacy, the most of the time. Usually she didn't try to see if some of the handsome guys who were flirting with her were well doted. But she used it a lot in her missions to verify if someone was transporting hidden drugs, weapons or explosives. Her family didn't agree, on the first moment her decision to leave the dance aside to become a sort of policewoman. Her parents had been professional dancers, and since she was a toddler they had projected on her all theirs expectations and frustrations. They wanted her to become a paranormal only to improve her dace skills. Her two years older, Selton, supported her to convince dad and mom to accept and respect her choice. They didn't understand why she was abandoning a career that would project her for a long time yet, argued she could do anything when she retired from the stage. But patiently she made them understand that her ideals were priority to her heart, and she couldn't dance well when her heart was committed with something else. Nevertheless she wouldn't stop dancing, she would just decrease it considerably. In her four years of company, she got to conciliate her schedules to have time to rehearsal and participate on shows and presentations with some famous artists who were still her friends, and maintain her promise to her parents, and soon became the third director assistant.

Pablo Hernan was a 28 years old Bolivian, very tall and very thin. His slovenly look gave him something of professor nuts, crazy and airy. But this impression was completely wrong. He was agile, fast thinking and impulsive. No detail escaped from his snoop eyes. His accuracy of mind made him a straight and inflexible man, and his obstinacy was as unbreakable as his strong convictions, and when he believed to be in the right way fought tirelessly to establish his point of view. From all the directors of the company, he was the most intransigent defendant of the human rights. It was almost an obsession to him, and for many times he canceled operations in the last minute for do not consider them sufficiently safe to the innocent people who could be around, permitting the flee of the suspects. But he was also the most ardent and rough director on the fight against the psychic criminality. More than his companions, he knew how much harm the human evil could do, because he felt it in his own flesh, through his family. His salvation was to have received a scholarship in the foundation when he was 05 years old. Two years later all his relatives were slaughtered by a drug dealers gang, as a punishment by the fact his father, a senator and chairman of a commission of investigation about the traffic mob, refused to receive a bribe to destroy evidences that incriminated many powerful authorities. The little Pablo never recovered completely of the trauma caused by the hideous crime. And yet became revolted by the fact the killings were never solved and the killers convicted. Throughout all his childhood and adolescence he fed hopes that, once graduated, he could make the justice to prevail, by punishing the assassins of his beloved beings. He didn't want a bloody revenge, his nature wouldn't allow that, but just wanted to see them behind bars for the rest of their miserable lives, and avoid they could continue to harm other people's families.

The long years of studies and training didn't cool his thirst for justice, and he was old enough, about 15 years old, helped by some mates, he began a self investigation, by distance, to identify and trace the profile of each one of the hangmen of his relatives. Hs greatest relief was to possess an ability which made easier this task, the capacity to get out of his body, in spirit, totally lucid, and do whatever he was pleased. He could even visit the spiritual colony where his family was living since they were murdered, and that usually brought great comfort to his hurt heart. They tried to make him understand how useless this work would be, and it was better to forget it all and move on with his life. Unfortunately he did not accept this idea. He didn't want to accept that the fact of his family was well could be used as an excuse to the impunity of those killers. He believed to be acting in the defense of their future victims. He guessed when people left this world, beside their bodies, they also left behind the all the passion and eager that made people fight for their ideals. But he was still made of flesh and bones, and couldn't simply abandon the emotions that were the strongest side of his personality, and this fight would be his greatest motivation to achieve his goals. After a long and tedious period of scrutiny he and his mates accomplished the work. But he was too young and did not have the required experience to face a powerful and violent organization. He had to keep exercising his patience and remain studying and developing is abilities until the right time shows up.

The opportunity appeared when at the age of 20 he achieved the maturity of his abilities. At this time Pablo was studying geology, just like his father, for three years, and thought it was time to put his plan in motion. He traveled to his hometown for the first time since the tragedy. He couldn't even come to the funeral, and for some years he lived in great fear the murderers could catch him in his school. To his deception he found out that the most of his enemies had already been killed, by the bloody dispute of rival gangs. The few ones who lasted were in a such state of physical and moral penury, that he understood that sooner or later they would be naturally swept out of the surface of the planet, and then he comprehended what his father, mother and siblings tried during years to make him see in his astral projections, that many times the nature is in charge to make the people pay for their crimes and mistakes. Pablo decided he wouldn't put the last shovel of soil in these criminal graves, and that rage wouldn't have place in his chest anymore, once he verified these poor devils were already receiving what they deserved, and should be let to their own luck. With the soul relieved he left behind his tragic past, and came back to his studies carrying only the heritage of a honest life lived in dignity of his family. His ancestors had taught him the believes that cosmic laws rule the universe, and all creatures would be agents of use and control of the ethic of the nature, and he returned decided to do his part to help society to transform itself into something better, where families could raise their children in peace.

When Pablo concluded his mastership was hired to work in a spatial agency, to utilize his ability to project his spirit throughout space, and use his scientific knowledge to analyze the surface of mars, collaborating in the work of reconstruction of a life environment in the red planet. His facility on abandon for some time his carnal organism was amazing. At any moment and place he could be absent, visiting somewhere else in the speed of the thought and returning before anybody could notice the fact. Many times he used this practice in places where they were not common, while he was driving, letting it in the "automatic pilot" to better see something that caught his attention on the road; or when he was dancing in a party, he let his skeleton shaking alone and flew back home to check out something. He just couldn't interact with the ambient, once he was in another dimension, but had total freedom of observation. After two years of work, he got tired of the monotony of walking through the deserts of Mars and quit. He wanted to do something more adventurous and when he heard about the company of the paranormals decided to become part of this project.

In the beginning, mister Vasconcellus didn't approve his option, for he intended to 6th level of his former student a great academic career, but after Pablo promises of continuing with the help in the conquer of Mars, he agreed. Then Pablo passed to utilize his abilities on the protection of innocent people from the perverted action of the paranormal phenomenon. His capacities were very well accepted by the corporation mates. Mainly his capacity of changing the color of his hair, eyes and cutis for some hours, as well as his astral projection power. After just few years he was promoted to forth director assistant. Once among his equals, felt again integrated to a community, just like in the old days of the foundation when he was part of the association young paranormals. In the company he found the woman who would become his great passion, the exuberant Suzanne Binoche, his former schoolmate, and the only girl that touched the core of his heart, when they had a short affair, despite the fact she considered him a little slow, as she liked to call him slow motion. But he became more and more bothered by her fad of asking him to turn into a blond man all the time they went out. At the beginning he thought she was fan of an old movie star, Brad Pit, but later he distrusted she wanted him more alike to Tharus Vendra. With his systematic refuses she got tired of him and broke up. Since then the lonely boy enjoyed just to keep a platonic crush on her, and now, to work with her would be an inexhaustible source of pleasure.

Suzanne Binoche, the fifth director assistant, was completely a hot woman. At the age of 26 and tall as a model, the powerful channel black hair girl awaken the greed of practically every men, and she used to say that only one kind of man didn't get hard with her looks, the dead ones, because even the gays felt regret for their option when they saw her. She had complete notion of the impact of her curves on the males of her specie, and since early age learnt how to take advantage on that, by increasing her seductive style, enhancing her perfect body in tight clothes and deep pruning, what she inherit from her mother, just like her inconstancy in love. Her mother got married six times, and had a child on each matrimony. Suzanne was a fruit of her third wedding, and had yet other seven siblings from her father's part. However, from him she was heiress of his sense of responsibility and honesty. This way she permitted herself to tease, play and date a lot, but she didn't do anything that would compromise her plans to the future, like not desired pregnancy or lousy husbands. She wanted to be completely safe of her feelings when surrounded to a real love, to whom she would love enough to give heirs. At the age of five, her stepfather enrolled her in the foundation's school, after she was approved on the mind exams, trying to get rid of a hyperactive child he couldn't stand. Once there she didn't receive many visits of her family, who seldom times remembered to pick her up to vacations trips, and the passing by of the time made her mates to become her unique source of affection. When she understood of her physical gifts, and their impact over the boys, she began to abuse of these features to get attention and respect, and even the girls, who normally were very envy, were happy on her side. The only school mate she would have given everything he wanted, and ever thought about getting married using a bride's dress, and have a bunch of brats was Tharus Vendra, her first infatuation. But he assumed a steady relationship with anybody. Since she was a young child, the perfection of his face and his magnetic character, created an indelible impression over her romantic soul, and once in the adolescence, they lived a brief but torrid love affair, the distant and strayed behavior of Tharus regarding to all women, caused much suffering and sadness in her sociable affective spirit, who was eager for attention and cherish. The boyfriend, who was till then charming, with his eerie aspect, became only introspective and taciturn on her eyes that didn't fit on her warmth and ardent personality. Even though, they had unforgettable moments of pleasure, until the moment she found out he was still going out with his former girlfriend. However she felt relieved with the situation, once she wouldn't have to deal with the consequences of a regular relationship, and she would be free to have experiences with other guys, what was her primary desire.

Her powers were as aggressive as her, in an amazing symbiosis. She had a fearless strong personality, and didn't accept to take any insolent answer back home, and was always "buying her friend's fishes", trying to solve their quarrels. She was always searching for trouble in the streets, and frequently get annoyed by rush drivers who were crossing the red light, or put other's people lives in danger, just to save some seconds. In these occasions, she used to stare furiously to the tires of the car, almost instantly a bang was heard and the tires were getting flat slowly. Then she passed by the incautious driver and looked at them with cynical smile. But when the transgressor let her more angry, she was capable to blast other parts of the vehicles. She didn't do it only in the traffic, but in another kind of transgressions, which let her outraged by the impunity of the criminals. Many times her mates tried to advise her to do not nosy in a straight way in other people's lives. She always agreed with them, recognizing her lack of self-control, but when another situation was presented to her, the blood began to boil in Suzanne's head and she did it again. Many times she stalked somebody, who had done something wrong and ran, to try to make them see what they had done, but in the deep of her mind she wanted them to react negatively so she had an excuse to beat them. She jumped over them, using her martial arts skills, and kicked and punched them violently, but not sufficient to cause great harms, and in a few minutes she had marked her point of view. Seldom times she was forced to use her psychic abilities to solve a fight, usually when there were more than five opponents or when someone was carrying a gun.

That was Suzanne, a vibrant and full of human heat woman, who loved life and freedom. Her friends adored her, for they knew how helpful and loyal she could be. That's why Hermes thought about her to integrate the lines of the company. Nobody better than him to know about her potential to fight for the justice, of any possible means, once he had been observing her since she was a teenager, and they even had a shallow affair when she got into college. The captivating charm of this "Walkiria" would be a great weapon on the combat against the crime. Her twelve abilities, between them the capacity to fly; the telekinesis; mental shield; electric impulse control and energy balls creation, allied to her boldness and courage, made her a complete policewoman and an outstanding agent, and she never worked in another place but the company. Suzanne loved to travel and have fun, that's why she coursed tourism in college. She would never fit in a monotonous paper work behind a desk. Her first dream was to manage a hotel company around the world, but the creation of the agency to control the psychic crimes made her change her plans. The perspective of joining her pleasure of traveling with her pleasure of kicking asses, and have permission to use her skills turned her head, and she couldn't conceive anymore another life style.

Argos Numy Buzzolor, the sixth director assistant, also known as the Joker, was the personification of the sympathy. As his alias suggested, he was always showing his teeth, even if he was tense or nervous, in large smiles or laughs, as if it was a sort of twitch. Extrovert and funny, he knew how to make the stories much more interesting. With friends, in the parties, he was always the center of the attention, amusing people with his gags an spirituous comments. Born in Angola, soon he lost his parents, killed in an endless civil war. He and his four older brothers were sent to a refugee camp, when a Swedish couple, who were volunteers in the doctors without border, fell in love with the little happy smiling kid, and as he didn't accept to be separated from his siblings, they were all adopted and taken to the new home. As his foster parents, at the age of five, Argos passed on the test and began to study in the foundation of mister Vasconcellus. The Joker had been always Peter's best friend, to who he always treated as an younger brother, who needed his guidance. His inclination to the studies was not very strong, and he wasn't worried about that. Very early he noticed the great financial potential of the paranormal phenomenon, and focused on that, to have an easier life with much money and always surrounded of beautiful chicks. He was always much more concerned about his appearance than with his grades, and as he knew he wasn't as any Denzel Washington or Lenny Kravits, decided to invest all his cards on the development of his muscles. He would sculpt it, and one day he would be known as the body. For years and years he practiced weight lifting, and built a perfect body, and even won some prizes in the professional circuit. Totally satisfied with his height and shape, he enjoyed enhancing his muscles with tight shirts, and to exhibit his iron carved abdomen and his thick legs in bath suits on the beach or at the swimming pool. Besides, with the self-confidence of a psychic level 06, his charm made him irresistible to the most parcel of women. The guys of the foundation were always looking for to be on his side on the Saturday night fever at the techno parties. Great dancer of electronic music, he knew how to be seductive on the right timing, and at these moments there would be enough girls to all of his friends.

When invited to join the company, in the beginning he saw it as just an opportunity to have a reasonable job, with a great job. Once he would have acquired experience as an agent, he could leave and work where he would have the chance to become millionaire. In a first moment he did nothing but filling paper work, having coffee with the mates, and to talking on the phone with friends. Yet, little by little he was getting taste for the thing, and began to use more and more his telepathic powers to help his mates on their investigations. His gift of transmutation of small objects, that was used before only to impress the chicks, became an important tool on the combat to the crime. However, as he used to say that wasn't born to become a saint, he didn't let to escape any chance to take advantage on anything. Iggy Sander, another childhood mate, who was a sensitive cop level 03, was always asking for his cooperation on the investigations of difficult solution. As the young Buzollor had the capacity to sense energy from the victims throughout their personnel objects collected on the crime scene, Sander used to consult him about the identity of the criminals. He was better than a DNA exam. Argos didn't want to take the credit, he let it to his ambitious friend, he was interested only in the gifts Sander used to give him. As the most complicated the case was the best was the present, which could range from exclusive tickets on important games to dinners in fancy restaurants and travels or clothes. Many murderers and drug dealers were behind bars thanks to their cooperation, and Iggy won many promotions and medals. Once as it was almost impossible to identify a serial rapist, who was frightening the dwellers of a small village, Sander asked for his help one more time. However the evidences weren't helping much, and the captain Sander entered in Numi's office with a plastic bag in a hand and two tickets to a show in the other. A tiny religious medal was enough to the concentration of Argos, who just took the relic in his fingers, and within a few minutes created a mental link with the rapist, raising all his file and his exact location, and as the den where he hid the souvenirs taken from the victims. The police officer got another promotion and Argos conquered the woman of his dreams during the presentation of the international rock band.

Nobody could guess that porcelain Japanese doll were actually a fierce and completely crazy woman. The small Kim Hiroko, 25 years old, amazed people all the time with her acts and the way she dressed up. Sometimes she was dressed up like a western businesswoman, acting like that, another times she wore out just like an innocent student girl or a subservient "gueixa", and even as an eastern "Madonna". And each clothing was followed by on of her multiple facets. Her personality presented very distinctive and exotic nuances, where some days she was expansive and talkative, and in others introspective and almost mute, in some occasions explosive and aggressive, in others very calm and tender. She was absolutely unpredictable, but two things didn't varied, her taste for the bizarre and odd, and her almost suicidal attraction for the danger. Many times she put her life in risk in a direct approach of some investigation just to make prevail her point of view. To jump over high speed cars, to cross gun fires in a linger walk, get into fights when she was alone, to swim with sharks, to challenge dangerous criminals, were some of her routines. Just like Lucy Liu, she had great facility to get rid of entangles, keeping harmless her perfect dawn skin. She was also famous for her astonishing legs, and her life style. The location and decoration of her flat depictured perfectly her eccentricities. She lived alone in a commercial area, and all the furniture and walls were dark green, and seemed like a Japanese futuristic comic book. In one of the rooms there were special gadgets for her erotic plays with her sporadic boyfriends. Addicted in television, she had plastic ones in each room, hung on the wall as big paintings, even in the bathroom, and the ambient sound ran each corner.

Kim and her older sister, Yoko, were completely different, what usually drove their parents crazy when they were young. While the second took a safe life with her husband and kid, Sato, working as chemical in a cosmetic factory, Kim's chores were in constant danger, where many times she seemed to be playing Russian roulette with the destiny, just to prove she could win, and even in her most noble actions there were a self destructive component, and a sadist-masochist behavior. Despite loving to live, or even because of it, she was always trying to test her limits to come back in total plenitude. The fact her family was away two generations from their ancient traditions, may have contributed to the shock of values that was evident in her attitudes, or she was simply crazy.

To leap from a moving car to another was a radical maneuver to a paranormal girl who did not have the capacity to fly, but she just loved to do it. One of the most used abilities of this psychic level 06 was the prompt cellular reconstruction. A wound that would take weeks to heal in a normal person required just one or two days to her. She had also lost the count of the times she was shot, acid or fire burns, perforations by laser shots and electrical shocks were "small coffee" in her language. She always enjoyed her capacity of hypnotizing almost every people. it was enough just a peer at the person, and in a second he or she was sent to a dream world. However, her most amazing gift was the capacity to create small objects by the manipulation of atoms of the atmosphere. Practically all her bangles were manufactured by this way. She had to concentrate in each detail, and within few minutes the molecules began to gather according to her wishes, giving shapes to her thoughts. The biggest object she had ever got to make was a gun she used to defeat a group of delinquents, who had kidnapped her to avoid their leader, a dangerous terrorist, was discovered. The revolver was so perfect, she created it while they were trying to strip her off, that the laser shots destroyed the entire warehouse, hurting the most of the delinquents, giving her the chance to flee and call back up. She also used it for a long time, without need to recharge. For these and other incredible feats, despite her bizarre methods and her peculiar behavior, she was promoted so young, and became the seventh of the directors assistants of the company, according to mister Vasconcellus, who always believed in her potential.

Denise Tanner could be considered the perfect woman in every sense. Of those girls men usually dream to take straight to the altar. Beautiful with a magnificent red hair, blue eyes and an ideal body, very intelligent, responsible and above all, a bright spirit and good feelings, she was the most reliable friend someone could ever have. She would do anything she could to help someone, without measure efforts. Since she was a child, Denise and her two younger sisters had shown interest on following their parent careers, becoming doctors. As they, the girls demonstrated intention to dedicate their lives to help poor people. it was common when her mates were traveling on vacations to expensive resorts on tropical islands or skiing in the most famous spots, she and her sisters were working with their father and mother in a humanitarian force in countries of the third world. When her healing capacity began to manifest, she understood it as a confirmation of her plans, as if they were in the right rhumb. Extremely dedicated to the studies, at the age of 16 she got to pass to the medicine school, and alongside with her paranormal trainings she started to occupy her time with visits to sick people in public hospitals. This way she was getting much experience of life condition, and early comprehended that many times the wounds of the bodies or the minds couldn't be cure simply with the use of regular medicine or mental energies, that frequently just cherish, attention and disposition to a long talk were enough to produce miracles in patients who rarely received proper consolation from their relatives and friends. For having her time compromised with several and exhaustive daily activities, the red hair girl didn't have enough time in her schedule to boyfriends and parties, and in her spare time she preferred the company of some friends and her family, despite being very harassed by the guys. She avoided getting in a more serious commitment, albeit she used to flirt all the time, but never passed over the preliminaries. Occasionally he used to have a more lasting relationship, and the longest lasted almost three years, but the poor guy didn't share her dreams and aspirations, and to make it worst, had some prejudice against the paranormal people.

The true love appeared when she met the gorgeous Peter Moll. In the instant they exchanged the first words, Denise knew he would have the lead role in her life. For a long time they remained just as best friends; once they were occupied with their studies and careers. However, the passion took over her heart exactly when her eyes were being opened to the true spiritual values, and she felt that her eager were in the ideal point so her need to share her destiny blossomed. There was a new time of development to her. The maturity of the woman raised at the same proportion the reality of the selfish feelings of men were stripped in front of her fresh agent eyes at the company of the paranormals, where she had begun to work after an invitation of her boyfriend. She was still naïve, and had the purpose to contribute with her medical knowledge on the humanization of the criminal investigations. The fact she could spend more time with her beloved was very important too. However, her confident personality wasn't prepared to deal with the raw reality of the streets, crowded by false and without any trace of scrupulous people, willing to do any kind of crime and to achieve their hideous goals. For several times her life was in unnecessary danger because of her trust on people who didn't deserve it, and if wasn't her capacity to become intangible, and the prompt help of her mates, specially Peter; who was always taking care of her, she would have perished victimized by the excess of sentimental actions. She had much difficult to act moved just by reason. Her other 11 abilities had only relation with the healing capacity and health maintenance. She had the amazing gift of the atomic reconstruction of the cells, simply focusing her sight to the area for some minutes. She also could fulfill people with disposition and will to work and enjoy life. Another skill was her facility to see internal organs and make precise diagnosis just like the ultimate Ionic exams. And another that connected her with herbs and plants, what allowed her to prescribe natural remedies to sick people. All that corroborated by her scientific knowledge. With all these qualities she was raised to be the eighth director assistant.

Anne Moss was the youngest director of the corporation. She was only 22 years old, and already occupied the job for one year, invited by Peter Moll. At the beginning nobody in the company understood or enjoyed the choice, because she was an outsider, very young and did not have experience as an agent. But after some months she overcame all the expectations and proved the director was right, once more, when he put such responsibility in her hands. Friends and mates since the adolescence, he knew very well the great potential beneath that brown eyes short brown hair girl. Extremely dedicated and hard worker, she possessed qualities he believed would be of great utility to the company, besides having some weird abilities even to the patterns of the agency, once nobody else was noticed as having them, as her strange capacity t accelerate her electrical impulses, what increased ten times her speed and agility, what resembled an old super hero, and granted her the alias "The Flash". In certain occasion, she ran after a car, of which a wounded agent had lost control, and when it was almost falling from a cliff, she opened the driver door and took out her colleague, while the car was in motion, and laid him on the ground. Unfortunately she couldn't come back on time to rescue the criminal. She also had the odd capacity to let her body as hard as the hardest metal, for some time. Once, when she was shut up in a corral by a psychic delinquent, who had the ability to create spontaneous fire, the moment she noticed he had put fire on her clothes, closed her eyes and got into deep concentration, and stood still like a bronze statue. Perceiving her maneuver, the bandit still tried to destroy her by other means, throwing heavy weights over her, beating her head with a bat, and even trying to chop her. However none of the tentative got to scratch the shell her skin had turned into. At this time, her back up team arrived and captured the criminal, and they even celebrated when they found out her clothes were burnt and she was bare naked. However, her most interesting gift was her capacity to transform the rests of ingested food into pure energy, what set her free from the basic needs, as to pee and to lee. This ability was first manifested when she was 14, and during a trip to cottage of a family's friend, she didn't feel comfortable to use the filthy bathroom, and she spent two weeks without answer the call of the nature. When it became unbearable, she had no option but to concentrate deeply, giving orders to her bowels to hold on, and little by little the she used to feel the typical relief of whom just urinated and defecated. When she came back, the researchers thought she could be very ill, when she related them what had happened, but exams showed she was completely healthy. They decided to keep her under observation while she kept the procedure, they were astonished when concluded her body had found a special way to disposal the waste. Anne was allowed to continue going to the bathroom only to have a bath, to put make up and to brush her hair and teeth, and only recommended her to sporadically use the toilet vase in order to avoid an atrophy in her internal organs. And they were also afraid her anus could get closed.

Only daughter of international war correspondent journalists, who were constantly traveling to work, always letting her under the cares of a nannies, who became even responsible for her growing and education, and who enrolled her in the tests of the foundation. When her parents noticed, she was already studying in the paranormal school, and didn't even bother to go there and check the installations, where she began to live in. The little Anne used to spend the most of her free time crying around the corners, missing her former baby sitter. In this period, her newly friend, Denise Tanner was crucial to her adaptation, and they became best friends. As Denise didn't live in the campus, she was always taking her to sleep in her house, and cherish of the Tanner family appeased the solitude of the young Moss, and she practically became a new member. Despite, some years later, she become friend of Peter Moll, never occurred to her that he and Denise could be a good match. Only when they were already in the same university they finally got together, when Anne introduced Denise to Peter. To her amazement, she discovered they already knew each other. As she knew very well the qualities of the two young friends, she spent the next two years trying to convince them to become a couple. When they began to date, they elected her as their official godmother. Anne was also a super gifted student who loved to study. At the age of 20 she had already majored in psychiatry, and with 12 powers urging to be used, she didn't have time or patience to get a boyfriend, what was very difficult, once the boys didn't give truce to that honey eyes curly hair girl, who conquered a legion of fans wherever she was, with her *mignon* body and shy look. But the restrained crush he felt about a former professor, 20 years older and married with children, let her disappointed with men in a general way, when he told her that he had given up to divorce because of his kids and broke up with her. Since she was 18 she decided to stop making sex until she find the perfect man, who would definitely conquer her heart.

With a team formed by the best paranormal agents, the government decided to use them as an example and prohibited the use of lethal weapons by the officers of the company of the paranormals. None electronic device that could harm normal people was allowed. Besides, the technical qualification of the agents excused them from the use of brutal force on the solution of the most of the cases. The competence of the member of the agency was gaining more and more respect in the world scenery, and enhanced the importance of a governmental agency to regulate the sensitive actions. Their activities helped on the control and adaptation of a new stage in the human evolution, avoiding dangerous conflicts that could degenerate into a growing bias. Psychic people and regular people should learn to sum efforts, to enrich the civilization and the mankind possibilities, living a pacific and fraternal life. Extreme actions from fanatics of both sides, who just wanted to sow war and disorder; to take advantages on the riots and chaos, should be contained and restrained.

Chapter 12

The blue jackets

Tharus, the Bat, barely could hold his rage while prepared the revenge against his opponents. All his allies were already waiting for his commands, well organized. He knew that the revolutionary movement would not have the necessary strength to jettison the actual govern, and that his actuation would be decisive on this way. He had decided to begin his revenge by destroying those that were allies of his former companions on the tentative to kill his brother, Iullus, and afterwards he'd go to attack those who conspired against him. The Bat desired to taste moment of despair that certainly would take over the "shop" agent spirits, while he was allowing them to understand the extension of his powers and his thirsty for their blood, after have summarily vanquished the resistance of the unfortunate dictator that the "shop" was obligated, by contract, to protect.

The brothers Vendra, for some time already, planned to create their own organization, that would help them to put in motion their beliefs to defeat the crime in any where or any sphere of the globe. Tharus took much inspiration from the teachings of an ancient secret society, denominated alternative great fraternity, or simply "AGF". The attempt promoted by the "shop" just precipitated its execution. Logically, they didn't intend to install their projects on that end of the world, they already had acquired a huge farm on a remote area of the African desert to settle the basis and had also hired a group of architects and engineers to project the installations. However, due the circumstances, they opted by the practical and fastest solution. Besides, they would count there the facilities they would never find anywhere else, with a regular army to support them and a new govern willing to share the power for their help. Kiria was the responsible to introduce the Bat to the second in command revolutionary leader, Dino Kubrusly, a 57 years old rough man, who already was informed about the presence of paranormals in the country, and was relief when they decided to review their position changing to the freedom movement side. Immediately he entered in contact with Rheno Zoff, a gentleman, who had studied in the best Swiss schools, and was the mentor of the liberty action, who was trying for 14 years to put an end to the abuses of the despot dictator, whose had the fame of being cruel and revengeful, and a somebody once a person attacked him you can't stop anymore or he will crash down this person. However, Zoff's efforts nor even had scratched the tyrant's structure alongside those years, the results were weak in the most important fronts; the battlefield and the media. Outside the country nobody seemed to give a damn to their claims, and they didn't allured enough sympathy of other revolutionary movements around the world to receive from them financial, material or technical support, and they were forced to fight with the resources of a twenty century guerrilla group, ragged and amateur. That's why Dino and Rheno celebrated with great joy the adhesion the some of the world most powerful men and women. Inclusive the revolutionaries accepted all their demands, because they knew very well that way the chances of victory would be almost one hundred percent.

Mister Zoff gave to Vendra brothers his second biggest camp, with soldiers and all the necessary material so, from there, they were able to organize their actions. The place was a waste land and the access very difficult and the life conditions very precarious, and if wasn't the gadgets the blue jackets had brought with them, there wouldn't have the minimum decent conditions required to shelter so many people. Even though, the place would convenient serve to their purposes, and the isolation would keep them hid from the secret police. They didn't want to be in the spotlight, because they knew that the authorities didn't believe that Tharus and Iullus had left the country so easily, and would try to trace their location at any cost. Besides, the revengeful character of the tyrant, that used to severely punish the smallest slip of his functionaries, wouldn't allow pass in "white clouds" the fact that the Bat ruined his plans, and worse, kept to himself a large quantity of the payment for the service that wasn't completed.

Several times he attempted against the rebel leaders life, and if wasn't his obstinacy on capturing them alive, to personally torture them, he would have been succeed all the onsets. However, in his ignorance about the psychic abilities, he had supposed that could capture the twins Vendra on his own way, and execute them with his own weapons. But while he elaborated his outstanding plans, trying to locate the whereabouts of his former assistant Kiria, who betrayed him in a hideous way, and principally, rejected his love and dedication, throwing away a luxury life as his mistress, his secret service of intelligence ignored the fact at that time, a legion of paranormals was invading the country. Once properly installed, the Vendra brothers contacted all the people of their extreme confidence, and let Savio Nog in charge of the task to gather all the groups and head them to the exact venue. Savio, a loyal friend from the times of the shop, for several times demonstrated to be in perfect syntony with the twins ideals, and had been the first person they talked about their purposes. Irascible as a guard dog, he was willing to follow them wherever they wanted to go, observing all the guidelines chosen by the Bat. In a few weeks he organized a emergency supporting phalanx, which would be the basic group of the Vendra boys, which Tharus named as the blue jackets. Hiring some jets, Nog transported all the integrants of this new militia and the required supplies, until a stripped spot of the frontier, which should be crossed by foot. They kept hiking until the camp. Ivana Minerva, who became Iullus assistant, had helped on the preparations, willing to follow her former lover wherever he was. In a few days they finally arrived in their destiny. Tharus was very content with the quantity of colleagues and mates who answered his called, and embraced and thanked one by one. The contingent only wasn't bigger because Savio thought that it could compromise the security, and only accepted those who were the most reliable people. two days after the arrival, when everybody were already settled and rested enough, Savio convoked the presence of everyone so he could pass more information and pronounce Tharus decisions about the function of each one.

_ Here you are, people. It is a great honor to have you here with us in this difficult moment. It is time of important decisions and actions. I salute you in the name of our leaders, Tharus and Iullus, and in my name. I know you've been told about the last events, and I won't waste our time repeating them. we can't even figure out what could have happened if wasn't this little angel sat by Tharus side, Kiria. However, this sad happening just precipitate the concretization of our plans, from which you are aware, and if you are here today is because you have chosen to become part of them. we all share the same ideals, to put some order in this riot created by the actions of vile men, who destroy the nature in the name of the greed, and jeer of those who want justice, once they believe they own the world and have rights and privileges over it, and they are above good and evil. In the last years we have been confronted with unthinkable abuses without having nothing to do to repair the terrible mistakes of these worms of the land, or because we could only act in the name of those who could afford, or because they were protected by corrupted governments. During many years we have been deceived by the president of the shop, who claimed to be a justice paladin, but who actually is nothing but filthy mercenary, of those who are capable to sell the own soul for a bunch of coins. Fair well, my friends, now we can! Now we can do whatever we think is more appropriated to the world. We've being forced to act before the schedule, but what a hell can we do? Therefore, be welcome to the pawn core of the blue jackets!

Everybody stood up and turned their heads to Tharus and Iullus, and for some minutes they cheered the brothers, in a huge lark, as a band of adolescences, which they actually still were. They demonstrated unconditional support to Tharus determinations, and after that they began to chill out and sat down again in the cold ground. Tharus was very introspective and didn't feel comfortable in a huge crowd. He didn't enjoy speaking in public, and preferred to pass that task to other people. He loved to rule, but didn't appreciate the contact with the masses, so the brother spoke in his name.

_ That's all, folks! Savio has said it all, and said beautifully. I just would like to apologize for the precarious accommodations. But that was what we could provide for the moment. I know you miss the Ritz and their champagne and caviar, but I believe it is for the greater good. I'd like to say some jokes, but I am not that good at that.

_ At last you found out! – Someone shout.

_ Ok, Castor! May I proceed? Thanks. Mister Rheno Zoff, here by my side, is the commander of the local militia, and answer for the national movement. They gave us guarantees that once the defeat of the actual government is assured, we'll have all the facilities to settle down our own agency in this country and they also gave us "white card" to help them to implement all necessary measures to create an experimental territory where we will be able to apply our theories which will provide a fair and strong development to all sectors of the society. in a small scale it will provide us suitable information to a precise implementation on large scale. I mean in the whole world. All our projects we have been developing in the past years, with much study and observation, will be here used to show us what practical adjusts are required, before being applied in more complex communities. Our militants will not use their uniform, after all we are civilians, but to distinguish us from the others, we'll have our own equable, and as our name indicates, it will be in dark blue. From now on we will be characterized for use only dark blue clothes in official missions. The raincoats must be in navy blue. Our manager, Savio, provide a large stock to us. Later you'll get yours.

_ And how we will finance our actions? – Asked a new member. – Of course each one of us has a proper saving, but a work of this port requires a considerable sum, once we are intending to implement long prize measures. How we're gonna live meanwhile?

_ Good question, Hans! And you deserve a good answer, which is the following. I do not know!

_ What?

_ I'm just kidding! Gosh, nobody laughs on my jokes. I am gonna be traumatized.

_ I was laughing!

_ Thanks, Ivana. Only you understand me. Let's talk serious. Initially, our operations will be paid by the money that me and Tharus have saving for so long. We are giving to the blue jackets something about 200 million dollars. All of you will receive a proper salary. We are still planning to get some more money from our missions. We'll have proper sources. When we vanquish these parasites that took over the government, we will return the most of what they stole to the public safes, but we will keep something for us. I think that's all. Thank you very much, and let's celebrate the creation of our agency! It's party time!

On the next day, the Bat called some of his collaborators and wanted to introduce them formally to the rest of the group, and convoked another gathering. This time he decided to talk by himself.

_ I won't be long everybody. I just want you to know the hierarchy that will temporally be established to optimize the works. I am the president, of course, and Iullus the vice-president. These people here are the directors you must know, and to whom you must report your concerns; suggestions and conclusions. I do not have patience to hear complains. So don't bother me, bother them. they are, Savio Nog; Ivana Minerva; Gisele Strauss; Antonio Maia and Noriko Sato. And for those who still don't know them, they will give a brief relate. Here you are.

_ Well, I'll be the first because you've already listened to me. I know that Tharus prefers to fight against an armed group than to speak in public. So I'll be his speaking-trumpet. As you know I am Savio Nog. I am 35 years old, and I am from Canada. I have the 6th level, and have been working for 10 years in the shop. I am graduated in environmental engineering, but actually I have never worked in this area, and must have forgotten the most of what I learnt. My dream was to become an ecological terrorist, and in a certain way I believe that is what I am. If I could, I'd grab all these motherfuckers who peel seal cubs, and would do the same with them. I must confess that I have, once or two. I am expert in tactical actions and do not hesitate on using violence to accomplish my orders. To me a good bandit is a dead bandit. That's what I think you should know about me. Next!

_ I think that it is my turn. My name is Ivana Minerva. I am thirty years old. I don't believe I just said that. Well, I also have the 6th level. I have been working as special assistant in the New York's office of the blue jackets for two years. I just work with papers, and do not have any experience in the kind of work we are developing in here, as the most of you. But I learn fast. I trust in Iulus and Tharus, and I know they will teach us properly. Each single of us is an import tool to the process. I am Russian and graduated in nutrition. I'll be in charge of the food, obviously. All my powers are under the blue jackets command. That's all.

_ Hello, people. my name is Nicholas Graff. I am 30 years old and I am from Germany. I have the 6th level as well. I began my studies beside this flying rat, and I am a mechanic engineer, and I've worked in the area for sometime. You have no idea how boring was this job. "You are not understanding"! I hated every minute of it, and if God permits, I'll never work again to greed businessmen, who are just concerned about the clients needs. I am sick of these marketing people, who just want to create new ways to consume. Thanks to my good dad I am free of these relationship management courses and lectures. I was reborn when last year I was invited to organize the structure of the blue jackets. I also have been trained by Iullus, and now I am to whatever it takes. The end.

_ Hi, I am Gisele Strauss, and I do not have any problem to tell you I a 29 years old, very well lived. I know that I look 20. I am from Aquarius, and like my friends in here. I am level 6. I've worked as public relations at the United Nations until recently, when I couldn't conciliate anymore my job with the cause of my dear Tharus Vendra. When he begged I used my skill to help his cause I couldn't say no. I may not have police or military training, but the vast experience acquired in the hard work in dozens complicated countries alongside these years qualifies my position. I have no more to say.

_ Fellows, I am Maia, Antonio Maia. I am from Portugal, and I am 40 years old. I do not have academic degree like the others, but I am also level 6. I just didn't want to continue my studies because I wanted to enjoy life, and I knew that my powers were enough for what I wanted to do. I never regretted that. I had been worked as secret agent to a certain government until I was hired to work at the shop, about ten years ago. I have a simple job. I am housekeeper. I clean the mess the other agents let. I also finish the tasks the others didn't get or didn't have stomach to finish. I had been loyal to my boss, until the moment I notice his crazy behavior. He just wanted to gather money and power.

I do not have principles, but I began to hate mister Price, and when Tharus, my dear friend invited me to join his cause, I couldn't refuse. In the time we've spent together I could notice how much in common we have. As I said I do not have principles, but my employers must have. Therefore, from now on I'll be tool to the will of the blue jackets, and who cross my way will understand my alias is pit bull. What I like the most is to break bones of who challenges me. I appreciate a good fight rather sex. And I like sex a lot, believe me. Thanks for your attention! I know we will form a powerful team. To those who know how to treat me I am a very good friend. Goodbye.

_ Good evening, my dear friends! I hope good energies flow freely around our chacras. My name is Vaivet Midral, I am 28 years old, and I am a mental level 06. I am also graduated in holistic therapies. I have always worked with the equilibrium of the vital energy of the people, animals and plants, positioning and distributing better the organization of forces that are the compound the personnel cosmos. Besides, I am one of the best energy trackers that exist. I can find anybody anywhere, independent if this person is paranormal or not. That's why my alias is GPS. I also have the capacity to analyze the inner body and I can see through solid objects. My parents are also psychic, just like my two brothers. As the most of you, I studied in the same school of Tharus and Iullus too, although we didn't share the same classroom, once they are much more older, but we have been friends for so long, and for three years they have been clients of my esoteric spas. Later I'll give some discount tickets to all of you, and when you're visiting San Francisco, you may lax in there. You're gonna love it. I am also their personal massage applier, and my magic hands have helped their energetic recomposing, after some exhausting missions. Therefore, if some of you is having a back sore or too much stress, I can relief your body. It will be a great pleasure. I am here to coordinate the search and recognizing group. May the universe allow you have a perfect and productive day, always conspiring on your favor, opening you energy cannels.

After the presentation, Iullus wanted to talk for a while.

_ Very well, people. I know you all are used to much comfort and perks, and here is too cold and the hygiene conditions are not ideals, but I think if we face it in a positive perspective, I don't know, as if we were in a reality show, maybe, just maybe, our discomfort will be minimized. Soon the action will keep us occupied and we won't have disposition to pay heed in these small details. Once we have accomplished our goals, the conditions will dramatically change to us, and then my friends, "the grill will get hot". To finish, I'd like to say that Savio and Vaivet will be in charge of the disposition of the agents into the groups, disposed according to their level, kind of abilities and filed experience of each one, so all the teams have equal powers, just like we used to do in the shop. Why to change what is working well? Tharus, Antonio and Nicholas are already preparing the action programs of each equip, and until tomorrow afternoon everybody will be noticed properly, so you can be prepared to enter in the arena. That's all for the moment. I would recommend you to stroll around here, to know better this country. Remember our theme, you've gotta fight for your right to party!

Everybody began to scream together.

_ Blue jackets! Blue jackets! Blue Jackets! Blue Jackets! Blue jackets!

On the following days everybody was completely absorbed in frenetic activities involving the planning of strategies, and the concern with about the terrible weather of that country became secondary. A single bath was a real challenge, a proof of courage to all of them, except to those luck ones who could fantastically control the temperature of the body, such as Nicholas Graff. To swim in semi frozen creeks was no problem to them. To the rest of the group, the simple changing of clothes was a cold torture. Other problems weren't so difficult to detour, as the washing of the clothes, once they tended to freeze while dried. Leon Reston, psychic level 05, had the ability to irradiate heat from his hands, and became responsible to keep the clothes warmed. The move throughout the countryside was complicated too, the mix of snow, ice and mud let the ground dangerously slip and dirty. Only those who could dematerialize or levitate didn't use to stumble or slide. The combination of a hostile environment and the lack of life conditions was creating an enormous tension between the group, letting the "nerves on the surface of the skin", what was raising a darker side of the personality of many of the members, and they were behaving in a more aggressive way. That seemed to be the exact intention of the Bat, who was deferring intentionally the beginning of the attacks, as if he wanted to let them more and more violent, pledging he was still studying the tiniest details to prevent flaws, and according to Vaivet, they should wait a better conjunction of some planets. Frequently he was using his ability of dematerialization to go to other basis of the guerrilla, to spend some days with them, drinking and having fun. Besides, he wasn't in a hurry to execute his plans of revenge, for the simple fact he knew his foes were terrified, without knowing what he was about to do, hidden in their filthy dens as rats, gave him additional satisfaction. He wanted to let them desperate, driving them to madness. He believed that vengeance is a dish to be eaten cold, what was ideal for a country covered by ice.

However, despite of all troubles in the camp, the militants were enjoying their new activities, and were excited with what was about to come. They believed they were living another Spanish revolution, that would attract a lot of sympathy of the world communities and that many artists; poets; writers; singers and others would still join them, willing to die for their noble purposes and ideals, just like in the war in the Spain. They were amazed by the perspective they were participating of a moment that would get into the history, a new kind of war that would bring a new world order. Psychic people that had never had a violent action in their lives, felt the huge increase in their adrenaline levels, by the simple perspective they would get into actions just like in the movies. The combat was closer. The contact with the local idiom and culture was creating on them a sort of identification with the problems of that poor people, and the relates hideous and coward behavior of the despot corrupt government, let them more and more revolted. If Iullus wasn't always settling them down, they would have began the hostilities by themselves.

Even though, every night they promoted parties and festivals, once they were still very young, celebrating with the rebels, dancing, singing, drinking and making other things too. They also used to play with their powers. In an infantile tentative to show the destructive extension of their psychic abilities, to make the rebels worship them as semi gods. The guerrilla got crazy, because they knew this time the victory was closer than never. Friendships and passions blossomed as weed, with alliances being formed and love promises being made among the confusion of the camp, in a profusion of feelings, as an answer to the stress and lack of life conditions. The coarse local inhabitants no way were used to the natural form the psychic people made use of their capacities, and easily confounded this things as divine phenomenon. They were abashed to see dishes; forks; spoons and glasses flying around or moving as if they were doing it for themselves, people levitating everywhere, or simply disappearing or appearing, young people swimming in lakes and streams side by side with ice rocks. They also didn't have a clue about the weird and incomprehensible games the paranormals practiced. The sensitive ones were seen by the superstitious and greenhorn locals as indestructible immortal beings, and if they kept beside these titans, working and living with them all the time, they would get a little of this overwhelming strength. Finally, certain afternoon, when Tharus came back from one of his incursions, gave orders to Savio, to gather all the brave combatants, because he brought good news. Everybody ran to his tent, to listen what it could be, and impatiently waited for his announcement.
_ My loyal blue jackets, the time has come. What we were waiting for so long is about to happen. Be prepared, because new times breeze is blowing. Warriors from the new order, the combat is about to begin! Onwards my friends!

Chapter 13

The flight of the Bat

Guided by the rebels, the blue jackets began to prepare quick incursions all over the country. By infiltration, and mixing with the locals, looking for the opportunity to create troubles to the government employers. Very well inserted in the landscape, they did not wake any suspect or interest from the part of the authorities. The very first part of the plan consisted on mining the state source of power, taking care to do not let be perceived the action of psychics. At least for the moment, the local secret service shouldn't suspect of their presence, putting all the credit on the guerilla's action, and it was being followed exactly had been determined, and the police and the army were treating the present situation with the same disregard they always treated the revolutionary group's operations.

Iullus was in charge of the countryside attacks, Savio Nog and Nicholas Graff leaded the capital actions and in the eight biggest cities. Initially, the missions were scattered and consisted basically on the systematic destruction of military convoys on the roads and ammunition supplies and equipments on the barracks, on the tentative of strangle the support infrastructure and supplying of the federal troops, using to accomplish the tasks several methods of energetic attacks. The sub-groups always released their power in unison, to raise the devastation potential. This way they didn't give any opportunity to strike back or defense to the enemy soldiers. Informed by rebel spies about the convoy schedules, the jackets quickly dislocated to the exact point on the road, preparing successful ambushes. Usually, Iullus used to stand still alongside the highway, to confuse the soldiers, who didn't understand what that gothic man was doing on the middle of nowhere, while the trucks passed by. Many of these militaries were seriously wounded, mainly on the stall of the vehicles that followed the huge explosions, but the only one that seemed to care about the casualties was Iullus Vendra. The vision of the suffering of these poor young men let him upset for several days. his colleagues always tried to cheer him up, saying that it was inevitable, that he should see the big picture, because once they had won this war the benefits to the rest of the population would overcome these sad episodes. What they were trying to do would result in good things to the rest of the world, when they were conquered their goals. But Iullus knew that those deaths would haunt him for the rest of his life. The other groups also waited to ambush the passing transport, but they adopted different strategies. Some of them levitated to the top of the trucks, without being noticed, when they were slower on the slopes. For some minutes they established mental links with the drivers, creating delusions on their minds, making them precipitate the vehicles on the abyss.

Meanwhile, the only tasks given to the local guerilla consisted on raising relevant information to the random attacks to the troops that made incursions through the fields on hopeless missions to vanquish the rebellion, to guide the blue jackets on their movements throughout unknown valleys, and taking care of general services in the camps. Tharus Vendra didn't trust on their abilities to fight or realize any relevant function. In consequence of that, the rebels had a lot of spare time, and they did not use it in an appropriate way. Their favorite pastime was to grow the belly with too much food and beverage, sleeping on the interval. Little by little, they were being dismantled by the ostracism and lack of perspective with the eminent victory, which for them represented only the end of a life style, lapidated throughout the years. They spent the days soaked in alcohol, in a stupid try to avoid thinking about what would happen to their lives from the victory day on, or if the new regime would have place to ignorant people that did not have time to study, because they were so occupied with ambush killings and hidings in the woods. In the cities, the teams read the minds of the militaries, searching the exact location of the barrack's warehouses, the kind of weapons they had, the routine of the sentinels and the passwords of the safes where confidential documents of the government were hidden. After they gathered these information, some members were materialized to inside and from there gave free access to the rest of the group, which split and each one went to do his part, taking what was utile and destroying the rest, using mental blasters or fire. More powerful ammunition, as missile, was taken by specialized psychic, who manipulated the sensors and all the electrical part, damaging temporally the projectiles, once there was no need to destroy unnecessarily something so valuable that could be reutilized by the new government, when they win. They also invaded air force and navy's basis, despite the country didn't have connection to the sea. Another dictator's extravagance. They took some pieces from the few planes and helicopters of combat, troops transportation, training and espionage. Old war tanks and fluvial frigates had their components also removed, strategically indicated by specialist, who knew which pieces couldn't' be replaced, once they weren't in the stocks. They blue jackets disappeared before they were detected by the sentinels. This way, they took the small power of the army, so it could be recovered once they were in the command of the country. To this purpose, the pieces were being catalogued and stocked, waiting for the end of the hostilities.

The intelligence of the secret service was having many difficulties to identify the motif of the sudden change in the combat characteristics of the guerrilla, and principally, they were astonished by the sudden efficacy of attacks of what before was only a mere exercise of incompetence. Hypothesis after hypothesis was being conjectured, but ironically, the participation of a large number of paranormal people wasn't even considered. They believed that if the Vendra brothers were still in their country, they were acting alone, and yet the twins were very powerful, they couldn't put in danger the national security. The government just woke up to the imminent disaster when, during an ambush, when the soldiers reacted hard, using weapons the guerrilla had no condition to stand up against. Surprisingly the rebels resisted more than was expected, and when they were finally defeated, the soldiers captured the only two of them who had survived. Taken to the basis, the rebels, who seemed foreign people, were hideously tortured, until they gave up and provided all sort of information. These two ones were members of the blue jackets, the group of Tharus Vendra. Immediately the high command and the president were informed, and the panic took hold of their souls.

_ Mister doctor president, don't you think we are over reacting the importance of these clones? I mean, they are only two, and our elite troops are formed by more than five thousands well trained men. Our regular troops are also quite prepared to fight them. These freaks can do much, but they can't do all.

_ I don't want to risk. I want that mister William H. Price take care of the situation. His organization did it, and he will have to solve it. I paid a fortune to him and what he did? Nothing, that's what he did, and now I have to deal with the remains of his lousy work. This looks like a hell's kitchen! How many other freaks got into my lands?

_ Unfortunately we have no clue, mister president. The rebels died before we had the chance to pluck out this information. But before you contact the shop, don't you want to listen our plans?

_ No way! You are a bunch of incompetent lettuces, who can't deal with a group of juvenile delinquents. You have no condition to fight a large number of macabre creations. Favor them with you absence, and go quickly do what I told you to do, before I promote you to seaweed.

In the evening the shop was informed of what was happening. However the directors of the agency seemed to be more frightened than the president of the country. They promised to take urgent providences, but what they actually did was to try to figure out how they would provide their own safety. They had a clear comprehension of what was about to come. They didn't care of what could happen to their business image, and simply abandoned the client, and didn't contact the government anymore. The dictator understood, when he couldn't talk to mister Price anymore, that he was alone, and had to deal with the problem by himself. He just didn't know how. On their turn, the blue jackets conceived they had finally been discovered, and them began to act openly, with much more dare and arrogance, trying to spread more panic among the authorities. They just avoided attracting attention of some international agency of news. Antonio Maia was in charge of the dirty job. He and his assistants ran out the country, identifying and erasing the principal civilian and military authorities, such as judges; generals; corrupt mayors and governors, who sustained the dictator regime. They perished in several ways, some were followed and had their habits noted, and in the right moment, a blue jacket made their houses or cars were exploded, also walls crumbled over another or cables of elevators were mentally cut when there was one of them inside. However, these methods weren't totally efficient, and they demanded too much time, and some of the targets survived. That's why Maia preferred his cleanest ability. He sneaked the targets and concentrated in their jugular, and within few minutes they had a sudden death. The terror took over these people, who began to flee in a hurry, without looking back, leaving behind everything they gathered with the sweat of the others.

Meanwhile, Tharus was in charge of the tasks that were more complex and involved more risks. Once he received the proper information, he went alone to the finalization of the action, and he was beginning to enjoy that. The sensation of power, the feeling he could do whatever he wanted, without need to press charge to anybody was bringing to the surface his darkest and dull side. He used to penetrate calmly at night in the decadent hydroelectric installations and dematerialized components of the turbines. Some of them were huge. In a few days practically all the country was without energy. He was aware the gloom he was putting the population in would bring too much suffering, once they couldn't heat their houses properly, and hundreds, even thousands of people would certainly die. But he believed it would inevitable, and the deaths would much less than if the revolution movement fought the government in a regular way. His excuse was that a cancer can't be removed without cutting in the flesh. The railroad system, hardly protected by the soldiers, was being bitterly damaged by the attacks of the Bat. The locomotives full of supplies to the troops didn't resist to his extraordinary powers. At night, he was playing as a innocent child on the railroad, holding a martini glass in one of his hands, the bottle in the other, and a cigar in his mouth, while waited for the train. When it was coming, he stepped aside and peered at the train dormant, destroying some of them. After that, he burst the junctions of some wagons, and when the security staff noticed his bleak presence was too late. They tried to shoot him, but it was useless, and in the next moment the train derailed. After verify the total destruction of the material, the Bat just turned his back and went away.

In a last and desperate effort to counter the steady advance of the guerrilla, the president ordered a huge strike of remaining forces to the central basis of the revolution, recently discovered. He decided to use everything he could, even the terrible chemical and biological weapons, which were the great pride of the megalomaniac of the dictator. As they couldn't measure the extension of the powers of the psychic enemies, nor even quantify them, the militaries had no idea they were being tracked by blue jackets stalkers sometime before their attack. When Tharus was alerted of the danger, he reacted in a hush way, as if he was enjoying this situation, once everything seemed to be working as his cognitive helpers had predicted. He knew that was the time to his final stroke, because he was beginning to get bothered of those jokes. An ambush was prepared, with the direct assistance of Vaivet, who was in charge to identify the possible venues to the siege, until she found an ideal point. A one mile extension magnificent ancient bridge that connected two parts of the country. It was in a cold deep canyon. There was no other passage to the convoy. Gathering all the militants, the twins went to what they knew was the final battle. To this spectacle, Tharus invited the leaders of the guerrilla. He wanted to give them a good picture of what he and his agents could do. While the sensitive members were on concentration to the enormous mental effort they were on the verge to make, hidden in the most inaccessible part of the opposite side where the troops should pass, Iullus demonstrated to be very unquiet. When he couldn't bare it anymore, went to talk to his brother.

_ Brother, I do not know exactly you're intending to do, but I think we should worry about the physical damage we can impose on the soldiers. I do not want to use unnecessary power.

_ Don't you worry, brother. I am also concerned about this bridge. It is too beautiful.

_ For god sake, Tharus! That's not what I meant! I don't give a damn to this thing!

_ Oh, I got you. Chill out, Brother, none of our jackets will be lost.

_ I am sure of that! I am worried about the soldiers.

_ In this case I can do nothing. Their fate is already sealed. Don't you forget this is a war! I don't give a shit for these men lives. I am worried about this bridge. Remember that they would kill each of us if they could, and wouldn't even feel remorse. Fuck them all!

Iullus knew that there would be no point on keeping arguing. The thing he feared the most was about to happen, and he would co-responsible for the death of hundreds, maybe thousands of men, which only crime was to belong to the enemy lines. He wondered how many of them were forced to join the army, by misery or by pressure. But there was nothing he could do. But what was bothering him the most, was the cold and distant reaction of his brother. He could even feel the restrained satisfaction in Tharus' look. A large number of lives would be reaped by his psychic friends, and could only watch the demonstration of the devastating fury they could unchain. He was trying to avoid thinking about what was happening with the idealistic and emotional guy he used to be. Iullus was afraid of the answer he could find out. Far away, the noise of dozens of motors announced the foe was approximating. The Bat determined that everybody took positions. Spread for several points, from a reasonable distance, the blue jackets waited, totally concentrated on their tasks. Some hours later, the first vehicle appeared on the horizon. The scouts of the army had no condition to perceive the plot when they authorized the passage of the convoy over the rigid construction, settled above a colossal abysm, on the end of which an untamed river that seemed to be claiming the despoils. Almost all the transportation and war vehicles were already on the bridge when Tharus called for Vaivet and told her to get into telepathic contact with the rest of the group, authorizing the start of the operation. Less than ten minutes of concentration were enough to produce small cracks allover the structure. With some energy the fissures became bigger and the bridge began to shake with more and more intensity, until it began to fall apart, with the excessive power acting over it and the weight of the convoy. The trembles were increasing until the soldiers were able to notice something was going wrong. The war men were taken by a paralyzing panic, what made the troops stand still. With the rising of the swing of the pillars, and recognizing they could do nothing, not even try to ran to escape, once there was no condition to flee, the soldiers began to scream their lungs out desperately, and between the cry, pray and mourning could be heard, brought by the cold wind. Suddenly, with a huge noise, all the structure broke down, taking to the deep of the abysm the lives of so many men and women, young ones and others not so old, some of them good people and others not necessarily so. Dreams and realizations transformed into ruins. None of the blue jackets felt the mood to celebrate what seemed to be the end of the struggles, the one that would put the revolution in the right path. They all looked incredulous with had just happened, and scared with the dimension of their acts. They also felt respect for the death of thousands and thousands of people. Silently they began to go away, avoiding looking towards the canyon. Iullus, the only one that didn't participate of the attempt, was feeling sick, with cold sweater and shivering. He tried to follow them, trying to flee as quick as possible from that terrible situation he hadn't helped to happen, but also hadn't tried to avoid. He walked some steps, but his legs reeled and fell on his knees, covering his ears as if he was still hearing the cries for help of those poor soldiers. However, the bleak silence was much more emphatic than thousands of voices, once it reminded him it was too late, that everything couldn't be undone. And them, crying, he began to spill.

The rebel leader, Rheno Zoff, who made it a point to witnesses the moment that would be recorded in the history of his country, was the only one that was celebrating openly, and didn't try to hide his satisfaction. He eulogized each member of the blue jackets, embracing and shaking their hands, as if he was already the new president of the nation. When he saw Iullus trying to stand up, he got closer and offered his arm as a support, trying to cheer him.

_ Why are you so sad, my lad? Nor always we are capable to avoid the worst. Fortunately life goes on, and I assure you within some time we will rebuild the bridge.

The young Vendra looked at him trying to figure out what kind of monster he was helping to conquer that country. If the situation wasn't so tragic, he could have laughed about that man's comments.

_ Don't you grief about the lives of the militaries? They are your folks too.

_ Once I was as naïve as you, my lad. But after have many of my relatives and friends tortured and slaughtered by these folks, just because they could know where I was hidden, I began to realize that nobody is innocent. They chose their path and I chose mine! They killed my family, so I killed them. It is tragic but it is true. I don't see the lives we have taken in here today, I see the lives we are saving allover the country, from tomorrow on. Let's go, I'll let you with your brother. It is time to rest.

Practically there wasn't a local press. The State had controlled if with its iron hands for so long that the new generation of journalists were too incipient to dig in for the truth of the news, and the few foreign correspondents who were interested on following the development of a monotonously long civil war, didn't comprehended what exactly was happening, and put the whole credit on the guerrilla's account . Ironically, if the government had permitted the free and independent work of the media, probably the UN had known earlier about the participation of psychics from abroad, and had decided to interfere through the company of the paranormals, saving the authorities from the catastrophic events that were about to come. The concourse of the blue jackets should remain undercover once the authorities who could witness their work were already erased. The few ones left were more worried about their own survive, and even the dictator was preparing his flee and of his family, taken by the panic to be caught by Tharus. Gathering just a tiny fraction of what he had stolen from the country alongside the years, he was just waiting his private jet be prepared to take off. Some of his main allies and cooperators, and their respective families, were hidden with him in a cottage in the woods, eager to go. After three days, which seemed an eternity to them, they all breathed relieved with the notice that everything was arranged to go, and the departure would be immediate. Without looking back they embarked in several pick-ups, believing they almost out of danger. In their rush to go, none of them perceived that in the roof of the enormous cottage, a linger blond man dressed in dark blue was lighting a cigar while observing the movement down there.

The sprint automobiles left through the road, and again nobody noticed that the blond man was now on the side of the road. Some minutes later, he was in the top of a cliff, and after that, over the roof of an old church, always escorting the fast procession, while blowing smoke calmly, until they arrived in a hidden airport, where the big fancy aircraft was waiting, ready to go. Without wasting time, the fugitive settled down on the large seats. They were still tense and silent. The strange man, dressed in dark blue, was sat in lotus position on the top of the plane, with a sarcastic smile in his mouth. When the pilot made maneuvers to take off, the passengers didn't noticed the presence of the blond man, sat on the last seat, lighting again his cigar. When the plane was very high, the passengers began to relax, clearing the ambient, and within few minutes they were already talking frivolities and even making future plans. Somebody stood up and began to serve beverages and appetizers to everybody, and for the last time nobody noticed the blond man sat comfortably in the last seat. For some minutes he kept listening the chat, curious, trying to find out if they had learnt something with the last happenings. Unfortunately he heard nothing that could make him change his mind and give up of what he was about to do. The people in there was just concerned about where they could live with more perks, and where was the best paradise to spend their money in. some of them were even planning their future back to power, when they had powerful allies.

Tired and sick of hearing this mount of follies, Tharus stood up and calmly was walking to the front of the aircraft. While he was passing, the people were growing dumb, scared by his unexpected presence. Without pay heed to that, he grabbed the lit cigar of a man, and the glass of whiskey of another, and stopped in front of the pilot cockpit. Without stare at them, he continued drinking and blowing the smoke to inside the glass, as if he was the only person in there. After some minutes of agony, the former president took courage and began to stutter.

_ You misunderstood me, mister Vendra. I was a victim of the shop just like you. They deceived us. you must understand. – Tharus seemed not to be listening. – Look, I am a very rich man. Extremely. I have too much money allover the world, and I can give a great part of it to you. Trust me, you just have to ask. My friends in here can contribute as well. Don't be sarcastic. We can hang along very well.

_ Why do you think you still keep this money, Jethro? That's very funny, I am sorry. The fortune you had stolen from the poor people is not yours anymore. I have to tell you it doesn't belong to you anymore. It already returned to its legitimate owner, and will be very helpful in the reconstruction of the country. My agents had identified all your accounts and passwords, and yesterday we had it transferred. You don't have money even to buy a cup of coffee.

_ For God sake, man! We're begging for mercy. We have innocent women and children in here.

_ How can you ask for something you never had? Besides, your families have made a pact with you all these years, enjoying the comfort this filthy money could buy and appreciating the perks the power was proportioning. I am sure that you had massacred many innocent families as well. This is called collateral damage.

_ I am just a poor accountant. I am not involved in any crime. – Interfered an old man.

_ I was secretary of culture. I was involved only with artistic projects. I never heard and I never participated on any felony. Trust me! – Begged a beautiful woman.

_ I tried to help the poor people. I was secretary of health. I am a doctor, and I respected my oath. – Cried another man.

_ I am touched by such innocence and ignorance. Really. I think that there are only saints in here. But unfortunately ignorance can not be used as an excuse. The fact is that you helped to maintain one of the most terrible regimes in the world, and you have to face the consequences. Besides, I can't set you free, because you will keep plotting from the exile. I am so sorry, but I have to cut the evil by the root.

_ No! I swear that these poor people are innocent. I give you my word. Let them go, and our families too. I can do whatever you want with me. – Asked the former president.

_ Your word is worthless than a dog's bark. I don't give a damn to what you or these people think or feel. I am just an instrument of justice. If you were still in the command of the country, all of you would remain doing the same things you were doing, regardless worries about the suffering of your own people. The citizens gave too much blood for you luxuries. It is pay back time!

_ You miserable! Do you think you're invincible? I want you to know that sooner or later someone will show the world you are not a sort of Mandrake, that you are really a filthy brat! – Cried the former dictator.

_ Who do think you are to judge our acts? Who are you to claim the roll of hangman? What you're about to commit is as hideous as what you pledge we have committed! – Said an old general.

_ Think for a while, mister! I beg you. Take us to the competent authorities. Let the proper judges decide for our guilt. – The dictator's wife opened her heart.

_ For God's sake! What's that noise?

_ Oh my God! What is it?

_ That, my friends, is the sound of your sentence. I think you have just lost the turbines of your jet. I'd like to ask to a courageous one to look through the window to certify. However, I was touched by your sincere revelations in here, and I decided to give you a chance. I had planned to tear the wings of this plane, but I won't do it anymore. I'll let you by your own, and if you can land these aircraft you are free to go.

_ How can we do such a thing? We are in a region of huge mountains. And even if we could land it, how can we cross the ice desert by foot, without proper clothes?

_ That my friend, is up to you. *Hasta la vista, babies!*

After these words, Tharus just disappeared, leaving behind people crying desperately. By far he could see the plane slowly begin to fall down, until disappear behind some mountains.

_ So far so good! – That was his only comment.

Mister Price, the president of the shop and his directors, for a long time believed that even without their support, the troops of the dictator would be enough to vanquish the pretensions of the Vendra brothers. They had no condition to know the twins were gathering a powerful militia, once many of their best agents were working with them behind their back or simply didn't want to fight against some of their best friends and work mates. For some time, mister price and his assistants believed the Vendra boys hadn't knowledge the shop had planned the betrayal, and for some time their routine remained the same. But after a while, it was impossible to deny that was very strange that many of their agents weren't back from their vacations, and they assumed that these people were already working with the brothers, and when some of their loyal employers confirmed that the twins had created a group named blue jackets, and they were working with the revolutionary army, mister William Price and his cooperators understood they were "in bad sheets". He knew his equips couldn't face the outstanding powers of Tharus. And it became more complicated with the desertion of many of his best men and women. He knew that Tharus wouldn't forgive what happened to his brother, and he had no illusion about his fatal fate, if he didn't take some urgent and desperate measures. Gathering what remained of his groups, he disappeared from the map, for mutual protection. He left everything else behind, his work; projects; investments. Everything could wait until plan some kind of retaliation or truce. He just wanted do survive. He understood he wasn't prepared to get into the spiritual word yet, once he had many enemies waiting for a chance of revenge. He thought he could defer it indefinitely. He knew the overwhelming ambition of the twins, and believed he could by their forgiveness, and later he would plot a proper punishment to these two and to those ones who were helping them. He would have his vengeance. Nobody would force him to abandon his beloved shop without tragic consequences. When he remembered that his agency was in charge of subaltern employers, his hate increased, and he almost wanted to attack these blue jackets. But he was a patient man, and would know the right time to strike back.

At the same time he was helping the revolutionary army to install a new political and social order in the country, Tharus sent a team, leaded by Vaived Midral, to stalk and find the whereabouts of the remaining members of the shop. The subaltern workers, who were operating the agency, didn't have a clue about what was happening, and couldn't help much. Tharus knew they were innocent and did nothing against them. for two months vaivet and her group searched in vain for tips in many parts of the globe. They ran through the official residences of the organization and other important dens, trying to find personal objects that could help them track the enemies, but everything was clean. Mister price had anticipated and ordered that all personal objects they couldn't take with them were destroyed. He also created a mental barrier using some of his best agents. Iullus had a theory that they were hidden somewhere on the sea, once they hadn't found the super yacht of the organization, which should be in maintenance in Norway. However, no technician knew where it could be. They had informed that sometimes the ship was sent to other countries, to other type of maintenance. Iullus knew that it was just a matter of time, once the shop couldn't maintain the mental block for so long, and at any moment they would commit a mistake. Within a few weeks his predictions proved to be right, and Vaivet was able to track the yacht, using some pieces of the ship taken from the house of one of the mechanics. Moving constantly, to difficult the location, the ship was found somewhere in the way to the Bikini islands.

The Bat exulted with the news. It indicated his revenge was next. He desired to finish it quickly to move forward with other projects. Leaving some agents taking care of his business in the country, he went with Iullus, Antonio Maia and Savio Nog. Using his ability of dematerialization and materialization about 150 miles each time, he went with his companions to the closest country where they met the rest of the group. During four days they looked for the yacht, until they finally found it anchored among two small islands, true paradises, hidden from the authorities and the blue jackets, ready to go at any time. The jacket rent a sprint boat to go to the venue, stopping behind an atoll, 10 miles away, to do not raise any suspect. Without rush, the group laid down on the rocks, to sneak the ship and to take a sun bath while observed the spectacular landscape. Iullus was the first to breat the suspense.

_ Brother, do you mind to tell me, what do you intend to do now that they are on our reach?

_ I just don't know, brother. Before anything else I want to enjoy every minute of it. After I talk to those nasty traitors, looking them at the eye, I'll decide. Maybe.

_ If you allow my intromission, I have to say that we don't have many options. – Interfered Antonio.

_ I agree in part with him. I just think that we have only one choice. And you know which one. – Completed Nog.

_ Hold your horses, friends. Don't you think that too much blood has already been dropped? What are we transforming ourselves into?

_ Don't be fool, brother. I know what Antonio and Savio mean. I know that William will never give up his plans to kill you. They are our enemies, and we can't have mercy because they won't, if they recover their forces. The less innocent people that may be between them are just in the wrong place in the wrong time. The rest is bullshit. End of discussion!

Standing up coarsely, the Bat called Iullus, Maia, Nog, Vaivet, Grummel and Starks to go with him, but his brother alleged lack of psychological conditions to go on.

_ If you permit me to say, Iullus is a great guy, don't get me wrong, but I think he doesn't have the necessary guts to some tasks. He should be in charge of some more light operations, maybe office work.

_ Shut your hole up, Maia! Or I'll do it for you. He is more honorable than me, and can do whatever he wants. Who disapprove his decisions will have to answer to me! Let's get back to the mission. I don't want anybody using cell phones. We must hack all the communications of the yacht. They can't call for help, and we can't let the authorities capture our signals.

Tharus convoked Aloma Dayrell to his place, and after that took everybody to the deck of the ship that was empty. Each one knew exactly what to do, and they split. Tharus walked for some corridors, while his crew immobilized the passengers that they were founding, until he stopped in front of the door of the meeting room, where he first met the president of the shop, and where the remaining people of the agency were. Probably trying to maintain the mental block. He gently knocked at the door.

_ Is there anybody in there? May I come in?

Nobody answered, but he opened the door and entered anyway. The jackets that arrived at that time began to cackle when they saw the terrified look in the eyes of their former colleagues. Antonio just looked at Vaivet and commented.

_ I hate this victim behavior. Specially from people that had been so powerful once. It is disgusting.

Mister Bill Price recovered a little his energies and stood up to talk to the visitors.

_ Tharus, my dear friend. Come along, we have too much to talk about. There have been some misunderstood between us, and I want to put it in clean dishes. Where is my dear Iullus? I missed him. I hope everything is okay with him.

_ You bet, Bill. He is very well, but not thanks to any of you.

_ That is what we have to talk about. I think somebody is trying to put us apart. I think we can fix it properly. Don't you agree?

_ I'll fix it my way. Don't waste your saliva, Bill. When I look at you I remember that if wasn't a girl named Kiria, Iullus would be dead by now, and I wouldn't even know who really was behind that plot. I would call for friends the responsible for the slaughter of my brother.

_ Things are not the way you're thinking. I can explain it all. The guilty is the dictator of that shit of country. He was too greed and tried to do a crazy maneuver. I never approved that. You know how much I like your brother. Please, you have to believe me. You have known me for so long. I would never harm a member of my staff. That infamous dictator is the guilty one. We are totally happy for you two. We can make him pay for his dare.

_ Don't you worry about him. We have already made a deal. I just wonder why you are hidden as rats if you were really worried about us.

_ Don't you think that. The point is that when we were informed about what was really happening, we thought that you could be so angry that we decided to be in the corners until you settle down. Don't do anything you can regret later.

_ Don't you worry. I won't regret.

_ I can imagine all the problems you have faced recently, and I am prepared to repair my fault generously. Let's chill down and maintain a civilized conversation about the damages.

_ Let me see, how much would you pay for may brother's life? Wait a minute, is everything alright, Vaivet?

_ Yes. Mission accomplished. We just identified all the accounts and passwords of the shop, and we have already transferred all the money. You have no idea how much it is. It is amazing. Some billions dollars!

_ I am sorry, Bill. You just lost your source of money.

_ You can't do that to me, Tharus. After all my dedication alongside these years! I taught you everything you know, you were just a dipper stinky brat. You can't simply steal all the money we gathered in a lifetime of hard work. It is not fair. You're so arrogant! I have showed the real world to you, that it is not that infantile colored landscape portrayed by mister Vasconcellus. I planned a bright future to us. Without me you'd be lost and probably would have become a loser. I put you in the right path. Me! Don't you ever forget it. I thought our friendship was stronger than that. You're a thief and a liar. I believe you have made it up only to grab my money. You disappointed me.

_ I disappointed you? You're such a cynical.

_ I thought we could conquer the world, to change it into something better, but you were just interested in power and money. I know you very well now. You're a great pretender. That's what you are.

_ I am ambitious, I must confess, but I am not as you. You have no measure. You may think what you want. I just want to get rid of rabbles like you.

_ What you're gonna do? Kill me? Kill us all? We are not so different, you know. – Jean Luc finally took courage to pronounce. – I never meant to harm you or your brother. He is my best friend. You should consider my word. I didn't know what I was doing. Mister Price deceived me. I don't wanna die.

_ Stop being such hypocrite, Jean. You're the one that cause me more aversion. I would never expect a betrayal from you. Now stop the bullshit.

At that moment Vaivet received a telepathic message of a jacket that was in the atoll with Iullus. Getting closer to the Bat, she whispered in his ears the note.

_ Take care of everything in here, Antonio. I'll be back in a few minutes.

_ Is there anything wrong, Boss?

_ I don't know, but I'll check it out.

Instantly he disappeared, and appeared besides his brother.

_ Why did you call me, Brother?

_ I just wanted to know what you're gonna do. Don't you think we have going to far already? Don't be hasty, brother. We can't go on like that. I love you, you're my dear brother, but I have to warn you. Please, stop this blood bath.

_ Unfortunately there is no other option, brother. You're my brother and I love you too, but stop being so weak and naïve. I won't tolerate it. I'll do what I have to do. It is for your sake. If I let them go you will never be safe. We can't leave evidences behind. Imagine what is going to happen if the entire world knows what we have done? The bad consequences will reach each paranormal in a general way. We have to hide all the proofs against us.

Iullus knew that his brother was right. They had gone so far, and the common citizens would get into panic if the knew the extension of what they had done. They would fear any psychic. Besides, the recent changes in Tharus mood, which made him more cold and without moral boundaries, wouldn't give space to further considerations, and again he wasn't strong enough to face his brother and save those lives, and just gave up. The Bat didn't care about the fact his twin didn't want to participate actively in the mission, and came back to the ship, and with the excuse that he would consider for more time what eh had discussed with mister Price and jean Luc, he gathered his team and returned to the rocks. They sat down in lotus position and began to stare the boat, concentrating in each part of it structure, in each piece and circuit of the equipments, while inside the group of the shop breathed more relieved, believing their arguments took effect in Tharus intentions. Now and then, small energetic balls were created in everywhere, and were growing and growing, increasing the shine while was spinning faster and faster, until finally they all exploded together. In seconds the whole ship was reduced into a disfigured mass of havocs; fire and smoke, till a last explosion spread for miles the remains of the yacht, and then, a total silence took over the place. Only the havocs that floated everywhere denounced a great tragedy had took place. Seagulls that weren't hit by the explosions, refused to fly, as if they were mourning the dead people and animals. Only the indifferent noise of the sea waves breaking on the rocks was heard. Tharus laid down on the big stones, breathing relieved, as if all his plans had ended as he had planned. No glimpse of remorse or pain in his conscience could be noticed in his countenance, and he was already considering his future objectives. Antonio Maia and Savio Nog seemed as well not have been affected by the hideous events, and began to chat about shallow subjects, and after some minutes, all the group was maintaining an animated conversation, but Iullus. After about three hours, when everybody was already recovered from the enormous spent of energy, Tharus decided that was already time to come back, and he wanted to pronounce the last words in that venue.

_ I'd like to thank you all, my brave companions. What we have done here today is something that could be interpreted as poetical justice. It is a day to remember and to relate to those that could not be with us today. From now on, the blue jackets will be known as the precursors of the new world order, and once again, the honored people will be proud to live in this planet. Let's go my warriors of the new order, because the work urges, and we have too much to do. New glories and new conquers wait for us.

With the chests full of pride, as if they were in a saint war, the sensitive ones embarked in the sprint boat and came back to the hotel, with the feeling of the accomplished duty embracing their spirits, as the dusk chill.

CHAPTER 14

THE COMPANY OF THE PARANORMALS II

The secretary of justice urgent convoked the presence of Peter Moll and two counselors to the meeting with the international police and army chiefs. The young director of the psychic agency was visibly unwillingly, after all, he had done plans to that Sunday morning and didn't believe that emergency could be so frightening to ruin his weekend. But orders are orders, and as he always obeyed, this time wasn't different. When that sort of thing happened he felt very luck, because working with his girlfriend made everything easier, once she was able to understand what was going on and this way become more benevolent with unpredictable facts.

At the meeting room of the minister, each one was asleep and irritated for being there in such bright day, without any further explanation for the urgency. Only the secretary of defense, mister Astor Powell, hadn't arrived yet, just the keeper of all the pertinent information. 20 minutes later he got into the room, escorted by his crew.

_ Gentlemen, good morning! Accept my apologies for the delay, but I was been informed about the ultimate facts concerned to the matter. I'd like to thank the agility on the cooperation of the justice secretary; the illustrious Misters Jardell and Hermes Vasconcellus; the directors of the international customs police; the director of the UN's secret service; the director of the company of the paranormals and the general Newt Deslock. I am aware how inconvenient it is to take you apart of your family and your programs to a beautiful day. However, time urges and the facts are truly serious to justify such setback.

_ Don't you worry, my friend. We are here to serve anyway is possible.

_ Thank you very much, mister secretary. So, I won't waste your time, I am going straight to the kernel of the issue. I am not sure if all of you are aware of the current subjects, so I will make a general relate: there is an international investigation and estate protection paranormal agency, titled "the shop". We have strong evidences to believe that this company operates outlaw for several years and became the greatest of the market. Its directors were target of a full investigation, but as they are involved with the business of manifold government agencies of important nations, they never could be annoyed in a proper way, for using illicit methods to solve their client problems. Many of these investigated directors were students of mister Vasconcellus's school, including the president, and one of them is the biggest active psychic in the whole world, mister Tharus Vendra, also known as the "Bat".

_ I believe that everyone in this room is aware of these facts, sir, once I made a report to them, last year. I was contacted by the members of this "shop" few years ago.

_ That came to my knowledge at the time, Peter. I just didn't know that you had reported it to the rest of these people present here today. So let's go on: We were led to suspect that this enterprise is direct involved in a legitimate constituted govern strike. Few weeks ago, the president of this country, some of his ministers and their families simply vanished without any trace. Right after a guerilla group, that had fought years without effective results, have assumed the control of the nation. But the most intriguing in this story, what changed our suppositions is that yesterday morning, were found remains of the wreckages of the yacht in the Pacific Ocean. Due to the difficulties of the recognition because of the awful conditions of the collected pieces, we could only guess that it could be Namor, the "Shop" Yacht. And we believe that every passenger that was on board on the last harbor stop is dead, including the president, mister William Price. Witness related that a group of men and women, all dressed in dark blue clothes, rented a fast boat the supposed accident. Apparently, they were leaded by the blond twin brothers. The criminal investigation agency has no conclusion till now, if there was an accident or a criminal attempt, or if there is reasons to it. It is more likely that regular investigations will never solve this case. However, is our intention to send immediately a super paranormal team to the venue, searching for prove and information.

_ If there was the participation of a psychic of the magnitude of Tharus Vendra, the only person in the world that could trace his energy is our friend Peter Moll.

_ I am ready to play!

_ I'd like to go as an observer.

_ Excellent idea, Hermes!

_ _ So, you two are in charge of this operation. Choose the integrants of the group and begin the investigation. If it is possible to yesterday!

In a few minutes Peter had already contacted all the people he wanted in this mission, and called his girlfriend to tell her what he had to do.

_ Hello pretty girl. Listen, are you interested in a travel to a beautiful island?

On Monday morning the group was already in the place of the sinister happening. To seize the wonderful sun, and to do not raise suspects, they were dressing swimsuits, once Peter didn't enjoy any formality. On Thursday afternoon. In a new reunion with the secretary, Hermes began to talk.

_ Very well gentlemen, our trip was very fructiferous. We gathered much data, however nothing conclusive that could help us in the court. However…

_ Speak up, man! We are not concerned about judgments. We just want to know what happened.

_ Yes sir! We are capable to fill in the blanks and elucidate many obscure points. To begin, I may affirm that actually there was an attempt. The hypothesis is completely discarded. We traced the energy of the main participants, inclusive Tharus Vendra. They tried to hide all the proofs very well, but my team is yet better. We just don't know why. My hint is that there was a crack in the shop. They were grossing too much, and for what I know of the Vendra boys, they would keep helping William price in his crimes for so long.

_ How these discoveries were made?

_ Well, we took four paranormal with the capacity to access the Akasic register. To who is not used to this term, Akasic register is the energetic impression of all animated beings and non-animated ones in the astral ether. As if it worked as a "big brother" in a planetary scale recording each movement of the atoms that the world is made of. Who is able to access these registers, watch a kind of movie in the mind. The most recent these events are, the best the registers will be. And the opposite also is valid. Depending on the level of the median, these images can be even recorded in a DVD, what can be used in a court. However, the action of Tharus didn't let this possibility, but gathering strengths, our crew could enhance the perceptions of our cooperators Francis wilde, Marcel Crom, Martin Scros and Alfredo Corsa, what allowed them to capture precise information.

_ Very well, but we could skip these technical part. What I want is the result of it.

_ Well, what we found out is that the Vendra brothers created a new organization named blue jackets, and that great part of the members came from a dissident faction of the shop. We supposed that, somehow, William Price plot an attempt against Iullus, in a mission in that poor country, with the help of the government. That explains why the motives why the twins are helping the rebel forces and why they attacked their own ship. However, I can assure that Iullus Vendra didn't participate on this crime, because he couldn't or because he didn't want to. That's all.

_ Excellent, my young friend! Excellent! Now the dossier we compiled before makes sense. We have already detected the formation of this new agency, but we didn't know by whom and what their purposes. It portraits a more dramatic scenery, because for what they elaborating, their intention is to break with the actual structure of the society, creating something that they called new world order. How it will be installed we have no clue yet. At first we considered as work of paranormal teenagers, as a sort of rebels without a cause, but now it assumes a scary meaning with the notice that their leader is the most powerful man in the whole world.

_ But how could that be? – Asked the assistant of the UN.

_ It is very easy to understand, my dear friend. – Answered the secretary. Mister Tharus Vendra and his brother created a new "shop", to work may as a mercenary paranormal army. This market is still very profitable. For the ride of the carriage, I'd say that it will be more powerful than the organization created by mister Price. Our spies had informed us that men and women dressed in dark blue walk freely through the corridors of the power in that country, more uninhibited than the members of the new government. Now you can have an idea of how far can go the dare and bravado of these psychic people. I am afraid of how they can grow their organization with the support of a country.

_ I'd say that the world is in a great danger. No mercenary group can be leaded by a paranormal level 08! – Completed the general Deslock.

_ At least the criminal world, I'd say. – Argued Peter. – For what I know of Tharus, I'd bet he is planning to sweep away the planet.

_ Don't get me wrong, mister Moll, but it makes us wonder if this paranormal phenomenon didn't bring more problems to the mankind than solutions, and it will lead us. – Completed the general.

_ I think it is a great waste of brain work, once the development of new technologies and new resources is part of the human history and inevitable.

_ How would he basis his criteria? – Interrupted the secretary Astor Powell.

_ That's right! And if tomorrow he decides who is against him is his enemy? – Said the assistant of the UN.

_ Definitely something must be done urgent, before these "humble fishes" get beyond any control. Completed the general.

_ If you excuse me, ladies and gentlemen. I am major John Hook, member of an elite group of the sensitive navies. I was convoked here by general Deslock! I have been elaborating an action plan, once we were already suspecting of the facts narrated here today. I can guarantee if we can count with the cooperation of mister Peter Moll, within few weeks we can erase the problem.

_ If you think so, I am in. I am childhood friend of the Vendra boys and other components of these blue jackets, and I'd like to have an opportunity to make them hear the voice of reason. I think I can convince them to surrender for their free will.

The major and the general exchanged looks, as if they were already expecting this reaction of the director of the company.

_ If everything is settled let's move on. We can't waste more time. – Completed the general.

For twenty days, the militaries prepared secretly, without any participation of Peter; who they considered just a powerful civilian they had to stand, the operation and the equipment they would need. Moll, without other alternative maintained his routine, disregarded to what he called mission to meet old friends. He was more worried about how the Bat would react to his offer than with the possible dangers involved in this task. He couldn't believe that a group formed by ex integrants of the foundation would represent any risk to his healthy. Moreover, in case of complications, his powers would solve them quickly.

In the day of the departure he was the last to arrive in the airport, and was astonished by the great number of gear the militaries were taking with them, but once again he paid no heed to that. He was upset because he would leave his girlfriend alone for so long.

_ Denise, don't forget to take care of my loft. Remember that you have to turn on the car each two days. I don't want to see the electrical part damaged.

_ Shut up, Pete! You've talked so much in my ears that I think something is going to be wrong. Take it easy and send regards to the people. I miss them. Now say goodbye to Puywacket. He is going to miss you.

_ Bye, Puy! Take care of my pussycat doll very well.

_ Take care, sweetheart. I want you back in one piece, okay? I love you!

_ I love you too, Deni. *Hasta la vista, baby!*

When the helicopter landed, he was still thinking in his life and how things would stay without in his absence, and how he would bare to stay so long without his beloved girl, without even the possibility to talk to her on the phone or in the internet or any other means, once he and the rest of the group should remain hidden. If weren't his friendship with the twin brothers, he would have given up to penetrate the woods, getting in a dispute that wasn't his concern. He didn't share the fears of the secretary of justice and the general, and considered it all an over reaction the measures that were being taken to face a problem that should remain in the police sphere. Only when they landed in a hill he began to comprehend the situation, when he paid attention to the mariners taking out all the equipments and weapons from the chopper. The cold relief of that desert brought him back to the reality.

_ Wow! How is cold in here. You didn't tell me that, major.

_ I forgot to include it in the tourism folder. I don't think it will be a problem to you, will it?

_ Not at all! I am a good boy scout. I just don't like this place. It is only my personnel opinion.

This was Peter's first impression about that desolated land. The militaries looked each other as if they were gibing, as if they regretted for having brought such dainty person. The buck men didn't understand the extension of the abilities of the director of the company, who they saw just like a burden. For five days the squad hiked through the country, under bad weather conditions, until they arrived on the suburbs of the capital. They had avoided any contact with the locals. Peter was visibly annoyed by the extreme lack of comfort, and the moody of the mariners. He had never walked so much in his life, and desired to make use of his ability of dematerialization or levitation, but major Hook didn't allowed that, because only other three soldiers had these capacities, and they couldn't transport the whole group. His companions in this mission, 14 tough men, very well trained in the arts of war and camouflage, ranged from the level 04 to 06, and didn't seemed impressed by the fact the director of the company was level 07, principally because they had never seen somebody with such power, and conceived the military training proportioned to them a bigger advantage. Definitely they didn't like him, and didn't hide this. They believed he was complaining too much and was delaying the mission. If the goals were compromised would be his fault.

By night fall, major Hook decided to inspect the city, using his capacity of instant transportation, escorted by a captain with the same ability. Peter was too tired and didn't show interest on going with them. he just wanted to get into his thermal tent the fastest he could and have a night of sleep. The two soldiers, in proper disguises, ran out through several hoods without being noticed or bothered, noting everything they found relevant to their mission, once the young captain was fluent in the idiom of the country of his grandparents. On the next night, they returned to the capital, until they found out a huge mansion; former residence of a minister; that had become the Headquarter of the blue jackets. Finished the first phase of the mission, major Hook decided to occupy the roof of one of the neighbor buildings, that was semi-abandoned, and make there his observation and strategy point, and he also decided that was time to make Peter contact his former mates, as previously planed, without revealing the presence of the UN soldiers. Peter didn't know that his intention was to attract Tharus Vendra into a trap, in which he should be quickly eliminated. Peter didn't understand the dimensions the mission was about to gain, and in the next morning he transported himself to the gates of the Headquarter and rang the bell, as if it was a courtesy visit. A maid came to him, but she didn't comprehend what he was saying, but when she heard the name of the twins, she resolved to let him get in. the curious young Moll was paying attention on the expensive furniture, left behind by the former dwellers. Suddenly he saw Bernadete Tinflas, an old mate of the school.

_ Peter Moll? What are you doing in here?

_ Hello Bernadete! It is nice to meet you too. How long I don't see you, huh?

_ Since I graduated. Did you join us?

_ No! I was just passing by and decided to visit you.

_ Man, it is really you! You became a grown man! And very beautiful one, I may add. You were so skinny. It is nice to see a friend's face. If you want to work with us I'll tell you that things are very good in here. We rule in the place!

_ I haven't decided yet. That's why I came to talk to the Bat.

_ Oh, unfortunately I think you're gonna have to wait a while, because sometimes he disappear for several days. He is really unpredictable. It is much easier to talk to his brother. Come with me, we will contact Iullus. While we wait for him I'll show you the place. You're gonna see many ex- mates.

Few hours later Iullus was already aware about the unwonted visit, and immediately he warned his brother. The two ones were very intrigued with Peter's presence, once they knew about his new job in the company, and didn't understand how it all fit in. Of course they knew he wasn't there to join the lines of the blue jackets, as a kind of double agent, once his weak character wouldn't required the necessary qualities. They didn't want to talk to him without comprehend better what his presence in that country meant, and told to their secretary to schedule a meeting to the next morning, while their agents were ransacking the town, searching for information about the steps of their former schoolmate. However, their best men couldn't track Peter whereabouts, after he left the Headquarter, and weren't even able to find out how he arrived at the city, or if there was somebody else with him. The twins were more intrigued. They just didn't take more radical providences because they trusted in the honesty of Peter, who they never believe was capable to betray them. on the right time, the young Moll came back to the headquarter, and was having tea and toast with some former mates and talking about the old days, when the Vendra brothers decided to get into the immense salon.

_ Peter, what surprise! What brings you here, old friend?

_ Hello, Iullus. It is nice to see you too. Hello, tharus. Won't you say hi to me?

_ Hi, Peter! I am just concerned about your presence in here. You know that I like to be straight, and I supposed that you didn't want to talk to me anymore after our last conversation. At least I don't have much to say to you. You know how much I care about you, who I consider as a younger brother, but unfortunately we are walking different paths.

_ Pay no heed to what he is saying, Peter! I know he is glad to see you again. Tharus's been a little bitter these days. You grew up, boy! Come here and give me a hug. You are welcome here!

_ Thanks Iullus!

_ Forget my manners, my friend. I am just a little paranoid. Let's go to our office and chat for a while. Are you still dating that beautiful chick? The one who was always with a cat in her arms?

_ Denise? Yes I am, Bat.

_ I heard that you are working in a new agency, isn't it?

_ Yes, Iullus. It is called company of the paranormals. It's been very good. I have a nice salary. You should see the car I bought. It is crazy. But Denise is the rarest jewel I've ever had. I am in a complete bliss. And how about you?

_ All the same! Many adventures and many women! We like to live in jeopardy.

_ I am happy for you, Tharus.

_ I am not as wild as my brother, you know. But I am having a great time either. My best friends are working with me, and I am beginning to make difference in the world. What else should I ask for?

_ I don't know, maybe a wife and kids.

_ You didn't lose your square mind, Pete. You sound like my grandfather. We are making history in here and come to talk about family matters. What figure you are!

_ I was just kidding, Bat. I am not so old fashioned. I just believe in the universal values that are the same of your grandpa's time. But I also knew things.

_ Be serious, man! On my grandparents time things were so different we can't compare with ours. We are developing new solutions to old problems. We are a sort of a new generation of mutants. That means a new step in the scale of the evolution of the mankind. We are the future, friend, and demand new approaches. Any determinant factor of the destiny of the planet must pass through us.

_ Tharus, you know how difficult is the formation of a new psychic student. Are required about 15 years of exhaustive training and studies so the abilities are under control of the will. Only those people above the level 04 have their capacities developed earlier, and more than 70% of the apprentices give up before the 10th year. However, the major of the human kind will never reach even the level 01, and will never know what is to be a paranormal person. I believe that will be necessary some centuries to make an expressive parcel of the population to achieve the psychic maturity. Thus, we will remain as minority for so long, who can contribute significantly to the future of the planet, but nothing as drastic as you may wish.

_ Surely you improved your intellect, Peter, and I appreciate that. I miss our long conversations. But you still remain so naïve. I agree that the most of the population is relapse, lazy, inept and so accommodated to develop something that would radically change their mediocre lives forever. And I am sorry for that, but I disagree as the difference we can make in the world. We are the evolution of the nature, and we will face the interests of the great corporations, who have been ruled the globe for so long. They never cared about the environment, and stop any tentative to preserve the ecology, that weights in their pockets. I am so sorry that the most of the citizens are nor prepared or desire to take part in this great and magnificent project, but there's nothing I can do about it. What nature teaches us is that when a new race of mutants appears, the pattern is that it didn't fit in the established behavior. So a dispute with the most powerful is inevitable until a new deal is arranged. I am sure that the most of the world population will understand that and will fit in this new world order pacifically. Even those who can't or don't want to develop their mental abilities will perceive the advantages that are being offered to them, to live in a better society, without the problems that the old model couldn't erase until now.

_ Now, who's being naïve? Do you really think people will accept dramatic chances without hard fight? People, in a general manner, tend to be afraid of innovations, and the line that split admiration by the powers of the paranormal beings and the fear of what these powers can do is very thin. I do not even want to think about what could happen if the whole world began to face our special abilities as threatens to the world stability. I am sure that it would unchain a process of rejection and aggression that would lead to bias and radicalization from both parts, with an unpredictable and catastrophic denouement. Somehow it is already happening. More and more people is starting to be lose their patience with the problems that some psychic ones are causing. However, I think that is up to us, the most reasonable people, to demonstrate a more tolerant and conciliator behavior.

To help the adaptation of the common citizen to the reality that the psychic beings are here to stay. We have to do it the less painful as possible. Besides, I don't have to remind you that we are all humans, and that this division between mutants and non mutants is irrelevant, it is something from comic books. We just have some other capacities. That's all.

_ In a certain way you're right, my friend. Unfortunately, sooner or later, people will began to use these differences as excuses to discriminate and segregate. It always happens, it is part of the human nature. You must be aware that many of us are treated in some communities as freaks. They are about to be put in ghettos. However, I believe that if there was a conflict, which I believe will be inevitable, the outcome wouldn't be unpredictable, because we simply can't be defeated if we remain together. Imagine what would happen if we ruled the world. I thing a new time of prosperity would began, and crimes; misery; selfish and violence would disappear of the surface of the earth, once it is almost impossible to pretend the vigilance of sensitive inspectors.

_ I think it is a waste of time to continue with this quarrel, Peter. My brother is a little extreme and pessimist on relation to all this. In part I agree with him, and I admit that in many aspects you're right. The usual manner that some men have been conducting the destiny of the planet is an irresponsible act of selfish. To put in danger the lives of the most of the population and the equilibrium of the nature just to satisfy the desires of a minority is the most hideous crime. And what can we do if we think that we have condition to stop it? Do you think that we should use our powers just to entertain? And if we could offer a more coherent alternative? one that conciliates development with preservation? I think that our capacities are able to do it. The problem is to offer our contribution without scare too much the conservative people. But we had enough of this "pub philosophy". Let's talk about something more concrete. What brought you here?

_ Very well, my friend Iullus. I think you're right. Actually I always had admiration for your pondered personality. Let's talk about objective matters. I was sent here by the UN secretary, as a sort of mediator. Your latest acts have been monitored by the police of several countries, and the authorities are worried about you have done to this country and to the enterprise where you worked in.

_ You don't know shit. – Cried an angry Tharus.

_ Unfortunately, my friends, they know a lot. You can't just deny your past actions. Do you think that the divulgation of your ideas on internet wouldn't attract the concern of the surveillances services? Interpol has being investigating your agency, these blue jackets, for some time. The incident with the yacht of mister William H. Price was object of much speculation. The president of your former agency, the shop, had many powerful friends, who want revenge. Tharus couldn't be connected directly with this crime, but many of his collaborators could, including you, Iullus. The international community is very, very worried about you participation on the victory of a revolutionary army over a constituted government. They fear for your future actions, and the impact you can have on democracy. The UN don't think that is productive to take you to the justice. the trial can be too problematic to the paranormal beings. That's why I was sent, to negotiate a pacific surrender of all of you. If you assume the responsibility for your acts you will receive the minimum penalty. What do you say?

_ I knew that it would happen, brother! We should consider this proposal.

_ I don't know Iullus. Things just precipitated a little. We hadn't predicted the unchaining of these happenings, but I think that is too late to come back.

_ Think twice, Bat. "The grill is getting too hot", and I think that you are too young to have this kind of complication. Think well, do you think that if the matter wasn't too damn serious I would have entered in this "B movie"?

_ Peter may have a point, Tharus. I think that we should at least consider this alternative. I think that things have been too far. I do not want to "buy this bull" now.

_ You don't understand, Peter. And you seem to be losing your faith, brother. There's no grill, there's no bull that will stand in my way. I will put in motion my plans. Who can face me? Nobody has entire idea of what I am capable of. This proposal is bullshit. Do you believe that these powerful people will let me go unharmed, after they had a small demonstration of what I am capable of? I am sure they won't! They are peeing in their paints because they know the potential we can reach with the join of thousands of paranormal people to the blue jackets. I just would like to understand your participation on all this, Peter. Or you're more ingenuous than I supposed or you are a tremendous rabble. But don't you worry, I am going to find it out. I have made up my mind. From now on we are political exiled people in here. Who dares to face me will feel the weight of my eager eyes.

At this moment, all the command that had followed secretly the frustrated tentative of negotiation got into the mansion, shooting everywhere, and hitting who was moving. Simultaneously, four soldiers materialized in the office where Peter and the Vendra brothers were talking in., shooting modern laser weapons, hitting the left leg of Tharus, who only escaped alive due to the prompt action of two of his blue jackets. They harmed the three soldiers before being killed. Numbed by the happenings, Peter, after have perceived have been superficially shot in his right shoulder, created a mental barrier around his body, and remained observing the battle, once he didn't know what to do and who he should attack. Iullus immediately used his ability to become to threw by objects, while his brother stared at the soldiers, pushing them against the wall, killing them instantly. Everywhere the blue jackets fought against the paranormal militaries that had the advantages of the surprise and the most modern guns. Explosions were heard all the moment, as well as furniture flying around were seeing. The bloody battle was being printed on the walls with the blood of the participants, and parts of bodies on the floor depictured the violence of both sides. Laser shots penetrating mental shields; materializations and dematerializations of people and weapons; balls of fire and balls of energy spinning around; magnetic discharges and much corporal fight were the terrible scenery of the hostility stage. Noticing that Peter was on his knees in a corner, Tharus screamed at him.

_ You filthy bastard! How could you do that? How could you betray me?

Peter was dizzy with all that, but he gathered strength to answer.

_ I didn't know they would do that, Tharus! You must believe me! I never menat to hurt you! I don't know what is happening!

_ I don't believe in you, son of a cockroach! I will kill you! Wait and see. I am sick of being stabbed in the back by the people who I trusted the most.

At that moment, when Tharus was prepared to vanquish Peter, two warrior-robots entered in action, shooting potent laser shots against the Bat, who was compelled to roll on the floor to escape, once his mental shield couldn't stop concentrated light emissions. He had to leap a lot to avoid the attacks, once the machines didn't give time to him to strike back. He didn't want to disappear from there because he still desired to kill Peter. Concentrated in his defense, on the first opportunity, he felt great joy when he could discharge all his anger over the robots, creating a pressurized field around them, and squeezing them as beer cans. While that, Peter seized the time to disappear from there, because he knew that moment was impossible to talk to his old friend. After certify that his brother was in safety, Tharus went after the other mariners, who were damaging his building and his companions. One by one they were being erased, and in the end, he was so irritated, that was enough a fast peer so the skull of the soldier was cracked. Only major Hook was spared so he could be interrogated. After a quick fight, the Bat immobilized him and told to some jackets to take him out of there. Tharus didn't know what to do when he saw the extension of the damages, and walked confused around the rooms, until Iullus embrace him, bringing him back to reality. They had to help the injured friends. In the final count, twelve jackets had been killed and others fifteen were seriously wounded. Within few minutes, ambulances and police cars arrived in the mansion to rescue the jackets. After some hours everything was under control. After drinking half bottle of tequila, while smoked a cigar, amidst the ruins, Tharus was calmly waiting for his men to bring to his presence the prisoner he didn't want to deliver to the authorities. When the military was put in front of him, Tharus waited for a long time to began to ask. For long minutes he stared at the man who commanded that attack. Special drugs didn't allow him to use his abilities to try to escape.

_ Who are you, who told you to do such insane act?

_ Go to hell, you crazy maniac!

_ I am the crazy one? You are pathetic! How dare you to get into my house to harm innocent young people?

_ Cut the crap, you idiot. I know you very well, and this your dangerous organization. Your days are over! I was only the first. You couldn't get Peter, could you? You can be sure that this mistake will cost you so much, you nasty man!

_ Don't you worry about Peter. I'll deal with him later. Worry about what I am about to do with you!

_ I am not scared. I am prepared to die. You can kill when you want to.

_ I won't do it. I had already too much diversion killing your lousy soldiers. I want to introduce you my friend Antonio Maia. He wasn't here when you attacked me, and he wants to have a bit of fun.

_ I am sorry for not being here at this tragic moment, boss. – Said Maia. – I could have helped you.

_ Don't you worry, pal. After all, it was a surprise attack. These morons must have had the support of a good group of psychics, once our people who have premonition didn't sense nothing. But let it be! They won't lose for waiting. Now I'll let you two alone. If you don't get any information from him, don't mind. Do as you please.

_ Let it with me, boss. I have some good techniques to use in this bastard.

_ That's fine. Now you Iullus. I want you to disappear with all the bodies of these soldiers. Burn them all. Their families must never have news about them. Later search the city to find out their den. Certify that there is nobody left behind, and bring to me the rest of their equipment. And don't you forget about Peter. I want all the jackets and the police looking for him. Don't let him escape using his ability of immediate transport. I want him alive, right?

_ Of course, brother. I don't want to harm Petey. I am sure he has a good explanation to all that.

_ Later we'll talk about that!

Peter had materialized himself in a unknown point of the city. He was confused and nervous with the path things had gone. Besides, his arm was bleeding and aching a lot. He almost fainted in presence of much blood, specially his. For some time he wandered between old and decay buildings, shops and shops of filthy aspect, and lanes full of strange people, talking in a language he had never heard. He was attracting too much attention due to his different biotype and clothes. He hid in a dark alley, and with much concentration he got to stop the bleeding and the pain. After that he went to a desert park and stayed there for some time, to figure out what to do, however he couldn't think about nothing but the hunger in his stomach and the cold in his bones. Some police officers, who were investigating the strange man, some people had related, surrounded him, to take him to the police department, once they were sure he was the man the jackets were looking for., but when they were about to catch him, he simply disappeared in a blink. After wander form some more time, Peter couldn't bare the cold weather, and got into a department store, which was already closed, and fighting against his principles, he stole some clothes that were more appropriated to the climate. To relief his mind, he swore that some day he would return to pay his debt. After doing the same thing in a grocery store, where he satiated his appetite, he tried to find out a safe place to spend the night.

Antonio Maia was in charge of the capture of the director of the company of the paranormals. He split the jackets under his command, into four groups, that began to sense every corner of the streets trying to discover his whereabouts. The relate of several witnesses, who said have seen a Latin man, who had blood stains in his clothes, headed them to the right path. Even the police found out that he was wearing local suit. The searches lasted the whole day and the next one. Under a tight siege, Peter was desperately trying to leave the city, but the action of many sensitive people, who were emitting powerful mental discharges, was frustrating his tentative, and he was able only to materialize some hundreds of meters ahead, and it was exhausting his forces. But finally his thick discipline prevailed and he could leave behind the limits of the old metropolis. During six days he tried in vain to abandon the country, but his sense of direction was terrible and his knowledge about the geography of that country was even worse, he was walking in circle. As he couldn't communicate with the local inhabitants, he couldn't find his way out, and he kept disappearing and appearing at random, and once more this inutile use of his capacities was exhausting his energies. He couldn't even think clearly, and was on the verge of a nerve attack, wandering through the lanes of a small village, as a hobo, receiving rests of food from people who were scared by his crazy dirty man aspect. Alerted by the rumors, a young member of the blue jackets decided to investigate the strange riffraff, and came around him with a sandwich in his hands. While Peter ate the meal, the young man dressed in dark blue observed him with much attention, and when Moll tried to go away, he just called Peter by his name, who turned around instinctively. In a flash, the guy gave him a punch in the cheek, and Peter feel down, fainted.

Two days later, he woke up in a tiny stinky cell, where entered a slice of light, coming from a narrow and dirty corridor. His jaw was dolorous, and the wound in his right shoulder had been precariously treated. His clothes had been changed, and he was wearing what he identified as a sort of equable of a sanatorium, and was not appropriated to that damp place, and he shivered all the time. Peter couldn't coordinate his thoughts properly, due to inhibitor drugs injected in his veins, that should be containing his abilities, and this way he couldn't comprehend completely his present situation. Now and then he began to scream, calling for someone, but there was no answer. From time to time, somebody sneaked around and pushed a bowl of soup for pigs through a small hole in the door. Starving, he used to eat it in a hurry. During one month he continued in that routine, without hear a single human voice. The only time he could see someone happened during the random baths, when some men just opened the door, holding a long rose, and squirted cold water at him for some minutes. After that, they dropped some dried clothes and left the jail. Usually, they medicated him when he was sleeping. After that time, Antonio Maia began to visit him regularly, to spank him for some minutes with a rubber bat or to spit him with electrical devices. Sometimes, at night, Zed Brugg, a potent psychic magnetizer, spent hours on his side, emitting low vibration mental waves, which created on him horrible nightmares. If wasn't his excellent physical complexion, thanks to the rigorous training, he would have died under these bad treats, but the constant rat bites were draining his healthy, and he began to share his disgusting meals with the animals, trying to avoid their attack, and he learnt to obtain vitamins through the ingestion from bugs and roaches that infested his cell.

After a long time, he couldn't precise, Tharus Vendra decided to appear to him. The Bat wanted to cool out his head before having a long conversation with Peter, to avoid a precipitated decision. He was about to decide the destiny of the man who was a childhood mate, and almost a younger brother. When they opened the door, he was scared by what he saw. He didn't like the conditions Peter was being submitted. Revolted with the supposed incompetence of the director of the institution, he immediately convoked Maia, and told him to take care personally of his guest, so he could receive better accommodations. After these deliberations, he entered in the cell, and sat down in a chair a assistant was carrying.

_ You may go now. – He said to his assistant. After some minutes staring at Peter, who avoided looking back; stooped down in the dark corner of the cell, he began to talk. – Peter, my poor friend Peter. Look at you! How could it happen to you? I am not talking about your present condition. Don't you worry, I have already given orders. Soon you will be put in a better place. I am so sorry for that. Iullus will be very upset with it. But I am referring to what put you in this situation.

_ I don't understand what you're talking about, Tharus. Everything is confused in my head.

_ That's normal. You've spent too much energy, but soon you will be recovered. Now I just wanted you to answer some questions. Why did you do that? What did you take those assassins to my house? Do you have any idea of how many dear friends I lost in that day? My men want to peel out your skin. I am trying to restrain them.

_ Tharus, I didn't mean to hurt you. Please, forgive me. I can't remember exactly what happened, but I want to apologize!

_ Apologize? It is so easy to say you're sorry. I don't know if I am capable to forgive. Sincerely. Many times I am capable to forgive, just like Jesus had taught. If somebody torture me, or cut my legs or worse, I think I am capable to forgive, but if this person hurt someone I love, I am capable to do hideous things, worth of Satan. Until now I hate those people who tried to kill my brother, even after I have had my revenge. I am aware of how terrible are these feelings to me, but I don't care. What I want is to feel them until the last drop of blood of the miserable people who harmed my protégées.

_ I don't understand what you mean.

_ Don't worry. You're not in condition now! I'll come back later.

Antonio Maia didn't observe Tharus orders, and Peter remained in the same condition for other two months, suffering all kind of abuses. Antonio had a special pleasure on spanking him, with the excuse he had lost many friends in Peter's action. He just took precaution to know when Tharus was going to visit him, so he could transfer him to a better cell, with better clothes, and diminishing the dose of the inhibitor. However, the bad treats had a devastating effect in the mind of the poor boy, and because of that, he began to lose his memory. Without distrust of what was really happening, the Bat used to visit him regularly.

_ You've seem much better today, man. – Tharus used to say. – It is good to see your recovering. Maybe today we can have a sincere conversation.

_ Tharus? What are you doing in here? I am innocent. Can't you tell that to the judge? I wanna go home!

_ C'mon, man! I am not a priest, but you will feel better after your confession. Plea your guilt, and things will begin to work to you. I must know who I am fighting against. It seems that the whole world is my enemy.

_ I am guilty, Tharus! I confess everything you want to!

_ That's a beginning, old friend. I can assure you one thing, I didn't lose the hope of having you working with me, on my side. Iullus would like that so much. I know what you will say, "unfortunately, Bat, I do not know how to act like you, free of responsibility with the consequences of my acts. I need rigid criteria of behavior to north my path". However, my friend, you have already crossed that thin like when you betrayed me. You've shown that you are also capable of hideous acts. Don't waste your time by holding false scrupulous. Do you still think that you are defending noble values? You're just a pawn defending the selfish interests of a few powerful men. You're just a puppet in their hands. I can say that because I met some of them. Do you remember that once I told you about Ivan Karak? He is one of the master puppets. He sent me a message the other day, asking me to do not kill you. Do you know why he interested in you? No? I didn't think so. He tried to control me once, and apparently he is controlling you now. You see, you will never be able to promote the changes in the society you dreamed about. I offer you the opportunity to really make a difference in the world with full freedom of conscience. You can still help me to implement the new world order. Think about it. Imagine the wonderful things we could accomplish together. Nothing nor nobody could stand up against us, if we join our forces. We can agents of the transformation of the whole mankind. If justice is with us, who could dare us? United we can be invincible. Nor even 13 armies or 13 times 13 armies could defeat us, because the force would be with us. We can create a lasting peace in the world. I just ask you to think about it. The planet depends on us.

While was talking, Tharus walked from a side to the other of the cell, gesticulating and shaking nervously, as if in front of his eyes there was portrayed the epics scenes he wondering.

_ Tharus, I think you have been reading too much Shakespeare! Please, don't get me wrong, I may not be with my mind functioning perfectly, but you're much worse than me. You should look for a doctor, man, because you know that the good and the evil are intrinsically mixed in each person. All of us are made of defects and also qualities, and to balance these two sides we can count on with an excellent instrument, the law, that in a general way protect our rights and charge our duties. But the law is not perfect, neither the people who apply it, and what is in our hands to do is to assure that both, laws and people who apply them, continue improving, getting better and better. We must fix, maintain and protect the mechanisms that regulate justice, and not try to destroy it to replace for something we think will be better. What do you intend to do? To erase all those who don't fit in you conduct criteria? This is not the way. We have to keep on working the democratic institutions and enhance the diplomatic negotiations. There's no other way.

_ I don't know if you're a complete idiot or you're just crazy because of the medication. You're just talking bullshit. Keep on thinking on what I told you. In my next visit we will continue this conversation. Till then I hope began to see the raw truth, that the nature evolves through radical and violent changes. People very well intentioned can do great harm to other people and to the world, and criminal ones can help the evolution, by sacrificing the rotten part of the mankind. Think about it, friend.

Another two months passed by without significant changes in Peter situation. He spent his time sat in the corner of his cell, trying to seize the hours he was not bothered by his hangmen. At these moments he realized that even the memories of his sweet Denise were vanishing in the haze, due to the constant torture and drugs. Would she have forgotten him? Was she worried about what had happened to him? Probably she believed he was dead, and probably he was, because Tharus would never permit he was released. The only relief he found was the weak reminds of the perfume of the elegant and sensual girl he had the luck to have as girlfriend. He never dropped a single tear when he was under torture, but tears usually rolled in profusion on his face when he dreamed about Denise. The vengeance of the blue jackets was being too cruel, and many times he wanted they could simply kill him. He had already forgotten his personal objects, which were so important to him, as his car; with its leather seats and metallic painting, his very well decorated apartment, his expensive clothes and jewels. Some glimpses used to cross his mind, making him remember of a time when he used to spend hours with friends in pubs; talking about the most varied and deliciously futile themes.

However, Maia's plans were beginning to show its effects, and alongside the endless days, they were mining his capacities. Peter was becoming a man without memoirs, forgotten of his values and ideals, and at last, he was just sat on the corner of his cell, looking to the dark side of it, with his mind empty. Once again Tharus didn't see or didn't care about the maneuvers of his men, and didn't understand why Peter's physical and mental healthy was getting worse.

_ It is pity to find you in this precarious state, friend. Unfortunately I am forced to comprehend that it is the result of your struggle to maintain yourself attached on the rotten values. I am still keeping you here because I can't afford to have you as my enemy. You're the only one in conditions to face me, and I can't permit it. Or you choose to help me freely or you will remain in here for the rest of your life. I believe that when you have expurgated all the conditioning you were submitted all your life, a new man will rise. As a sort of phoenix. And I am sure that this new Peter will be my great ally. I know that when you reach the freedom of thinking and choice, which only the illuminated spirits receive access, your ecstasy will be bigger than any suffering you may have passed in the process. I just ask you to have more patience. In this time you will be truly free, as I am, when you're untied from the falsely puritan education; and from the hypocrisy of the authorities that have the only purpose to completely annihilate the spontaneous talents. They want to transform us into pawns; submitted on the whims of these pretense kings. No my friend, you don't know the true sense of the actions disconnected of feelings such as guilty and remorse, nor even the clarity that comes when you began to see through the shallow human interests. The real man rises when the layers and layers of low self stem is removed, and the ancient fear and prejudices are gone, and you comprehend that there's no such thing as hell. It is just the creation of people with lack of imagination, that didn't think about something better to control the primitive impulses of the mankind. Heaven is also an empty promise. Have one thing in mind, old friend, wherever you go, you take with you your nirvana, and you die, you will remain in this place in have been creating with your existence. Dare to take the reins of your destiny! That is what I want to you.

CHAPTER 15

THE FUGUE

Since the moment the command of major John Hook did not keep contact at the predicted time with the operation basis on the other side of the border, colonel Anthony Nelson was certain something went wrong. For about 18 years they had been uniform companions, and better than anyone else, he knew the methodic habits of his subordinate, that only for a major contingency John Hook wouldn't accomplish his missions. Immediately he set in motion the rescue team, and using the most modern devices, such as insects micro robots, that roamed the country capturing images and sounds without being detected; nano satellites and DNA scan, began to spy the main govern members movements, hoping to identify those the belonged to the blue jackets row, and this way, discover the task force whereabouts. However, after two months search about the destiny or any other information that would lead to what happened to them, the rescue operation had to be officially aborted, and the team was given as disappeared, probably killed, and the central command gave start to another action plan to infiltrate the country.

However, none of the company of the paranormals members accepted passively that version of the facts. They simply didn't conceive Peter could be slain so easily. Besides, they didn't understand how a diplomatic mission, apparently simple, could have degenerated into such catastrophe. Bitter with the military weak explanations, decided to organize their own rescue group. All the agents offered themselves as volunteers to save their director that before everything was a dear friend. But, to have a better chance of success required a small number of integrants, and this way, it was accorded that only psychics with abilities that would help the work, would go with Hermes Vasconcellus, who after study the case with his father, decided to take with him Denise Tanner; Suzanne Binoche; Argos Buzzolor; Dan Lee; Pablo Hernan; Steven Damme; Silvester Cobra and Arnold Conan.

They began the operation on the neighbor country, setting the Headquarter in the only hostel of a poor small village, less than 80 miles far from the border. From there, they began with mental incursions, searching for Peter's whereabouts, and the militaries that were with him. However, the mental shield over the country, imposed by the blue jackets, was making difficult the task, and even Pablo, with his exceptional out of body capacity, couldn't penetrate with total freedom the domains of the Vendra brothers. After some weeks of exhausting efforts, the only confirmation they got was that he was still alive and in the country. After that, Hermes understood that only with a work *in loco* would be possible a precise identification, for the most dangerous it could be. Thus, the group, in proper disguises, entered the country, heading to the Bat's cave. They hired a local guide and a translator, so they could have the maximum of freedom of locomotion and seek. From time to time, police patrols used to stop them, to check out documents. Prepared to that, Hermes was taking with him three powerful psychics level 06, specialists on the creation of thoughts-forms; a sort of delusion, what made the police officers believe that the piece of papers they were given, were legitimate documents and visas. However, after some days, one of the soldiers that participated on the patrol, noticed something strange with the group, and began to stalk them. Distrusting their weird behavior, the soldier contacted his captain, who asked for the help of some jackets. For two days they waited for back up, and them the siege was closed. Sergey Gagarin, was the psychic level 06 in charge of the jackets team. Best friend of Antonio Maia, Sergey loved a struggle, so as his mates, Casper Van Die and Hutger Lenox; both level 05. They heard relate of the local police officers about their intentions, and decided what would be the best approach to end the suspects. Sergey wanted to wait the dawn to surprise them while they were having breakfast, to do not give them the chance to offer resistance.

Hermes and his companions were camped in a meadow, discussing where they should go, while having breakfast, when a patrol with 12 men; escorted by the three jackets; leaped over them. Immediately the guide and the translator stepped ahead to begin the conversation.

_ Freeze! Everybody raise your hands! – Shouted the captain.

_ Calm down, mister commandant! – Replied the guide. – We are just archeologists searching for an ancient site.

_ Shut up, you retard! Who asked you something? Limit yourself to obey my orders! Otherwise I will have your tongue cut!

_ Yes, yes, my dear commandant! Whatever you say. My lips are sealed. You don't need to worry about me. I know how to obey orders. I am the best one. My mother was always saying that, and my old man never needed to kick me. If you need my services, just ask.

_ Shut this hole up, bigmouth! I am not interested on what you have to say. If you make me lose my patience I guarantee you will regret. And the rest of you, why are you hiding your faces? I want you to take your clothes off.

The guide granted them enough time to prepare the counter offensive, once the disguises where about to be discovered. They had understood that there were psychics with the soldiers, because they recognized the blue raincoats. Suzanne, Pablo and Argos would fight the three jackets, and the rest of the group should defeat the patrol. In a flash, the three agents of the company leapt over the jackets, while Dan over heated the weapons of four police officers, burning their hands. Denise became intangible and hid behind the captain, hit a karate strike in his back, putting out of action. Kevin, Sly and Arnold jumped over six soldiers, putting them under knockout in a few minutes. Hermes, who was participating in a combat by the first time, defeated his opponent, despite being wound in the belly. After some time all the patrol had been defeated, and only the jackets were still offering resistance. Using mental shields, they were protected against the attacks of the agents, but with the help of the other agents, there wasn't more possibility of fight to the jackets, and within some minutes they were exhausted and gave up. Sergey had been responsible to assist Antonio during the torture sessions on which Peter was systematically submitted, and was still impregnated with the energies of the director of the company, and they were sensed by Denise. Argos and Dan didn't have much trouble to tear information from the jackets, and finally the location of Peter was obtained. They also plucked news about the tragic destiny of the command leaded major John Hook. While that, Denise did an emergency surgery in Hermes, using hypnosis to anesthetize him. After that she stopped the bleeding and pull out the tip of the knife, disinfecting the wound with her energies. She also spent three hours applying magnetic hand imposes to reconnect the vases and tissues, and in the next morning Hermes was almost completely healed.

The three prisoners should under their custody until the end of the mission, at least, otherwise they could be uncovered by the police. This way, only Denise and Pablo could go on, while the rest of the group should return to the Headquarter. Suzanne suggested that she was better prepared to continue with the mission than Denise, but Tanner wanted to find Peter any way. She was visibly shaken by the news that Peter was prisoner in a mad house, and nobody could convince her otherwise. On the same day, they; escorted by the translator headed the Venue where Moll was captive. For three days they traveled fast, almost without stopping to rest, until they reached the big and old gates of the state asylum. The huge decaying building seemed a concentration camp, due to the precarious conditions the patients were submitted. Within few hours, the translator, Lipad Prenal, had obtained some answers about the accommodations of the installations, after offer some bribe to some employers. That was enough to Pablo, and he could project his spirit and walk through the corridors of the hospital. During some minutes he ran cells, nurseries, salons, galleries and patios, until he found his goal. He couldn't believe that feeble skinny sick dirty man was the gorgeous Peter, who was always elegant, but the energetic recognition didn't let any space to doubts. Pablo comprehended that in that physical penury of the young Moll, was almost impossible a tentative of flee. Returning to his body, he related the sad picture he saw and his impressions to Denise. However, she wouldn't give up now she was so close of the love of her live, and ran to the gates, and before she could be detected by the security guards became intangible and almost invisible. Walking through all the way indicated by the colleague, the trembling girl quickly reached the immense cold soil yard, where she promptly identified the one for whom she would move earth and sky to protect. He was walking in circle, around a broken fountain, in the middle of a great number of sick men. As it was a visit day, she could return to her normal appearance, and mingle with the rest of the visitants, who were crying for their relatives. Absolutely shocked with weakness of her dear Peter, she couldn't hold the tears that were falling from her beautiful eyes. But he didn't notice her presence, and continued his walking around the fountain. Recovering her strength, she realized that would be inutile to try to make him recognize her, and she just pulled his hand until a dark corner and hugged and kissed him, without care about the bad smell from his clothes and mouth.

_ Finally I found you my love! Thanks God!

_ Mom, is that you?

_ Yes I am, my dear!

_ Mom, I wanna go home with. Please, take me with you. I promise I will be a good boy from now on.

_ That's fine, my love. Listen, mom is here to protect you. Put your head in my lap. I will make you get better soon.

_ I like that, mom. Your hands are so hot! I am not cold anymore.

_ Unfortunately I can't go on with it, my dear. Can you see those men over there? They are paying heed on us, and we can't let them notice what we are doing. Do you understand me?

_ Yes, ma'm!

_ Very well, I energized you a little, and the rest is up to you. Pay attention on what I am about to tell you. Now I have to leave you, but I will be waiting for you.

_ How am I going to find you?

_ Follow your heart! I will leave a trace of light to guide you to me. Do you swear that you will come?

_ I swear!

_ Look, take this. This bottle contains pills that will cut the effects of the medications they are giving to you, and you will begin to feel better. Take one each day, and within few days you will be able to escape. Now hide it very well, for it is your passport to the happiness. And always remember that I love you so much.

_ Goodbye mom!

With her heart broken she left Peter behind, but she knew it was indispensable, and quickly she came back to her companions. As they didn't have anything else to do, Pablo and Denise returned to the Headquarter and wait for the result of their efforts. Peter still remained sometime looking at the small bottle in his hands, without comprehend the extension of what had happened. Afraid that somebody stole it, he put it in his pants and returned to his exercise, to enjoy the short period he was allowed to stay with other people. for almost six months he couldn't have a normal conversation, besides his hangmen, who from time to time conceded some minutes of relative peace among the crowd, as in that day. Back to his cell, he took one of the pills, when the vision of that beautiful woman came to his mind, and decided to hide the bottle in the only place nobody would search, between the pages of an old book Tharus had given him. Without other thing to do, he kept looking at the letters of the cover of the book. He couldn't say how many times he had read it, the biography of an ancient wizard; who died in the fire; in the Spanish inquisition; on the XVI century, accused of witchcraft and heresy, for purpose a govern system based on the qualification, where the power wouldn't lie in the hands of the noble men, but in the hands of those who were more trained in the most different forms of arts and science, and principally, without any participation of the members of the clergy. This kind of druid, Allan Taliesin, also known as the Dark Wizard, for only leave his castle at night, had influence under many European courts, and there was who believed that his powers would spread his domains for the whole continent. However, the love of the daughter of the richest men of Venice; a merchant, Catarina de Lamborghini, destroyed all his plans. When he saw her beautiful blond appearance, during a carnival ball, he fell completely in love, and was corresponded, although her father; richer than many kings, had plans to marry her with a local noble, and because of it Lamborghini elaborated a plot to put Allan behind bars, using the cooperation of Taliesin's enemies and the inquisition, that was eager to pluck all the estate of the wizard. Believing he was betrayed by the woman he loved, Allan became depressive and gave up to fight for his life. Since the first moment the Bat got into contact with the rare edition in the private library of the president of the shop; the only copy that was still entire in the XXI century; it became his desire object, and William Price used it to make Tharus obey his orders for a long time. When finally price presented The Vendra boy with it, the book became a bible to Tharus. Printing many copies, he used to give them to his friends, relatives and cooperators.

Every day Peter took one pill, as Denise had recommended, and slowly he began to feel the diminishing of almost all symptoms of the strong medication he was being poisoned by Antonio. Only his memory continued in a blur. He was becoming more agile, and the shivering ceased completely. Decided to find that pretty woman, he kept steady in his determination to escape from that place, and began to practice physical exercises regularly, and was amazed with his facility to execute the most strange movements. His mind had forgotten his skills in many martial arts, but not his body. He was also astonished by the speed his legs were gaining muscles, and how fast they developed. Ready to try to flee, he was just waiting for the best opportunity, and he didn't had to wait for so long. Tired of visiting him in the mad hose, Tharus decided that the best thing to do was bring him to his presence, and from time to time he sent people to pick him up, and in these encounter he used to spent hours monologuing in Peter's ears. After that he sent him back. The poor Moll stayed all these time sat in the ground, as a little pet, without comprehend what was happening, while Tharus, without care if he was understanding or not, made a speech about his crazy ideas, while smoke cigars drinking the purest scotch whiskey.

_ We, my friend, are co-creators of the universe! Believe me. Otherwise, why the Lords who made all this would give us free will? I finally comprehended it, and I will tell you. They want us to create our own path, creating conditions to influence the way of other people, and even the world we live in. everything that the men invented until now is fruit of their own decision, or do you think that some kind of divine force created the transgenic food? Holy shit! What is the advantage of having so many capacities if we can't use them to improve this damn world? Learn one thing, friend, we don't need to press satisfaction of our acts to nobody! Did you copy? To nobody! Because the Lords want us to experience our free will. They know that in the end everything is right. We are children who need to learn from their own experiences, the good and the bad ones. Ivan Karak told me once, you remember him, don't you? He told me that the laws of the universe aren't so perfect, and we can and we must help to improve them, and even create some of our own. We can create a whole new line of evolution. And he is working for that. I confess that it let me a little scared, imagine, the man is crazier than me. But I understand the guy, I mean, why we should follow rules and laws that don't fit to us? I won't play the game of a group of people who think they are above all and everyone. What is wrong to someone may be right to another. No my friend, I will be the lord of my destiny!

Peter knew that was visit day when a nurse picked him up to a bath and to put some clean clothes a car was waiting for him in the parking lot. He had been so debilitated, the jackets began to disregard his surveillance, and to escort him only three soldiers were sent. No psychic was present. Due to the pills, he was controlling better his mind, although he had forgotten his paranormal condition. He didn't let the rest of the people realize his real state, and even pretended to be weaker. He felt the best moment to try to escape was close, and wanted to be prepared, and not even the hostile climate would discourage him, because he would bear anything to flee from the constant torture sessions. The car took the road, and the guards didn't understand why a crazy man would require that kind of vigilance. They had never seen him in action. They considered that the hand and ankle cuffs were exaggerated to hold a man who couldn't even stand up by himself, besides, the snow storm would be enough to inhibit any tentative to run away, if he had conditions to do so. However, they had no condition to know that Peter was in a stoic determation to put an end to all that, independently of any obstacles, thanks to the pills; to the mental emissions sent by his people and to desire to meet the pretty woman. After about riding about one hour and twenty three minutes, he felt that it could be a good moment to try his luck, and that place would put him in the right direction. He noticed that the guards were talking as if they had completely forgotten of him, and despite the great velocity of the vehicle, he kicked the door, with his two legs, and before the soldiers understood what was happening, he jumped out. He closed his eyes, expecting the violent impact with the asphalt, but to his surprise, he seemed to float smoothly over it, and when he opened his eyes again, he was laid down over a frozen bush. Rolling to behind of it, he spent some time thinking about how he would get rid of those cuffs, but the vision of the guards returning to look for him distracted his attention, and when he believed that was time to run, he noticed that the cuffs were already broken. He didn't stop to analyze that, and immediately began to run. The soldiers started to cackle of his tentative of flee, and remained driving around him, stimulating him to go faster. When they realized that his arms and legs were free, they comprehended that something was wrong and decided to end the play, and drove in his direction to crash him, to give him a lesson he would never forget. When Peter sensed the car was coming over him, in high speed, he was so scared that his preservation instinct liberated a so strong energetic charge, so the impact made the vehicle stall several times, before to fall from a cliff.

His helpful spirit spoke higher, and he went to the car to help the soldiers, but when he reached it, he verified they were already dead. He didn't understood what had happened, and didn't fell guilty by the accident. He grabbed the coat and the boots from one of them and a pack of snack from another, and went away, following an invisible track. Quickly he devoured all the fruits and sandwiches, tasting them as if they were the most delicious meal in the world to someone who spent months eating nothing but remains that even the pigs had rejected. While he was walking and chewing, tears were rolling through his face, and he thanked God for it, remembering a passage in the bible he read once " I was hungry and thou gave me what to eat", or something like that. At that moment he comprehended nothing could be worse than seeing a human being without the minimum conditions to be fed. During two days he wandered through the valleys euphoric with the new regained freedom, and didn't even cared about the terrible weather, and the snow that fell fiercely. During the nights, he looked for shelter in caves in the mountains, and amazed discovered that when the hunger attacked his stomach so badly, he could eat almost everything to apply it, without being intoxicated. The only problem was the terrible taste of some roots, stones and woods.

In one of these days, while he was feeding by shoots of plants he dug under the snow, a strange noise interrupted the silence of the valley. Paying heed to that, he could distinguish the bark of dogs, that were becoming louder and louder, and ran away in the opposite direction. However, the barks of the beasts were each time closer, and he began to imagine the fierce animals dilacerating his flesh, and this vision made him give even more work to his legs. But it was in vain, because while he had only two legs, the dogs had four, and within a short time he could already see their powerful jaws, thirties for his blood. When he realized the beasts were about to jump over him, he closed his eyes, waiting for the inevitable bites, praying for, somehow, the animals were eliminated before they did some harm to him. However he just felt the sensation of his shoulders hitting the ground, when his legs trembled, and for his astonishment, the beasts didn't attack him, on the contrary, a silence and a total absence of movement took care of the place. Finally he took courage to open his eyes, and looked around, trying to figure out what was happening, and for his surprise he saw, few meters far from him, the animals laid down in a pond of blood, possibly dead. He looked around again trying to see who had saved him, probably a hunter, but he didn't see anybody. He peered at the animals e perceived they were huge and dangerous, and that the two rottweillers were well treated due to their appearance, and the owner shouldn't be far, and concluded the best he could do was to keep following his way. Sometime later he sensed that someone was stalking him, and began to run and hide, so he could distinguish who was around. In a few minutes he noticed two people dressed in dark blue, and understood it was the equable of the people who were keeping him captive, and understood they couldn't be friend. He just didn't comprehend why they were after him. Probably they believed he had killed the soldiers who were escorting him. He notice there was a man and a woman, and they were on the top of the hill staring at him. By their arrogant look he understood they wouldn't let him go, and that was inutile to try to flee. But he didn't care, and begin to run without look behind. Less than one mile ahead, while he was crossing a semi-frozen creek, he felt a strong arm punching his back. The man was hidden behind a tree. Peter fell in the cold water, and it helped to keep him aware of what was happening. The man grabbed him by the coat and threw him against a stone. Peter almost fainted, but he new that if he gave up would be the end of his dream of freedom, and he fought against the dizziness. Without a word, the woman held his left arm, while the man held his right one, and at this moment, when Peter was desperately trying to get rid of them, he felt a electrical wave runs through his body, and the two jackets were thrown far away. Dazed by the unexpected attack, they stood up. The woman was angry.

_ So you want to play? Let's rock and roll! – She said.

_ Tharus wants you alive, but I think if we take just your head he won't be upset for so long. – The man completed.

_ Please, I don't want to fight! Let me go!

_ How can you go away with your neck about to be broken?

_ What?

Suddenly Peter felt his a strange force in his throat. The two jackets were doing a mental turnstile, and began to suffocate him. Feeling the huge weight in his neck, the scared Peter looked around, trying to understand what was happening. He fell on his knees, trying to get rid of the invisible rope that was squeezing his throat. With the face buried in the snow, he tried to catch some stones to throw against the jackets, but he couldn't reach them. Desperate, once again he wished the two people were dead as the animals were before, and suddenly the pressure in his neck just disappeared. He was free once more. Crawling, he could see that the jackets were in the ground, inert. Getting closer, he saw that some stones had broken their foreheads.

Shivering of fear, he stood up and left with his head spinning with the inexplicable things that were happening with him. Some miles ahead, a sudden storm of snow brought him some other problems, and he had to look for shelter in a small grotto. Forced to spend the rest of the day in that hole, he started mental games to make faster the perception of the passage of time. He closed his eyes and began to conceive about what could be his foods of choice, once he remembered nothing about it. At the same time, a great will to eat chocolate took care of his stomach, and he began to imagine till the smallest details of a delicious half bitter bar. Even the smell he created in his mind. After sometime, he felt a little weight in his left leg, and believed it could be a small animal, and that plucked him out of the altered state of mind, and he couldn't believe in his eyes, when he saw it was tablet of chocolate identical to the one he was conceiving. Only when he held it in his hands, he believed that somehow it had actually happened. He guessed that it must have fell from a hidden pocket of his coat, and the smell of it made him imagine about the pastry. But he didn't waste much time with these conjectures, because he had a better thing to do with it. On the next morning, he returned to his way, happy for being still alive and free, and the desire of see again that pretty woman became stronger, and he struggled with the ruthless cold with great joy. The monotony of the landscape made him to think about his condition, about how he could have lost his memory, and what he was doing in such uncomfortable place. In the next morning he did the same thing, and a strong determination was the only thing that kept him fighting against that terrible weather. After some hours of hard hiking, he began to hear voices, it sounded a female voice, he heard a woman's voice. He tried to find out where it was coming from, but it was in vain. He thought that probably was becoming crazy, as his folks in the asylum, and it began to bother him. He just stopped thinking about it he distinguished, far away, a gray line hacking the whiteness of the horizon, while he was getting closer he saw that it was a road, and his chest got full of hope, and he stepped faster. If he continued with luck, he could even find a hitchhike. Who knows?

Chapter 16

Joseph Prometeus Souz, the Ziggy

Prometeus had been always a skinny and fragile boy. Son of university professors of a poor country of the European east, as needy as bright, his four older brothers were equally very white and very lean, trace of lack of nutrition during the childhood and genetic inheritance. His parents immediately embraced the foundation full scholarship proposal to little five years old notable kid, for they glanced the possibility of having a better life style with the generous wage they were offered to help the rest of the family. Besides, they couldn't afford a health and dental insurance as good as the one the foundation was offering. And God knew how much they needed medical care, specially in a miserable nation with serious socials problems. Offerings like that were very rare to someone in that condition to disdain. They also had knowledge of the excellent level the foundation school was in, with remarkable teachers and very good discipline, that forged marvelous psychics, well prepared in all aspects of the life. It would be outstanding to Joseph keep the familiar tradition and become a mathematic or history teacher with a good reputation, with a strong academic character. The Souz were compromised with teachings for generations.

The shy and introspective boy never had attracted attention to himself, and in the foundation school wouldn't be different. He preferred to always walk alone, sneaking off by the corners and shadows of the school. As he didn't have any sportive skills practice, his major joy was the reading and studying of ancient Greek and medieval history electronic books. For several years this routine remained the same, and Joseph didn't made a single friend, and nor even his roomies paid heed on his presence, for they had nothing in common. This way he practically talked only with the teachers and the foundation employers. The institution psychologists tried to make him approach of his mates, but all the tries resulted in nothing, for he didn't possessed any quality that could attract girls company or create bonds with the other boys. He used his spare time to read in the library, spend hours in front of his laptop or listening MP5 music. He only attended to the events promoted by the school academic center when he couldn't slip away. On the school recess period he went back home, but even then he didn't escaped his isolation, once his relatives were always compromised with work and studies, and he lost contact with the few neighborhood mates. This way, his childhood passed in a melancholic void, without everything that make the children lives memorable, and his adolescence without any contact with the opposite gender. Most of the time, his presence in the classroom, the refectory or the club was completely ignored. He was so used to this loneliness that even in his birthdays he didn't want any celebration, preferring to spend the day alone, watching movies in the cinema, and later, having a meal in a fast food restaurant. And he came back to the dorms he ate the small chocolate cake crammed with fudge that his mother always sent. His family didn't worry about this because they knew that deep in his heart he was happy with this life style.

But everything changed when he completed 12 years old. His mind powers became much more intense, attracting the attention of everybody around him. As much he developed his abilities as much notoriety he achieved. He didn't like that, mainly when they used to bet on how big his powers could raise. But his sense of responsibility always kept him on the same path. All the students wanted to get closer to him, and did not accept his refusal to their invitations, always insisting until he give up and participate of their programs. They didn't want to understand that he was naturally lonely and desired to remain like that. The shy boy saw with a great dose of sadness his quiet and hush world turn into a big hurricane of parties and all kind of activities the young boys and girls used to practice. His personnel universe was expanded, against his will, to a level that he could never conceive. Lab tests, lectures, conventions, interviews and travels to exotic countries, fulfilled his agenda, and at the age of 16 his chores looked like more a big company CEO chores than a regular teenager's. but there was at least one advantage, all that compromises brought in a good sum of money, that he used to help his relatives, and he had found an excuse to himself to keep on standing that total lack of privacy. He always called his mother to tell her the peculiar places he was in:

_ Mom, can you guess where am I?

_ On the other side of the video phone, of course!

_ Right, but where the telephone is?

_ I have no idea, son! You know that I am not fond of this kind of jokes.

_ I am in New York, Mom! Can you believe it? You can't imagine how wonderful this city is! Yesterday I'd been to the statue of liberty. It is amazing!

_ That is great, Joseph! I am so happy for you. Enjoy your stay.

_ As they say around here, "Dabrat", Mom. It means that everything will be fine! The day after tomorrow mister Shenell will take to Thailand. There is a kind of prince there that wants to meet me. Is that right or is that right?

_ Very right my dear.

_ Ask daddy if he received the money I sent yesterday.

_ Don't you worry, my son. He commented with me that it was credited in our count the day before yesterday. This is blessed money! Only God knows how much we needed it. Your father paid the lasts installments of the house and there still enough money to replace our old furniture. You are aware that the salary of a teacher is miserable in any country of the world. Our damn country doesn't valorize the academic field, and if wasn't the foundation help, and now yours, we would be starving by now. The way things are going, we can even return to our plans to move to Brazil. You know how the cold weather bothers your father. And we would have the advantage of receive a dignifying treatment. I heard that the Brazilian people is very kind with foreign people. Your aunt Gertrudes, your uncle Hans, and your cousins Christian and Andersen are perfectly adapted. Another they sent me an e-mail, they wrote that country is a true paradise. It is a beautiful horizon. I am envy. I can't wait to go out of this freezer.

_ Don't you worry, mom. Things are getting better to me, and soon I will realize your desire. I'll provide everything you deserve.

_ You're an angel, Joe. Listen, your father and brothers aren't here now. They will be upset because they couldn't talk to you. Now it is better to you to rest. God bless you, my dear. Kisses.

_ Kisses, mom. See you soon!

At the age of 17, Joseph had already reached the 7th level. Till then, nobody had reached that level, and as amazing as his development, were the kind of capacities he possessed. He had developed abilities that let the researches disconcerted, such as his incredible healing gift. In a unknown manner, some illnesses disappeared in minutes, and he could even recover dead tissues, in a small scale. He could gather atoms and molecules, and this way, he was able to create small objects of manifold colors. His new friends didn't let him rest, when he had a spare day, and took him everywhere, as if he was a miracle of the nature they wanted to exhibit to exhaustion. When he demonstrated his gifts to the public, in parties, through games and plays, he used to let the audience drooling, and as he was so sweet and sociable, his friends convinced him to do all kind of crazy acts. Aware of that, Joseph couldn't help being such proud of his gifts, mister Vasconcellus controlled steadily all the steps of his inconstant pupil, and when he couldn't avoid Joseph to hang out with his pals, he put somebody to follow Ziggy. The technicians didn't know at that time all the mechanisms that composed the extra sensorial perceptions, and were afraid that the linger use of these faculties could overload the energetic centers of the paranormal people, what could develop serious damages to their brains, and that's why they recommended to the apprentices to use their abilities with much caution.

However, how to control a 18 years old paranormal teenager who had achieved the 8th level and was eager to trespass all his limits and seize life as if the world would end on the next day? He seemed to be exceeding the boundaries imposed by the technicians just to see how far he could go, mainly when his fans dared him, pushing the limits. The shy boy, humble and opposite to the frivolities of the world, was being replaced by a buck challenger young man, proud to be the only one in the planet with such power, vanity for being surround by so many people trying to please his tiniest wishes. The influence mister Vasconcellus and his assistants, and even his family, had over Joseph, who desperately wanted to compensate his lack of attractions to the ladies with the ostentation of his gifts, was getting weaker each day. Right after have completed 19 years old, he went to Brazil, where this family had emigrated to few months before, to celebrate having achieve the exceptional mark of paranormal level 09. He was just one degree far to reach the maximum level in the scale developed by the researches of the foundation and of other hundreds of institutions that studied the paranormal phenomenon to the human beings. He was treated as the ultimate celebrity by the world media, and awakened ambiguous reactions on the common people, who were sometimes wondered by his feats, and were terrified other times with his dread possibilities. He was enchanted by the luminosity of the country and the extreme sympathy of the people, and during the few days he were with his relatives, the press and local authorities didn't left him in peace, and he felt compelled to realize many presentations and shows, organized by the city halls of the main cities. He could notice that the metropolises could be poorer than the European ones, but the women were much more beautiful and sensual. Their astonishing curves conquered all his admiration. He loved the hood his family was living, named Pampulha, where they taught in a federal university.

_ It is a pity you have to go tomorrow. As your older brother I'd like to show you all the landmarks and attractions of this incredible city, principally the female ones. It is unbelievable how hot are the women in here.

_ That's it Christian! The boy must know life is not only made of trainings and compromising. There is too much diversion out there waiting for him. We should take him to some beach, so he could spend sometime with some ladies.

_ I'd like to know what your wives have to say about that! You're too naughty!

_ Wait a minute, mister! Include yourself out if this. You're a healthy bachelor student who has the right to enjoy your life. Seize the day!

_ That's fine, Andersen. You won. Pack your bags! The weekend is on me! But unfortunately I can't go with you! I have some appointments on Friday night.
_ That's not funny! It should be your time.
_ Don't you worry about me. Make up some excuses to your wives and seize the larks.
_ Only if you promise us you will join us soon.
_ Deal!

Many times in his trips, Ziggy was escorted by his three childhood mates, who shared for many years the same room, and who had now become his best companions, those he could rely on, because their friendship didn't depend on the level of his abilities. Frank, Joshua and Fez were so without physical attractions as Joseph, and the four were dubbed as the geek group. If they weren't paranormal apprentices, they would be the typical students known as "nerds". And would be stigmatized by all the inconvenient happening and difficulties faced by those who were in this condition. Even with all the perks and privileges he was treated, Ziggy had never had a true girlfriend. He had given and received some French kisses, but that was all, and he remained as virgin as the day he was born. He had had some opportunities to get laid, but when he noticed the repulse in the eyes of the girls, who were going to bed with him just because of his fame, he gave up, romantically believing in the ideal woman, who would appear some day. The one who would let him so infatuated that everything else would lose importance. He met her before he could conceive. As he had promised to his siblings, Ziggy returned to Brazil with his geek group, to do nothing but spree a lot. For twenty days they wandered throughout the country, enjoying beaches; mountains; waterfalls and the rainforests, where they met much interesting people. However, the withdrawn Joseph was still afraid to get involved with a girl who could be only thinking about the advantages she could gain from him, and his eager heart desired a true love, and didn't allow him to fall in love easily. On the twentieth day, all the guys went to the wonderful city, Rio de Janeiro. Joseph was petrified by the agitated nightlife of the metropolis, and each night, he and his geek group ran through a true *via sacra* between lust hotels, fancy restaurants, dance houses and nightclubs. The alerts of caution about the extreme violence that contrasted with climate of permanent party , didn't bother the most powerful man alive. Thus, they used to go to places that were forbidden to the majority of the foreign tourists, and in one of these nights, while they were drinking in a vintage bar; which was full of delinquents; but also full of good food, a band of bad boys; attracted by their accidental tourists look; decided that Joseph and his friends wanted to get rid of their belongings. However, they weren't in a good day, because Ziggy was extremely moody, and thought that facing that band would be a good way to relief his anger. When the bad boys announced the assault by making the other costumers, who didn't want to witness mayhem, to run away, he just stood up and challenged the criminals.
_ Look, I don't talk you language properly, but I don't care. You just got me in a bad day, and you will suffer the consequences.
_ Shut up, *gringo*! Don't you know how to talk a macho man's idiom? So talk to my gun, you son of a pig!
_ I am losing the patience I don't have! This is your last warning!
_ Show me the money, you queer! I'll make you eat my bullets!
_ I love when it happens!

At this moment, Joseph looked at them, at these moments he enjoyed to blink as Jeanne or to shiver his nose as Samantha Stevens to create a spooky impression, and the bandits fell down, crying out in great pain. Ziggy had broken many bones and ribs of them with his mind capacities. After that, he paid his bill and instantly disappeared with his friends, back to their hotel, as if nothing much had happened. His brothers were bothered by his lack of remorse for what he did to those men, but they didn't knew that this wasn't the first time he made use of extreme violence to solve a quarrel.

Sometimes he just lost his temper. On the next evening, his siblings and friends decided to take him to a ballet festival, trying to undo that bad impression. They wanted to believe that somehow he was feeling guilty for what had happened. When the curtains were opened and the spectacle began, he held his breath for a long time, enraptured by the quantity of beautiful women in front of his eyes, specially one, who captivated his attention. A 23 years old girl, with a gorgeous face, black hair, thick lips and incredible tanned body and amazing green eyes. The boy was so touched for her, that in the middle of the presentation, he materialized himself in a flower shop, and bought all the stock of tulips and materialized them in her dressing room, after having checked her name out. At the end, he used his celebrity prerogative to promote a meeting with her, and after the proper introductions, she asked him to have dinner with her troupe in a near restaurant. He accepted immediately, and his mates laughed about it, because they had never seen such impetuous behavior. In front of her, he was metamorphosed into a new man, and he didn't lose his voice, as usual in front of a beautiful chick. To impress her even more, in the end of the night, he asked for the attention of everybody and raising his right hand, he concentrated for some minutes, and suddenly a small ring began to take form in his palm, and when the task was finished, a diamond rings laid down between his fingers, with her name carved in it, Carmen Claudia Hera Cintra. When put it in her finger, he knew he was already in love, unconditionally.

As was written, he conquered impressionable girl's heart, and this time he wasn't worried about her motives. His feelings were enough to him, and if she corresponded it a little, this would be more than sufficient. The girl, who completed her income by working in a shopping mall, in a teenager clothes store, was completely dazzled by his power and the perks that came with it., and despite the difficulties of the communication, which he was solving quickly by deciding to learn the Portuguese, they lived a powerful passion. Ziggy was crazy of love, when she decided that was already time for them to sleep together. He rented a huge yacht, and had produced romantic climate to the occasion. Liberating a sexual energy restrained for so long, he spent the best night of his life, loving all night long the woman who had awakened on him feelings he didn't know that existed. The insatiable Carmen had already had a relationship with another paranormal man, and was enchanted by his second level abilities, and supposed she would melt even more in the arms of one level 09, while dreamed with the magnificent life she would have by his side. On the next weeks, Joseph satisfied even her tiniest wishes, not only those that could be bought by the money, but specially those that could be created by his powers.

The young Prometeus had never been so happy. Nor even his capacities were capable to proportion such ecstasy. He even believed that destiny had given him these powers only he could provide a great life to his beloved Carmen. Everything lost the glow to him; his job; studies; volunteer work; fame; and even his family. He neglected even the healing works he used to do in public hospitals. Everything else was relegated to second plan. The overwhelming infatuation dominated his mind and body just like the most potent drugs, and didn't allow him another alternative, but remain on her side 24/7. For her, Ziggy was disposed to renounce to all his projects and ambition, and beginning to live they way she believed would be more appropriated to them. Wishing to have her always on his side, he invited her to live in his wide apartment in on of the most fancy cities in Europe, and this way, she wouldn't have anybody else to depend on, but him. She accepted on the same time, and neither the tears of her family and friends were capable to make her consider the decision. She wanted to travel the fastest possible, to begin her new exciting life, and during some weeks, the couple ran through the most beautiful towns of the old continent, in a true honeymoon. Little by little, the intense rhythm of crazy adventures was ceding space to the routine, and the relation was gaining more ordinary appearance. Joseph had lost completely the interest on his old habits and duties, and the compromising that was motif of great joy before, became extremely boring and without grace, and if weren't the appeals of his wife, who was tired of his constant presence, he would have quit all his activities to remain on her side.

His only goal was to realize each extravagant desire she manifested or even insinuated. And when he noticed she was missing her hometown, he materialized himself in Rio de Janeiro to pick up some friends of her, and within a few minutes everybody were in the Cayman Islands for a season of diversion. He didn't have the necessity to present passports, visas or any other documents, once he could transport instantly within a distance of 800 miles each time. Tired of receiving the same kind of presents, jewels, clothes and garnishes, she challenged him to materialize something really impressive. So he began to study the fundaments of craftwork and after sometime he began to create of the air, beautiful sculptures of ivory, marble, crystal, jade, gold and diamond. These last two were forbidden to be created by the psychic people, so the international market wasn't affected by the over production of the products. He didn't care about the laws, and even created a gold statue of her, of a natural size. However, the spoiled Carmen Claudia wasn't excited by these gifts as she used to be, and the only thing that let her up was the fact that it was a crime. It used to have a great effect over her sexuality, and she normally rewarded him properly, by realizing his most hidden fantasies. Joseph was each day more obsessed by the woman he split his bed with, and he decided to make a big surprise on her birthday party, and began to study car mechanic manuals. That would be the greatest feat a human being had ever done. Prometeus would require from his mind a giant effort that could costs his sanity, but he was disposed to run the risks. His chest was full of pride and jubilee when he conceived the repercussion it would have in the world, and how happy his beloved wife would be. When he felt secure of his knowledge about vehicles, he began to prepare her gift. He entered in deep concentration, until he reached a trance state, and during some hours a white mass was growing, expanding and taking form until the outlines of a car could be identified. Finally a real yellow Ferrari was materialized shined in front of his eyes, perfectly copied in its minimum details. He put gasoline in it and proved it could ride as any other automobile. After that he wrapped it and took it to the salon where her party would take place, and during the celebrations he offered it to her. So distracted by her new present, and the attention it attracted, she didn't noticed Ziggy was burning of fever, and the Hercules effort cost him ten days in bed, without energies to heal himself, and without courage to ask for the help of one of his friends, afraid of what mister Vasconcellus would say about it. But the nurse hired by Carmen Claudia, who didn't have the minimum vocation to be baby sitter, restored his healthy in a couple of weeks. Carmen didn't even stayed on his side, she was disappointed by the fact he was weaker than she supposed, and she occupied her time with more interesting things, and was enjoying the sudden freedom. Joseph always excused her excessive frivolous behavior, who was truly in love with him for a brief time. However, she was a young ardent beautiful woman, who loved the company of handsome imposed half bad men, qualities Ziggy was far to possess, and he was already driving her crazy with his constant night stroll some miles over the ground, as if she was some sort of Louis Lane flying over the city with a man who had no resemblance with Clark Kent. She was so selfish to be interest on the altruist use of his abilities, and wasn't touched by his volunteer work, which he had remained doing because he though it would impress her. The shallow Hera was visibly becoming bored by his behavior and capacities, once they were no more new things to her, and when she met one of his friends, who had been traveling and recently had returned and came to have a dinner in their house. Savio Crio Nogg, a 21 years old Canadian psychic, who came back to the foundation to realize complementary tests, sent by his paranormal school in Quebec. Despite he wasn't as powerful as Joseph, once he was only in the sixth level, he had all the other qualities she admired in men. He was tall, strong, confident, and his red hair and blue eyes enhanced his cute virile face, and he knew exactly the impact his appearance caused in the women and he also knew how to be extremely seducer and how to woo them.

Carmen, besides being very beautiful, was also very exotic to the European patterns, and her traces, typical of the Brazilian miscegenation was a great success between men, what used to let Souz completely crazy and jealous. However, sick and weak, he couldn't do much to control his insatiable wife, who seemed to have the chest and other parts of the body in permanent ebullition, and during his recovering she was dangerously free to extrapolate her limits, and the opportunist Savio offered to be her host in this work. After a short period of time they became lovers. They used to spend hours in his flat, and Carmen used to make up the most unbelievable excuses to justify her constant disappearing. She didn't break up her relation because she was afraid of his bad temper, and his reaction could be uncontrollable. She knew very well that Nogg was the man her heart was beating for, but she kept her double life, trying to gain time to think about how she would get rid of her inconvenient husband. Savio didn't encourage her to leave Joseph because he wasn't sure about his feelings, and just wanted to seize his time.

Feeling relegate to second plan by his wife, Prometeus began to distrust that something wrong could be happening to the woman he had so far judged totally faithful. She was always absent when he was sick and became distant and distracted after his recovering, and avoided his presence constantly. She used to react bad to his cherishes, and became annoyed when he wanted to make love to her, as she had never been before, and stopped asking him to realize her extravagant desires. The fact that the woman who had an almost uncontrollable sexual furor passed to deny more intimacy with him let him crazy of jealous, and he asked for the help of a former school mate, Leonard Bogart, a former private detective of few scrupulous and much ambition, that worked as consultant, who could read the mind of people, ability Joseph wanted the most to possess in that moment. The dull Bogart had been worked for so long as private investigator, when the investigation methods of his class were forbidden, and he began to act undercover to a select group of clients so his activities couldn't be detected by the authorities. He was sent to prison. A single afternoon was sufficient so he could find out the truth. While Carmen went shopping, he followed her to establish a mental connection, and when she stopped in a fancy café, to have a snack, he could unfold her deepest secrets, bringing to the surface all the mysteries of her conduct. When he reported to Ziggy the situation, he became desperate. His mind went into a blur, and his body almost exploded, and his throat became as dry as a desert, his heart bit faster, and a cold sweat wet his clothes, the whiteness in his face expressed the distress that was in his soul. The mighty paranormal, the most powerful man alive, the one who could control all the organic functions of his body as the most powerful fakirs, who could be as impassible as a Tibetan monk, was replaced by a regular man, who could be cheated by his wife, a man with all the flaws that can be unleashed by strong emotions. Without being able to control his thoughts, he understood the best would be to get out of there, until he knew what to do. In seconds he was in the lobby of a hotel in Romania, as far as he could be from the source of his torments. He had much trouble to hide the feelings that were burning his core, and check in without let being noticed his state of mind. Once alone in the room, he let all his sadness being expressed. He rolled on the floor, as if whips were tearing his flesh, crying like a baby, begging for his toys. Hours passed by until he could recover partially the control of his acts, and shrunk in the corner of the room, in fetal position, he spent the rest of the night, trying to understand the tragedy that stroked his life. His deepest fear had become true, and his appearance had spoiled his relationship. He tried to figure out if he could have done something different that would have kept her in the right path, once he believed that was his great part of the blame. He remembered again and again each detail of his love story, touched by moments like when he became a real man.

_ You're precious, Joseph! Don't you worry, because you were better than the most of the experienced men. It is hard to believe this was your first time.

_ Are you sure, my precious? I think I was too nervous. You know, I wanted everything to go perfect.

_ I'd say you were the best lover I ever had. So far! You let me tired, boy. Keep on like that and I think I'll fall in love.

_ Is it a promise? Because I am already in love with you! I don't need to say that I had never had a woman like you, because you know it is true. You are unique to me.

_ You're really precious!

He also relived the day when he invited her to live with him.

_ My precious Carmensita, I'd like to talk to you about a serious issue.

_ What is it, precious? I am all ears!

_ You know how complicated is to me to live in here with you, in Brazil. You know, I am too busy. But I don't want to be apart f my gorgeous girlfriend. It is too painful. So I decided to make a proposal, why don't you come to live with me in Europe? I'll give you everything you want, and when you think the time has come, we will get married. What do you think?

_ Of course I accept, precious! I always dreamed about living in Europe.

And the day he gave her the Ferrari.

_ Precious, I don't deserve it! You're too kind. How can I compensate you?

_ Just give me a heir!

_ Wait a minute! Nobody told me about kids. You know, I am still too young to deal with brats. I don't know if I will be prepared some day.

_ Don't you want lots of kids with you appearance and my powers?

_ I don't know, precious. Can you imagine if they come with my powers and your appearance? What a bunch of losers we'd have! No sir, I don't want to risk.

_ you're funny, girl. You're too "Eminen". Don't you worry, we have a whole life to decide it.

_ Get used to that. If you really want to be father, my advice is for you to find another mother to your brats! Don't get me wrong, but I ever conceived having children with a blond blue eyes man, a sort of Brad Pit. Imagine how beautiful our kids would be. You're far from it, and I will be very sincere, to live with you is one thing, to have children who will be alike you is another one, completely different.

All the reminds seemed to converge to the same point. She loved him, and even cared about him. The only problem was his appearance. And how could he blame her? He was always aware how grim he was. The great problem was a lack of communication, and in great part it was his guilty. Probably they should rethink about their relationship, trying to mend the broken pieces, talking about their feelings. Who knows, maybe there would be some procedures to remake his appearance. Maybe they could overcome these problems and move on, as if nothing had happened. He would make her love him again. Besides, he couldn't even consider the hypothesis of living without her. The simple idea was a great torment, and all his emotional fragility came out again, and he began to cry. He understood he couldn't talk to her until he was totally equilibrated, and therefore he stayed for some days in the hotel. He also had the illusion that if he disappeared for some time she would miss him and find out how much she cared about him. He believed he knew her, and despite her slips, he thought that wouldn't rest until she knew he was well, and probably he would find her sick in bed when finally returned. From that day on he would put an end on her provocative skirts and tops, and when she was dressing more properly, like a lady should dress, men would stop dreaming about her. She would fit in a wife's behavior. She would also have to stop being so kind to guys in general, for they used to understand it wrongly, believing that she was flirting with them, as it usually happens to pretty women. However, he wouldn't give the same treatment to his former friend Savio. That deceiver would suffer all the consequences for challenging the most powerful man alive. Nogg had seduced his naïve woman, and would receive what he deserved. Joseph wouldn't hesitate in using his psychic attributes just like Savio hadn't hesitated on using his physical ones.

Four days later, Souz decided that he had already tortured sufficiently his beloved Carmen, and that was time for them to mend their broken relation. He went to the most expensive store in the city and bought a fancy suit to him, what should awake her interests again, and with his heart full of hope and disposition to put a stone over the past, trusting in their future happiness, he materialized in one of the rooms of his immense apartment. While he was gathering courage to get into her bedroom, he created beautiful artificial flowers to present her, putting them allover the corridor until the door of his spouse. In these few days he discovered how big was his love for her, and didn't care anymore about the bias against the female desire, and as most of women were capable to forgive a love affair of their husbands, he would grant her the benefit of a second chance. If normal people could be so abnegated, so could he. He had witnessed so miracles of the nature and had realized many wonderful things, that he should be the master of his destiny, and create his own personal conduct, without care too much about other people opinions, which many times are truly sincere but could also hide selfish interests, that would end up sabotaging the better feelings of the other person. He had been always proud of his incredible bride, and should be able to deal with the stumbles this nature gift brought with it. He could even conceive the kind of harassment she was exposed to, and how difficult should be to her to linger such temptation. Since the very beginning of his relation, he noticed that the most of his acquaintances didn't comprehend or didn't accept that a guy without physical attractions could conquer the heart of a goddess like that, and they usually believed she was with him because of his powers, fame and money. Thus, the most of his male friends, and even some women, didn't respected her much and were always openly wooing her, as if they wanted to let clear despite Joseph's powers they were smugger. That's why he laid off these people. This man, Savio Crio Nogg, was exactly like that, and always pointed out their physical differences, to humiliate Ziggy, imposing his presence in the most inconvenient situations. Joseph knew that probably Savio came to visit him only to try to steal the woman everybody talked about, as if was a sin Joseph have a woman like that. But Prometeus wouldn't lose his trophy to that Casanova, and was disposed to give him a trailer of the real extension of his abilities. Savio should suffer the consequences of his acts.

Confident of his resolutions, Ziggy opened the door, but the kind of noise he heard in the twilight broke definitely his hopes. Nothing in the world could have prepared him to what he was about to see, and the impact was devastating. Twisted in a position he didn't know could be possible to a human being, Carmen and Savio were surrendered to the most basic carnal pleasure. They were so eager they took too long to notice Prometeus presence. Who was stood still, without knowing what to do. They were so scared they didn't even try to cover their bodies, and for a long time the three remained in silence looking at each other. Carmen was the first to talk.

_ Precious, where were you? I was so worried.

_ I can see how worried you really were.

_ That's not what you think. There's a reasonable explanation to that.

_ I am all ears, as you used to say!.

_ Wait a minute, Ziggy. Things are not like you're thinking.

_ Shut up, Savio! You can't keep on deceiving me. I have already found out your hideous betrayal. I decide to take a time to mull things over. In my delusions I thought that this cow wasn't that guilty, that I could even forgive her if he showed some level of regret. But what I see is that she didn't even had time to notice my absence.

_ I don't know what to say, precious. I am human and I need to be loved, just like anybody else.

_ Shut your hole up, you bitch!

_ You don't need to be rude, Ziggy. She is not a child. You will respect her properly. – Savio said in a defiant way.

Prometeus couldn't believe that after everything that happened Crio could still try to control the situation. He was so cynical. Joseph looked angrily at Savio, who was violently thrown against the wall.

_ You liar! You pretender! Your time will come, bastard, but not easily, and not here. – Souz shouted.

Before Carmen could say something, Prometeus transported the three until a distant point of a thick forest. When she realized that got so desperate she lost her voice. Ziggy was dizzy and sat down on a rock to breath better, while observed with hate in his eyes the shaking couple in front of him. He couldn't believe when Carmen got closer to Savio to tenderly check his wounds out. He began to cry.

_ Why did you do that to me? Why? I gave you everything!

_ Forgive me, precious! I am weaker than I supposed. You didn't give the attention I needed.

_ How can you say such thing? I even tried to guess your thoughts to satisfy you. Be honest, at least one time in your life, bitch! You never hid you didn't feel physical attraction for me. Savio is the kind of man you always dreamed about.

_ I won't lie to you, precious. Actually he is. I will as sincere as I have never been. I love you, precious. In my own way, but I love you, but I also love sex, I love to be dominated, and I love the men who excite my imagination. Unfortunately you don't fit in it. You give me much pleasure, but I need much more. I need somebody to fulfill my fantasies.

_ You broke my heart!

_ Why? I mean, did I rip out any part of your body? I don't think so. If you hadn't discovered that, we would have continued as happy as we always were. What is the matter if one of us has an affair once and while? I'll be honest with you, you asked so and I will be. Savio wasn't my first case since I met you. You never found out the other men, and you kept quite happy. I am sure you have done the same, and I don't care. I must confess that Savio is too much beautiful and charming. I am in love with him, and I even considered the possibility to break up with you and marry him. But I think we can have some kind of arrangement. We can be happy the three of us.

_ No, I won't share a woman with this ogre. – Savio interrupted.

_ Don't you do that! – She asked. – I beg you, don't tease Joseph. I am afraid of what he can do to us.

_ I don't give a damn! I have to say, Ziggy, nobody likes you. It is not only your appearance people despise, it is your personality too. God made such a prank when He put so much power into a havoc vessel. You don't deserve a woman like Carmen, but if you want her you can keep. I already had enough of her.

_ What? You don't want me anymore? And the promises you've made?

_ Don't get me wrong, sweetheart. I like you. I really do, but I am too young to get deeply involved with only one woman.

_ I thought that you wanted to have kids with me. You can't just leave me.

_ Shut up you two. I am still here, and I won't witness your quarrel. I hate you! I hate you both! You can't keep on making plans because I won't let you free! I will have my revenge!

For a moment prometeus seemed to be hesitating. He sat back on the rock to analyze what they had talked about, but he couldn't. He couldn't focus his mind, and while he was lost in thousand of thoughts, Savio looked at Carmen, and she understood what he wanted to do, and gave she agreed. Crio stared at a stone behind Ziggy and moved it with his mind, heading it to his head, but making use of his amazing instinctive reflex, Ziggy detoured in the last instant, and the stone just scratched his nape. When he put the hand in the back of his head and felt the blood, Joseph became more furious, and lost completely the rest of the reason that had remained in his mind, and was taken by such hate, that seemed his powers had ran off his control. Another time he put his hand in the back of his head, and miraculously the wound was healed, and after that, what could be seen was a unchain of overwhelming forces, such as a group of hurricanes spinning around, plucking out trees, soil and rocks. Savio and Carmen tried to protect themselves from the terrible storm, but it was inutile. The only person immune to danger was Prometeus, and the two tried to beg for mercy to the man who was giving outlet to all the pain that was killing his soul, and he couldn't and wouldn't hear them, because of the catastrophe and because his mind and heart were closed to the outside world. Nogg tried but he couldn't reach Joseph anymore, his powers seemed fireworks in comparison to Ziggy's, and each tentative of escaping was frustrated. Savio neither could get closer to the slender guy who was as powerful as a Greek god, who was shouting with all his lungs his restrained rage. Small tornados were formed from energy discharges that emerged from the ground, raising a dust curtain that extended through some miles. Nobody had never seen demonstration of such power.

When he felt relieved, after have put out everything that was burning his chest, Joseph began to regain control over his abilities, and decided that was already time to stop the hostilities. He was tired, and his knees leant forward and he fell on the ground. For some time he stayed in that position, with the two hands covering his face, as if he wanted to erase the recent negative thoughts. When the dust settled down, some minutes after, it seemed like if an atomic bomb had exploded over the place. Lifting his head, Souz could have a glimpse of the overkill he had unleashed, and was terribly impressed with his acts. After a huge effort, he stood up, and began to walk through the devastated field, until he stopped in front of the bodies without life of Savio and Carmen, interlaced. He got desperate.

_ What have I done? – He cried. – What have I done? I didn't want that. I didn't want them to die! I am not a killer! Oh God, please, please wake me up from this nightmare!

But the vision of the harmed corpses imposed the cruel reality. He had acted like a madman, against all his tenets and beliefs, transforming into a bloody monster in the very first tribulation life had presented him.

_ What have I done with all the studies and trainings? I'd be better if I had been born with some mental disease, thus I could do no harm to another human being.

He had already forgotten all the infamy, and only felt remorse in his heart, that would destroy all the good things practiced till then. To get rid of it he would be capable to give his won life, if he could repair all the evil he had caused. But there's no solution to death, and after some time he understood that the best thing to do was to return to the apartment with the bodies and then call the police. He should suffer the consequences of his lack of control. And so he did. Lying them down in his bed, he barely could control his despair all the moment he looked at those young beautiful bodies that until few hours ago were burning with passion. He went to the corner, sat down, and remained there, peering the sinister picture of his drama. He felt like a Dostoieviski character, a person who believed himself an outstanding man, the true superman that finally discovers that he was nothing but a reptile, the last of the human beings, a man who will never do great feats. He began t comprehend how difficult it would be to the paranormal communities, who would suffer prejudices because of his insane act. He stared at the pale face of Carmen and couldn't imagine how he would look her parents in the eyes, and how he would justify his actions. And what could he say about Savio, the poor guy had no obligation to him, and had just done what any other man in his age would. Joseph finally understood he was the only criminal in this whole story, and nobody would excuse his behavior. He would deserve everything that happened to him, and even if he was convicted to life sentence, it wouldn't be enough. The only way to pay completely all his debts would be by bringing them to life.

_ I am not a murderer, and I shall not be!

When he was young, he was able to relive small animals, but he had quit that, because it used to extenuate his strengths. But now was different, and if he had to risk his like to bring them back, he would try. Even if he had to use all his energy he would do it. Decided the matter, he kneed and held strongly the right leg of Savio and Carmen. He concentrated for some minutes, and then he started to donate his forces so the spirits could be attached once again to their respective carnal organism. The quietness of the scene was just superficial, there were enormous emanations of cosmic fluids; kundalini energies; mental emissions and ectoplasm energy circulating around the whole ambient, strengthen the bonds that connected the two dimensions. After almost one hour of exhausting donation of his vital forces, Joseph finally made them breath again. While they were regaining strengths, Ziggy was losing his, until he fell down, mindless. Some time else passed by until the two young reborn couple began to shake violently, coughing and mourning. As if they were awakening from a terrible nightmare they jumped off the bed, trying to figure out what had happened with them. Carmen didn't retain any memory of the time she spent dead, but Savio, due to his excellent training, remembered almost everything, and was aware about the huge sacrifice Souz had made for them. Carmen didn't understand why they were covered of blood, but without any apparent wound, and Savio tried to explain to her, but suddenly they saw Prometeus laid down, and immediately they ran to get help for him, in some gesture of gratitude. They called an ambulance, and while waited, they cleaned all the clues that could portrait the sad facts that unchained the incident. Savio dressed up and went away before the arrival of the paramedics, and in a last conversation, they decided that they'd better to do not meet again, to honor the Joseph's sacrifice.

Specialists were intrigued by Souz's condition, who remained in coma for three weeks, although no harm could be detected. After that period, he woke up in a morning, almost completely recovery, thanks to his strong and healthy organism. However something was different, the intelligent and well articulated guy had been replaced by a silenced lost look man, who was not capable to express what was going on in his soul. All his friends, family, work mates, former professors and foundation staff were stupefied by his sudden illness, diagnosed as sort of cerebral paralysis. Mister Vasconcellus sent his best researchers to analyze the case and try to find out a cure or at least a reasonable explanation, but none reliable result was possible. Only some paranormal level 06 who had the healing ability were able to produce a insignificant alleviation. Allover the world, the news caused surprise and unchained an endless series of speculations, until the media lost interest in the case, and the most powerful man alive was almost forgotten.

Joseph Prometeus Souz was sent to a healthy clinic, maintained by the foundation, where he would probably spend the rest of his days, under the action of powerful medication, that should restrain the action of his powers, that were still active, but out of control. The young student who was fluent in several idioms and dominated many abilities couldn't even recognize his own name, and spent his time scrawling in a notebook or watching cartoons, without notice what was going on around him, without condition to recognize his relatives. For almost two years Carmen Claudia visited him, trying to help the nurses to take care of him, but slowly she was losing interest, and other occupations were gaining her attention. She was his widow, and in a certain way she inherited not only his fortune, but also his fame, and she was always been invited to talk shows around the globe to talk about his condition. The statues he create with his powers were no longer considered a felony, because of his sickness, and she sold them and returned to Brazil, where she passed to live in great style. Savio Crio Nogg returned to Canada even before the news of Joseph's mental disease. He tried to put all that behind and continued with the normal rhythm of his life and plans, and some years later he was invited to work as agent in a organization of psychic investigation, known as the shop.

CHAPTER 17

BACK TO THE PRESENT III

With a bit of sadness in his heart, Peter returned to the country where passed the worst moments of his life. A mix of excitement and anxiety dominated his feelings, and the cold in the belly contrasted with the certainty that his thick discipline, allied to his intelligence, could supplant the might, but out of control, Tharus, the Bat. Also now, he was in charge and was commanding the whole situation, and had his best agents standing by him, and not a bunch of full of testosterone and nasty soldiers. He looked to his companions and amused himself with the excess of will they were demonstrating, and the most animated was undoubtedly Suzanne Binoche, that was eager to defeat the rival group. The most dangerous the mission was, the most she enjoyed. Also she wanted to revenge all the suffering they inflicted to her, and in those moments, when she was ruminating the hate in her chest, a name always let her out of her guts, Antonio Maia. Suzanne deeply desired that the conflict was led to a negotiated solution, but she wouldn't be sorry if the diplomacy fails and she have the opportunity to get a bloody retaliation. The cold and sly Maia was far the most dangerous "blue jacket", for being adept to extreme violent even cruel acts to solve the problems. And frequently he was the one who would use those methods. She wanted to have the chance to use these tactics against him. Binoche had charged her subordinates to just track his den. She didn't want to expose them to unnecessary risk.

The members of the company of the paranormals were waiting to find a very well structured organization and totally functional, due to the support of a vast mount of money that had arrived to the country and the capacity of its integrants. Nevertheless there was some kind of general deception when the first informants reported that the government was in a total operational disorder into the outline set by the Vendra brothers. The most of the Jackets seemed to be acting without a major motivation, and the lack of purposes were clear on their great interest on spending in personal riots the money that should be spent on the propaganda and raising the ideas of the "new order". They seemed to have succumbed to the folly caused by the excess of power, influence and impunity. The lack of central command let them even more exposed to all sort of temptations, which strayed those who were not sufficient prepared to deal with this overwhelming responsibility.

Tharus Vendra rarely left his base, allowing the burden to his crew the task of pass his determinations that were growing more and more confused and without direction. He didn't have the hurry to fulfill his plans, and the facilities of the country were very attractive to the members of the party, and he had allowed that everyone enjoyed some of the unimaginable perks, such as beverages; drugs; fancy food; sex; gamble; luxury and all the freedom to realize the most odds fantasies. All that and much more was on the grasp of those who now were controlling the national territory, and who were supposed to look after the public interests. However, the people, free of a civil war that had last so long, preferred the total lust of a docile government instead a new wave of violence, and they did not protested or made any efforts to stop the official riots. But the long months of crazy acts ended up to scuffed the relations between the blue jackets and the members of the government, and between those ones and the population, that had demonstrated a growing dose of intolerance with their debauchery. They were afraid that began a vehement protest against their policy. They had no manners to invest in what was needed to develop the nation. There was no way to get international financial support, but the citizens wouldn't understand that. They would believe that the ministers were completely incompetents on economics and social matters, and that it would generate an uncontrolled anger.

One of the blue jackets that weren't contaminated by the "mermaid enchantment" was Iullus Vendra. He had a deeply commitment with their cause, and wanted to see implemented in the country the "new order", so they could identify the positive and negative points of the program. In some way, he felt guilt for had not tried with more emphasis to stop the massacre of the members of the old regime and the members of the "shop". He didn't want that was in vain the sacrifice of so many lives. One of his most important decisions was to look for Ivana Minerva and date her once more, whose moral equilibrium he took his strength to keep doing what was necessary to go on with the cause. They were a well centered couple, with one complementing the determination of the other, and this way, together they were stronger than separated. Just like the bronze, that is stronger than the sum of its parts; copper and brass. The sympathetic and reliable Ivana brought stability to Iullus's life, that was beginning to think for his own, and did not want to remain as his twin brother's shadow. He wanted to step his own path, and did not wish to follow Tharus's mistakes. He began to see that his brother wasn't the person he had conceived, and besides it, other interests were growing in his heart, such as settle down somewhere; get married and raise a family with lots of kids. Just like his parents did, and he knew those plans wouldn't fit in Tharus's scheme. But the blue jackets, and in great part also Iullus, weren't being successful in their challenge, and they were failing on their purpose to make this country into an example of good behavior to the rest of the world, just like an ancient Greece, perfect and idyllic. Instead, they were facing the raising of a corrupt decadent and debaucher Rome. He didn't know what to do.

The Vendra's siblings used to visit very often the new action field of the twins, because they were in charge to bring all the belongings of Tharus and Iullus, once they couldn't travel abroad anymore. The Bat received with great joy his holographics dvds of his vintage idols: Depeche Mode; Kraftwerk; Ultravox; Joy Division; New Order; Echo and the Bunnymen; Eminen; Talking Heads. He was going crazy without them. Tharus used to rock his megalomaniac delusions with these old classics, while dancing and tracing guidelines to restructure the society in a global scale. However, he was visibly losing his contact with the reality each day, until that his only link with the outside world was his companion Kiria Eolo, who became an excellent strategist and coordinated the weak structure that connected the blue jackets and the new government, trying to make up the madness of her beloved Bat, who among puffs of his cigarettes and sips of scotch whiskies, confiscated from the unbelievable cellar and tobacconist of the former dictator, prayed crazy ideas to create what he denominated as the only possible salvation to the human race, his new world order, that would unite paranormals and other ethic minors that would willingly break up with the status quo. He used to say that he wasn't alone in this job work, that another organization had the same purposes, and sooner or later they would join forces, and nobody and no nation could step up he and Ivan together.

Obviously no one understood what he was saying, or which other group he was talking about, or who this enigmatic Ivan was.

Peter had combined to meet Suzanne at Gilda's farm, because it was a friendly place, hidden enough to the operations, and of course, he wanted to see again the person that had saved his life once and that became his spiritual relative member. He passed all the coordinates to Binoche's group find it easily.

_ What's up, Sue? Was it hard to find?

_ We could have found it with tied hands! Don't you know that our psychics are the best trackers?

_ Yes I know! And I also know that you're so proud of your agents that you always give them more credit than they deserve.

_ Whatever bossy! What are your orders?

_ For the moment we'll have to wait. We need the locations of the blue jackets that are responsible by the intelligence.

_ That won't be long. The people that are tracing their location are very clever!

_ Right now let's go inside and have a nice cup of coffee, because this chill is heavy. Let's go people! There is a cozy place to everybody. You're gonna meet some close pals. This nice lady is Gilda, my guardian angel. This gentleman is Glen Ariel fuond, her husband, and those shy fellows are Jono Querplex; Iberna Tuplor and Smor Fraggen. They are gathering allies to our cause.

_ My dear Peter, ask your friends if they have some problem with a person like me, because I can see their deception faces.

_ That is my fault, Gilda. I've always talked about you as a ordinary woman. They don't have any prejudice, believe me. Time will show them how outstanding person you are.

_ Tell Gilda that she is very nice, bossy! A bit fancy, but very nice.

_ I'll tell her, Sue. Don't worry. After hang out a little with her you will notice that she is a bright human being. Not only in her dressing way, but in her heart!

After some hours of pleasant chat, with the ultimate gossips, Moll received a message from Pablo:

_ I haven't good news, Peter. We had located this mister Maia, as it was established, but unfortunately, in the last three days we lost his track. However we could check his habits and found that lately he had done nothing but drink, get drug and sex. Not necessary in this order. He looks like a turkey on thanks given's eve. We have some possible dens, but we'll need more time to check it out.

_ Don't worry, Pablo Ulisses. You've done enough. Now is my show time. Pass me the addresses where you didn't look for yet, and continue with your other requests. Cheer up, my friend. Things are going on as predicted.

Peter had a deep breath, as if he desired to flee from what was about to begin. Gilda noticed his concern and approximated.

_ Is everything ok, my dear?

_ Everything is very fine, gilda. Don't worry.

_ You tell everyone to do not worry. But I can see that you're the worriest one in here.

_ I tell them things are gonna be fine, but I know that it is a lie. Many people will suffer until it gets to the end. I just can't avoid that! I wish I could have more time.

_ We know that you've prevented that if you could. But it is not in your hand. There are things you can't control. One thing you can do is to use the time the best way you can. I know you give your best. You are powerful, but you are not God.

_ Thanks, Gilda! I know that God moves in mysterious ways, and that everything will be good in the end. Excuse my weakness moments. Now I have to go with suzanne. I'll let my crew in here. They have some procedures to follow. Can you provide everything they need?

_ Perhaps, perhaps, perhaps! I'm just kidding! Don't look to me like that! Of course, my dear I'll do anything you ask. Don't you worry!

With the information in their hand and ready to get some action they just disappeared. Less than a second later they were in front of the first place to be inspected, the apartment of one of Maia's mistress. There was nobody in there, they just took a look and vanished right after. They also visited an old warehouse, where he used to do his felonies, but again they found no single clue. The next target would be a bar frequented by outlaws, where he used to find his informants and where he used to find all kinds of drugs and riots partners. The place was very dangerous. Not even the police officers had the guts to go there without a huge and well armed squadron. With a badboy's face, Peter was the first to get in. he went straight to the botton, trying to do not attract too much attention, but everyone in the salon turned their heads to see his good looking silluete. He went to the balcony and asked for a drink. After some minutes was Suzanne's time to get in. she didn't give a damn, and walked as if she was in a catwalk, as a super model. Step by step, enjoying what her arrogant presence was causing in the costumers. Her tied leather clothes and high heels boots, and a sexy raincoat and her mysterious look were the fantasy came true of every man in that room. A general silence was made in the place. Peter knew that she would behave like that, and in a certain way it was in their plan. Lust eyes were following her to the balcony, where she took a vodka's bottle from someone's hand and drank a long swallow, in a sexy gesture. Immediately several men surrounded her, offering all sort of beverages while trying to harass her. Calmly, she put a hand in her pocket and took an Antonio Maia's photo. The most of the men got scared by the single glance of that face, and walked away in a hurry. They seemed to know very well the anger of that rough paranormal, and did not want get into his business. She gave a disappointed look at them:

_ What is going on, my boys? Just now that we are becoming close friends you go away? That's outrageous!

One of them seemed not to bother! He was so excited that he didn't give a damn to what Maia would do if he knew what was happening. He very much wanted to take his chances. This big man, with a nasty appearance, came closer and put down his grim face to hers:

_ Family girls don't usually come to such place. But a true lady wouldn't carry a photo of a hideous man like this Antonio Maia. Someone could harm this pretty face of yours. Whispered in threaten tone the hulk man, shutting his fist.

_ And this someone could be you, darling?

_ If you wish, my hot woman. You remind me Sidney Bristow, from "Alias", the old tv program, do you know?

_ Oh, that is cute! I am a great fan of her since I was a child! Because of that kindness I won't hurt you much!

_ But I will hurt you a lot, Barbarella! After all is not every day that we can find a first class material like you to realize our worst sins.

_ I am so flattered. Unfortunately I have to say that I ugly man to me is like herpes, I want to be miles away, Shreck! In second place, if I'd like little worms I'd be fishing right now. But if you give the proper information I won't let you uglier than you already are. C'mon, spit it out, I don't have the whole night!

_ You bitch, you are really turning me on! Keep on saying those exciting words and I promise you will find out why I am dubbed Grotto, the butcher.

_ I am officially scared, Dumb ass! I believe that you will dance according my music. Otherwise you will be known from this day forth as Grotto, the gelded.   - She roared in an anger tone.

A huge pressure in the "balls" made the hulk man bend down due the great pain, while she kept swallowing her drink slowly. E didn't understand what was happening, and desperate because of the growing ache, that seemed rip his pelvis off, looked at his mates, asking for help, who assumed that he was being threatened by a hidden weapon, took some chairs to fight that strange woman. However, Peter was paying heed to what was happening and with a simple peer made all the chairs into small fragments. Before the rat pack could notice what had happened, with another peer, he threw them out of the establishment.

_ I thought you could use some privacy, Sue!

_ That's why I like you, Pete. I think our friend didn't understand the dainty situation he is in. I think I'll have to use extreme force.

A crash followed by a cry, and the hulk put his hand in his left leg, and noticed that it was broken.

_ I am not kidding, asshole! This is your last chance. Next time you can say goodbye to your friend, the dick. I don't think you will miss it, but anyway I think you don't want to lose it.

_ Take it easy, young lady. There's no need to be nervous. I'll say what you want to hear. That loser doesn't deserve my loyalty. You can even do us a favor if you get rid of that crazy jerk. Now let me breathe a little, please.

When the information was obtained, the two agents went to a condo in the suburbs. The condo was literally falling apart, with tons of garbage amounted on the corners. They walked slowly, trying to identify the right building, what wasn't easy due to the bad conditions of the venue. When a group of kids running and playing on the lane passed by them, Peter couldn't help remembering about his own childhood and about all the difficulties his neighbors passed through. In that place shouldn't be different. For some moment his mind flew away, and he imagined what had happened to his old childhood mates, and he felt a bit of guilty in his heart, because till that moment he had done nothing to try to help his former neighbors, who had been a important part of his life, and mainly of his parent's lives. But Suzanne didn't let these thoughts take care of him for so long, she shook his arm, bringing him back to reality. The kids, when saw the agents, they ran away screaming, as if they were there to harm those children, and one of them returned with an old tomato in his hands, and without saying anything, he threw it against Peter. The young Moll began to laugh, while he observed the fruit come closer, and when it was only some inches from his head, Peter made it stop in the air, remaining spinning. The young boy was afraid, and he tried to run away too, but this time Suzanne didn't allow. She stopped him with a stare, lifting from the ground and bringing him to her presence. When she smiled at him, the kid told them everything they wanted to hear. Immediately they let him go, and Peter grabbed her hand, and in the same time they were inside the small apartment, and were face to face with Antonio Maia, who was drinking in company of two young girls, Iksa Bentley and Georgina Plovs. Maia was drunk, and for a instant he thought that they were also jackets, and invited them to join to his birthday celebration.

_ NO, thank you very much Antonio. I didn't know you appreciated 16 years old girls. In my country that is illegal. Now get rid of them, we have important issues to discuss. – Peter said in anger. When he saw that man, he remembered all the tortures he suffered.

_ Not today! My head is twirling. I drank too much, I smoked too much and I sniffed too much. Now sit down and try to relax, that is an order. Later I am going to taste that woman you brought. – Maia wasn't thinking properly.

_ Don't you remember me? We were so close few months ago. You treated me very nice and I came in to thank you.

_ I get drugged and you're the one who get high! Man, I don't remember you at all, and besides, my specialty is not to cure people, but to hurt them. – He began to cackle.

_ I see that it is not working, so I will be straight. My name is Moll, Peter Moll. Now you remember me?

_ Moll? Of course I do. I thought you were dead. Man you are different. Have you been working out? What fancy clothes!

_ Cut the crap! We are not here to chat.

_ Do you think you scare me, boy? Don't you underestimate me! If Tharus had allowed me to use all my skills in you, I'd be seeing a ghost at this moment. Did you bring your girlfriend to try my methods? I can use some help of her.

_ Unfortunately I have to say that is you who is underestimating me. Your time has come, hangman. I won't let you hurt anybody else.

While he was talking, Peter's anger was growing, so as his desire to kill that man. Antonio noticed the danger, and in the fog his mind was, he tried to remember exactly who Peter was. But he didn't have much time to think, because Suzanne was behind him, and she gave a violent kick in his back, throwing him in the other room. The stroke worked as a start, and Maia recalled everything about Moll. Frightened and agitated, the jacket stood up quickly, and showing an incredible agility, he got his gun from within a vase and shot on theirs direction. Impassible, Peter just peered at the bullets, which detoured in his mental shield. Once again, Suzanne was behind him and kicked another time, sending him to another room.

_ I forgot to tell you to take care. This girl also loves to hurt people.

Scared, the two girls began to scream, because they thought they would be killed too, and they grabbed Peter's leg, begging for mercy. While that, Maia took advantage in the confusion, and ran through the fire ladders, going to the terrace. Without care about his escaping, Peter, gently, took their arms and asked them to leave, and after that he joined Suzanne in the stalking.

_ I am beginning to enjoy that! – He said.

_ Welcome to the club, my dear!

Once in the terrace, Antonio had much difficult to concentrate enough to be able to levitate to the next building and from there to the next one, because of the excess of alcohol and other drugs in his blood. He tried to hide behind some water pipes, and when he felt secure, he opened a bourbon bottle that was in his pocket and drank it in just one swallow, without notice that Peter and Suzanne were already sat on the bigger pipe.

_ The view from here is amazing, isn't it?

_ How? How did you arrive here so fast?

_ I asked you to do not underestimate me, pal. Do you think that I am still that undefended boy that you tortured? Please, I ask you again to do not commit this mistake.

_ Stay away from me, you jerk! I have already contacted my colleagues. This time I won't have pity, little boy! Wait and see! I will kill you both and spit on your corpses!

Trying to scare them or to hypnotize them with his shouts, Maia was prepared again to run away, when Suzanne stopped him. He took a knife from another pocket and jumped over her, but she disarmed him easily. Furious, he jumped again over her, but another time she proved to be a better fighter, and she punched him to the ground. Mad of hate, he tried to jump over her once more, but she shunned and he stumbled and fell from the roof. Peter was too distracted with the struggle and he couldn't react on time to save the jacket, and he hit the street with a big bang and a clatter.

_ Is he dead? – Suzanne asked.

_ I think so. After all he fell from seven floors. It is that old saying, if you're gonna fly don't drink, and if you're gonna drink don't fly. That wasn't the end I had I mind, but goes as predicted.

_ I won't be sorry for him.

_ Me neither. Now let's move on. You insisted to come with me, and I agreed, but now I have to go on alone. You must come back to your group and continue with your part. This is just the beginning.

_ I must confess that I am a little frustrated, because things are going so easy. I could use more adrenaline.

_ I wanted to agree with you, but I know that we will have a difficult time ahead. This organization of Tharus and Iullus may have been over estimated. We already perceived they aren't professional, but anyhow, Tharus is too powerful yet. I can't imagine how he will react. May the force be with you!

_ May the force be with you too!

Within few hours the groups under the command of Anna and Suzanne began the abduction of the jackets located by the psychic trackers. The agents of the company couldn't restrain their testosterone, and after a last check on their gear they got into action. The teams of Pablo and Kim spread through the country, raising the whereabouts of the members of the blue jackets. After that informed all their habits, routines and addresses to the agents in charge of their apprehension, who counted with the surprise element and the numeric advantage to close the siege, acting in syntony, to immobilize and capture them, without let a change to a counter reaction. Simultaneously, several incursions were made allover the territory. Vaived Danae Midral had just taken her bath, in her cozy hotel room. Relaxed and asleep, after had napped for thirty minutes in bathtub, she was dressing the robe when two agents held her arms, at the same time a third one shot her a powerful sedative, while another agent was blocking her abilities. All the raptors possessed the capacity of instant transport, and using a group effort, they materialized her to the place where another team was waiting to take her to the group of Argos, who should take her to the base where Hermes Vasconcellus was in charge to keep them arrested. The procedure was almost the same to all members of the organization of the Vendra brothers.

Kim was in charge to track Iullus, and when discovered his whereabouts, she conduced Peter to the place, but he was too cautious and wanted to wait for the nightfall to look for the old friend. Tharus's brother woke up about two in the morning, with a strange sensation in his belly. This sensation was going up to his chest, throat, and finally stopped in the back of his brain, and he felt that somebody was calling him. Intrigued, he didn't have the gift of telepath, he decided to follow this felling, and went to the porch. If there was nothing he would breath some fresh air, at least. First he took a generous dose of cognac, and when he went out to the cold place, he almost fainted, when saw the man he loved as a younger brother; who was supposed dead; sat comfortably in an armchair.

_ Peter, is that you?

_ In flesh and bones, my dear friend! More flesh than bones, actually.

_ I thought I was seeing a ghost! I was told that you were dead! You have no idea how it hurt me. It is so nice to see you. Come in! Give me a hug!

The two friends embraced each other for a long time.

_ Thanks! I needed that. I knew that you had no participation on what happened to me. I know how sincere you are, and exactly because of it I came to you.

_ I think I know what you want to talk about. Do want to drink something?

_ Yes I do! A dry martini, please.

_ Here you are, Peter. You don't know how relieved I am.

_ Iullus, you know me for 20 years, and know that I would never betray a friend. You have to believe me. I didn't know what that militaries were planning. I thought I was sent here to negotiate. As your brother would say, I was dangerously naïve.

_ I know you very well, and I believe in you. I just couldn't see you as a traitor. I must confess that in the first moment I believed that the little boy that I knew could have changed his character through out the years. It happens all the time, and we hadn't had contact for so long, that I let myself go with the evidences. After sometime, when I was checking out what had happened, I concluded that you were manipulated. I know what that is, I had already seen that when I worked at the shop. I was feeling terrible for not having interfered for you in that prison, and when I was informed you had died frozen in the mountains, I felt terribly guilty. If I could turn back in time I would have even fought my brother to defend you.

_ I am so glad to hear that, Iullus. I always trusted in your good feelings, and that's why I am here today. I want to offer again the old deal. But this time it is true. I am in charge of the operations now, and I assure you there's no trap this time. I guarantee all the points of the negotiation, because if we don't have a deal, the consequences will be terrible to this poor country.

_ I know what you're talking about, and I kind waited for that to happen. We have scared too much powerful people with our crazy actions. Nobody could prevent the extension of the powers of my brother, and how many sensitive people he could gather. It is totally understandable, and I must say that I am scared too. We took hold of this country so easily, that it makes me wonder what we're going to do next. The presidents of lots of nations must be thinking they're the next. And I think that if you don't stop us, we will spread our revolution. Tharus wants it, and the most of the blue jackets too.

_ I know what you mean. You gathered too much power, and you brother was always eager to save the world. But I must confess that I am a bit disappointed with the structure of this organization of yours, the blue jackets. When I was caught and spent all those months captive, I thought I was dealing with a very well orchestrated group, that would represent in the future a great risk to the company of the paranormals, once it became more solid. However, what I see now is a bunch of drunk prankster college students that just want to spree and have fun in the country they conquered. You became an empty promise. What happened to you?

_ I don't think we were prepared to what came after the conquest. You see, our plans were to create the blue jackets in the future, but the attempt of the shop against me precipitated everything. Tharus thought that we had enough structure to achieve our goals, but I knew that wasn't true. Some of our members are professional, but the most of the blue jackets is formed for students who just finished the university. We dreamed a lot and acted a few. Our members aren't compromised with the future. They think that they can come back home after the revolution and continue with their previous lives. They are too young and want nothing but diversion and adventure, and when the new government gave us a great part of the country, we got lost with the great facilities. Even tharus revealed himself a weak leader, who doesn't have patience with the implementation of the new order. It is a beautiful dream this new order, but hard to be put in motion.

_ That's why I am here, my friend, to help you to get out of this mess. You have to work with me to convince him to give up these plans. The Unite Nations are prepared to consider his good will.

_ I don't know, Peter. He believes that if we give up now we will be erased by the militaries. He thinks that now the world discovered the potential of his powers, he must be eliminated. He is stuck to this idea. You're gonna have problems to convince him the otherwise.

_ If we fail to convince him, we can still capture him to show that we do not intend to kill him. With your help it would be less difficult. I am allowed to promise you that only all the accusations against you will be erased, and your brother will be sent to an institute, to be neutralized for some years, until they understand he is no longer a hazard to the society. the Bat is like a brother to me, and I prefer to see him in a recovering center than practicing more brutal and hideous acts, until he is eliminated as a mad dog.

_ I understand your point, Peter. My heart is torn by it, but I must conspire against him. For his own sake! Unfortunately there's no other way. You can count on me. Ivana too.

_ That's all I wanted to hear, my friend. I must leave now! It is dangerous to stay for more time. I'll keep in touch.

Iullus couldn't say anything. His throat was suffocated, and before disappear Peter saw tears rolling through his face. After ten days, almost all the jackets had been captured and the most was convinced to abandon the cause, by means of the promise they wouldn't go to trial, once they had not committed a more serious crime that could be detected. The few ones that remained loyal to the Vendra brothers were aware of the presence of the agents of the company, and they looked for shelter in the Tharus's barrack, who hadn't began yet the retaliations because his brother had convinced him to wait the exact moment, to do not compromise their future intentions. Nichollas Graff and Savio Nogg were radically against a possible deal, and rather to go with all their forces combined in a frontal attack, to show the world they should be respected and feared. They believed that it would bring the sympathy of millions of people to their cause. But Giselle and Kiria were on Iullus side, and supported his considerations. Peter had put Suzanne in charge of negotiations with Tharus girlfriend, who should help Iullus to put some rational judgment in his head. Suzanne knew Giselle very well, and comprehended she would have perceived by that moment the actions of the Bat had gone so far, and he should be stopped, and Binoche looked Giselle's help to intermediate her encounters with Kiria. A reunion was scheduled in an abandoned factory, so they could establish the best manners to help Tharus.

_ Did you come alone, Sue? – Giselle asked.

_ Of course!

_ You know how dangerous is this situation, don't you?

_ I am aware of it.

_ But it is too good to see you, darling.

_ Dido! Come here and give me a kiss.

_ I missed you so much, Sue. How long have we been apart?

_ I think since our fight for the Bat. But that is all past. Did you bring the girl?

_ Sure! Come in, Kiria. It is safe.

_ So you're the famous woman that grabbed our Adonis?

_ I think so. Nice to meet you!

_ The pleasure is all mine.

_ So, what are your intentions? You know we can't linger in here.

_ The most noble ones. We just want to avoid a bigger disaster. We don't want to shed more innocent blood.

_ I know. I want you to know that I am accepting to help you because I love Tharus so much to see him commit this suicide. I just want to take care of him because he is totally lost. In the bottom of his heart he is a good man, and his intentions are elevated. But he took the wrong way, and he must be conduced to the right path again.

_ That's all we want, Kiria. We are Tharus friends, and I can say that I even sympathize with the most of the ideals of these blue jackets. I also think that the mankind needs a profound change, otherwise we run serious risks of destruction of the planet. I also agree that the interests of a minority can't damage the future of everybody. If the circumstances were different, some companions and me had enjoyed this organization of yours. But unfortunately destiny put us in opposite sides, and we must solve it the best way we can. Nobody in here wants to witness the disgrace of our beloved blond Bat.

_ I am glad to hear this. Now tell me what you want me to do.

_ Not much! You have to convince him to deal with us. He trusts you and will hear whatever you have to say. Even Iullus is helping us.

_ Iullus? Now I am totally relieved. I have already been talking to him about these matters, but he gets angry all the times. I need more subsidies to argue. I have noticed he is confused with all this situation, and he is losing control of what is happening, what let him even more confused and disappointed. I am afraid he end up hurting too much people, people he loves and that love him. That would destroy his spirit. I have noticed he's been exasperated with his brother lately, and I just didn't understand why. I am afraid they face each other.

While the three girls were talking, Nicholas Graff was spying the suspect fact. Annoyed because he couldn't hear their conversation, he decided to appear to them, escorted by other two jackets. Savio had been angry with Giselle, after she have rejected his woos, and it made his distrust her intentions, when he perceived her constant whispered chats with Kiria, and he asked Nick to put somebody to stalk her.

_ What an interesting picture we have in here, don't we? Three exuberant girls gathered looks like a modeling event. Are you being shot to Vogue magazine? – He interrupted, intentionally scaring them.

_ What is that about, Nick? How you dare to follow me? – Giselle cried.

_ Why? Am I interrupting something? Does the Bat know that you are talking to the enemy?

_ You're completely wrong, Nick! We are just talking to an old friend. We must leave some options opened.

_ That is not up to you to decide, Traitor! Savio already suspected of your behavior. When the ship begins to sink the rats are the firsts to flee! But if we sink, everybody goes with us. we haven't yet launched our most lethal attack. Boys if any of these cows try anything, don't hesitate to kill them all. Keep them under your aim. You will rip up Tharus heart, Kiria.

_ Don't you do that, Nicholas! I would give my life away to protect him. The government asked me to deal with the UN. We are trying to save Tharus.

_ Then it means that things are even worse than we thought. The government is also involved in this plot. What a shame! The Bat is being sold by those people that should have been the most loyal friends. Did you hear that,Savio?

_ Loud and clear, Nick! The transmission is perfect. Tharus is here on my side.

_ Now we have to wait to hear his decision. If that was up to me, I would kill all of you, after you have satisfied a whole army, as the whores you are.

_ Why, aren't you man enough to entertain us? – Suzanne asked.

_ I am a real buck, you know. I can even show you that now if you want to. I always wanted to break you. You are too arrogant.

_ You were jealous of the men I had, you limp faggy.

_ You filthy bitch, you will pay me!

In a rage, Nichollas shot a energy ball on her direction. The explosion didn't have much impact, once he hadn't enough time to prepare it, and Suzanne, protected by her fast mental shield, immediately stood up and paid in the same currency. But hers was more potent and it threw him against the wall. He had his left arm broken, and decided to use his laser gun, but before he had time to aim it, she burnt all the circuits of the weapon, with just a peer. Meanwhile, Giselle took the chance to attack the other jackets, who were level 05. Easily she defeated them. Breaking their mental block, she set fire on their clothes, and desperate they jumped from the lift hole. Using the instants Giselle was paralyzed by the hideous scene, Nicholas stabbed her in the back. Felling the blood in her throat, she stared Suzanne in the eyes, frightened by the sensation that she was dying. In a last effort she whispered to Binoche.

_ Say to my family that I am so sorry. Tell them that I loved them so much. Goodbye! – After that she fell on the ground, dead.

_ I am not guilty for that! – Nicholas said. – She had what she deserved.

_ you bloody dog from hell! I will kill you! – Suzanne cried in despair.

In a assassin fury, she jumped over him, using all her knowledge in martial arts, without give him chance to recover, and when he was wounded enough, she gathered all her energy in a ball of energy and sent it to him, to expurgate all the hate and frustration in her heart. The explosion was so strong that heavy machines fell over him, creating a sort of gravy. Exhausted and shocked by the tragic unfolding of the things, she fell on her knees, without conditions to get out of there. She began to cry. Hidden in a dark corner, Kiria was petrified, without knowing what to do, and the two girls remained in that position for some time, until they heard noises of steps. Behind the shades of the warehouse, Tharus emerged as a kind of death angel, in his dark blue coat.

_ My pretty Suzanne, how long I don't see you. What a mess you did in here! I am admired for what you did to my friend Nick, my dear Giselle and other two jackets; Fred and George. You're an amazing girl. There was a time when I had a crush on you. I even thought we were twin souls! How stupid I was. Do you remember our games and plays? Why don't you answer me?

_ I am scared! I didn't kill Giselle. She was my friend!

_ But you're the only one standing in here! You're fearless! I don't think you're worried about me. How many times we made love in the most weird places? I think that somehow I am guilty of what you did to Giselle, because if I hadn't dated you both in the same time, probably you wouldn't hate her for so long. Believe me when I say that I'd rather to meet you in a different place under different circumstances. I want you to know that you were an important part of my life and that you occupy an important part of my heart, but I can't let you go. My duties are bigger than me, you or anybody else, and I just have to erase who get into my way. My soul is ripped, my heart is bleeding and my eyes can't produce enough tears to mourn you. I just hope that someday your spirit will understand my motives and will forgive me. Now it is time to die! Goodbye, my spice Sue!

She stared him at the eyes and noticed a mix of cruelty; sadness and compassion. He turned back for a moment, knowing that she couldn't escape, and began to concentrate until a small ball of electric energy was formed, he didn't want to use his regular energy balls because he didn't want to harm her body. While it was growing, Kiria watched the coldness of the man she loved, and couldn't believe how he would kill that defenseless woman, who was his girlfriend once. She understood that only she could save Suzanne, that he wouldn't have courage to kill that woman in front of her, and she ran out her den, and jumped over Suzanne in the exact moment he turned around and shot his killing sphere. The shock hit her chest, and when Kiria hit the ground she was already dead. When Tharus understood who he had actually murdered, he got crazy. His legs trembled and he began to cry out loud.

_ What! Kiria, no! Don't you do that to me! Where did you come from? What have you done Suzanne? What have I done? What have I done!

Stunned and hallucinated by what had just happened, he fell on the ground and began to crawl in the direction of her body, and when he certified that the beautiful Kiria was really dead, he grabbed her and laid her in his lap, kissing her face and crying desperately.

_ Forgive me, my love! How could I know that you were still here? How could I have done that to you? I will be disgraced for the rest of my life. You saved my brother's life and I destroyed yours.

Touched by the atrocious suffering of the unique man she had ever loved, Suzanne even forgot for a moment that she was the one supposed to be there laid down, dead, and she was dragging herself towards him when two strong arms held her, and pulled her back, cautiously. When she turned her head back to attack the person that was trying to capture her, she saw Peter's face.

_ Shut up, Sue! I came here to save you. My intuition rang, and I understood that something could go wrong with you. We have to get out of here before Tharus recalls you. We don't know what he could do. He is so instable. There's nothing else to do in here!

When the news spread through the agents of the company, a general sadness took over their spirits. Hermes was too apprehensive with the death of Tharus's girlfriend, because from that day on, his acts would become even more unpredictable, and he understood and any pacific surrender would be impossible at that time. The secretary of the UN comprehended that things could go even worse if the mission last any longer. They had to act immediately, because Tharus Vendra would go against them, when he was recovered, to have revenge, as he did once with other enemies. Peter Moll concluded that was time to bring Joseph Prometeus Souz to the core of the action. Meanwhile, Tharus whipped his woman. Despite he felt for her a felling closer to the gratitude than to love, he was completely shocked by her tragic destiny. He didn't comprehend completely her participation in that case, he was just informed by Savio that she was sent by the government to negotiate with the enemies. In his rage, he blamed all the authorities he put in the power of high betrayal. They couldn't have plot behind his backs, and decided that he would began his vengeance by killing them. He asked to Savio to schedule an urgent reunion with all the ministers of the state. Without distrust his intentions, they immediately answered his call, and the meeting was organized in a fortress in the countryside. They believed that he wanted to discuss the terms of the surrender of the blue jackets. They didn't know Kiria was dead. They couldn't hide their satisfaction with the departure of the paranormal people, who had been helpful during the civil war, but were becoming a hindrance with their intention to take part of the new regime. Tharus was sat down, when they got in.

_ Good morning, gentlemen! I called you here today because we have important issues to discuss. I'd like to inform you that our association is over from this day on. – The Vendra said with irony in his voice.

_ I have to agree with you. – Said the president. It was good for us and for your organization, but I think you have to move on.

_ That's right, mister president. As your prime minister I must express the opinion of all the authorities, and we agree that it is time for us to rule our own country, without the interference of foreign people.

_ And you must be anxious to get back to your families, aren't you? – Said another minister.

_ We are sure that you, mister Vendra, took the right decision. Certainly the United Nations will see with generous eyes your good will. – Said the president. I want to express our deepest gratitude. In here you will be remembered as heroes, and someday we will create a holiday to homage the brave blue jackets.

_ I am really touched with all that demonstration of gratitude, but you got me wrong. I never said that I was leaving the country nor that I would surrender to the enemy.

_ But you said that our partnership was over!

_ Yes I said. I said it because you are the one who are going away.

_ We? Going away? Where to? When? – Asked another minister. – Where do we go?

_ Yes, you have to go. I just don't know where you are going to, and I don't give a damn! Probably to hell! Who knows? Goodbye!

Without wait for any other answer, he disappeared, while the authorities began to comprehend what was going on. Outside the building, he concentration on the gas pipes, and after some minutes, dozens of explosions set a devastating fire that burnt all the construction and everybody who was inside it. Protected from the flames by his mental shield, Tharus watched all the destruction, while havocs passed near him, thrown by the violence of the infernal heat. When he certified that everything was reduced to ashes, he lit his usual cigar, took a small bottle of rum out of his pocket, and toasted the dead. After that he dematerialized. He came back to his barrack a little disturbed and anxious with himself, when he understood that he was feeling a strange satisfaction with the elimination of all his disaffected people, as if he was just killing bothering filthy insects.

CHAPTER 18

THE CLASH

Hermes Vasconcellus had surrounded himself with all the possible cares to bring in safety Joseph Prometeus Souz to the operations field. This would be the very first time he was absent of the mental health hospital. His mind debility let his powers too much instable, and even with the strong medication that the doctors used to apply on him, it would be possible something go wrong, bursting a chain reaction that would release his capacities into spontaneous manifestations, with unforeseen unfolding acts. To let Joseph more comfortable, Denise Tanner was designated to scort him during the whole path, once he was used to the company and relied on her, besides, she was out of duty, result of the relative tranquility the agents were conducting the operation. The young girl was very attached to Joseph, because since the beginning of her medicine school training she volunteered to assist him, touched by the mystery involving the circumstances of his sickness. She cherished Ziggy, and in a certain way he reciprocated, once she was the person he used to smile at. Whenever possible, Denise used to spent hours beside him, reading E-newspapers, E-books and magazines, applying comforting energetic hand impositions, or just talking to him while supervised his clinic evolution.

Even with all her dedication, his treatment seemed to do not accomplish any effective result, and his situation was practically the same along the years. He was a definite cerebral paralysis that prevented him to be the master of his actions and thoughts, only allowing a precarious interaction with the surrounding environment, by responding to certain kind of pricks. But his small alleviation was able to permit his active participation on the risked plan to capture Tharus Vendra. His medicine was in a gauge replacement of other weaker to prepare him to the moment when his talents would be decisive to the total accomplishment of the mission. The plan was to force the Bat to use the maximum of his capacities, until he reached his critical point, what would led him to a complete exhaustion, giving them time to immobilize and drug him. However, to tease a man with that kind of potentiality would be as risky as to challenge a hurricane during an earthquake. To reduce his power of destruction was imperative that all the agents worked together, as a ballet group, without give chance to any kind of improvisation. Ziggy's participation would be crucial to the accomplishment of the mission, and since the first moment that was decided he would have to help, the doctors and psychic healers began several therapies to try to put him reasonably aware of the situation. However there was no way to know if they were making progress, for everything about his mind was a great incognito. Denise Tanner was the only person who could make him respond to determined stimulations, once only in her presence he demonstrated some level of awareness.

During this time, Iullus tried to control his brother, believing that this would be his only chance to help to restrain his madness. Aware of each detail of Peter's plans, through constant contacts, he moved into the base of the blue jackets, while Ivana was safe with Hermes. Every day he made up something to make Tharus to postpone his ideas to attack the agents of the company of the paranormals.

_ You have no idea of what I've passing through, brother. – Tharus used to say to him. – Everything seems to be falling apart around me, and when I try to put things in order again they end up breaking down once more. Life is complicated even for special people like us. events are intrinsically linked and if a tiny detail get out of control, all the result is wasted. Are you following me?

_ Sure brother! Don't you forget that I have been witnessed all your development. I thing that you began to think like that when we watched those old movies, rebel without a cause and the savage. I even lost the count of how many times you watched them.

_ I don't know either. Maybe 50 times.

_ we identified ourselves with the main characters and we even used some gestures of them for some time, do you remember?

_ Yes I do!.

_ Marlon Brando and James Dean, They were special actors! We used to see ourselves throughout them. but I must confess that from some point I began to notice that you were identifying yourself with other Brando's character, Kurts, from apocalypse now. But he was evil, brother!

_ You're funny, brother! Do you think that you can sum the choices of a whole life in a simple influence of some movies or comic books?

_ Oh, yes, I had forgotten peter Parker!

_ Shut up, brother! The truth is that nobody is already prepared to hold such power, while the planet is in the middle of such disorder and destruction, without commit some mistakes. It is normal and even predictable that the most of the people remain in silence in front of brutality, for they fear for their lives, but how can someone act like that when he is in condition to face and win the cruelty of men and bring some order to the world?

_ I understand you, brother. I am much less powerful than you, and I already feel like that. The problem is that despite our capacities, we are not prepared to fix the world, simply because we do not have the moral qualities, enough wisdom and scientific knowledge to face this huge work. The lack of discernment compromises our best intentions. We got into this maze and we can't find the way out. I think that we are finding out too late that the abuse of our abilities will never even scratch the surface of problems of our civilization. Unfortunately there are too many people trying to obtain advantages over the nature and the rest of the civilization. We can't make difference by just eliminating some criminals that disgust us, because other ones would take their places. Life and evolution are complex matters. I am beginning to understand Peter's ideas. I think that only a collective effort and lots of negotiations can produce effective and lasting results.

_ I think I read this speech in some novel of the x-men, I think doctor Charles Xavier said that. Evolution is made of tentative and error, tentative and error. We do not have the rules, and we have to use what we've got. I can't do it other way. I have good intentions, and my mistakes are part of the process, and the corpses that I've left behind are necessary casualties. I can't just quit now, because if I do so everything that I struggled for will have been in vain. No, brother, now I have to fulfill my destiny till the last drop. My way is a one way lane, and I have to keep in mind that my ideals are right. This is the end of the world as we know it! Someday somebody will complete what I leave unfinished. But it can wait! Now we have to celebrate life! So let's drink and smoke and eat something. Let's celebrate the memory of our friends and companions that became legend.

While Tharus prepared the meal, Iullus contacted Ivana so she could tell Peter that he couldn't hold his brother any longer, and that the company should capture him the quickest possible. Preferentially before he left the barrack, because outside it, would it be much more difficult to restrain his actions. He also informed that besides Savio Nogg, only few jackets remained in the venue. Iullus knew that he was acting like that to protect his brother, but he couldn't help feeling a traitor, even understanding that Tharus was mentally ill. He comprehended that his duty to his parents, siblings and friends was to prevent his brother could harm more people. After receiving the message of the Vendra, Peter mobilized his agents and contacted the psychic schools that were helping the mission to increase their mental emissions to difficult the use of Tharus abilities, because the time had come to the checkmate. 40 agents would act directly in the offensive. 10 would be in charge of the immobilization of the remaining jackets and the soldiers that protected the barrack, while other 05 would capture Savio Nogg. The rest of them would help in the confrontation of the Bat. At six in the morning, it was still very dark when the agents materialized in the fortress. Silently, the guards were being put down, one by one. Savio was still sleeping when they break through his room, but he was very agile and strong to be captured so easily, and after some minutes of intense physical and mental fight, with objects flying around; small energetic explosions and fire, and the use of a short gun machine and a laser weapon, he defeated the opponents. Exhaust, he tried to get out of the room, to inform Tharus they were under attack, but he fainted in the corridor.

Tharus had spent the night awakened, in a immense dark salon, drinking, smoking and listening music, sat in a small bench. During hours he remained in the same position, leant forward with his elbows supported by his legs and the hands holding his head. He was immersed in dull thoughts. Who had a glimpse of that squalid shaggy hair man, and noticed his old tired sad worried aspect, wouldn't recognize the gorgeous charismatic guy, who caused commotion among men and women wherever he passed by. The young confident sympathetic elegant paranormal had become a bitter man, corroded by feelings of remorse, guilty, hate and distress, and his clothes, methodically dark just enhanced his sick appearance. His look let transparent the despair that took hold of his soul, caused by the incessant fight between his will to recognize his mistakes and give up everything and his overwhelming pride, that compelled him to go on with his insane plans, because few people would be in conditions the ideals that moved him, once the most of the population would never have such powers. He was even cursing the day he joined the shop, getting into a world of intrigues, betrayals, violence and unmeasured ambitions. He wasn't prepared to pluck out of his eyes the veil that covers the diseases of the human conscience. The naïve angle and futile of the fashion circus that had been his point of view for many years was radically put down, and he began to see a filthy ground full of rats, cockroaches and garbage, the real dimension of the relationship between the people.

However these dark thoughts lasted for a few time, because in the deep of his being, he considered himself a kind of missionary. He was convinced that his noble intentions would let him invincible, and believed that sooner or later the hypocrites would be defeated by his steadiness, and he would fulfill his destiny. He remembered a man he knew when was a teenager, Ivan Karak, and his explanations for the injustice in the distribution of the bliss in the planet, and despite he was in a comfortable situation, the problems faced by the most part of the population reached his young spirit and he even used to forget the proper issues of boys in his age. For some time he desired to be a journalist, to bring to the surface the scandals people wanted to sweep to under the rug, but after sometime he understood that his mission would be even bigger, because he had to promote deeper changes, the kind of ones that only direct and fearless actions could produce. In his innocence of spoiled kid, Tharus dreamed about an earth more human and coherent, as if could be accomplished by the actions of a few people, who should be living examples to be followed, of courage and great realizations, and somehow he never abandoned these ideas. But all this dreams turned into nightmares with the lasts happenings. The deaths of Giselle, Nicholas and Kiria, and the vanishing of so many other companions worked as water in the fire of his enthusiasm and determination, and he was lost for the first time in his life. He knew that Moll had survived to the terrible tortures he was submitted, and certainly was between his enemies, plotting against him, and the time had come to face Peter Moll. He told to himself.

_ Now is the time to be ruthless!

He had deceived by fair words the ideal of bringing the director of the company to his side. The young man he considered a younger brother. But the course of the fate showed him it was impossible, once the young boy demonstrated strong convictions, and nothing would pluck out these ideals from him. But how could Tharus destroy somebody he considered a member of the family? The tired Bat clearly remembered of the first contact he had with that frightened shy boy, who used to see the Vendra boys as heroes. Alongside the years he got used to the respect glow of admiration in the boy's eyes all the time he reached a new level in his powers, and he was also proud of the achieves of the little Peter, who he was more connected to than he older siblings. If Iullus was his blood twin, Peter was his energetic one. Their powers were almost identical, what became things even more desolators.

Peter was the first one to find out where Tharus was. He got into without being noticed, and for some time he observed his ancient idol, staring at the bitter man he became. He barely could identify the powerful haughty formerly guy, who was an inspiration to young paranormal allover the world. Tharus always represented a freedom symbol of thoughts and attitude, with his rebel resemblance of someone who wasn't intimidated by contrary or threaten opinions. To the disciplined and obedient young Peter, who couldn't break through his conditioning, the Vendra was a semi-god. It was a terrible irony of the destiny that Peter, who worshipped his lack of compromising, was being responsible for the prison of that free spirit. But unfortunately children grow up, and their ancient idols do not resist to the eyes of adult people, who judge things without enchanted eyes, and they become normal people, with the same qualities and flaws. However, to the young Moll, the enchant wasn't totally broken, and while he peered at the Bat, his eyes were still glowing as when he was a child, and his heart beat increased as it usually does in the presence of some member of the family that isn't seen for a long time. In his mind Peter asked himself if he would have enough courage to combat this man who was a sort of older brother, while tears rolled on his face. Maybe if the circumstances were different, probably he wouldn't raise a finger to threaten Tharus, on the contrary, he would be capable to put his life in danger to save a member of the Vendra family, but he also remembered the miserable people of that country, that would suffer the consequences if he didn't arrest the Bat, and besides that, he knew that in fact he was protecting Tharus, protecting him from himself, who was out of control and would harm innocent people sooner or later. Reassuring his convictions, Peter filled his lungs of air, controlled his nervous and stepped inside.

_ May an old friend get into your room?

_ Peter, is that you? C'mon in! I was waiting for you. There is a chair for you. Sit down!

_ Don't get me wrong, Bat, but you look awful. What happened to you? It seems that don't take a sunbath for ages!

_ I am aware of that. I am even considering vacations in some tropical island. All this cold and ice are driving me crazy. But you, my dear friend, you look amazing! You're better than the last time I saw you. For what I can see your girlfriend is taking care of you very well.

_ I can't complain.

_ I see. I truly wanted things remained like that. It is a pity things got to this point. You have no idea how it hurts me when I see you against me.

_ I have never been against you, Tharus. And I never will. I am here to prove that. I never meant to hurt you, but I can see that you do it to yourself. It hurts me to see that things are in a dead end, and if I am not able to convince you to surrender, the authorities will take more drastic providences, and I am afraid that it will cause much suffering to this poor people. Your parents even asked me to give you this holographic message. They understand my reasons after they talked to mister Vasconcellus. They appeal to your sensibility. We assured them that if you surrender peacefully you would be a free man within a few time. Everybody knows that this is the best way out for you.

_ I don't want to see this message. If my family is so naïve I can understand, because they haven't our experience. But you my friend, you can't be such an idiot! I trust in your good intentions, and after some time Iullus made me comprehend that you were deceived by those militaries, but I ask you to do not let yourself being manipulated like that again. We both know that I reached a dangerous level to the people who like to play this power games. These faked world leaders will never fell safe while I am still alive and kicking, because at any time I can decide to rip them out of their positions, as I did in here. I am uncontrollable and they know it, and you know it. So there are only two alternatives, to kill me or to keep drugged in prison for the rest of my life.

_ No, that is not true! You're completely wrong! I will protect you. Mister Vasconcellus will protect you, and many other important people. Everything is negotiated, and if somebody someday tries to sneak into your room to assassinate you, he or she will have to face me.

_ Nice words, my friend. I appreciate them, but they arrived too late. I just can't go back.

_ There's nothing that you can't do, Bat!

_ You're right, but I've gone so far, and I must continue coherent. I have to stop pretending. I am sick of being so nice, of being a gentleman, of being obedient. It is time to let rise the real Tharus, the black Bat! I have to exteriorize the emotions that I have been keeping locked under seven keys. I have been unhappy for trying to suffocate this conflict that let me ashamed, making me hide from myself a great part of my personality. The most honest relevant and strong one. However, my friend, if you want to know the truth, I will tell you, I won't surrender, and I won't give up my plans. I don't care! I want to see how far my energies will take me. I will not regret my acts, and I will not answer to anybody. I won't submit myself under corrupt governments. Let them dare to face me. The real thing is that I love to be powerful. I love to be the number one in this planet. It is such an huge pleasure to be able to do whatever I please, without fear. And you with this aura of good boy don't deceive me. I know that in the deep of your heart you feel like me. How many people in this damned world can share these feelings? C'mon, admit it, it is too good to be strong enough to forge our own destiny, isn't it? We don't get sick. Our biological control lets us immune to virus or bacteria. I can't recall the last time I felt pain, may was when I was 09 years old, and I had to go to the dentist to pluck out two healthy milk teeth, that were blocking the passage of the definitive ones. We can smoke, to drink, to use drugs, to eat anything spoiled that it won't harm us. we are not exposed to the common accidents like the ordinary people, because our capacities not only protect us, they inform us about dangerous situations. Our abilities are too odds to be comprehended by the rest of the mankind. We are semi-gods, and we have to act like that. The gods from mythology must have been people like us, and just like them we have the duty to protect the planet, by eliminating any insect that that dreams to be important the sufficient to threaten the environment. Men and women that do not hesitate in front of nothing to satisfy their stingy and sordid interests, are under the bugs in the scale of the evolution, and must be treated like that.

_ I have said before, and I will say again that I agree with you in many aspects, Tharus. I won't deny that many times, in front of unfair situations, I feel just like you. But the difference is that for me, this sordid people remain humans, doesn't matter what they did. It is not up to me to decide their condition. I have to insist that we are not in the position to judge anybody. What we can do is to assist the justice in its process of organizing and disciplining the citizens. We have to fight for the democracy. I know that I am not a god, I will not allow that anybody pledge this position. We have boundaries to respect just like anybody else. You have become a huge head ache to the United Nations, and I have no other alternative but to take you with me, because if I do not do it, you will be hunted like a crazy cow, and everybody that are around you will perish in this chase. You have to understand the risks you're putting innocent people into.

_ I am so sorry, Peter. And don't be tricked, once they have erased me, they will turn their eyes to you. You will be the next in their list if you do not behave like a pet. They have to control any powerful paranormal, and in the end we will not be seen as divine blesses, but like a threat and burden to the survive of the regular people, for they tend to destroy everything they can't get advantages over. But I am not an easy target, and if the hazard is that serious as you're talking about, I will have better chances if I strike first, and that is what I am going to do!

_ Can't you see that you're paranoid? There isn't and there will never be any conspiracy to dominate the world. Mulder was just a character from a tv program. We will be well while we are in the path of the peace. In the end everything is right, and if it is not right now is because we are not in the end. That used to be your philosophy.

_ Give up Peter! Don't waste your saliva. This conversation is over, and if you have something else to try, please try it before I go.

Perceiving that would be useless to keep talking, Peter gave a sign, and immediately dozens of agents got into the room, behind him. The last one was Iullus Vendra, he was visibly affected by the betrayal. When Tharus saw him, he couldn't hide his surprise and frustration.

_ At last you chose your side, brother. I knew that you didn't have the guts to follow me. Everybody alerted me about it. You were never a blue jacket. But I forgive you. I think that is better for both of us, because I won't have to waste my time protecting you anymore. You're on your own from this day forth. Don't you forget that I love you, and tell dad and mom that and our siblings that I love them so much, and that someday they will be proud of me again.

Slowly, the Bat took a glass of bourbon and drank it, and while he put it back on the table he glanced at the agents, and a huge wave of energy was liberated throwing away some men and women. In this moment, Dan Lee; Gutt Morenz; Lana Gimenez; Andrew Wannay and Phosen Sanders began to produce small fires around him. Kim Hiroko and Chico Cruz created an electric filed over him, while Debora Spitz; Karl Tet; Jeffrey Morgan; Emilio Steves; Lucy Moretzon; Cindy Craw and James Goldblun shot energy balls, at the same time peter made the ceiling to crumble. However, any of these tries scratched his mental shield. Tharus was even amused by them. At least, the heavy attack wasn't allowing him to strike back, or even to dematerialize himself to escape from them. this way, he was only able to deal with one agent of each time. He tossed one against a pillar, another was dematerialized, other he killed with an energetic ball; he hit another with an electric dart, while dropped another with a heavy wardrobe. While that, Savio Nogg was waking up, and hearing the row of the battle, he ran to help his leader. Entering in the gallery almost completely destroyed, he surprised everybody, and seized that to throw his energy balls. He neutralized an agent and hurt the knee of Debbie Spitz, and gave enough time to the Bat to recover his strengths. Staring at Iullus, Tharus dematerialized him to a safe place, and after that he grabbed his loyal companion and disappeared, leaving behind an enormous ball of destruction. However, before it exploded and devastated all the barrack, Peter ordered to his agents to get out of there, taking those ones who did not have the ability of instant transport.

The mental shield produced by the equips of Diana Maris and Anne Moss allied to the efforts of the students of the schools around the world that were participating on the operation were producing strong effects. Because of the exhausting waste of energy the Bat was being compelled to do, the mental block didn't allow him to go too far, and the constant monitoring he was being submitted by Pablo hernan and Argos Buzzolor, within few minutes the whereabouts were traced, and Peter and his team reached him before he could make a plan up. The Valiant Moll protected partially his staff from the fierce attacks, and gave them time to strike back with maximum force, but he knew that was just a matter of time until the remaining jackets could harm his agents, and then he decided to attract to himself all the fury of the Vendra, to give his team enough time to neutralize the rest of the fugitives. And for some minutes he was able to hold the deadly attacks in the same proportion Tharus held his ones, for his strong conditioning and discipline were surpassing the slovenly capacities of his opponent, who had stopped training long time before. However, a tiny headache that was throbbing with more and more insistence indicated he was in the verge of the critical point in the use of his abilities. His legs were beginning to get weaker and he decided to get on his knees to save energy and to concentrate better. Dan Lee understood what was happening to his boss and contacted the support team, and gave green signal to the use of Joseph Prometeus Souz in the hostilities. Immediately Denise got closer to Ziggy and, who was peacefully eating a pack of candy bar, some miles away from the battlefield.

_ My dear friend, it is time to you to do me that favor, do you remember it?

_ Me remember! Ziggy do what pretty doctor ask! Keep my candies, please!

_ Of course, Ziggy! When you finish it I will give you some more. But now you have to do as I showed you. Try to concentrate on the venue I am thinking about and imagine we are in there. Just close your eyes and imagine it hardly.

_ Ziggy can do that. It is easy.

Almost instantly they materialized few meters away from the battle core.

_ Congratulations, Joseph! You deserve a kiss. Now forget about the things that are happening around us, and concentrate only in my voice. Just let me conduce you. Be cool!

Tenderly holding his hand, she led him to where Peter was. Suddenly Joseph began to be annoyed by the mayhem in there, and he lost control, beginning to scream, begging to Denise to get him out of there. He was so agitated that he attracted the attention from everybody, including Tharus and Savio, who were surprised by the unusual intromission, and for some time the hostilities ceased.

_ What a hell is that? – Tharus asked out loud. – What is Ziggy doing in here? Aren't you ashamed of using this cripple man? How low can you go down? Do you want to sacrifice this retard? Can you believe in such thing, Savio? You won't have my mercy if it is that your intention.

Savio didn't even listened to the gibes of his leader, because he was shaken by the condition of his former friend. It was the first time he saw Joseph since the tragic day. he heard about what had happened to Joseph but he tried to do not think about it anymore and move on with his life, because he understood how guilty he was. And now, when he was seeing in that situation the man who had been the most powerful man alive, he couldn't help the burden of all the remorse to fall over his shoulders. He started to walk toward Souz, as if he wanted to beg for forgiveness.

_ Ziggy, what happened to you? I can't express how sorry I am. I have to talk to you.

Joseph stopped screaming when he heard Savio's voice and peered at him. For some time he stood still, as if he was taken by old memories. Nobody around understood what was happening, and intrigued, they even forgot about what they were doing in there, and remained in total silence. Little by little, Souz's face regained his normal appearance and seemed that he had recovered his reason. Tears began to roll through his cheeks, and the only one who could understand the meaning of all that was the sorrow Nogg. For some time Ziggy could recover the control of his mind and comprehend the whole extension of his tragedy, and the promises non-realized, the personal goals drastically interrupted, and the affect he wasn't able to give and receive anymore. Suddenly he got desperate by an entire life wasted for such a small thing, a satisfaction reached with so much suffering. While he stared at Savio, who was still handsome; arrogant; healthy and challenging, he comprehended all he left behind so that inconsequent man could throw away his life, causing more suffering to the world. His sacrifice wasn't helpful. He wished he hadn't saved Savio's life. In that moment he hated Nogg with all his fibers, and that hate was transformed into something uncontrollable, and he cried out loud, as he hadn't for 14 years.

_ You treacherous worm! How could you do that to me twice? I sacrificed my life for you two, believing that you could be someone better than I had been. I consumed all my energies to bring you back from the reign of the dead, and now I realize that it was in vain! I should have let you rotting in that forest. I think that she didn't seize her second choice properly either. But at least with you I will fix my mistake.

Savio Nogg didn't argue because he knew inutile, and because he knew Joseph was right. He just sensed what was about to happen and conformed with it. He only nodded his head and waited that Joseph consumed his anger, by hitting him. Prometeus became numb with the huge quantity of energy his brain was producing. Around him the nature seemed to portrait his state of mind, and reacted, giving a glimpse of how devastating his powers could be. When his capacities reached the critical limit, he opened his arms and released an overwhelming wave of transparent fluids, so strong that it was almost tangible, making the atmosphere vibrate, as a lake's surface hit by a stone. The ground began to shake in a vigorous quake, ripping out grass; bushes and trees, rolling them in a giant dust cloud. The noise was terrible, and when it stopped and the dust dissipated, everything in front of Joseph in an area of half a mile had been destroyed; dragged and heaped up in a enormous pile, that could be seen by far as a small hill.

Tharus had gathered all his strengths to maintain himself steady while all around him was breaking apart, but he end up being dragged with Savio by the energetic hurricane. Nobody had never witnessed such devastating creation of a human mind, and the agents of the company had to run away to do not be sucked by that phenomenon, and by far they were astonished by such vision. Exhausted by the fierce effort, Joseph sat down on the ground, back to his old condition, alienated of everything that had just happened. Recovered from the scary scene, Denise ran to him, to verify his conditions, putting a sack of pastries in his hands.

_ Thank you, Denise. Crispy chocolates, crammed of mint; strawberry and almond. I love them!

_ Are you okay, Ziggy?

_ I've never been better in my whole life!

Peter couldn't believe what had happened, and turned his head to Suzanne, asking.

_ What was that, an atomic bomb?

_ Boy, I had never seen such a thing in my entire life!

_ I am still astonished by that. – Debbie talked.

_ I just wanted to know if everybody survived this overkill. – Dan said.

_ I think so. – Diana answered. – I can see all the agents from here.

_ But the main question is: What had happened between Ziggy and blue jacket?

_ I think it is quite obvious, isn't it?

_ It doesn't matter right now. – Peter observed. – We don't have time to speculate, we have more urgent questions to answer. Let's go people! Let's see if there is somebody alive in that mount of soil.

Everybody ran to it, and using their capacities altogether they began to remove the rubbish. They removed a lot, but it seemed that they had done nothing, because of the volume of was still remaining. They found many wild animals that were inadvertently involved in the plot. While the agents were digging, the most of these animals, once free, ran away, frightened but unharmed, and it fulfilled Peter's heart with hope, that his old friend could be still alive. And it made him work even harder, because he didn't accept that a strong and powerful man as Tharus could die that way. One hour had passed by without the agents could find any sign of the blue jackets, but nobody wanted to give up until the last rock had been removed, or until they could rescue at least the dead bodies. Even wounded, Kim was helping the digging, by directing the efforts, and where to look for. When the agents began to show the signals of tiring and dejection, for it seemed that nobody could have survived under that immense pile of soil, she sensed a tiny vibration coming from an specific point of the rubbish. Kim's ability was better than a search dog. Immediately she told her companions where to work, and they, once more fulfilled of hopes, created a whirl energy, of considerable size, that within few minutes revealed the dead body of Savio Nogg. In the same place, after some more minutes of search, they found out Tharus Vendra, mindless but alive. Carefully he was removed, and in the same moment Denise Tanner began to treat his wounds. He had been saved by his mental barrier! It protected him against the overwhelming weight of rubbishes over him. He had tried to also protect his companion, Savio, but he couldn't, because he had to use all his forces to save himself. After the works, the agents of the company gathered to pray for the success of their operation and for the souls of those who gave their lives for it. They knew that despite the loss of many lives, a bigger tragedy had been avoided.

Tired and sad, Peter didn't want to go with the rest of the group, he rather to go to the farm of his friend Gilda and rest some days there, with his girlfriend, Denise. During 10 days they recovered their body and mind energies, by strolling without worries through the countryside and visiting the poor people who had helped him before. By the first time he could walk around without further concerns about his enemies, and enjoy everything good that the country had to offer. Moll and Tanner even helped in the beginning of the work of reconstruction that would bring back democracy to that suffered nation. New winds were blowing in that region.

_ My dear Gilda. – Peter said one day, during a philosophic conversation. – The best way to help yourself is helping other people! If everybody had any idea of how much we can be beneficiated when we help to solve the problems of the others, they would spend much more time of their lives doing it.

_ I've learned that by the worst way possible. When we are involved with the concerns of other people we forget our own pains, and after some time we began to see our sorrows from certain distance, and we see them in their right dimension. That's how I surmounted the loss of my beloved son.

_ That's exactly what I am talking about, my dear friend. You don't know how many people you helped when you decided to risk your life by saving me. And in my name and in their names I wanted to thank you, from the bottom of my heart.

_ Stop it silly boy! You don't have to thank me. On the contrary, you've done so much for me and for my country. If you agree, from now on I will consider you a nephew of my heart.

_ I will be so proud of it, aunt Gilda. You're part of my spiritual family.

_ So you have to come to visit me regularly, ok?

_ You bet I will do it whenever I can. Despite I want to have a close look in the return of the democracy in this nation. If somebody tries to get some dishonest advantage over it will have to face me.

_ I am not sure about what exactly happened in here, Peter, but one thing I know for sure. The citizens of this country have a due to you. May I kiss you in their names?

_ Of course Aunt Gilda! But I want you to know that I just did what I had to do. There's no merit on it.

_ Anyhow we got rid of two dictators of shit!

_ Certainly! But now we have to look forward, to the future. The past is legend.

_ I am sure you will be too much happy aside this pretty girl, despite she doesn't talk too much.

_ Me? I usually talk too much. I just wanted to let Peter enjoy the maximum of your company.

_ I know, I am just kidding my doll. You're a special girl, anyone can notice it, and you deserve a special boy like Peter Moll.

_ You're right, ma'm. And I'd like to call you aunt either. I already admired you from everything he told me about you.

_ I'd be honored by that, my sweet girl.

_ That's way we all will be inflated by the eulogizes. We'd better change subjects. – Peter joked.

_ So let's go to the church because the whole village is waiting in there for your farewell party.

_ That's what I like, too much fun; good food; good drinks; good music and good friends gathered. Can life be better than that? – Peter asked

CHAPTER 19

A LIFE LESS ORDINARY

The church was crowded. All the ritual of a religious wedding was fulfilled. The bride was beautifully dressed, the groom was elegant and anxious, smiling people in impeccable suits, weeping toddlers or running everywhere, a large number of flowers of ornate the ceremony and a coral chanting classic themes. Argos Buzzolor was shining. After all it was his first marriage, and the wedding had been postponed twice due to his completely exhaustion because of the last mission. Six months had passed by since they had captured the last of the blue jackets, and everyone involved in it had received worthy vacations as award, and that was all they received, because the government determined that any information about that case should be classified as confidential. This way no official homage could be programmed to celebrate the victory. However, nobody bothered by that, because they just wanted to rest and forget about all that. Some of the agents even needed psychological treatment during some months, due to traumas developed by the fact they were harmed and they harmed lots of old schoolmates. After these time they were all recovered, and the marriage of Argos was being a sort of collective expurgation, as a triumphal return, because it was the first time everybody was gathered after that mission.

Mick and Tommy had come from Australia to watch the wedding of their loyal friend. They didn't believe Argos could find a bride that seemed to have so many qualities, as he liked to emphasize. They had to mock him a lot, and as always he reacted to that with a great sense of humor. The happy ambient was a portrait of how confident in the future the agents of the company were. None of them had believed in the dull predictions of the Bat, and nothing better than a wedding party to show that tomorrow can be even better, and Argos bride provided a beautiful celebration. In a castle, surrounded by beautiful gardens, the guest could taste the most exotic and expensive food and beverages, while dancing with the best DJ's. in the end of the night, the directors of the company, comfortably sat around fancy tables, gathered together to chat a little.

_ I always knew that Argos was elegant. – Anne said. – but now he overcame.

_ I am still astonished by that. – Pablo commented. – He must have spent two months of salary in those clothes.

_ Leave him alone. – Said Debbie. – He just have to be as gorgeous as his bride.

_ I agree with you. – Said Kim. – I just think that her mother is too "Britney".

_ Hold up your poison, Girl. – Completed Dan.

_ Forget about me, boy! You're too square to appreciate our conversation. Don't you know that the best think on a wedding party is to talk about other people's clothes?

_ That's right, Kim. – Said his wife. – Why don't you go to take a look at the kids?

_ You have to obey your boss, Man!

_ Keep kidding, Peter! Someday will be you're your time. Wives are all the same! Listen to me.

_ You can count on that, Dan. – Said Denise. With me, men have just one alternative, to obey.

_ are you crazy, woman?

_ You are a boy scout, Peter. You do whatever I want.

_ You two disgust me. – Said Pablo.

_ Shut up! Your time will come.

_ Stop saying shit, Sue. Women are only bosses of me in bed.

_ I have to correct you, they are your bosses "from" the bed.

They used to laugh even about the poorest gags, as a bunch of kids baking potatoes in a summer camp. For some time they wanted to forget they were some of the most powerful people in the world, with great responsibilities over their shoulders. Then mister Vasconcelus and family approached to them.

_ Do you have any news from Tharus? – Asked the president of the foundation.

_ I think he is crazy for losing such party.

_ That is not fun, Sue. – Reprimanded Peter. – You know he lost his reason.

_ That is true, Denise? – Mister Vasconcellus asked. – Has he actually lost his mind, as our poor Joseph?

_ I am afraid he did. The ultimate exams have revealed a great damage in his brain. I am not capable to heal that. It is pity to see such handsome man in that state.

_ What? So you think he is cuter than me?

_ Of course not, my dear Pete! I am just saying that he is also very beautiful.

_ Chill out, silly girl. You don't have to worry. I am just kidding. I also think he is a handsome guy.

_ I knew it. – Said Dan. – when you drink a little you reveal your own nature.

_ Don't be jealous, Dan. I also think you're too cute.

_ Stop you two. Mister Vasconcellus is waiting a serious answer. I think he can get better a little with a proper treatment. With lots of physiotherapy he can recover the movements of his arms and legs. The support and help of his siblings and parents are being decisive.

_ That's fine, Denise! But I am sure that your cares are being also very important.

_ Thanks, mister Vasconcellus! I am doing what I can. Besides there are many paranormal healers trying to help. I am just a medicine student. Remember that!

_ She is so humble! – Peter said.

_ The most important, my darling, nobody have taught you. It was born with you! It is your dedication to your patients! The bond you create with them. – Continued mister Vasconcellus. – Since the first moment he was taken out of that rubbish, all hurt, you began to heal his wounds, and avoided a bigger damage. That first aid was crucial. And it has been like that since then.

_ Ok you won. I am really very good. Can we change subject now, please? It is so sad to know that I can't fix his brain damages. He will be like that for the rest of his life.

_ Who can predict the future? – Pablo asked.

_ I can!

_ Who are you?

_ I am Ian Balder Hanussen.

_ Shut up Balder! You're just a trainee. You have only to listen and learn! – Peter joked – These interns are becoming very exhibited.

_ But Denise, I am so sorry, because I heard that you are leaving us. – Mister vasconcellus continued.

_ No, I am not! I am just changing my perspectives. I am leaving the direct work. I want be in the backstage. I just want to take care of people. this thing of living in danger is not to me.

_ I also prefer like that. Once she is safe I won't be that preoccupied.

_ And Iullus, Peter, do you have news from him?

_ Yes I do, Suzanne! Last week I was called to help to contain a small problem. The Bat's capacities were out of control. He was been taken to do some exams, when he felt a terrible pain. The remedies weren't enough to contain it, and a succession of explosions destroyed a dozen cars on the streets. Fortunately nobody was seriously wounded. We had some difficulty to restrain his abilities, and when we came back to the hospital, Iullus was there.

_ And how is he, man?

_ He is very fine. Unfortunately for you, Sue, he is going to marry Ivana in a couple of months. But she is already pregnant. He is living in a farm that belonged to tharus, in the patagon desert. They are planning to live in there.

_ Who told you that I would be sad with it? It is better her than me!

In that moment Argos entered in the salon.

_ At last, old friend! I thought you had forgotten us. – Peter Said.

_ What's up people? I am so sorry that I am not giving you the proper attention, but I have too many guests, you know. Are you been well served?

_ Don't you worry, boy. It is everything alright! – Diana said.

_ Argos, you naughty boy! You have to sit down with us for a while.

_ I am here for it, Anne. What a beautiful necklace, Denise. Are these real diamonds?

_ We have already repaired on it, Argos. Our boss is getting rich. – Kim observed.

_ It is not like that, people. Another day I was walking Ziggy when he asked to sit down. Then he took some stones and held strongly in his hands, closed his eyes and within some minutes they were being transmuted in these diamonds you're seeing. As I do not like anything illegal, I went to the proper department and had them registered, and they were considered worthless. After that, Peter ordered the necklace, and presented me.

_ That is a honest girl! – Argos said.

_ But tell us, Argos. Have you already regretted? – Pablo Asked.

_ What kind of question is that? – Diana complained?

_ Don't you worry, Di! I know the sick mind of this *latino*. But I tell you man, that I will never regret. Pollyana is the woman of my life.

_ I bet it. Of course the millions of her father have nothing to that.

_ I didn't even know that her father was that rich.

_ I believe that!

_ Shut up, you two! Have you noticed how talkative Diana is today? – Suzanne asked.

_ She is always saving saliva!

_ it is nothing like that, Kim. Sometimes I just want to observe people around me. Another times I want to talk. Today I am wondering that life could be always like that, an eternal party. Why do we have always to complicate things?

The night was running in perfect celebration. The fiancées had seized the moment and ran away, hidden, and the satisfied guests began to go home. In a distant table, the Vasconcellus family observed the happy agitation. With the last happening, the president of the foundation had seen his influence increased, what transformed him into a shadow of many governments. The greatest paranormal people the world had ever seen were formed in his school, and the actuation of them in all the spheres of the society were integrating the sensitive people. As a rigid control over these people should be done, nobody better than him to make this link, to orientate the task. The old and idealistic man that had proved his ideas would have still much breath tom exercise perfectly this new role, and he was still training his only son to take his place one day. They were respected by psychic beings of all levels around the world, and the politicians and businessmen who show up in the ceremony did it because of the Vasconcellus family, and they made their point by bowing, one by one, to Jardell, as if it was some Masonic ritual, and he was a sort of godfather. The old man was visibly bothered by that, once he didn't want toadyism, he wanted to see practical actions to have the sensitive people well integrated in the society. his greatest fear was that his accomplishments were used to bring great disorder to the planet, and he wouldn't rest until mechanisms to avoid that were created. When the movement finished he called his best student and his girlfriend to his table.

_ Come here, Peter! There's a long time that we do not have a good conversation.

_ Is that there are too many things happening, that I do not have much time. But I miss our conversations, mister Vasconcellus.

_ That's nice, boy! But tell me, how do you feel now that you are the most powerful man alive?

_ I don't know, it is a little weird, if you want to know. I try not to think about it.

_ That's the best thing you can do. You can't permit the proud to take hold of your soul. You've seen what happened to Joseph and Tharus. You'll have always to watch out your powers. I know that you are more centered, but you can't be too cautious. I just want you to know that we are here to help you, mainly to deal with the press. Now forget about these worries and seize the moment, you deserve it.

_ Thank you very much, sir! I never desired that position. I'd rather to see Ziggy and Tharus occupying the first two positions. I was glad to be the third.

_ If I can give my opinion, I think that Peter deserves to be where he is because nobody is more disciplined and dedicated than him. In the foundation or any other school in the whole world.

_ Less, Denise, less!

_ I am serious, Pete! Don't you agree with me, mister Vasconcellus?

_ In Genus, number and degree! The young Peter is far the best student I've ever had. I never worried about him, neither the other instructors. And we never will. Besides, I'd like to say that the disease that destroyed the life of Joseph and Tharus will never haunt Peter, simply because he know all the extension of his powers, and the time to stop pushing them. That's why I say, my lad, seize the moment. You've reached that position throughout uncountable incarnations, and now is time to receive the awards. God gave you a lot, as He have always given to us all, but you knew how to multiply these gifts the universe has presented you better than anybody, and your time has come, be happy!

_ I hope you're right, sir! – Peter agreed.

_ My dear love, I had never thought about it. – Denise asked. – Did you really spend so many time practicing the occultism?

_ As far as I can recall. The most ancient regression that I have ever done, remounts to the times of the old Atlantis, and at that time I was already dedicating my studies to the esoteric world. By the way, all the paranormal beings must have began a long time ago.

_ There are clues that the most elevated sensitive people had begun their training in other planets, specially one named Capela. – Hermes said. – They came to earth in exile, when people in that planet achieved a higher moral level. Those who were still tied to power, violence and other low instincts were convicted to live in our planet and help the development of the beings that were giving the firsts steps in the evolution scale. They would only have permission to return to Capela when had learnt their lesions. Rumors have said that many of them have already returned to that planet, however, some of us preferred to remain in here to continue helping the people from earth.

_ I think you're right! – Peter agreed. – I've received some information that corroborates your version. I just know that I never was a warrior in the sense of this word, as if somehow I could know that men would never control their destiny, for the strongest they could be, until they learnt how to control the forces of the nature. That's why I had chosen to follow the path of the wizard, and that way I would be apart of the iniquities that destroy the dreams of ambition of those who live by the sword. And so I kept developing my mental skills, incarnation after incarnation, in the old Egypt; China; India; Greece and other civilizations. The weird thing is that I found a gap in that line. There's a complete blank in my spiritual memory, and I can't access a certain period of my other lives. I don't have the registers of a period over than ten thousand years, as if I or somebody else had erased it. And I can't have access about the period I lived in other planets, like this Capela. It is we totally weird, because the level of development I've reached should grant me full access to my spiritual memory. But what I can say is that while the humanity was struggling in bloody wars, I was training and practicing in the solitude of monasteries, while men and women were enjoying riots in the ancient Rome I was preparing my skill in the silence of old temples, and while atrocities were committed under the shadows of the middle age, I was meditating in the darkness of the caves.

_ How dedicated you were, boy! – Hermes joked.

_ You have made so many sacrifices, my darling.

_ No at all, Denise! To me it was never a sacrifice, the otherwise. I've dedicated all my heart and good will to these trainings. My greatest ambition was always to discover the greatest mysteries of the universe. I never dreamed that I could reach this power.

_ But that is exactly why you've reached such level. – Mister Vasconcellus completed. – I believe that if your parents had received an adequate alimentation, when they were young, and even you, when you were a toddler, certainly your carnal organism would be in better shape to receive and to manifest the potent charge of energy your spirit was bringing to it. I am sure that you could have reached the same level of Joseph Souz, and even trespass him. But thanks God you haven't, because I think that we are not prepared yet to deal with these higher energies. Our researchers are developing better gadgets to measure the capacities of the students, and the best level to their fragile brains, according to their genetic conditions. Probably in your next life you will reach the ninth level. In my studies I created the theory that a dedicated apprentice pass to a higher level after two incarnations of severe studies, and I can say that in your previous life you had latent powers in this same stage, so if you continue practicing, who can say how far you can go?

_ I hope so! I have lived already 25 years, and I intend to live another 125, this way I will have too much time to continue my development.

_ God bless you!

_ He will, you can be sure, Hermes!

_ Now if the young people excuse me, it is my time to go home.

_ But is too early, mister Vasconcellus! – Denise complained.

_ My time of sprees is over, my dear lady. And I also hate to say goodbyes, so I will go out like the French people.

_ We are used to that. – Peter completed.

_ I almost forgot it, Peter. – Hermes said. – I hate to ruin your night, but I have no other alternative. I've just received an urgent call from the first secretary. It is a matter of world security, yet more complicated. This way, tell to your agents to go home, because tomorrow morning we'll have an important reunion.

_ You must be kidding, Hermes!

_ I wish I was, my friend! But the threaten is real.

_ But it is only two in the morning! Everybody is still having fun. It is not fair! Can't this matter wait until Monday morning?

_ No way! You are not understanding the situation. The grill is very hot. It is tomorrow! Bye.

_ Don't you worry. I will give them the bad news.

Denise was looking angry to her boyfriend.

_ I don't believe you are going to ruin this party.

_ What can I do, sweetheart? As a doctor you know about professional responsibility, don't you?

_ I comprehend, my love. I don't agree, but I comprehend. We have the right to party as anybody else.

_ Come here, everybody! I have news to you. – All the directors surrounded Peter Moll, to hear what was so important. – I just want one minute of attention, please. Hermes just told me that we have an urgent mission, however enjoy the party, because we will have too much to do on Monday morning. Thank you very much!

_ So let's celebrate today, because tomorrow nobody knows what is waiting for us! – Said Suzanne.

_ Let's keep on partying! – Shouted Diana.

_ Life is short, and we just live one at each time! – Completed Pablo.

Denise was still staring at Peter.

_ What? Don't you agree with me, sweetheart? What are they going to do? Take out my badge? This weekend is ours and only ours.

_ You're my hero! I didn't know this part "Ferris Bueller" of yours. You're surprising me. Now I think that your case has solution.

_ Thank you very much, my red hot girl!

_ I just don't know if you're becoming a little devil or a little bat!

_ Only time will tell. Wait and see!

Printed in the United States
by Baker & Taylor Publisher Services